War With Russia

General Sir Richard Shirreff

Born in Kenya in 1955 where he spent his early years, Richard Shirreff commissioned into the British Army as a cavalry officer after reading history at Oxford. In his 37 years of service he commanded soldiers on operations from the most junior to the most senior levels. He saw combat as a tank commander in the First Gulf War, experienced many of the complexities of Northern Ireland during his three tours there and learned first-hand the challenges of bringing peace to the Balkans in both Kosovo and Bosnia. He returned to Iraq as a multinational commander in 2006-7. When not in command he spent time either being educated in the art and science of war on a succession of different command and staff courses or in a range of posts as a formulator or executor of policy in the Ministry of Defence and Army Headquarters. His last seven years in uniform were spent in two senior NATO command posts: Commander of the Allied Rapid Reaction Corps and Deputy Supreme Allied Commander Europe; the Alliance's deputy strategic commander and the most senior British general in the Alliance.

Since leaving the Army he has set up Strategia Worldwide, a risk management consultancy, He and his wife have two adult children and one grandchild, and live with their two springer spaniels in Hampshire. This is his first book.

War With Russia

GENERAL SIR RICHARD SHIRREFF

An urgent warning from senior military command

CORONET

First published in Great Britain in 2016 by Coronet
An imprint of Hodder & Stoughton
An Hachette UK company

First published in paperback in 2016

3

Paperback ISBN: 978 1 473 63225 7
Ebook ISBN: 978 1 473 63226 4

Typeset in Bembo MT Pro by Palimpsest Book Production Ltd, Falkirk, Stirlingshire

Printed and bound by Clays Ltd, St Ives plc

Map drawn by Rodney Paull

Hodder & Stoughton Ltd
Carmelite House
50 Victoria Embankment
London EC4Y 0DZ

www.hodder.co.uk

To my friends in Latvia, Estonia and Lithuania. Men and women who understand the price of freedom.

Contents

Foreword   ix
Preface   1

Prologue   19
Part One: Reckoning   25
Part Two: Recovery   275
Part Three: Riposte   331
Epilogue   432

Glossary   439
Acknowledgements   445

Foreword

Admiral James Stavridis, US Navy (Retired), former Supreme Allied Commander Europe

A T HIS CONFIRMATION hearing in the summer of 2015, General Mark Milley, the new Chief of US Army Staff, was asked by the Senate Armed Services Committee what was the greatest threat to the American – and Western – democratic way of life. He answered, 'I would put Russia right now as the number one threat . . . Russia is the only country on earth that retains a nuclear capability to destroy the United States. That is an existential threat.' General Joe Dunford, the new Chairman of the Joint Chiefs, expressed the same view to the same committee during his confirmation hearings.

I fully agree with that assessment. It is also an assessment shared by a select group of top military leaders; people whose experience puts them in the best position to know the facts of the case. In particular, I applaud my former comrade-in-arms and Deputy Supreme Allied Commander at NATO, General Sir Richard Shirreff, for laying out the risks America and the West currently face in this brave, timely and important book.

As the Strategic Commander of NATO, the North Atlantic Treaty Organization, I saw Russian aggression first hand. Of all the challenges America faces on the geopolitical scene in the second decade of the twenty-first century, the most dangerous is the resurgence of Russia under President Putin. Yes, Islamic jihadists pose a massive threat to our security but, until the jihadists can defeat us on the battlefield, they cannot destroy our nation. The Russians are different – and this is the truly terrifying bit – as they appear to be prepared to use nuclear weapons, based on recent, very public comments by Vladimir Putin.

Under President Putin, Russia has charted a dangerous course that, if it is allowed to continue, may lead inexorably to a clash with NATO. And that will mean a war that could so easily go nuclear. As the Prussian general Carl von Clausewitz once said, 'War has its own grammar but not its own logic.' I would add that it has its own dynamic. If American and NATO soldiers find themselves in direct combat with Russian troops, that conflict will escalate. And that means the ultimate option will be on the table: the use of nuclear weapons. This book describes brilliantly how this horrific scenario could develop 'on the ground'. These are the sort of scenarios that many senior civilians, and especially politicians, throughout history have consistently failed to understand or have wished away.

But this dynamic can be stopped and war averted if NATO, under the leadership of America, shows the necessary resolve and determination. It is a war that can be prevented, but only if the Russians believe we are serious about being prepared to fight to defend our freedoms and those of our allies.

2017 War With Russia tells the story of a war that could result from a failure to stand strong in the face of Russian aggression. It tells the story of how, thanks to a series of misjudgements and policy blunders, NATO and the West stumble into a catastrophic war with Russia; scenarios that I can attest are all too possible and which make for chilling reading. But it also tells the story of how the tide of history can be turned when good men and women stand up to be counted. Above all, the message is that it is not too late to prevent catastrophe.

This is no ordinary 'future history', for it is told by a brave and seasoned warfighter, a former senior NATO commander, who served the NATO Alliance brilliantly as my deputy, and whose judgement I learned to trust; a man whom I, as an admiral, would have leaned on for his judgement on how the land battle should be fought. Moreover, a man who really does understand the geopolitical realities and risks and who has proved that he is not scared to tell it as it is. It is very rare that such a senior and experienced general is prepared to put his reputation on the line, but Richard Shirreff is that man. He correctly called the consequences of the Russians' invasion of Crimea and annexation of parts of Ukraine back in 2014. I fear that he has again correctly called the Russians' next moves in *2017 War With Russia*.

Some will say that the warnings of our most senior American admirals, generals and the author of this book are a predictable response from men with an interest to protect and they are no more than crying 'Wolf!' I would remind the naysayers of this: in 2017, it will be a hundred years since the United States committed four million young Americans to the slaughterhouse of Europe, of whom 110,000 gave their lives. Twenty-five years later, America had to do it again – and the cost was much greater in the Second World War. Had it not been for NATO and the determination and sacrifice of a new generation of Americans, the subsequent Cold War could have had a very different outcome.

At a recent top-level convention of senior political, diplomatic and military figures in Europe, an attendee asked, with reference to Russia's military adventurism and muscle flexing in Europe, was the present situation with Russia more like the slide to world war in 1914, or the failure to stand firm against Hitler that led to the next conflagration of the Second World War. The chilling answer was: 'No, this is Europe 2015. With nuclear weapons.'

2017 War With Russia lays out a plausible and startling case of the potential peril ahead – it deserves a serious reading indeed.

Preface

THE WAR WITH Russia began in the Ukraine in March 2014.

At that time I was a four-star British General and the Deputy Supreme Allied Commander Europe (DSACEUR), deputy to NATO's American Strategic Commander. Based at NATO's strategic headquarters (Supreme Headquarters Allied Powers Europe or SHAPE in the NATO vernacular) situated just north of Mons in Belgium, I was an experienced NATO man having previously commanded NATO's Allied Rapid Reaction Corps.

I had been in post as DSACEUR for three years and I confess that, along with my senior military colleagues, I accepted the received wisdom that, despite the Russian invasion of Georgia in 2008, NATO should aim to foster a strategic partnership with Russia. I visited Moscow on several occasions to build relationships with the senior Russian military leadership and happily welcomed General Valeri Gerasimov, now Chief of the Russian General Staff and Commander of Russian Armed Forces, into my home.

However, the invasion of Crimea, Russia's support for separatists in eastern Ukraine, its invasion of that country, and the President's self-proclaimed intention in March 2014 of reuniting ethnic Russian speakers under the banner of Mother Russia, has changed my view of Russia's intentions fundamentally. Russia is now our strategic adversary and has set itself on a collision course with the West. It has built up, and is enhancing, its military capability. It has thrown away the rulebook on which the post-Cold War security settlement of Europe was based. The President has started a dynamic that can only be halted if the West wakes up to the real possibility of war and takes urgent action.

This book is that wake-up call – before it is too late.

So, back in March 2014, there was a sense of incredulity among us western military leaders when it became increasingly clear that the 'annexation' of Crimea was no less than a Russian invasion. Put bluntly and in context, this was the first attempt to change the boundaries of Europe by force since Hitler's invasion of the Soviet Union in 1941.

Not only were we witnessing a brutal return to the power politics of 'iron and blood' in Europe, but we were also seeing a new form of state-on-state warfare. Rather than merely applying brute force, Russia instead undermined the integrity of Crimea from within and without the need for a conventional attack. I watched the TV shots on CNN and BBC News 24 on the widescreen TV in my office in SHAPE. It showed soldiers in green uniforms, with no identifying unit insignia, faces obscured with balaclava helmets, driving similarly unidentified vehicles. As my fellow commanders and I watched, we all knew who those vehicles belonged to and who was operating them. But proving it was another thing. It was highly professional and expertly implemented and we couldn't even consider doing anything to counter it as Ukraine was not a member of NATO.

In the days that followed we received regular updates from NATO's Intelligence Fusion Centre, as they listed the Russian tank armies and airborne divisions now preparing to invade the rest of Ukraine. At the same time, we witnessed an unprecedented buildup of Russian forces on the borders of the Baltic States of Estonia, Latvia and Lithuania. Now this was very much our concern, as 'the Baltics' – as NATO refers to them – had been NATO members since 2004.

Then President Putin spoke in the Kremlin on 18 March 2014 and formally admitted Crimea into the Russian Federation.

The next morning I sat with my direct boss General Phil Breedlove, NATO's Supreme Allied Commander Europe, the SACEUR, for the daily operational update in the Comprehensive Crisis Operations Management Centre at the heart of SHAPE, which is NATO's strategic military headquarters. This newly refurbished, state-of-the-art command centre was built to replace an old-style Cold War bunker. It is NATO's strategic nerve centre and it is specifically designed for the challenges of twenty-first century conflict. Manned by its mixed military and civilian staff from the twenty-eight nations of the Alliance, it is also able to integrate its planning with the multitude of different international organizations and other agencies with whom NATO does its essential business. With its banks of computers, multiple media feeds from different 24-hour news channels and social media, and its real time satellite and drone surveillance imagery, it allows SHAPE's Command Group to think, plan and act strategically.

The glass walls and open-plan architecture of the brightly lit conference room made the atmosphere more like the trading floor of a City of London investment bank than a traditional military headquarters, as successive 'briefers' outlined the developing situation on the ground to the Command Group and its supporting staff.

Despite the shock of the Russian invasion, the tone was measured and matter of fact. There was a sense of purpose, a recognition that this could be, if the opportunity was taken, NATO's moment to show how relevant it still was. After all, this was the very sort of scenario that the Alliance had been formed to confront sixty-five years earlier. Conversely, fail to match the moment and there was a real risk that this might be the point that NATO's inherent weakness – the requirement for all twenty-eight member states to agree on a course of action – was laid bare for all to see.

Which was it to be?

I remember well the air of unreality as the detailed contents of the President's Kremlin speech were analyzed for us by the Operations Chief, a US airborne forces major general, a veteran of the wars of the past decade and a man not given to hyperbole. He quoted the sometimes bizarre, always hyper-nationalistic, words of the President: 'We have all the reasons to believe that the policy of containment of Russia which was happening in the eighteenth, nineteenth and twentieth centuries is still going on.' Followed by the President's chilling warning to the West: 'If you press the spring, it will release at some point; something you should remember.' It ended with the unequivocal statement that Russia and the Ukraine were 'one nation' and 'Kiev is the mother of Russian cities'.

As I listened, the implications were clear. The annexation of Crimea, and the President's vow to reunite 'Russian speakers' in the former republics of the Soviet Union under the banner of Mother Russia, was little different from Hitler's annexation of the Sudetenland in 1938. Would future historians judge this as our generation's Rhineland and Sudetenland moment? And to continue the analogy to its logical conclusion, would an implicit Russian attempt to reincorporate the Baltic States – with their significant Russian speaking minorities – into a new Russian empire in a couple of years' time be our Poland? My answer was an emphatic 'yes'. If NATO failed to step up to the mark.

In the following days we watched the continued Russian build-up of troops on both the borders of Ukraine and the Baltic States. This was not in the modern NATO script or the way 'the West' – meaning broadly Europe, the US, Canada, Australia and New Zealand – viewed the world either.

Eminent western military thinkers were even now proclaiming the end of state-on-state industrial war. But if my passionate study of history has taught me anything, it is to take no apparent 'certainty' for granted, together with our inability to learn the lessons of the past. I felt as if I were back at Staff College in the Cold War days of the late 1980s. We were once again talking of Russian tank armies and airborne divisions and calculating where and when they might attack across the border into Ukraine.

My first concern was for the Baltic States and what this display of Russian aggression would mean for them. I recalled, with some discomfort, my interview in September 2012 on Latvian TV, in which I had said so confidently, in response to some sharp questions from my interviewer, that I saw no threat to the Baltic States from this Russian government. How wrong I had been. All the Chiefs of Defence of these freedom-loving, western European-orientated countries were my friends. All had family members who had been deported to Siberia or liquidated in the purges of the Soviet era. The previous Estonian Chief of Defence had himself been deported to the Russian Gulags with his entire family as a child, aged nine. All had experienced the brutality of conscription into the Soviet military and, as the Soviet Union collapsed in 1992, all had put their lives on the line and answered their country's call to break away from the Soviet empire. They understood the horror of what might be coming around the corner in a way that I, as a Brit, or SACEUR as an American, could not even begin to do. These were men who really understood the meaning of the word 'freedom'.

I phoned them all in turn: Riho Terras, Raimonds Graube, and Arvydas Pocius. They were calm, but utterly realistic. They reported unprecedented levels of Russian military activity in their airspace, seaspace and along their land borders with Russia. These, they reported, were clearly designed to intimidate them. This was the way the old Soviet Union did business and they were under no illusions as to what they were witnessing now.

It turned out that the Americans had been there before me. General Marty Dempsey, Chairman of the Joint Chiefs, had conference-called them earlier that day. In the face of their concern he had ordered the immediate deployment of a squadron of F-16 fighter-bombers to the Baltics. With that one gesture, I knew that America was continuing to underpin and guarantee the freedom of Europe; if Russia attacked, however far-fetched that might seem, it would mean them engaging those aircraft. And that would mean America was also being attacked. Nevertheless, my friends expressed disappointment, some bitterness, but no surprise, that none of the major European NATO powers – Britain, France or Germany – had shown any solidarity with them. They could have said to me, 'I told you so.' But none did. They didn't need to.

Back at SHAPE, our daily lives quickly became dominated by the crisis in Ukraine and how NATO should respond. At the end of one briefing, SACEUR, NATO's strategic commander, a genial, Harley Davidson-riding, US Air Force fighter pilot from the Deep South, asked me for my thoughts as a land commander. 'Phil,' I replied, 'the NATO nations won't like it, but now is the time to deploy a brigade to the Baltic States to show the Russians that we're serious about defending them.'

Sadly, and in the course of this book you will see why, this was a political bridge too far for the North Atlantic Council. But militarily and, I would argue, politically, it was the right thing to do. An all-arms brigade of 5,000 men with tanks, armoured infantry, attack helicopters and artillery would have sent a powerful message to the President: 'Thus far perhaps, but no further.' It would also have irrevocably bound all NATO nations into the defence of the Baltic States.

I quickly made two more phone calls, to Air Chief Marshal Stu Peach, the UK's Vice Chief of Defence Staff, in the Ministry of Defence in London, and to Mariot Leslie, the UK's Ambassador to NATO in Brussels. I suggested that now was the time for Britain to show solidarity with the Baltic States and particularly with Estonia, whose lion-hearted soldiers had fought and died alongside British soldiers in faraway Helmand. The wheels of government turned and, shortly afterwards, to his credit, the British prime minister authorized the deployment of four RAF Typhoons to Estonia. But the question remained: would the effort be sustained?

And then, at the end of March, my thirty-seven-year military career was over and I left SHAPE to start a new civilian life. I was, however, interested to note that, in May 2015, just over a year after I had first suggested it, the Estonian Chief of Defence called for NATO to deploy a brigade to the Baltic States to show its solidarity with those small and vulnerable countries, as its massive and ever more aggressive neighbour continued to ramp up its military activity on their borders. Sadly that request fell on deaf ears.

How had it come to this? How was it that Russia, whom NATO considered its most important strategic partner as late as 2014, was ripping up the post-Cold War settlement of Europe in our collective and shocked faces? And how had we been taken so much by surprise?

We have only to look at ourselves to find most of the answers. NATO itself set the scene for what followed in Ukraine. Back in 2008 it gave Ukraine its naive promise of NATO membership; a promise of collective defence that could never have been implemented militarily. The logistical challenge of assembling sufficient NATO combat power to protect Ukraine's eastern border should have been blindingly obvious, even to politicians who had grown up in a time of peace and knew nothing about war fighting. Put simply, Ukraine is just too far away to defend if attacked by Russia.

Furthermore, this posturing by the West only fed a deep-seated Russian paranoia about a perceived NATO strategy of ever-increasing containment. After all, during the Cold War, the Eastern Bloc countries had stood as a buffer between the borders of Mother Russia and democratic Europe. And be under no illusions, the Russians know all about being attacked from the West. This promise to Ukraine of NATO membership would have put yet another NATO country right on the Russian border. So, add to this Russian fear of encirclement the sense of profound dishonour following the collapse of the Soviet Union, and the subsequent chaos in Russia in the 1990s, and the result for proud Russians was a toxic brew.

We in the West might struggle to understand that real sense of personal dishonour felt so deeply by patriotic young officers who had served in the military and KGB at the apogee of Soviet power – men like the President – but that sense of dishonour is real and we need to accept it and factor it into our calculations.

Of course, the President had already shown himself to be a ruthless opportunist when he took the cool and brutal decision to invade Georgia back in 2008, at the exact moment the world's attention was focused on the Beijing Olympic Games. Despite this, after some perfunctory initial protests, the West quickly returned to business as usual. After all, Georgia was so far beyond NATO's sphere of influence and so deep in Russia's, there was little we could do. So an initial Russian toe in the invasion waters had shown the President what he could get away with; Hitler and the reoccupation of the Rhineland in 1936 came strongly to my mind, even as far back as 2008.

If this were not bad enough, there were other political and military blunders which, compounded together, gave an impression of growing Western weakness to the ever-watching Russians.

There was President Barack Obama's much-vaunted new 'Asia–Pacific pivot', which demonstrated Europe's reduced strategic importance to the United States. It was signalled by the massive reduction in American forces stationed in Germany. How ironic it was that, a month after Putin invaded Crimea, the last American tanks left German soil after sixty-nine years.

Once there were over 6,000 NATO tanks in Germany, most of them American: a massive statement of America's determination to protect Europe. It is a simple fact of military life that, once you cut capability, it requires a superhuman effort to regenerate it. Storing mothballed tanks and other vehicles of war in Eastern Europe, as the Americans first did in 2015, does not by itself create a credible military capability. That requires manpower, training, logistics and commitment and, equally important, enough time to pull everything together so they can operate as an effective team.

The impression of America's decreasing interest in Europe was further reinforced by Obama's abdication of diplomatic efforts to contain Russia in Ukraine in 2014. Don't forget that America, together with Russia and the UK, were signatories of the 'Budapest Memorandum' of 1994, under which Ukraine agreed to give up its nuclear weapons in return for US and Russian guarantees of its territorial integrity. Russia had torn up the Budapest Memorandum and Obama had chosen to forget American promises; not a good signal to send Russia, or the world.

In Europe, the United Kingdom, Europe's premier military power since the Second World War was led, from 2010, by a coalition Prime Minister, David Cameron, who appeared increasingly backward leaning on the international scene. His Defence Review of 2010 was nothing more than a gamble based on an assumption that the international scene would remain benign. Wars and conflicts that threatened the security of the United Kingdom were declared a thing of the past. The UK's national strategy proclaimed that there was no existential threat to these shores. How irresponsibly naive that sounds, as I write these words today.

Having unilaterally decided that this was the way the world would be for the foreseeable future, the 2010 Review then emasculated British military capability. The consequences are far-reaching and difficult, if not near impossible, to reverse: 20,000 experienced regular soldiers were axed from the Army. Royal Navy frigate and destroyer numbers – the work horses of any fleet – were cut right back. Some ships came off station from the Libyan maritime embargo in 2011 and sailed direct to the breaker's yard. It seemed quite extraordinary to me at the time to see our warships being broken up at the very moment they were most needed. The unravelling of Libya and the deepening turmoil of the Arab Spring ought to have told any politician with any sense that the world was not as safe and predictable as they were busy assuring us it was. Not only were RAF fast-jet numbers removed from the inventory, but that essential capability for a proud maritime nation, maritime patrol aircraft, was also disbanded. It would be difficult to overstate the disbelief of our allies or delight of our enemies at this shortsighted decision.

When I said in the *Sunday Times* at the end of March 2014, as I stepped down as DSACEUR, that this was a 'hell of a gamble', the Defence Secretary was so infuriated at being questioned in public that I was summoned by General Sir Peter Wall, the Chief of the General Staff and head of the Army, and told that the Defence Secretary had wanted 'formal action' taken against me. However, formal action would have involved a court-martial and, fortunately for the latter's political reputation – it also seems he had not appreciated that I reported to NATO and not to him - wiser counsel had prevailed. But the damage to our armed forces and, through them, our ability to defend our national interests – the first duty of any government – had already been done.

This failure to understand the realities of dealing with bullies was further reinforced during Britain's response to the crisis in the Middle East, caused by the eruption on the scene of the so-called Islamic State in the summer of 2014. Both the Prime Minister and the new Foreign Secretary, Philip Hammond, recently moved into post from Defence Minister (where, after threatening me, he had continued to oversee the rundown of British forces) waxed apocalyptic on the threat IS posed and yet did nothing credible to confront that threat. Foreign Secretary Hammond's hubristic boast that 'Britain defined itself by the extent to which it punched above its weight' was proved hollow.

So, when the Prime Minister himself wrote in a Sunday paper in 2014 that 'Britain should avoid sending armies to fight' – strongly implying that the Army's primary task was now humanitarian relief – I saw how the impact on the thinking of our allies and potential adversaries was profound. This pronouncement signalled that Britain was led by a government terrified of being seen to commit, but nevertheless yearning to be seen as bold and resolute. A country famous for once 'walking softly and carrying a big stick' – meaning that British governments did not make threats they did not fully intend to implement – now had a leadership that shouted loudly but, thanks to ongoing defence cuts, carried an increasingly tiny and impotent stick. And be in no doubt, nobody in the military was fooled by the 2015 Strategic Defence and Security Review with its creative accounting to maintain the Defence budget at two per cent of GDP and the 'jam tomorrow' – and most of these are many, many years in the future – of its big-ticket equipment items.

Since I wrote the preface for the hardback edition, everything I predicted has come to pass and we are now in an even more perilous situation. Russia has been ramping up its so-called 'snap' exercises with up to 30-40,000 troops at a time, suddenly and without prior warning, practising the overthrow and occupation of the Baltic States. American naval ships have been buzzed at low level by Russian fighters in the Baltic Sea and there has been a massive build up of Russian military force in the vicinity of the Baltic States with three Motor Rifle divisions (around 60,000 personnel) since January 2016. In the words of Dmitri Trenin of the Carnegie Moscow Centre, the Kremlin has been in a state of war with the West since 2014. While not yet in the Baltic chicken coop, the wolf is prowling around the still very flimsy fence. We are, de facto, in a new, and much more dangerous, form of Cold War.

Meanwhile, the international institutions on which Britain's, Europe's and transatlantic defence and security depends, NATO and the EU, are coming under increasing pressure. Yes, NATO has now agreed to send four individual battalions from the USA, Canada, Germany and Britain to the Baltic States and eastern Poland. While this is a start, no-one should be under any illusions that this is anything but a political token. First, it will take some time to deploy those battalions, which may itself encourage the President to conduct a pre-emptive strike before they are in position. Second, without proper command and control and the artillery, engineers, attack helicopters and logistics to turn individual battalions into an effective fighting brigade, and spread over four countries, those four battalions would be picked off piecemeal should Russia attack. At the same time, NATO is itself unexpectedly weakened by the fall out from the attempted military coup in Turkey which threatens to emasculate its second largest military power and render it ineffective and increasingly unstable as a result of the swinging purges against its armed forces.

Most recently, in July 2016, Republican Presidential candidate Donald Trump in an interview with the New York Times cast doubt on America's willingness to come to the aid of a NATO ally under attack. At a stroke this comment has undermined the notion of NATO's founding principle of collective defence. NATO is totally dependent on strong US leadership and peace in Europe will only be maintained if there is absolute certainty that the US will always be there to defend its allies. Trump's comments will embolden the President and make the nightmare scenario in this book more likely.

At the same time, the EU is itself faced with an existential crisis following the British vote to leave in the June 2016 referendum. Britain itself not only faces a potential break up of the Union following the resounding Scottish vote to remain in the EU, to say nothing of the risk to the Northern Ireland peace process, but faces political and economic uncertainty with inevitable implications for its international standing and its armed forces as the full fiscal impact of BREXIT is felt. At the very least, maintaining Defence spending at even a creatively accounted 2% of GDP will be little comfort if GDP shrinks as a result of the economic consequences of BREXIT.

Meanwhile, the one man doubtless rubbing his hands in glee at this turmoil has been the President sitting in his office in the Kremlin. Britain, once Europe's premier military power, seemed set on a course of moral and physical disarmament. As a young KGB officer in East Germany during the Cold War, the President recalled the respect in which Britain, under its 'Iron Lady' prime minister, was held by Russia for its bold recapture of the Falkland Islands in 1982. Britain had said they would do what seemed the near impossible and had gone ahead and done it. That combination of a show of arms, and quiet but grim political resolve, had given Britain huge political capital. Clearly that stubborn resolve, so respected and admired across the world, had evaporated. Britain was now little different from any other semi-pacifist, European social democracy; more interested in protecting welfare and benefits than maintaining adequate defences.

If Britain's enemies concluded that it was fast losing the will to fight for what it believed in, much of Europe never had the will to start with. Moreover, the US was now looking to the threats and opportunities of the East, instead of the old world of the West.

So this is the story of how the West failed to heed the warning signals from Russia, unwittingly emboldened its President and, through a succession of disastrous policy decisions, blundered over the edge of the precipice to war.

'So what?' you may say. Of course, it will be grim for the people of the Baltic States and Poland, 'faraway countries of which we know little', to paraphrase Prime Minister Neville Chamberlain in 1938. But will it really affect us in Britain and Western Europe if NATO is rendered impotent and we are unable to protect the Baltic States and Poland from Russia?

The answer to that is a resounding, 'Yes'.

First, the most terrifying scenario is that, without strong conventional deterrence – tanks, planes, artillery, ships and boots on the ground – the only remaining line of defence for a NATO facing imminent military defeat is nuclear weapons.

The growing weakness of our conventional forces means that the only way Russia can be deterred, or defeated, is by the threat, or use, of nuclear weapons. However, the consequence of the release of Inter-continental Ballistic Missiles, such as Trident, on Russia would be Armageddon; a result so terrible that the Russian President will calculate that the US, UK (despite the strong statement of intent that she would have no hesitation ordering the use of nuclear weapons from UK's new Prime Minister Theresa May) and France – the only nuclear-armed states of NATO – would never risk the near total destruction of human civilization in Europe for the sake of three small Baltic States.

And he is probably right. Which is why he would get away with it.

This is why maintaining an effective conventional deterrent – military forces that can fight and hold off the Russians if they attack, but above all to persuade them not to attack in the first place – is critical. It is only by having strong conventional forces that we can hope to ensure there is never a need to use that final option: nuclear weapons. Put another way, weak conventional forces make the use of nuclear weapons as a last, desperate, line of defence, very much more likely.

Even without the release of nuclear weapons, if we do have to fight a conventional war, prepare yourself for appalling casualties. These would be infinitely greater than anything suffered in recent wars in Iraq and Afghanistan. There could well be casualties on a Second World War level of horror. Be under no illusion whatsoever: war has a grim and uncontrollable logic of its own. Once the first bombs and missiles are launched, who can say where the next lot will end up landing? If we are hitting Russians, why should London, Edinburgh, Berlin, Paris or Warsaw not end up being targeted in return?

It does not need Russian soldiers marching though Berlin and Paris for the world as we know it to cease to exist. A militarily victorious Russia, able to dictate to a defeated Europe and NATO from the end of a barrel as to exactly what will and what will not be acceptable to them, will be enough for life as we now know it in Western Europe to come to a very abrupt end.

'To the victor the spoils'. Always.

As DSACEUR, Deputy Supreme Allied Commander Europe, I sat in the council meetings with defence ministers and the decision makers of NATO; I was part of the discussions and decisions on how force should be deployed, and walked the corridors of power in NATO HQ Brussels, the White House, No. 10 Downing Street and the Pentagon. In this book I will take you into those corridors as the politicians agonize over whether to send in Special Forces, order air strikes or deploy armies and navies.

I will show you, based on my personal experience of NATO's campaigns in Afghanistan and Libya, the posturing, the vanity, the political cynicism, and the moral cowardice which all too often characterizes those decisions. I will also highlight the occasional statesmanship and how the leadership and moral courage of one individual of stature can change the course of history. I know, too, the reality of combat, so I will show you how decisions taken at the highest levels affect the men and women who fight the battles and who, together with innocent civilians, pay the price of war.

When I was DSACEUR, I led exercises in which we war-gamed these scenarios, based on our own capabilities and what we knew about our enemies. What follows in this book represents one such, entirely feasible, scenario, however unimaginably awful it may seem. But just because something is unimaginably awful to Western political leaders, that does not mean it is not considered a viable option by the Russians.

This is fiction, but it is fact based, entirely plausible, and very closely modelled on what I know, based on my position as a very senior military insider at the highest and best-informed level. Why write it as a future, fact-based fiction rather than a polemic? The answer is simple. I have contributed to at least three think tank papers in the last six months highlighting the threat from Russia. But who reads think tank papers but other think tankers? My aim has been to explain the very real danger we face to the general reader with no particular interest in defence and to make it accessible. At every stage I have shown how the political and military decisions we are currently making, and have already made, are now propelling us into a future war with Russia. However, this is a war that could yet be avoided, if we act right now.

That is why this story needs to be told before it is too late. Because, in Trotsky's chilling words, 'You may not be interested in war, but war is interested in you'.

Of one thing I am absolutely certain: the President in the Kremlin knows all this and, even as you read these words, his admirals and generals are also war-gaming these very scenarios.

And they have every intention of winning the war.

General Sir Richard Shirreff
Laverstoke, Hampshire
August 2016

Prologue

I T IS MAY 2017.

A new US president was inaugurated in January and immediately reversed President Obama's 'hands-off' approach to Russia. The first new foreign policy decision was to arm Ukraine with the counter-battery radars, drones, electronic warfare equipment and secure communications, armoured HUMVEEs and medical equipment it so desperately needed if it was to defend itself against the Russian separatists, supported by Russian regular forces. But equipment is rarely enough and, on the advice of the generals, US military personnel were also deployed to train the Ukrainian army in how to operate this highly sophisticated equipment.

This allows the President to tell the world that the US is in Ukraine only in the role of 'trainers' and not as combatants; an obfuscation that the American president believes will deter the Russians and their proxies without over-inflaming existing tensions.

However, the absence of US soldiers on the ground to protect the 'trainers' leaves them vulnerable to attack. The compromise solution is to provide US fighter air cover, although the generals warn that there is little a fighter aircraft, however sophisticated, can do to protect a few men on the ground from 20,000 feet. Only too aware that the American people in general, and the House of Representatives and the Senate in particular, will not countenance US 'fighting' soldiers stationed in Ukraine, the

President tells the generals to stop complaining and make it work. Anyway, the 2014 Minsk peace accord is still holding and not even the most hawkish US general is suggesting that Russia is about to attack.

The equipment and the trainers are sent, their mission specific: get the equipment installed and working, get the Ukrainians trained and then get out as quickly as possible.

In the UK, the new Prime Minister is distracted by the consequences of the UK electorate's vote to leave the EU in the June 2016 referendum. On top of this, Nicola Sturgeon, the SNP leader, is threatening a second independence referendum. In an attempt to rebuild their 'special relationship' with the United States, the UK timidly sent a small team of medics and supply officers to help train the Ukrainian army in 2015. However, far from sending a signal of strength and resolution, the UK's effort appears weak and the force a potential hostage to fortune. Just as bad, this move reinforces the Russian narrative of NATO trainers being Ukraine's 'foreign legion', an insult that plays particularly well with nationalist forces at home.

In Ukraine, despite the political ambiguity of the 2014 Minsk ceasefire, major fighting has ceased and the war settled down to a semi-frozen conflict, with both sides – Ukrainian Army and 'Russian Separatists', although supported by Russian regular forces – occupying entrenched positions. Behind Ukrainian government lines a form of normality has emerged, which allows US and UK trainers to work with the Ukrainian army under near peacetime conditions.

Unaccountably, the strident Kremlin propaganda of two years ago, portraying the deployment of trainers as evidence of the NATO threat to Russia, has recently gone quiet, helped no doubt by increasingly close cooperation between Russia, America, France and Britain over air strikes in Syria. This absence of vitriol and threats gives the US president further confidence to send more US equipment and trainers, although still without proper 'boots on the ground' protection.

Meanwhile, in Russia, the President's personal ratings have begun to suffer as a result of the troubled economy and falling ruble, under ever-increasing pressure from continued sanctions and the volatility of the oil price, Russia's main foreign revenue earner. GDP has fallen by around four per cent annually since 2014. Despite this, defence spending has risen, as planned, by forty per cent in the last three years. The President's popularity has never recovered properly from the humiliation in 2015 of a Russian tourist jet being blown to pieces by jihadists over Sinai and a warplane being shot down by the Turkish Air Force, and his failure to take revenge. The President knows he needs to balance the economic books, or do something remarkable, if he is to regain the massive levels of popular support he enjoyed in those heady days after the successful invasion of Crimea in spring 2014.

His solution: to resolve, once and for all, the Ukraine problem and so fulfil the blood-stirring promise he made to the Russian people in his Crimea victory speech in 2014, that Russia and Ukraine are 'one nation' and 'Kiev is the mother of Russian cities'. The President now needs to engineer the circumstances to allow him to do this.

Thus it is that a potentially dangerous situation has been made very much worse, because the President has been emboldened by the continued disunity and weakness of the West in the three years since he first annexed Crimea and captured parts of Ukraine. In the face of this, rather than being persuaded to abide by international law, the President has decided to attempt further foreign adventures, particularly when his analysts in the FSB – Russia's external intelligence agency and successor to the KGB – assure him that the promises made in 2014 at the NATO Summit and ratified in Warsaw in 2016, 'to strengthen collective defence', have not been met. They tell him that, its decision to deploy four battalions to the Baltic States and eastern Poland, far from building a credible deterrence, NATO is erecting a Potemkin village.★

In short, NATO has failed to send the necessary strong signals that it is ready and capable of implementing collective defence and, in time of crisis, manning up to the Article 5 Guarantee that decrees that an attack on one NATO member is an attack on all NATO members; the very cornerstone of the NATO alliance.

The President's principal military advisor, the Chief of the Russian General Staff, has further assured him that NATO lacks the knowledge, capability and military hardware necessary to match Russia's ever-improving conventional capability. The Americans have disbanded their two heavy brigades in Germany, reduced their stationed forces in Europe to a handful, and would be hard pressed to redeploy to Europe quickly enough to respond to a potential Russian ground threat to NATO territory.

The Chief of the General Staff also pointed out that, while the Americans may have forward-based tanks and other military hardware in Eastern Europe and the Baltic States, it will be impossible to man them with trained crews quickly enough to prevent a Russian grab of the Baltic States. The Russians can dispatch an airborne brigade onto Riga from their aviation base at Pskov, only fifty minutes flying time from Riga. They would be in control of the Latvian capital before any Americans managed to even take off from their base at Fort Hood, Texas. Once the Russians were in control it would be game over. It is one thing to deter an attack with a credible force, quite another to mount an invasion from over 5,000 miles away.

★ 'Potemkin village', derives from the deception efforts of Prince Potemkin, statesman and favourite of Catherine the Great, who erected dummy villages along the banks of the Dnieper River in order to fool the Empress into thinking that the area was settled and prosperous during her visit to the Crimea in 1787.

Furthermore, in stark contrast to NATO's ageing armoury of attack helicopters, tanks and artillery – much of it dating from the 1980s and 90s – the Russian army now boasts state-of-the-art equipment, exemplified by the new T-14 'Armata' tank, first unveiled in the Red Square Victory Parade in May 2015.

But the Chief of the General Staff has also assured the President that Russia's conventional capability is only there to threaten and intimidate. Of equal importance, and far greater subtlety, Russia has continued to refine its asymmetric or, as they call them, *maskirovka* ('deception') tactics, as deployed so effectively in Crimea three years before; undermining the integrity of a target state from within, but keeping such actions under the threshold that might trigger a NATO response.

Despite warnings from the now, very worried Baltic States, NATO has failed to even recognize that *maskirovka* and under-cover operations are being actively used against those member states. They are the next obvious targets and it is only too obvious to them what is going on. To most United States and Western European politicians, however, these are annoying distractions on the far borders of Europe; incidents that rarely merit even a mention in their media. Their more immediate concern is to satisfy their electorates and keep themselves in power.

The President and his advisors in the Kremlin have watched and noted this ever-growing western malaise. So the scene is set for the President to complete his strategic intent: to reunite ethnic Russian speakers in the former states of the Soviet Union under the banner of 'Mother Russia'.

PART ONE

Reckoning

1730 hours, Tuesday, 9 May 2017
Kharkiv, Ukraine

AFTER THE DARKNESS and bitter cold of the Ukrainian winter, spring is a time of optimism for the people of Kharkiv. And this Victory Day holiday afternoon was no exception. Warm spring sunshine set off the white walls and golden domes of Pokrovsky Cathedral. In Maxim Gorky Park, groups of students from the many universities in the city played football, or lay on the grass chatting, while extended families gathered to picnic and barbecue to celebrate the holiday.

In the city, the cafés and bars in Freedom Square were full of people making the most of the weekend and the weather. It seemed a long time since the 2015 Minsk ceasefire effectively froze the war of 2014–15. Since then, the provinces of Donetsk and Luhansk had become *de facto* Russian protectorates, now known to their Russian 'peace-keepers' as the province of Novorossiya. An uncertain peace prevailed, regularly broken by flare-ups along the front line between the Ukrainian army and Russian-backed separatists.

A lone man made his way through the groups of revellers, scanning the crowd as he walked. Unobtrusive at around medium height and in his early thirties, with close-cropped dark hair and a black, zip-fronted fleece jacket over a newly laundered white T-shirt, he moved with an easy, sinewy stride; a man used to covering ground with minimum physical effort, always keeping something in reserve. However, Anatoly Nikolayevich Vronsky was not enjoying the sun. A driven, utterly focused man, Vronsky accepted nothing but the best, and things looked as if they might be unravelling before they had even started.

First, his contact at the base had telephoned to warn him that the group he wanted had left earlier than expected. Then, ten minutes earlier, the idiot tasked to follow them had reported in that he had a blown tyre and had lost them on the outskirts of the city. Vronsky's best guess was that they had to be heading here, the tourist part of town, which is why he was now searching Freedom Square for them, methodically breaking down into sectors the vast, café-lined square, surrounded by huge Soviet-era concrete buildings. Each sector had to be surveyed in turn; slowly, not rushing it, just as he had once been taught and how he taught those who now followed him.

There. At a pavement table: one woman and four men. Now he saw them, the group was easy to spot among the Ukrainians. Uniformly clad in jeans and polo shirts, the men sported the distinguishing mark of any American soldier, the crew cut.

Vronsky slowed his pace, relaxed his shoulders so that he was almost slouching and made his way to an empty table right beside them. As he waved to the waiter, he took out his mobile and made a couple of calls. Minutes later another man and an attractive, younger woman joined him. They shook hands and he kissed the girl on both cheeks, sat down and ordered coffee; a typical group of young Ukrainian professionals relaxing on a day off. Then the three of them argued about the most likely winner of that season's Premier League: Dynamo Kyiv or Metalist Kharkiv. All they had to do now was wait.

The moment came when one of the Americans at the next table pulled out a tourist map, looked around to orientate it and placed it on the table. 'Well, we're obviously in Freedom Square,' said one of the group, with a marked Texan accent.

It was what Vronsky had been waiting for. 'Where are you heading?' he asked, in faultless, American-accented English.

Surprised, the American turned and looked at him. 'Hey, you speak pretty good English . . . you ever been to the States?'

'Sure.' Vronsky smiled. 'I was at the University of Texas in San Antonio for a couple of years.'

'You don't say . . . that's where I'm from!' was the delighted response from the American.

'Hey, you don't say. Is the River Walk still the place for a beer?'

'Sure . . . the best.'

'We'd better celebrate then. I can't offer you an Alamo, but let me buy you one of our local beers. Have you ever tried a white beer? Perfect on a sunny evening.'

'Well . . .' the American hesitated. 'I guess one won't do any harm. By the way, I'm Scott Trapnell.'

'Anatoly Nikolayevich Vronsky,' he responded and they shook hands. 'I lecture in English at the University of Kharkiv. What are you guys doing here?'

'Great to meet you, Anatoly,' enthused the friendly American. 'We're US military. 1st Battalion, 15th Field Artillery, US Army. Here to train your army in how to use the AN/TPQ-36 weapon-locating radar. That's the mobile radar system our government has given your guys to help track incoming artillery and rocket fire. I'm Master Sergeant Scott Trapnell and these guys are my training team.'

'You don't say, Scott. That's amazing. We owe you guys so much! Without you here, well . . .' Vronsky's voice trailed off. Both men knew that it was only the presence of the American trainers that was stopping Russia from overrunning this part of pro-Western Ukraine.

'So, where are you based?' Allegiances confirmed, Vronsky picked up the conversation again.

'We've been out at Chaguyev training camp, east of Kharkiv,

for the past couple of months . . . We're in town today for some R and R.'

'I suspect you need it,' Vronsky commiserated. 'Being stuck out there must be boring and uncomfortable.'

'Well, you know what it's like.' Trapnell caught himself, not wanting to complain in front of a friendly local, but Vronsky was right. That was pretty much all they did in private: complain at the conditions and count the days till they got back Stateside.

'I do. I did military service too and those old Soviet barracks were dumps.'

At that moment the waiter brought the beer and they sat and chatted at the pavement table. Soon, General Order Number 1 – the rule preventing American military personnel from drinking alcohol while on duty or while deployed – was set aside and the Americans were able to relax for the first time in months; imagine themselves as simple tourists for a few moments, enjoy the sun and the exotic beer, and watch with obvious appreciation as long-legged, ash-blonde Ukrainian girls strutted past.

In no time the Americans were at the centre of a group of admiring Ukrainians, all keen to buy them beers, practise their English, and express their gratitude for what America was doing to support their beleaguered country.

Vronsky lifted his chair and placed it between Trapnell and his neighbour, the only female soldier in the group.

He turned to her. 'Hi, I'm Anatoly. Thank you for what you're doing for us.'

'It's a pleasure, Anatoly. And I'm Laura Blair. But please call me Laura,' she replied, a typically open, friendly, pretty all-American girl. 'I guess life has been very tough for you with the war and everything.'

Vronsky looked at her. 'You're not wrong . . . All war is dreadful but civil war is brother against brother, fathers against sons.'

'What about the Russians?' asked Blair.

'Sure, they're involved, but how can they not be? Ukraine and Russia are inseparable. Like twins joined at birth. The tragedy was the separation after Soviet times.'

Blair persisted. 'But the Russians have invaded your country, broken the ceasefire, attacked your soldiers.'

'If young, innocent conscripts, forced to fight against their will, is an invasion then yes, the Russians invaded. The Kremlin will tell you they were volunteers. Don't believe that propaganda. The truth is everyone in war loses, is a victim. There are no winners. Everyone's lives are blighted; young, old and always the innocent. It's the women and children who suffer most . . . But enough of us and our troubles on such a beautiful day. Where are you from, Laura?'

Vronsky saw her look up at the sun and then at the happy crowds around them. She smiled. 'Amherst, Massachusetts,' she replied, 'and you?'

Vronsky ignored the question. 'Amherst? Home of the poet Emily Dickinson?'

'Exactly. I'm impressed that you know. My dad was a janitor at Amherst Academy where she was at school. I guess you know about her from teaching English?'

'For sure,' said Vronsky, eyes softening, 'and she's one of my favourite poets. My time at school in the States left me with a love of American literature and a passion for Emily Dickinson. There's a line of hers that has brought me through the dark times of the war . . .'

He leaned close to her ear and whispered:

> *Hope is the thing with feathers*
> *That perches in the soul –*
> *And sings the tunes without the words –*
> *And never stops at all.*

Blair was entranced, unable to trust herself to speak as tears formed in her eyes. At that moment she felt a very long way from home and, besides, no man had ever talked to her as Vronsky was doing now. She smiled and closed her eyes, anxious not to show the handsome Ukrainian how deeply his words had affected her.

Vronsky used the moment to steal a glance to his right. Anna Brezhneva, his attractive female companion, had already focused on another, younger American, Sergeant Jim Rooney. 'I am study English at the University. I have girl friends who love to meet your friends.' She put her hand on his arm and gave it a slight squeeze. 'Is that good expression, Ji . . . im? You teach me if I say it bad?'

Rooney grinned. 'I like this idea. And you say it real well . . .'

Vronsky looked around the group and knew it was time.

'I tell you what,' he suggested with a broad smile, addressing them all. 'We have so much to thank you for. Why don't we all have dinner together? My cousin owns a great restaurant not far from here and he'll look after you like family. This is no tourist restaurant. This is where only locals go. You can't come to Kharkiv and not try our local food. You won't eat better *holubtsi* anywhere.'

The younger Americans looked at Trapnell for guidance. He hesitated, impressed at the offer but not quite sure.

Vronsky continued, 'And, as our honoured guests, it is of course our gift to you.'

Trapnell looked at the others, who grinned back. It is a rare soldier who can refuse the offer of high-quality, free food. 'Sure. Why not? But we can't stay late.'

'Don't worry. There'll be no problem. The restaurant is on the east side of the city and on the way back to your barracks. We'll eat, have fun, and get you back to your base in plenty of time.'

Anna Brezhneva waved her phone at Vronsky and shrugged, as if she was asking him an obvious question.

Vronsky smiled. 'Anna wants to know if you would like her to invite her girlfriends to make for equal numbers.'

The American men gave him a thumbs up, while Laura Blair sighed tolerantly.

'Make the call,' he said to Brezhneva, and she immediately starting talking into her mobile phone.

Vronsky summoned the waiter and demanded the bill. As he handed over 500 hryvnia, a couple of Mercedes taxis cruised past.

Brezhneva jumped up and waved them down. If the Americans noticed the fact they were the only two taxis in the square, then they gave no sign of being unduly worried.

Vronsky kept a fixed smile on his face, as he listened to the men discuss whether Anna's girlfriends could possibly be any prettier than she was. What was it with foreigners? They knew he spoke their language, but surrounded by others who could not speak English, they seemed to forget that fact. He caught Laura's eye.

She pulled a face as if to say sorry.

He smiled and nodded gravely in response. She was an intelligent and sensitive person and, in another life, he would have found himself warming to her.

Vronsky stood. 'Shall we?' he asked, as he helped Laura put on her jacket and indicated the two waiting taxis.

They all squeezed in. Unaccountably, once they had split up to do so, a big man got into the front seat of the second vehicle.

'Don't worry,' Vronsky announced to the Americans. 'He is here to make sure your friends are safe. There are some bad people in this city.'

Slightly heady from the unaccustomed beer and friendliness of their new friends, Rooney and Blair sat back in the taxi.

Vronsky ordered the driver to move off. Behind him in the rear view mirror he saw Laura tense. Perhaps his command had been that bit too sharp. Not perhaps what you would expect from a university lecturer. 'As I said,' he explained, 'the restaurant is not in a tourist area and the driver was surprised we were going there. I had to tell him twice.'

Reassured, the Americans started chatting and pointing as the taxis pulled out into the evening traffic, heading down Ivanova Street before hitting the main road west, Pushkin'ska, on their way to the east of the city. Soon they had left the city centre, crossed the Kharkiv River and entered the grim suburbs. Vronsky sensed a growing apprehension and announced that he was ringing his cousin to confirm they were nearly there. The neighbourhood might be awful, he explained, but the food was superb and getting a table was not easy. Vronsky saw Trapnell smile and the others followed his lead and relaxed with him as he made his phone call.

Fifteen minutes later, the taxis pulled up outside a tall 'Khrushchev' apartment block, one of many built across the Soviet Union in the 1950s and designed to pack as many people as possible into as small a space as possible. If getting the Americans into the taxis in Freedom Square had been the riskiest part of the operation – one shout of alarm and the cars would have immediately been surrounded by inquisitive and hostile locals – this was the second most difficult moment. Vronsky did not need a problem here, where unfriendly eyes might witness what was to happen next. Although there was nobody on the street at the moment, people could well be watching from the surrounding buildings.

'We're here,' he announced with a smile, stepping out of the car.

Trapnell looked up at him from inside the car and wound the window down. 'Where's the restaurant? What the hell are we doing here?'

Vronsky looked down at him, no longer the friendly university English lecturer. He needed the Americans to do exactly what he told them and that meant he was now cold-eyed, his voice ice-calm and ruthless. 'Do *exactly* as I say. Come with us. Quietly. *All of you.*'

The Americans were aghast, shock taking over their faces as they began to absorb what was happening. With their eyes locked onto his, they did not see the four men who were now emerging from the ground floor of the apartment block.

Vronsky motioned to them to surround the cars. In moments the Americans were being hauled out of the vehicles, arms locked behind their backs, mouths gagged with gaffer tape, heads covered with blankets, and then dragged towards the building.

All but one.

Master Sergeant Scott Trapnell was a man apart. Not for him the interminable muscle building in the gym favoured by most American soldiers; small, wiry, seemingly the most unobtrusive of men, he was an Aikido sensei and black belt and trained obsessively. Instinctively, in the face of an attack, the long hours of Aikido practice kicked in. A quiet calm came over him as his assailant yanked him out of the car. Then, using the other man's weight, the American dropped a shoulder and swung his assailant, applying the classic bent-armlock technique to turn his arm at the elbow and throw him onto his back and onto the road. As the man fell, his head snapped back against the tarmac with an audible crunch and he was silent.

The next man whirled to face him, hands up, ready for another such move. From his stance he was obviously well trained in martial arts.

Trapnell, wearing a sharp pair of leather cowboy boots for his big trip downtown, instead kicked him full force between the legs. Nothing subtle, nothing ninja, just a good, old-fashioned kick for goal, with all the force of his anger and betrayal that he could put behind it. 'Fuck *you*!' Trapnell screamed, as his boot connected with his balls.

The man dropped. Gasping. Eyes bulging in speechless agony.

Satisfied that the man was staying down, Trapnell looked around him and saw his fellows already being bundled away. For a moment, and with two men down, there was nobody to hold him on his side of the car. He ran. Hard and fast. And he was a good runner. Half-marathon was his speciality, but he was still very useful at a full sprint.

'Get him!' Vronsky yelled from the other side of the car. But there was no-one to get him.

The tower blocks around them were full of their enemies. In a few more seconds the American was going to start yelling for help. And that would bring people out onto the street, some with guns, who might help. The American would get away and the whole plan would be blown.

Without hesitation or remorse, Major Anatoly Nikolayevich Vronsky of the 45th Guards Spetsnaz Regiment reached under his jacket and, with the practised coolness of a Special Forces soldier, pulled out a PSS silenced pistol, issued only to Russian Special Forces, KGB, FSB and MVD. He took careful aim at the centre of the sprinting Trapnell's back and fired two successive bursts of two rounds in quick succession at twenty-five metres.

Trapnell was bowled forward and over like a shot rabbit. He twitched a couple of times and then lay still.

Vronsky turned, no emotion on his face. There would be ample time for blame and punishment once they were safely across the border. 'You two, fetch the body.' He indicated behind him with his thumb. 'Clear up any blood.'

'Praporshchik Volochka.' He pointed to the woman who had called herself Anna Brezhneva. 'We are moving straight to extraction. Get the vans here *now*.'

0800 hours, Wednesday, 10 May 2017
The President's weekly defence and foreign policy meeting
The Kremlin, Moscow

FYODOR FYODOROVICH KOMAROV, the President's Chief of Staff and regular judo partner, was below average height, stocky with the pale blue eyes and fair hair of a northern Russian. He was usually the most unruffled of men but he was troubled that morning. In line with his KGB training he was systematic, paid careful attention to detail, and took nothing for granted. He was also utterly single-minded, whether in his service to the President, or as a key player in the group of St Petersburg-based former KGB officers – known as *siloviki* – who had effectively taken over Russia from the reformers after Boris Yeltsin's demise; men who bitterly regretted and resented what had happened to their beloved country ever since.

Komarov knew only one way: ruthless control. That was the old Soviet way. He also knew that the price of failure was high and that morning he had to manage the President's reaction to yesterday's kidnap of the Americans in Kharkov and the un-anticipated death of Master Sergeant Trapnell.

Clutching his briefing papers and notebook to his chest, he knocked twice on the ornate, gilded double doors of the President's office.

The doors were opened soundlessly by two soldiers in the

ceremonial uniform of the Kremlin honour guard; tall, imposing and specially selected for their impeccable Slavonic looks, they were the men of the 154th Preobrazhensky Independent Commandant's Regiment, the men who protected the President.

Komarov entered, paused momentarily, dipped his head in salute and then walked forward. The room was spartan, minimalist, the only concession to extravagance being the green curtains edged in gold and tied back with gold ropes. Behind the President's chair there was only one decoration, the gold double-headed eagle of Russia on a red shield. The desk was huge but empty of any papers except, he noted, the report from Kharkiv. A long conference table jutted out at right angles from the desk towards the door.

Behind the desk sat the President; pale, bloodless face, high cheekbones, oval eyes cold, menacing and light blue. It was the face of a watchful fox with sparse, short, white-blond hair; a wiry, tough physique under his usual dark suit, plain navy blue tie and white shirt. Here was a man who worked out regularly and fought in the judo hall twice a week, described by his press spokesman as being, 'So fit, he could break people's hands when he shakes them . . . If he wanted to.'

However, his voice never failed to surprise Raskolonikov. For such an alpha male it was slightly high-pitched and nasal.

'Why did they kill the American, Fyodor Fyodorovitch?' the President demanded, using the formal patronymic. 'The mission was to capture the group. I wanted them all alive on television so that I can show the world that NATO and the Americans are attacking our people from Ukraine. Not in body-bags with the Americans screaming terrorism.'

'I agree, Vladimir Vladimirovich,' Komarov replied, putting his papers on the table in front of his chair. 'Typical of those Special Forces prima donnas. Always promising the earth, but when they cock up, they do it spectacularly. I talked to Colonel General Denisenko, Commander, Special Operation Forces

Command, this morning and left him in no doubt of your displeasure.'

The President said nothing, which meant he was still assessing how he was going to react.

'He tells me the Spetsnaz commander had no alternative once the American started running.'

The President frowned. 'They should not have let him escape in the first place. Who was responsible?'

Komarov looked at the President. As an old and trusted associate he could say things others could not but he still had to be careful. 'They underestimated the American. He was small but he fought like a devil. We now discover he was an Aikido expert.'

'So I see.' The President nodded at the file on the desk.

Komarov knew the President was a man who got into the detail and, as he had suspected, he had studied the report on the capture of the Americans.

'And I see he destroyed any prospects of fatherhood for the man he kicked in the balls.' The President smirked.

'We can turn this to our advantage, Vladimir Vladimirovich,' Komarov replied. 'Our people can make much of his injury in the news bulletins. Insist the shooting was in self-defence.'

The President nodded agreement. 'Who commanded the team? The report omitted that important detail.'

'It was led by one of our best, Your Excellency, Major Anatoly Nikolayevich Vronsky, 45th Guards Spetsnaz Regiment. Awarded Hero of the Russian Federation twelve years ago for his gallantry in North Caucasus. Son of a Soviet tank officer who had to become a taxi driver to feed his family after the fall of the Soviet Union. He went as an exchange student to a US university after doing his military service. When he finished in America, he became a professional army officer before passing the selection process for Special Forces.'

The President was silent for a moment, his earlier anger

dissipated. 'A tricky operation, I accept, and Major Vronsky seems to have recovered from the initial setback in an exemplary fashion. He did well.'

He looked up at Komarov. 'Convey my displeasure to General Denisenko. There must be no more mistakes if he is to remain as Commander of Special Operations Forces Command. Is that clear?'

'Very clear, Your Excellency.' Komarov would pass on the rebuke, but he knew the President well enough to see that he was secretly pleased. The execution of Trapnell would send a strong signal of Russian determination. 'Your Excellency, may I now call the meeting?' He passed an agenda and updated brief to the President, who nodded his agreement.

The double doors were opened by the guards and the President's Deputy, the Foreign Minister, Finance Minister, Interior Minister, Defence Minister and the Chief of the Russian General Staff entered.

The President remained seated.

'Sit,' he commanded.

Komarov took his habitual seat as note taker at the foot of the table. From there he could see the President directly. The others took their usual places at the conference table.

They waited for the President to speak, faces strained, wondering who would be his first target. He was a man who applied the principle of divide and rule to his allies and subordinates as much as to his enemies.

They did not have to wait long. The President looked hard at the Defence Minister who, despite his background as a minor Communist Party functionary and never having heard a shot fired in anger, was resplendent in the uniform of a General of the Army, complete with the ribbon of Hero of the Russian Federation displayed prominently among the multiple other ribbons on his chest.

'Alexandr Borisovich, I've read the report on the capture of the Americans in detail. I am not impressed that one was killed. We will turn it to our advantage but, be in no doubt, I will accept no more mistakes.'

The Defence Minister shifted uneasily in his chair. 'Understood, Vladimir Vladimirovich. It will not happen again.'

'I have also read the report on the situation in eastern Ukraine and am content that it remains relatively quiet,' said the President, looking at Komarov for confirmation.

Komarov nodded and the President switched his laser-like stare to the Finance Minister, 'You next, please.'

From his position at the end of the table Komarov saw the sweat on the back of the minister's bald head. He cleared his throat and swallowed hard. 'Vladimir Vladimirovich, it pains me to tell you that the economic position is getting increasingly difficult. American and EU sanctions continue to have a deeply negative effect on the economy—'

The President interrupted, 'These are old excuses, Boris Mikhailovich. EU sanctions have been toothless since the Italians, Greeks, Hungarians and Cypriots vetoed them at the EU Summit last June. The EU remains deeply divided.' He smirked, and then added, 'My strategy of increasing the flow of refugees into Turkey by bombing civilian targets in Syria and so putting ever greater pressure on the EU has worked better than I ever thought possible.'

'Of course, Vladimir Vladimirovich,' continued the Finance Minister. 'Nevertheless, the price of oil remains a problem. You will remember that my budget was based on a price of one hundred dollars per barrel, but the price has been consistently lower than that. There's a glut of oil on the market following the easing in sanctions against Iran after the nuclear negotiations in Lausanne two years ago. Iranian oil is pushing prices even lower. That means we are losing around forty billion dollars a year because of sanctions and around ninety to one hundred billion dollars a year because of the low oil price. On top of that, the increase in defence spending has put a huge strain on the budget.'

The minister removed his spectacles, polished them with a white handkerchief and summoned up his resolve. 'Vladimir Vladimirovich, there is no other way to describe the economic situation than very difficult.'

'What are my economic options?' demanded the President.

'In economic terms it is simple. Unless the price of oil goes back up, which no economist believes it will in the near future, we either have to cut spending or raise taxes to keep the deficit down to our projected zero-point-six per cent of GDP. And if we don't do that, we have no option but to borrow at increasingly expensive rates, which will only make the situation worse. The ruble is losing value. The forecast for growth from the Central Bank is zero and GDP is static at best.'

The President reflected silently and looked at Komarov with a raised eyebrow.

This was a moment the two men had rehearsed the day before. 'I suggest we ask the Interior Minister, Vladimir Vladimirovich,' Komarov responded. 'The economic picture is important, but it is the impact on your popularity which remains the key.'

The President turned to the Interior Minister, a man born in a remote village in the heart of Russia, near the River Volga, who, despite his rural origins, had made his career as a Moscow policeman. After rising through the ranks of the Criminal Investigation Department, he had eventually became Moscow's Chief of Police through peasant cunning and driving ambition, before being appointed Interior Minister. On his way he had uncovered, and now held close to his chest, the secrets of the most powerful, including the President. Behind the grey, close-cropped hair and the broad peasant face, the Interior Minister maintained a tight grip on the levers of power.

'Boris Vadimovich, what impact is this having on public opinion?' demanded the President.

'Vladimir Vladimirovich, you know better than anyone the resilience of the Russian people. We know how to suffer and even take pride in being able to endure the hardest conditions. But even the most resilient are beginning to tire of high prices, the shortage of consumer goods in the shops, the . . .'

'Don't give me that,' the President interrupted, voice dripping sarcasm. 'You can't call a few shortages hardship! What you describe may affect the Moscow middle class, but it is irrelevant to people in the heartland of Russia. *Our* people.'

'Vladimir Vladimirovich, you are, of course, correct,' the Interior Minister said. 'But people are no longer as tough as in Soviet days. They have been spoiled. The middle classes have travelled abroad for holidays and know what they are missing. But to hell with them! What does concern me is increasing unemployment and increased levels of poverty among the jobless.'

The President waved a hand in dismissal. 'This is a fact of Russian life. It sets us apart from the softness and excesses of the West. But what about the so-called opposition? They can hardly call themselves credible if, two years later, no-one has yet emerged to take that agitator Boris Nemsov's place.'

Komarov saw the Interior Minister frown and decided to support him. 'I regret, Vladimir Vladimirovich, that his killing two years ago created a martyr and a focus for those who dare to oppose you.'

'It had to be done,' the President snapped back. 'He was a dangerous and destabilising figure.'

'Of course,' Komarov equivocated. 'But the minister is correct in highlighting the threat his name still poses. The memorial to him where he was killed is regularly cleared away by the police, but it is always replaced.'

'I won't have it!' The President was getting annoyed. 'The bridge is to be guarded and anyone daring to replace the memorial is to be arrested!'

'It will be done, Vladimir Vladimirovich,' said the Interior Minister, who then turned to look squarely at the Deputy President. 'Don't forget I counselled against the liquidation, but others thought differently. If he had been left alone, he would have burned out on drink and women.'

'Enough!' directed the President. 'We must give the people pride in Russian power . . . as we did when I took over the Crimea three years ago. That is the way to restore morale and to neutralise the opposition.'

'Exactly right, Vladimir Vladimirovich!' the Deputy President exclaimed loudly.

'Thank you, Viktor Anatolyevich. I take that as your support,' the President said drily to his deputy.

Komarov liked the Deputy as much as he liked any man at that table. He was a former Ambassador to NATO and knew the West well. On the face of it he was a charming, open internationalist, a fluent English speaker married to a beautiful former Russian pop star. He gave the impression of being one half of a star couple, who wowed the Brussels dinner party circuit with their glamour and ability to set even the stuffiest diplomatic dinner party alight with their dancing. In reality, the Deputy President was a hard-line nationalist, very much one of the *siloviki,* appalled by the collapse of the Soviet Union, humiliated by the accession of the Baltic states to NATO, and determined to re-establish Russian power in its traditional 'near abroad' by whatever means were necessary.

'You, Vladimir Vladimirovich,' said the Deputy, 'you alone have restored Russian pride after the disastrous end of the Soviet Union at the hands of that traitor Gorbachev. Your leadership has restored Russia to the status of a great power after the chaos he caused. The economic position may be difficult, but now is the time of opportunity, the time for boldness!' He slammed his hand on the table for emphasis.

The President gestured at him to continue.

'The West may have great economic capability, but they think only of social welfare. They have forgotten how to stand up for themselves. I know from my time as your Ambassador to NATO that this is an alliance which is all talk and no action. But, nevertheless, it continues to pose a danger to Russia. It continues to encroach on our borders and its long-term strategy of encirclement of the Motherland is plain to see.'

As Komarov recorded these words, he noted the President tightening his jaw and clenching his right hand into a fist as if crushing his enemies. However, he also noted how the President avoided seeking reassurance from the others at the table, as that was a mark of weakness. He nodded at the Deputy President, saying nothing. Instead, he turned to the Foreign Minister, 'Yevgeney Sergeyevich, have we succeeded in dividing our enemies abroad? If so, is now the time to exploit those divisions?'

The Foreign Minister was tall and grey-haired, with the look of a distinguished international diplomat. 'Vladimir Vladimirovich, you have nothing to fear from the European Union. Yes, the sanctions regime has hurt us, but it hurt them, too. Besides, the mass migration crisis is well on the way to causing its collapse. So your efforts to undermine them, to divide them, particularly your bold decision to conduct air strikes in Syria, are having precisely the effect we anticipated.'

Komarov intervened. 'Yevgeney Sergeyevich is right. Not only are Greece, Hungary and Cyprus in the bag, but we can also assume division in France. Our banks have been giving loans to Marine Le Pen's party for some years. Now they will need to show sympathy, or we will demand immediate repayment of those debts.'

The Foreign Minister resumed, 'Yes, and in Germany we

can count on the willing fools who believe what they read about Russia in *Spiegel*. There are plenty of Germans who have a natural sympathy for us and see NATO as a dangerous aggressor.'

'We are all agreed then that NATO is an existential threat. But what about its capabilities?' asked the President.

'Therein lies the paradox, Vladimir Vladimirovich. Even as it expands eastward, NATO is like a marshmallow: soft at the centre. It talks and talks about the principle of collective defence. However, while we are increasing defence spending, NATO nations can only promise to try and raise spending to the agreed NATO levels within ten years. I do not for a moment believe that Britain, France or Germany will risk the lives of their soldiers to defend NATO's eastern member states. Their elect- orates will simply not allow it. Yes, the Alliance has a minimal presence in the Baltic states, but it shows no sign of wanting to antagonise us by establishing anything permanent.

'However, while the Alliance is weak, the bottom line is that NATO could, in time, pose a real and present danger to Russia. And just as worrying, the Baltic states could offer them a convenient launch pad for an attack on us. Right now though, NATO does not possess the physical capability to counter anything we might do. Almost as important, it also lacks the political and moral will to do so. While that is true of its leaders today, it might not be the case tomorrow.'

The President stared at the far wall before speaking again. 'I agree that Britain, France and Germany will do nothing. And Britain has become an international irrelevance.' The President at last gave a caustic smile. 'So, those countries don't count. But what about America?'

'Still the strongest military power on the globe. However, since the Obama presidency, they show no appetite to re-engage in Europe. We have no need to fear the few tanks they have placed in storage across Eastern Europe, from Estonia to Bulgaria. They are only for show. Without crews, ammunition, spare parts and maintenance teams they are so much useless metal.'

The President held up his hand for silence. 'Are we making the mistake of underestimating them? After all, what about last year's exercise in Poland, just before the NATO Summit? What could be more aggressive than deploying over twenty-five thousand troops as a show of force so close to our borders?' He shifted in his chair and then added, 'You may be right about NATO's present weakness, but I see mortal danger to Russia from America one day . . . and that means mortal danger to all of us.' He looked meaningfully around the small group of men who were his inner circle. 'My first duty is to defend Russia by preventing NATO encirclement. And the way to do that is to seize eastern Ukraine and the Baltic states.'

The Foreign Minister thought before answering. 'I accept that this deployment was a display of aggression against Russia. But it is still early days for the new president. We think that while they are talking big, they do not have the will or the mandate to engage overseas.'

Komarov looked at the President. 'That opinion is reinforced by the latest FSB report.'

'So I saw . . . but I repeat, beware of underestimating the Americans.'

Next the President turned to the Chief of the General Staff, his principal military advisor, rather than to the ludicrously bemedalled Defence Minister who sat alongside him. 'Are Russia's armed forces ready, Mikhail Nikolayevich?'

'Without question, Vladimir Vladimirovich,' the soldier replied.

As ever, Komarov noted how out of place he looked at this meeting. He was an ethnic Tatar from Kazan who, unusually for a Tatar, sat at the head of the Russian Armed Forces. Steady eyes, high cheekbones, dark greying hair, a man hardened in combat in Chechnya. He was the holder of the Military Order of Valour First Class, and a man who looked younger than his fifty-nine years.

'Our forces are ready to finish this business in Ukraine. At your command we are ready to move into the Baltic states. Our recent snap exercises have ensured that the Baltic and Northern Fleets are prepared for war, as are our air and ground forces. Our nuclear forces are on high alert and all five strategic submarines of the Northern Fleet are at sea with full complements of submarine-launched nuclear missiles. We have just reinforced Kaliningrad with nuclear-armed Iskander missiles. Once the final logistic outload is completed we will be ready for war.'

The President nodded and considered his options. Then he spoke, looking around the table as he did so. 'I understand your concerns about the increasingly difficult economic position, but we have an opportunity to seize the initiative here, to secure the eastern provinces of Ukraine and incorporate them as Novorossiya – New Russia – within the Russian Federation. To that end, I believe that the presence of American and British trainers in Ukraine indicates a clear and present threat to Russia and is more evidence of NATO aggression.'

The Finance Minister raised a hand. 'If I may, Vladimir Vladimirovich . . .' He faltered.

The President did not like being interrupted. 'What is it?' he said, with some irritation.

The Finance Minister seemed nervous. 'Please forgive me for saying this, but I must put on record my concern that any increased risk of hostilities with NATO will send the ruble into freefall and put the economy under even greater pressure than it is at present.'

'That's enough, Boris Mikhailovich,' the President cut him off. 'You had your say. My decision is to strike now, while we have the opportunity. Once we have Ukraine's Donbas region, we will have secured a manufacturing area of critical importance to our economy. NATO will be hopelessly divided as to what action it should take and may well start unravelling as we apply ever greater pressure and the nations argue among themselves. We will take more US and UK trainers as hostages and that will further divide them. What we leave of Ukraine will be a defenceless rump under our control. Russia will once again be pre-eminent. And . . . ,' the President now glared at the Finance Minister, 'with all this going on the world will take fright. Gold prices will soar and oil prices should go through the roof. That's exactly what you say our economy needs. Isn't it?'

The Finance Minister nodded.

The President turned to the Defence Minister. 'Alexandr Borisovich, I want to be briefed in detail on the plan for breaking the ceasefire tomorrow morning.'

'At your command, Vladimir Vladimirovich.' The Defence Minister bowed his head as he said it.

Komarov gathered up his papers. 'I'll work the briefing into your programme for tomorrow morning. I also suggest we warn this group for an on-call meeting to review developments once the plan is initiated.'

'Agreed. And I'll see you in the gym this evening. Now, I have a helicopter to catch.'

'S IT DOWN, PLEASE.'

General Sir David McKinlay, the Deputy Supreme Allied Commander Europe, or DSACEUR as he was called, entered the conference room with a pronounced limp. A grey-haired Scot, he proudly wore the distinctive Lovat Green trousers of the Royal Marines with his shirtsleeve order. He might be a four-star general, but the vagaries of the British military system meant he continued to wear his Royal Marine uniform, much to the confusion of his allies. Indeed, he recalled with amusement the Portuguese general who had asked him, on the day he had replaced a crimson-trousered cavalryman, if British generals were allowed to invent their own uniform. *Vive la différence*, he thought as he looked around the room, and McKinlay certainly did not fit the usual mould for such a senior British general.

He had come up the hard way and was commissioned from the ranks. A former Navy rugby prop forward, he was moustachioed, bulky, if not a touch overweight – but battle-hardened as befitted a veteran commando. He looked older than his fifty-seven years and spoke with more than a hint of his native

Falkirk accent. He was a man who saw things as they were and unless there was a compelling reason otherwise, and those instances were rare, he believed it was usually better for everyone in the long run if he told it as it was.

After over two years in post at Supreme Headquarters Allied Powers Europe, known as SHAPE, he had a good feel for the idiosyncratic world of NATO and the political and diplomatic complexities of high command. In addition to that, in common with most senior Royal Marine officers, he had impressive credentials as a commander up to brigade level. Indeed, his two DSOs from Iraq and Afghanistan bore witness to his extensive combat experience, as did the prosthetic he wore to replace his right leg, amputated above the knee as a result of an IED strike in Helmand province ten years earlier.

This morning McKinlay was in the chair for his boss, Admiral Max Howard, the Supreme Allied Commander Europe, the SACEUR. A strong-minded and politically savvy US Navy Admiral, Howard was currently in his personal plane over the Atlantic, en route to a Congressional hearing in Washington. SHAPE's other four-star general, the Admiral's Chief of Staff, General Kurt Wittman, a politically well-connected Luftwaffe logistician with no operational experience, had been called back to Berlin. That made McKinlay the senior general there that day and the man on the spot.

'Well, ladies and gentlemen,' he said, taking his chair at the head of the table, 'please proceed.'

But he got no further.

'Excuse me, sir.' Group Captain Jamie Swinton, his Principal Staff Officer, or PSO, was at his shoulder. 'We've just had a call from SACEUR's comms team. He is still mid-air, but wants to talk to you immediately. We've fixed up for you to take a call on the Tandberg VTC in your office in five minutes.'

'Thanks, Jamie. I'll be with you right away. Ladies and

gentlemen, I do apologise and I know how much work has gone into preparing this briefing. Please proceed, Skip,' he said, turning to Major General Skip Williams, the Deputy Chief of Staff, Operations, a crew-cut, hawk-faced, athletic-looking young American major general, who wore the Screaming Eagle insignia of the 101st Airborne Division as the combat patch on the shoulder of his battle fatigues. 'You take over and backbrief me later.'

'Sure thing, Sir,' said Williams.

With that McKinlay stood up and stumped out of the room with the Group Captain.

Five minutes later, he was back in his office and seated behind the desk installed by the very first DSACEUR, Field Marshal Bernard Montgomery. His Royal Air Force PA, Sergeant Lorna Bevan, first brought him a mug of the Scottish Breakfast tea to which he was addicted, and then ensured that the American-provided Tandberg secure VTC – Video Teleconference – system was up and running and that he was connected to SACEUR's comms team.

'Dave, are you receiving me?' Admiral Max Howard's finely drawn features, the thoughtful face of an Ivy League historian rather than a war-fighting admiral, filled the screen. 'Things are moving fast in Ukraine and we may lose comms, so I'll be brief.'

'Go ahead, SACEUR,' said McKinlay.

'Dave, I've just heard from my European Command HQ that a group of Americans are missing in Kharkiv. They were part of the training team sent to support the Ukrainian army and it looks as if they have been kidnapped by Russian Special Forces. We expect the Russians to put them on TV any moment now, claiming that they are US Special Forces, captured after crossing the Ukrainian border into Russia. Even worse, it looks as if one of them was killed trying to escape.'

'Hell, this is bad news,' responded McKinlay.

'It is. I've tried to brief the NATO Sec Gen,★ but I can't get through to either him or the Chairman of the Military Committee.† At present this is a US-only issue, but we can expect the Russians to claim it is evidence of NATO aggression.'

'I'll get on to the Chairman of the Military Committee soonest and be ready to brief Sec Gen . . . But it would be useful to know the US line.'

'I've talked to the White House,' said Howard. 'The President has accepted my advice that we show strength and, in fact, is all for going on the front foot. I hear the Brits are talking about pulling out their trainers, but the US is not going to back down in the face of Russian provocation like this.

'I've persuaded the President that the US should not over-react, but we will provide reconnaissance and surveillance top cover for all trainers deployed in the field in support of the Ukrainians as protection for our people. We've also agreed pretty robust defensive rules of engagement. More than that, the White House is tasking the US Permanent Representative to put a motion to the North Atlantic Council, the NAC. We want to agree a NATO training mission to Ukraine to demonstrate Alliance solidarity in response to this Russian attack on US soldiers. I want you to be ready to brief the concept and planning we've already discussed.'

'Roger to that, SACEUR. I'll talk to the Chairman of the

★The NATO Secretary General (Sec Gen): invariably a distinguished international figure who is responsible for leading the North Atlantic Council (NAC), the decision-making body of NATO, coordinating the effective working of the Alliance and leading the NATO staff. The current incumbent and his predecessor are both former prime ministers of their respective nations.

†The Chairman of the Military Committee (CMC) is NATO's senior military officer and the principal military adviser to the Secretary General and the North Atlantic Council. He also directs the daily business of the Military Committee, a body made up of senior officers from all NATO members and responsible for providing advice on military policy and strategy.

Military Committee now and will also touch base with the US ambassador before the NAC meeting.'

'Thanks, Dave. I'll aim to get back just as soon as I've testified over—'

And with that the screen went blank as communications were lost.

Group Captain Swinton, who had been monitoring the call from a remote set, stepped into the office. 'Sir, I understand the news has got through to Brussels and the Sec Gen has called an emergency NAC meeting this afternoon at 1400. They're expecting you to brief the training mission plan. The planning team are stood by now to take you through the briefing they've prepared.

'Sec Gen and the Chairman of the Military Committee would like to see you at 1330 for a chat before the NAC. Sergeant Jones is stood by with the car and police escort for 1230. And we'll make sure there's a sandwich in the car.'

'Thanks, Jamie. The briefing should be fairly straightforward as we've already war-gamed this scenario. But getting the Alliance to agree to a NATO training mission?' said McKinlay. 'That sounds to me like one hell of a long shot.'

An hour and a half later, briefing with the planners completed, McKinlay had put on a tie and slipped into his formal, bemedalled, Lovat green tunic to conform with the normal custom for military officers attending the NAC. He was now sitting in the back of the BMW 7 Series F01 four-door sedan, the designated staff car for DSACEUR, as Sergeant Taff Jones, his Welsh Royal Logistic Corps driver, gunned the gears to stay close to the Belgian military police motorcycle outriders, who were carving their way, blue lights flashing and sirens wailing, through the heavy traffic on the N27 Brussels ring road.

'I suppose we have to travel like this,' mused McKinlay to himself as he tried to read through his slides and notes, while the top-heavy, armoured vehicle swung sickenly every time it cornered.

He arrived at NATO HQ, in the Boulevard Leopold III in the north-east of Brussels. As the car swept up to the main entrance, guarded by the flags of the twenty-eight member nations, he was met by one of SACEUR's forward-based liaison team, an improbably tall, former professional basketball player, who had signed up to serve his country in the US Army following the attacks of 9/11.

'Hi, Sir. I'm Dan Rodowicz. I'll see you through security.'

Two minutes later he was on the first floor of the utilitarian building and was shown into the Secretary General's conference room.

Already waiting in the room was General Knud Vahr, Chairman of the Military Committee, a lean, wiry Danish cavalry general wearing parachute wings and with the piercing blue eyes of a latter-day Viking. 'Greetings David. Thank you for making it over here so quickly.'

With time so short, McKinlay came straight to the point. 'How do you recommend I play it with the Sec Gen and the NAC?'

'Play it straight. Sec Gen will open the meeting, commiserate with the Americans on the loss of their soldier, then ask me for the formal advice of the NATO Military Authorities. I'll make a couple of points and ask you to brief us on the plan. Then Sec Gen will ask the ambassadors for their comments and questions and then there'll no doubt be the usual lengthy discussion. As you know only too well, these guys just love the sound of their own voices and they'll want a say. Just remember that you are a military professional and they are not. Do what you always do and stay in your lane and you'll have no problems. And anyway, Sec Gen will keep a tight grip on the meeting. He thinks he's running a government and that the ambassadors are his cabinet who'll do as they're told.'

At that moment the Secretary General entered. Radek Kostilek was a former prime minister of Poland. Grey-haired, high-cheekboned and with a humorous glint in his eyes, he was inclined to wear his heart on his sleeve and prone to overreact emotionally – particularly where Russia was concerned.

He sat down. 'The Americans have got themselves into a hell of a fix this time and the Russians will use this as an excuse to have a go at NATO. On top of this kidnapping crisis, this American proposal for a combined NATO training team is just not going to run. The Germans for a start will see it as a knee-jerk reaction to the kidnap and they will push back. They pontificate about the importance of Alliance solidarity and then undermine it the moment the Americans really need their support. And as for the usual backsliders . . .'

The three men looked at one another and said nothing. Each knew the depth of frustration the others felt.

'General, what does SACEUR think?'

McKinlay updated him on his mid-air conversation with SACEUR and the key elements of the training-team proposal: multinational, based in Kiev and focusing on professionalising the Ukrainian armed forces at the senior levels. He stressed that it met the lowest common denominator criterion of NATO and that all NATO Chiefs of Defence Staff had bought into the idea that morning. 'I understand the political concerns,' he continued, 'but I think we can allay ambassadors' worries by emphasising that this is not front-line support, nor any form of NATO boots on the ground.'

The Secretary General's aide tapped his watch. It was time to move to the Council chamber.

At that moment, McKinlay saw, on the TV screen in the corner of the room, a CNN newsflash. Four pale, shocked figures in green jumpsuits; three men and one woman under a Russia Today news channel headline.

'Secretary General,' he said, 'you might want to listen to this.'

The aide turned up the sound in time for the three men to hear the strident tone of the Kremlin's chief propagandist, the Russia Today presenter Dimitry Kiselev, announcing in Russian, with English subtitles, that three American Special Forces, with a female signaller, had been captured inside Russia, having infiltrated across the Ukrainian border. The picture then cut to the smug, round-faced and smooth-cheeked Kiselev himself, working up an anti-NATO rant.

'We've seen enough. Time for the NAC,' said the now grim-faced Secretary General. 'Let's see if we can hold the Alliance together over this one.'

The three men left the conference room. The aides who had been waiting outside fussed around them like mother hens and they walked towards the Council chamber.

0700 hours, Friday, 12 May 2017
Briefing Room, Boryspill Air Force Base, Ukraine

'ANY FURTHER QUESTIONS, Phil?' asked the intelligence officer, as he concluded the briefing.

'No, thanks, I'm happy and good to go,' replied Major Phil Bertinetti, US Air Force. 'I guess this should be fairly straight-forward. We'll get up to fifteen thousand feet and provide surveillance and reconnaissance overwatch for the American trainers looking after the Ukrainian weapon-locating battery operating behind the front line near Debaltseva.'

'Situation over the past few days has remained pretty quiet. There's been the usual sporadic shelling from both sides, each reacting to the other, but the Russians are lying low after kidnapping our guys in Kharkiv. Any problems and you have the Quick Reaction Alert flight on the tarmac at immediate readiness,' the intelligence officer added.

Dark-haired and of medium height, while Bertinetti might look the part of a typical 'top gun', he was also a keen moun-taineer who had summited the highest peaks in each continent, the Seven Summits challenge, before graduating from the Air Force Academy. A professional flyer to the core, with nearly 4,000 flying hours as a fighter pilot under his belt, his combat experience included Libya, Afghanistan and Iraq.

However, he reflected, those were conflicts where there'd

been no-one flying against them. He knew the Russians were good and he knew the Russians might be looking for him and his wingman that day. Here in Ukraine, it was his Exercise Red Flag 'Top Gun' training above the Nevada desert – American pilots training against American instructors, simulating Russian tactics – that he might need to rely on now, if the Russians decided to take them on.

'Remember what they told us on Red Flag?' he said to his wingman, Captain Leroy MacDonald, a good-looking Floridian from Tallahassee. 'Survive the first eleven missions and you'll survive the war.'

'I'll follow your lead, skipper. You've been around. I'm the learner here.'

'We're all learners . . . *All* the time. That's the only way to stay alive as a pilot,' said Bertinetti. 'Come on, Leroy. Let's get airborne.'

Fifty minutes later, the two F-16 Fighting Falcon, single-engine, multi-role fighter aircraft were airborne at 15,000 feet over the flat, black-earthed expanse of eastern Ukraine.

'Zulu One, this is Apollo flight.' Bertinetti called MacDonald. 'Are you in contact with friendlies?'

'Affirmative, Apollo, I've got them covered with my pod.'

'Copy that, Zulu. Slewing my targeting pod up now. Looks pretty quiet, but we can take nothing for granted.'

The pair of F-16s screamed across the wide blue arc of the Ukrainian sky, describing a wide orbit as they maintained cover over the Americans working with the weapon-locating battery on the ground. If any Ukrainian separatists decided to mess with the American trainers below, they would have one of America's most potent strike fighters to deal with.

'Apollo, Apollo. This is Giant Killer, are you receiving me?' Bertinetti's radio crackled in his ear.

Unusual for Ground Control to call without a reason, he thought.

'Affirmative, Giant Killer. I'm reading you five by five.'

'Apollo. Bogey one o'clock, inside five miles. Single contact descending to one four thousand.'

'Copy. Apollo is no joy – I cannot see target – standby.'

Bertinetti put his aircraft into a steep turn to starboard, simultaneously putting his radar and weapons into dogfight mode with a deft flick of his left thumb on the throttle. He vigorously scanned the sky through the bubble canopy and suddenly picked up the contact visually: an Ilyushin Il-76, a multi-purpose, four-engine, strategic airlifter, the Russian air force insignia clear to see. And it was heading west, for central Ukraine.

'Giant Killer, this is Apollo Two. Tally one. Russian Ilyushin Seventy-six, heading west. Do you want me to intercept?'

'Apollo Two, affirmative.'

Bertinetti slowed down and circled the Russian plane. He rocked his wings from side to side and as he came up alongside, he could see the pilot in the cockpit of the large Russian aircraft looking back at him. With a subtle pressure against his sidestick, Bertinetti flashed him the weapon-coated underside of the Falcon, while transmitting on the VHF Guard international frequency for the Russian to turn around and head back into Russian airspace.

Meanwhile, as per SOPs – standard operating procedures – MacDonald was providing cover for Bertinetti from above and behind.

Suddenly and unexpectedly the Russian dived.

Perplexed as to what the Russian was doing, Bertinetti followed it down. Next moment he heard an exclamation over the radio from MacDonald.

'Holy shit, Lead. We've been bounced. Four bandits at six o'clock.'

From the corner of his eye Bertinetti saw a flash as a missile streaked towards them across the sky, doubtless a passive infrared K-74M2 – brutally manoeuvrable due to its advanced-thrust vectoring, which made it almost impossible to escape from and the primary close-range missile of a Russian Sukhoi T-50 PAK-FA stealth fighter.

Stealth fighter! Christ! That's why my systems didn't see the son of a bitch!

Bertinetti's brain was scrambling to absorb all this new and unexpected information. Even as he accepted what must have happened there was a blinding flash and MacDonald's F-16 vanished into a million pieces at the centre of a fireball.

The Ilyushin Il-76 was the decoy and the Americans had been ambushed.

Bertinetti's survival instinct kicked in. All the hours of flying drills and exercises and avoiding rock falls and breakages ensuring that he acted rather than froze. Survive!

He first rolled his aircraft upside down and then pulled it into a steep dive, buying himself that survival time. As he did so, the blood drained from his brain under the G-force and he felt the suit inflate and tighten around his thighs. No missile alarms. That manoeuvre had thrown them off balance, as he hoped it might.

Now they would be confident. Only him left. They would assume they could take him down easily.

Out of the dive and now he climbed, pushing the throttle through the afterburner gate and feeling the kick in his back as it lit behind him. As he did so, he saw four distinct dots on the horizon, despite his vision greying out from the G-force.

Four of you bastards. No wonder you are so confident. But I'll take one of you with me. Leroy was my friend.

He turned to face them, and sure enough, there they were: two pairs of Russia's very latest 'super weapons', as the aviation press had dubbed them when they had made their first international appearance at Britain's Farnborough Air Show. But this was no air show, this was for real.

As the F-16 streaked across the sky, Bertinetti's brain seemed to slow down, initial brain-freezing panic over, as he started to analyse the data his aircraft's computers and his eyes were feeding him. It was the same as on his beloved Honda Firebird motor-cycle; the faster he drove, the slower the world seemed to move around him.

He sensed the Sukhoi T-50s were inside his missile range and by moving his head and looking at each target in turn, he could slew the reticle, the fine sighting lines on his joint helmet-mounted cueing system. As he put the reticle onto the first Sukhoi the 'lock on' tone sounded in his helmet until, when it reached a crescendo, he released an AIM-9X Sidewinder infrared missile with a solid, steady trigger pull. 'See how you like that, you fuckers,' he muttered.

There was a fractional pause, a white streak across the sky and another fireball where, a split second earlier, there had been a Russian fighter.

One-all, thought Bertinetti as he put the reticle on his next target. *That's levelled things a bit.*

'Lock, Lock.' The radar warning receiver sounded in his ear. He instinctively pulled the throttle out of afterburner and then rolled his left hand onto the chaff-and-flare button on the cockpit wall by his left knee, in a desperate attempt to decoy the incoming missiles from the Russians.

Too late. Next moment his aircraft was being blasted violently to the right and, out of the corner of his eye, he saw a chunk of his left wing disintegrate.

Without realising he had done so, his right hand was already grabbing and then pulling up on the ejection-seat firing handle, set in between his legs and next to his crotch. Then his head was violently compressed into his spine as his ejector seat fired, followed by a sudden blast of ice-cold air, as he was hurtled up and out of the aircraft. His first instinct was one of blessed relief at being clear of his aircraft, followed a couple of seconds later by the sickening sensation that he was beginning to fall.

'Deploy, you bastard. Deploy!' he started screaming to himself,

as he began to accelerate towards the earth, still strapped help-
lessly into his seat. And then he was jerked upwards. He heard
a sharp crack above his head and the seat fell away below him.
Looking up, he saw the wide silk of his parachute canopy. Now
instead of noise and wind, there was instant peace.

He was alone in the sky. The Russian planes had vanished
and, below him, he could see his plane tumbling, left wing
missing, before it smashed into the open cornfields of Ukraine
below. There was a split second, perhaps he imagined it, perhaps
not, when he thought he saw the F-16 shatter on the ground,
like a plastic toy dropped onto a stone floor. Then the fuel
tanks ruptured and it disappeared in a massive red-and-yellow
fireball.

Then came the exhilaration of survival and the joy of the
descent before the ground rushed up to meet him. He landed
with a thud, which knocked all the breath out of him. He
must have blacked out for a moment, because the next thing
he saw was the blue of the sky and, in the periphery of his
vision, people running towards him from a small village nearby.

Bertinetti lay still for a moment to collect his thoughts. Then
he undid his harness and rolled to his feet. He could stand and
he could walk. He rolled his shoulders and everything seemed
to work. That was good, because that meant he could get
straight back into an F-16.

He took off his helmet, gazed around him and breathed
deeply. He had cheated death. But he was pissed. Oh boy, was
he pissed.

1900 hours, Friday, 12 May 2017
The Kremlin, Moscow

'NO, VLADIMIR VLADIMIROVICH, the American pilot landed in Ukraine. He was shot down inside Ukrainian airspace. As was the other American pilot, who was killed.'

Komarov stood before the President's desk. He had been practising judo in the President's private gym when the call had come through. As instructed, Russian TV news was saying that a Russian aircraft had been shot down, but not before it had first destroyed two American aircraft, which had attacked it.

Komarov had quickly put on a track suit, hastened to the Kremlin's situation centre, been briefed by a senior air force general and was now briefing the President.

'Damn,' said the President. 'Never mind. It is enough. We are telling the world the Americans opened fire on our pilots first and, thankfully, the wreckage of the Sukhoi fell behind our lines. That proves it was shot down over our airspace. Our friends are saying that this is not only naked aggression by America, it is also NATO attacking Russia. Russia is justified in defending herself. The only response is war. Get me Merkulov on the telephone. Now.'

'He's on hold already, Vladimir Vladimirovich.' Komarov had thought ahead and warned the Director of the FSB – the successor to the KGB – to be on standby.

Merkulov, a career KGB operative and old colleague of the President, was too crafty a beast to be caught out by a surprise phone call. Furtive, with the expression of an animal looking warily out of its lair for predators, he was ruthless and deadly. He was ready for the President and prepared for his order when he came on the line.

'Lavrentiy Pavlovich, it is time for you to start stirring up our ethnic Russian comrades in the Baltic states. We need to get them back where they belong. Under Russia. But first, the ceasefire in Ukraine must be broken . . . And it must be the Ukrainians who are seen to do it.'

'With pleasure, Vladimir Vladimirovich,' said Merkulov reflectively.

COLONEL 'BEAR' SMYTHSON ran with the smooth, effortless rhythm of a natural track athlete, despite being a big, broad-shouldered wrestler. Although it was still an hour before sunrise, it felt good to be out and running hard on such a lovely spring morning. There was enough dawn light to pick out the Iwo Jima Memorial with its heroic depiction of marines raising Old Glory, while on his left shoulder, as he headed back towards his married quarter in Fort Myer, the myriad crosses on the green slopes of Arlington Cemetery gleamed white.

Bear needed this time to himself. Not only was his early morning run around Arlington Cemetery the only exercise his job permitted, but it also gave him time to think, to plan his day, and to get things into perspective before the tsunami of work hit him in the office. As Executive Assistant to the US National Security Advisor, he was a busy man in a key post. Today might be a Saturday, but most Saturdays were working days. Sundays too, when needs required.

While some of his predecessors had found the pressure too much and been quietly 'returned to unit', Bear flourished on the challenge. A tank commander by background, he had been noticed not only as an inspirational leader in combat, but also as a highly capable staff officer, a rare combination in any army.

He had spent much of the previous decade fighting America's wars in Iraq and Afghanistan. Indeed, on his left wrist he wore a silver bracelet with the names of the soldiers killed in action under his command, an ever-present reminder of the human consequences of war.

As an African American, Bear had had his own mountain to climb in the US Army. A native of Atlanta, Georgia, he may have grown up after the segregation era, but he had never forgotten the humiliation of waiting for the white boys to finish on the fairground rides before the black boys were allowed their turn. He might be a 'bird' colonel, who wore a Silver Star for valour proudly on his chest, but when he went to visit his mother in her care home in Atlanta, the few whites he saw in the area looked as if they still expected to push in front of him to get to the fairground rides. There might have been a black president for the previous eight years, but sometimes it still felt as if he was back in Atlanta in the 1970s. The secret to success, he had discovered, was never to let anyone see the hurt it inflicted.

Suddenly he focused on the voice in his earpiece: 'We are just picking up news from the BBC's correspondent in Ukraine of an attack on a primary school in Donetsk, capital of the separatist republic in eastern Ukraine . . . It appears that over eighty children have been killed in a rocket attack, which the Kremlin is claiming was fired by the Ukrainians. The Russians are saying that this is a direct attack on their people and must be punished. This places the ceasefire in Ukraine in serious jeopardy . . .'

Bear did not need to hear more. First he slowed to a gentle jog, getting his breath back as he did so. It was never a good move to sound anything but measured and in control when he spoke to his boss. Next he punched a name in the Favourites list on his phone.

Moments later, Abe MacWhite, the President's National

Security Advisor, answered. 'Got it, Bear,' was his drawled response. 'I've heard the news from Ukraine. I'll be in the office by 0600 hours. I'll want to see the CIA and NSA reports and who they think is responsible when I get in.'

'Roger, Sir,' said Bear. As he started to run back home, he called the duty officers in America's two principal overseas intelligence agencies, the Central Intelligence Agency and National Security Agency, followed by the White House car pool. Calls finished, he accelerated into a sprint, relishing the pain in his legs and the burning in his lungs. If this incident in Ukraine developed as he thought it might, it could well be many days before he next had the luxury of an early morning run.

Forty-five minutes later, after a quick shower and a change into his day uniform, crisply pressed by him the night before, a hurried farewell kiss to his wife Tonia, still drowsy in bed, a look at his still-sleeping children and a rapid dash by car into the White House, Bear was at his desk in the West Wing with his first coffee of the day. As he sipped it, he studied the CIA and NSA reports on the attack on the school in Donetsk, conscious that the time for quiet reflection would end the moment his boss arrived.

Then General Abe MacWhite walked into the outer office where Bear was sitting. A four-star general and Commander-in-Chief, Special Operations Command before retiring from active military duty and in his younger days, a feared Delta Force operative, MacWhite was well over six foot tall, as rangy as a Wyoming cowboy.

Bear braced to attention, as the man described by Secretary of Defense Robert Gates as 'perhaps the finest warrior and leader of men in combat I ever met' nodded a good morning, but said nothing. He knew the man would have already run ten miles before dawn and would eat but one vegan meal later in the day. Bear was in awe of him but, he acknowledged, he had no desire to be anything like him.

MacWhite picked up the CIA and NSA reports and scanned them. Only when he had finished did he speak.

'Morning, Bear.' The tone was quiet, laconic and full of authority. 'How was your run?' There was a glint of amusement in MacWhite's eyes and Bear grinned back. 'A bit more of a sprint than usual, Sir . . . and yours?'

'Something doesn't add up here.' MacWhite was scanning the CIA report again and his mind was obviously now in the grim suburb of Donetsk. He looked at the satellite photo of the shattered ruins of the primary school destroyed by a series of devastating salvos from a BM-30 'Smerch' heavy multiple rocket launcher, capable of firing twelve, 300-millimetre calibre rockets in thirty-eight seconds.

'We know the Ukrainians have used this weapon system in the Donbass previously, but we're pretty sure their heavy weapons are still situated well away from the combat zone, in line with the Minsk Two ceasefire agreement. This says that none of our satellites picked up any firing from Ukrainian territory . . . and yet it also says this attack came from the direction of Ukrainian lines.' The general was not so much asking a question as making a statement.

Bear nodded. 'I saw that, Sir. The signal traffic picked up by the NSA and corroborated by the British suggests that the Russians are behind this. Either they fired those missiles or their proxies did. The only explanation for a horror on a scale like this, is that the Russians will pin this on the Ukrainians to give them a reason to break the ceasefire.'

MacWhite grunted agreement.

The phone on Bear's desk rang. He picked it up, listened and nodded. 'We're coming right on over.' He looked at MacWhite. 'The President's ready for your morning update now, Sir. She'll be in the Situation Room in fifteen minutes.'

Soon afterwards they were sitting in the neon, strip-lit Situation Room in the White House with its widescreen TVs,

PowerPoint presentations and banks of computers. A grim-faced President was being shown photos of broken children's bodies being lifted into ambulances or laid out, faces and bodies covered, awaiting transport to the mortuary. Just as the staff briefer was saying that everything pointed to Russian involvement, the live feed CNN cut to an emergency broadcast from Moscow's Russia Today.

The cameras had closed in on the vulpine face and cold blue eyes of the President as he sat at his desk in his office in the Kremlin, the gold double-headed eagle of Russia filling the background. This was obviously part of a longer speech, but the English subtitles of this short soundbite could not have been more chilling.

'The Motherland cannot stand by while our children are massacred. On top of this outrage American jets have attacked and shot down one of our pilots . . . The ceasefire in Ukraine is worthless . . . Ukraine must pay the price . . .'

Then it cut back to the CNN newsreader and there was silence in the Situation Room.

Bear watched the President as she looked round the table at the guarded faces; nobody as yet prepared to stick their neck out and speak. Lynn Turner Dillon had only been inaugurated as 45th President of the United States of America five months earlier and this was the first serious military crisis of her presidency. Bear had also been in Washington long enough to know that, until the politicians around the table knew how she would react to such an incident, silence was the best way of not incurring her disfavour.

And who could tell how she would she react to this carnage? Sixty years old but looking twenty years younger, a former chief executive of a giant Canadian gold mining company and a tough businesswoman who had risen to the top in a man's world, she had been the surprise winner of last year's Presidential elections. She was neatly dressed with highlighted blonde hair and preferred to emphasise her femininity by wearing skirts rather than a trouser suit. This morning, however, she was learning the hard way that while it took tough decisions to reach the top in business, lives were rarely lost by those decisions. Now, two men she had ordered to Ukraine were dead and their comrades had been kidnapped.

Bear's thoughts were broken by a tap on the shoulder. A Situation Room staffer had come up behind him and he now handed Bear a codeword-classified CIA report marked 'Top Secret'. Bear quickly scanned the headline, stood up and placed it in front of MacWhite.

MacWhite speed-read the first page and leaned forward, breaking the silence. 'If I may, Madam President?'

'Please, General. I need your advice,' she replied.

'Madam President, what we are witnessing are classic Russian tactics: intimidation and manipulation of events. CIA agree that Russia launched this attack against the school in Donetsk. As we have just seen,' MacWhite gestured at the television, still playing but now turned to silent, 'the Russian President is using it as an excuse to ramp up the fighting in Ukraine by claiming it is the Ukrainian government which has broken the ceasefire. This latest CIA report,' he held up the document Bear had passed to him, 'is very clear on the indicators we have been picking up for some time now. The Russians are about to launch an invasion of eastern Ukraine. Their immediate objective will be to open up a land corridor to Crimea.'

The President narrowed her eyes.

'As you'll remember, Madam President,' Bear saw that MacWhite had noticed her momentary confusion as to the geography and strategy and was covering for her, 'the Ukrainian government still holds the territory between Crimea and Russia. That's about two hundred and forty miles, border to border. The Russians want to connect it up and make it all part of Russia. Hence the invasion.'

The US president, the most powerful person in the world and Commander-in-Chief of the world's most powerful armed forces, digested the information before responding.

'General, what do you suggest we do?' Her voice was steady, betraying no emotion.

'Madam President, apart from ensuring all our trainers are extracted to ensure no more hostages for the Russians, there is little we *can* do. Ukraine is not a member of NATO, so we're not going to war with Russia over this. That means they *will* get away with it. But I do have two recommendations. First.' He held up the forefinger of his left hand and grasped it with his right to emphasise the point. 'We must try to ensure the West is united. That means calls to our key NATO allies. I suggest you start with the French President. After all, France has consistently delivered in the Middle East and in Africa in the last couple of years. I guess you ought to call the British Prime Minister for old times' sake, but the Brits have not delivered on the ground ever since Afghanistan and even then they needed to be bailed out by the US Marine Corps in Helmand.'

'No, General. The Brits are beginning to show a bit of their old spirit lately, despite being so late joining in with air strikes over Syria. But they remain our most important strategic partner. It's vital that I call the Prime Minister first. And your second recommendation?'

'Ma'am, I don't like what is developing here. There's something about this belligerence of the Russian President . . . his rhetoric . . . We believe he might want to spark something in the Baltic states. Perhaps capitalise on the tension in Latvia and Estonia between the locals and their ethnic Russian, so-called 'non citizens'. We know the Russians have been hard at work fomenting discontent for some time now, hence the wave of recent labour disputes and strikes. It's not even impossible the Russians make a grab for the Baltics while we focus on Ukraine.'

'What is your recommendation, General?' pressed the President.

'Call a meeting of the Cabinet. You'll also need the Chairman of the Joint Chiefs. He needs to give the requisite orders, not me. Meanwhile, we should ask the Pentagon to prepare a proposal to take appropriate measures to ramp up military readiness.'

'Military readiness . . . Such as?'

'Such as preparing to man the brigade's worth of vehicles we have warehoused and spread across the Baltic states and Poland,' replied MacWhite. 'They are currently mothballed and it will take at least a fortnight to get them prepped, manned and concentrated in one place should we need them. Then we need to ramp up the readiness to move of 6th Fleet, 18th Airborne Corps, Special Operations Command and US Air Force Europe.'

'Meaning?' the President interrupted, obviously unfamiliar with this military terminology.

'That these forces are currently at normal peacetime readiness. Personnel are on normal leave rotas or away on courses, equipment is being routinely dismantled and serviced. Start by reducing notice to move; lead elements reduced to forty-eight hours with the remainder at graduated readiness out to seven days. That means giving the necessary notice now so we ensure we can get people, equipment and forces to the right place in time if we need to. Also, it sends a strong signal to the Russians.'

The President nodded. 'Makes sense. Agreed.'

The general continued, 'And, given this could be the start of something larger and the Russians will probably play the nuclear card, we need to send a warning order to the "at sea" Trident boats in the Barents Sea. But we've got to be circumspect about this. We mustn't give the President any excuses to claim that we've provoked him.'

'Isn't this overkill, General? Warning the Tridents. Calling back the fleet? And all on the basis of a rocket attack in eastern Ukraine?'

'Madam President, we have been watching the President very carefully ever since his 2014 invasion of Crimea and his move on eastern Ukraine. We've been waiting for something just like this to happen. In fact, we're surprised it has taken him this long to make his move. Our predictions . . .'

Bear saw the President give her National Security Advisor a hard look and his boss take a deep breath.

He and the general had war-gamed these scenarios. They both knew what was probably going to come next; what the Russians wanted, what the Russians had in mind. But call this wrong, and his boss would lose the President's trust and would soon be out of a job. And it would not be only his boss who'd be looking for a new job. His own career would go into free-fall.

Without thinking, he gave his boss an almost imperceptible nod of support; calling this right was far more important than jobs or careers.

'*My* prediction, Madam President, is that events are now going to start speeding up. We need to get ahead of the curve or we will be playing catch-up. We'll be subtle. That I promise you. But . . . blowing up an infant school. Killing one of our soldiers and kidnapping four others. Not forgetting shooting down two of our fighters and killing a pilot. If that is the Russians' idea of subtle, I think I probably have a bit of leeway. Anyway, the only way we might get them to back off is to show we mean business. Any failure to react will be taken in the Kremlin as a clear green light to invade Ukraine, and that's for starters. That is the way the Russians think.'

'Agreed. Please will you fix?'

This was the first time that Bear had seen the President under real pressure and he was impressed at how she absorbed information and how quick she was to make a tough decision.

'Yes, ma'am,' MacWhite said. 'And then there's NATO. We need to try to get more NATO troops on the ground in the

Baltic states to send a message to the President not to try it on. We also need to ensure NATO reserves are mobilised. I'll talk to our NATO ambassador in Brussels, but I recommend you call the Secretary General. We've got to get the North Atlantic Council on board, so the State Department needs to get active on the diplomatic front. Showing determination and unity now will stop lives being lost later.'

0700 hours, Sunday, 14 May 2017
Residence of DSACEUR
La Belle Alliance, Erbisoeul, Belgium

THE PHONE IN the kitchen rang. General Sir David McKinlay, just back from walking around the extensive garden of his residence with his springer spaniel and still clad in his dressing gown, put down the two mugs of tea he was about to take upstairs to the bedroom, where his wife still slept. He picked it up.

'Yes, Jamie,' he grunted, seeing that the call came from his Principal Staff Officer, Group Captain Jamie Swinton.

'Morning, Sir,' replied Swinton urgently. 'Sorry to bother you, but we're picking up reports that the Russians have broken the ceasefire in Ukraine. Seems they launched an early hours assault with airborne forces and they're now attacking towards Crimea. The picture's still pretty confused. There's an Ops update at 0830, with a NAC called in Brussels for 1400 hours. I've tasked Sergeant James to collect you at 0800.'

'Thanks, Jamie, I've got that. See you in the office,' said McKinlay, switching on the TV in the corner of the kitchen as he put down the phone and picked up his tea. As the BBC World channel came to life, he was shocked to see the sleek, low silhouette of Russian T-14 Armarta tanks, newly in service from 2016, with their smoothbore 125 millimetre guns traversing menacingly as they raced unopposed through a burning Ukrainian village. As Jamie had just warned him, this looked different. This was no longer 'proxies', or Russians pretending to be Ukrainians causing trouble in Ukraine, these were elite Russian forces crossing the Ukrainian border and advancing towards Crimea.

He put down his wife's mug of tea and sipped his own as he continued to watch, appalled yet at the same time fascinated, as television news reporters brought him a raw flow of images of the unfolding strategic and humanitarian disaster.

1400 hours, Sunday, 14 May 2017
North Atlantic Council Conference Room
NATO Headquarters, Brussels

T HE LAST TIME the North Atlantic Council had met on a
Sunday was six years previously, during the Libyan crisis
of 2011. None of this crop of NATO ambassadors had been
around back then, as McKinlay knew full well when he stumped
into the NAC Conference Room. From the looks on their
faces he sensed their shock and disbelief that, yet again, the
President had taken them all by surprise with this morning's
attack to open up the land corridor to Crimea. The question
they were all asking was whether he would stop there.

McKinlay was also only too aware of the importance of his
position as he took in the flags of the twenty-eight NATO
nations hanging on poles around the walls in alphabetical
order. And there, in the centre of the Council chamber, was
the circular table around which the NATO ambassadors sat
and at which so many questions and crises concerning the
defence of Western Europe and the North Atlantic area had
been discussed, shelved and occasionally resolved, since its
formation in 1949. Somehow NATO had always come through
in the past and he was determined that it would not fail on
his watch.

There was the usual noise and bustle as ambassadors took

their seats and their aides and note takers crammed themselves into the chairs behind them. McKinlay saw that US Navy Admiral Max Howard, the SACEUR, was already seated next to the Chairman of the Military Committee, the Danish general, Knud Vahr.

SACEUR beckoned him over. 'I've brought David in to brief the NAC on where we are with getting the nations to stump up the necessary forces,' he explained.

'Good idea. How does it look to you, David?' Vahr looked at McKinlay with his piercing blue eyes.

'Not so good, Knud, I'm afraid, and it's down to the usual suspects,' replied McKinlay, taking his seat beside Howard and organising his papers.

At that moment Secretary General Radek Kostilek entered. His hair had been recently cropped to his usual crew cut and, at sixty-two, he looked fit, youthful and tanned from his recent holiday in the Maldives. He took his chair and the conference room fell silent as he looked around to ensure he had everyone's attention before opening the meeting.

Kostilek got straight to the point. 'Ladies and gentlemen,' he said gravely, 'as you all know, Russian forces, responding to a so-called terrorist attack on a school in Donetsk, invaded Ukraine this morning. In New York the UN Security Council will shortly be meeting and we now need to consider our own response to this aggression. Before we do so, I call upon SACEUR to brief the Council on the military situation.'

Admiral Max Howard leaned forward in his seat, his aquiline face, gold-braided uniform and extensive medal ribbons giving him a presence that immediately commanded attention.

'Secretary General, ladies and gentlemen, NATO faces an exceptionally dangerous situation. We have already seen Russia attacking and shooting down US aircraft engaged in lawful training activities in Ukrainian airspace and claiming it a provocation. Our assessment is that the attack on the school in

Donetsk was Russian-executed to provide the pretext for breaking the ceasefire. In the early hours of this morning, Russian regular forces attacked Ukraine, a valued NATO partner. The Russians started by launching an airborne operation by 98th Guards Airborne Division to secure key communications nodes along their axis of advance in southern Ukraine towards Crimea. They followed that up with an attack on land by 20 Guards Tank Army, supported by air and naval forces in the Sea of Azov. I have to tell you that the Russians appear to have secured all their initial objectives. The key town of Mariupol has been captured and the land route from Russia to Crimea opened up. At this stage it is too early to say whether Russia will advance further into Ukraine, but we cannot rule it out, as the Ukrainian army has effectively capitulated.'

Howard looked around the NAC table in case of any questions.

'What is your recommendation now, SACEUR?' asked Kostilek.

'Secretary General,' continued Howard, 'there is little NATO can do militarily to stop Russian aggression in Ukraine. The imperative now is for the Alliance to demonstrate its resolve and readiness to defend itself. Above all, we must ensure there is no spillover of the crisis. I recommend that NATO's immediate reserves are mobilised to deter any aggression against any Alliance member. In practical terms, this means reducing notice to move times for the Very High Readiness Joint Task Force and the NATO Response Force. It would also be prudent to deploy forces to the Baltic states to pre-empt any Russian surprise attack there. But none of this is possible unless member nations provide the necessary troops and equipment.'

Looking around the table, McKinlay could see a number of the ambassadors nod in agreement: Latvia, Lithuania, Estonia and Poland, which only made sense as they were probably next on the Russian wish list. Others, notably Germany and Italy, sat with their faces as if frozen, giving nothing away. Not good news. He looked next at Dame Flora Montrose, the elegant, erudite, Oxford blue-stocking with the flawless complexion, who was the UK's ambassador to NATO. Her body language was important. If she showed any sign of sitting on the fence at this moment of crisis, his own position, even though he was a NATO rather than a UK officer, would become very much more difficult. With some relief, he spotted the most imperceptible of nods from his fellow Scot in support of the Eastern Europeans. He would not have to take issue with Whitehall. Yet.

Howard looked at Kostilek. 'Secretary General. I suggest that DSACEUR, the man responsible for ensuring NATO has the means to implement strategy, tells the NAC where we stand in generating such forces.'

Kostilek turned to McKinlay. 'Very well, DSACEUR. The floor is yours.'

McKinlay looked around the table at the assembled ambassadors. This might be a moment of high drama for NATO, but the Scottish Royal Marine remained practical, down to earth and focused.

'Secretary General, ladies and gentlemen, I will be brief. First, let me point out that NATO has a small maritime presence in the Baltic already. The Standing NATO Mine Countermeasures Group, or SNMCMG, is currently exercising in the Baltic with ships from Germany, Poland, Norway, UK and Belgium. However, while an important demonstration of NATO's presence in the Baltic, it is not a deterrent force as such, as it only has very limited offensive capability. As for the would-be "Very High Readiness Joint Task Force", the VJTF if you will forgive another NATO acronym, the reality is that, despite the best of intentions, it is a long way from being ready for anything. It is an *ad hoc* formation of units from fourteen different nations and it has never trained together properly in the field, so – and I'm going to put this bluntly so there are no misunderstandings – it is simply not ready for combat. Not only that, while the lead element of the Task Force is at high readiness to move, the reality is that we'd be doing well to get it ready in place within twenty-eight days.'

McKinlay looked around the room. None of the ambassadors looked surprised.

He continued, 'And then there are the force levels. Of the nations who have offered troops to the Very High Readiness Task Force, only the designated Danish, French and UK units are ready for deployment within three days. I have spoken to the Chiefs of Defence of the other contributing nations, but none can give me any assurances that their forces will be ready in less than two weeks. Or at all . . .'

Now a few of the ambassadors began to look unhappy at the implied criticism. Kostilek intervened. 'Thank you, DSACEUR, for the reminder about the NATO minesweeper group. But you do not bring any comfort with your comments about the problems with the High Readiness Task Force. What about the NATO Response Force, the NRF?'

'I'm afraid the situation doesn't get any better,' replied McKinlay. 'The aspiration to deliver forty thousand troops as part of the NRF is just that. An aspiration and one which only exists on paper. Things are better for the maritime and air components, but we have to be realistic about the land component. Even if the Very High Readiness Joint Task Force of five thousand could be made available in time, it would not amount to a credible and capable deterrent to the Russians. But . . .' and he resisted the temptation to laugh sardonically, 'we do have a headquarters which could command the force if, that is, it had a force to command. However, even that depends on the framework nation – the country responsible for providing the bulk of the manpower and equipment to ensure that the headquarters can operate – being prepared to see notice to move reduced.'

'So?' questioned Kostilek. 'Why is there a problem with at least doing that?'

McKinlay had been long enough in NATO to know that he should avoid any direct criticism of a NATO member state. He said nothing.

At this point, the German ambassador, a large man, with the grim demeanour of an Osnabrück landlord chucking out drunken British soldiers at closing time, scowled and raised his hand. 'Secretary General, I must protest at this implied criticism of Germany. Yes, Germany is currently framework nation, but we insist on the correct procedures before we can reduce the notice to move of the VJTF. And we have yet to be convinced that Russia poses a sufficient threat to NATO to justify such a reduction. In fact, it may just ratchet up the tension. Furthermore, we are not convinced that the necessary consensus is achievable. To reduce NATO forces notice to move requires a unanimous vote in the NAC.' As he said this, he looked hard at the two ambassadors to his immediate right, the Greek and Hungarian ambassadors.

McKinlay could see from the body language that both were clearly unhappy at this talk of deterring Russia. Of course, both nations were in thrall to the Kremlin; Greece thanks to the bailout of Russian cash, and Hungary as a result of the sizable nuclear deal agreed a couple of years earlier with the President. Neither would want to jeopardise those deals by voting for anything that might antagonise Russia and the President.

McKinlay could see that Kostilek knew just where this was going and sensed him trying to control his irritation. Nevertheless, like the consummate politician that he was, he stepped back to ensure that the ambassadors had their say. He looked first at the US ambassador. As de facto leader of the Alliance, the US usually spoke first on matters of importance. He declared, 'The United States has the floor.'

'Secretary General, the US takes this situation very seriously.

Indeed, we cannot recall a more serious state of affairs in Europe, certainly since the end of the Cold War and probably not since the construction of the Berlin Wall in 1961. Russia has started a highly dangerous dynamic, one which could lead to a military clash with NATO. The way to guarantee that does not happen, and that Europe remains secure, is to show strength. Now is the time for Europe to prove it can defend itself. For too long European defence has been underwritten by US taxpayers. We have carried the burden of protecting you. You can be sure that the US will continue to underwrite the security of NATO, but we expect European nations to carry their share of the burden. You now need to deliver the reserve forces you agreed to generate at the Wales summit in 2014 and ratified at last year's Warsaw summit. As we have just heard from DSACEUR, this has clearly not been implemented.'

McKinlay could feel waves of collective irritation coming towards him from the European ambassadors for spotlighting what had been promised but had not been delivered.

Only the US ambassador looked approvingly at him, before continuing, 'The USA accepts the NATO Military Authorities' recommendations in full. The USA expects other member states to do likewise.' The US ambassador stopped. He had made the American position very clear.

McKinlay then listened to around twenty statements from other ambassadors supporting the US position, but without committing to actually doing anything. As each one spoke, he reflected on how many different ways there were of saying the same thing in diplomatic speak.

Then it was the Greek ambassador's turn. Newly appointed, he was a political appointment of the Syriza government; a shaven-headed, former Marxist sociology lecturer, who dressed in a leather jacket and T-shirt rather than the conventional suit and tie.

'Greece is bound by ties of fraternal Orthodox brotherhood

to Russia. We believe that Russia is only responding to provocation from NATO. Any stationing of NATO troops in the Baltic states, or reductions in notice to move times of NATO reserve forces, will be rightly seen by Russia as further provocation and proof of NATO's aggressive intention to surround and contain Russia. Greece cannot accept the recommendations of the NATO Military Authorities.'

There was a resigned silence around the table. McKinlay watched as the US ambassador rolled his eyes, while Kostilek's jaw tightened in frustration.

Then the Hungarian ambassador, a rotund little man with an incongruous fixed grin on his face, raised a hand and was given the floor. Reading from a note passed to him by an aide, all he could manage in heavily accented, broken English was, 'Hungary takes the same view as Greece.'

The Secretary General broke the silence. 'I see we do not have agreement,' said Kostilek evenly, although McKinlay, who knew the Polish former prime minister socially, could see from the heightened colour of his neck that he was well beyond irritation and now getting angry. However, he controlled himself. 'I regret that without full agreement from all member states, the NAC can do no more than condemn the perpetrators of the atrocity in Donetsk, condemn Russian aggression against Ukraine and continue to monitor the situation. And, of course, NATO will continue to maintain the minesweeper group on its current task in the Baltic. Do I at least have your agreement to that?'

He looked at the Greek and Hungarian ambassadors, challenging them to come back at him. There was silence.

'I see we have agreement,' said Kostilek shortly. Then he gathered up his papers and left the Council chamber.

Anatoly Nikolayevich Vronsky shivered under the leaden grey skies as a cold northerly wind off the Baltic blasted an empty plastic Coca-Cola bottle across the path in front of him. He removed the daysack from his shoulders, placed it at his feet and pulled his black, zip-fronted fleece more closely around his body. To his right the River Daugava, a quarter of a mile wide at this point after its thousand-kilometre journey from its source in the Valdai Hills, in the heartland of Russia, looked dark and forbidding. The wind sent showers of icy spray across the path along the riverbank. 'So much for spring,' he muttered to himself, as he checked his watch. Then, sure enough, and exactly on time as ever, he saw the slim, blonde-haired figure of Anna Brezhneva, cover name of Praporshchik Volochka of the FSB, seconded to the Spetsnaz for this mission and his favoured operating partner.

Vronsky re-shouldered the daysack, strode towards her and enfolded her in a passionate-looking embrace; to anyone watching, two lovers greeting after an absence. However, his voice was brisk and matter of fact as he murmured in her ear. 'You're exactly on time, Anna . . . We'll head for Moloney's now. That'll give me time to brief you before we meet them.'

Vronsky placed an arm loosely, but proprietorially, around

Brezhneva's shoulders and steered her past the entrance of the Riga Technical University, up Ratslaukums, and then they were amid the elegant art deco buildings and weathered, green copper church spires of the old city of Riga. They continued towards Riharda Vagnera Street and Moloney's Bar.

'What news from Ukraine?' Vronsky asked. He had been in Riga for a week, since the kidnapping of the American army trainers.

'Total success, Anatoly Nikolayevich,' murmured Brezhneva, pulling Vronsky's arm more closely around her shoulders. 'The land bridge is being opened up to Crimea. Ukraine has been dismembered.'

'Excellent,' replied Vronsky. 'That'll distract the West from what we're planning here.' Then quickly, as they walked towards Moloney's Bar, he briefed her on how a major demonstration against the Latvian government was being planned in two days' time, after weeks of increasing tension between Latvians and their 'non-citizens' – ethnic, Russian-speaking Latvians, many of whom had lived there for generations, but were not permitted Latvian citizenship and were therefore not citizens of the European Union either.

A massed crowd of non-citizens, whipped up by the barrage of propaganda and misinformation broadcast into Russian-speaking Latvian homes from Kremlin-controlled TV, would assemble and march to the Soviet-built Monument of Freedom, erected to mark Latvia's purported 'liberation' from fascism by the 'fraternal forces' of the Soviet Union in May 1945. It would end with speeches and the laying of flowers.

However, since arriving in Riga, Vronsky had been preparing the ground for inciting violence by infiltrating the demonstration with extreme nationalist elements of the Latvian Russian Union, the political party representing Latvian ethnic Russians. In addition, there was an active Latvian 'non-citizens' militia, set up and trained by Spetsnaz undercover operatives, also directed by Vronsky. This was the self-styled 'Russkiy Narodov Zashchita Sila' (Russian Peoples' Protection Force – or RNZS). The RNZS would play a key role in controlling the demonstration or, more to the point, ensuring it got out of control.

'After that,' Vronsky mused, 'anti-Russian feelings are so high among the Latvian nationalists that anything could happen . . . But first we have to meet the two guys who are leading the demo. They're at Moloney's Bar.'

'Is that a safe place to meet?' questioned Brezhneva.

'It'll be full of British stag parties. No-one has a chance of overhearing us.'

'Stag parties?' she asked.

'Groups of young British men celebrating an impending marriage by getting drunk and shagging as many women as they can afford. Decadent—'

'Westerners,' Brezhneva interrupted, with a smile.

Vronsky smiled back despite himself.

As Vronsky had predicted, Moloney's was full of raucous, sweating Brits determined to enjoy the Latvian beer and attempting to chase Latvian girls – with little success. Later they would end up at the Nightclub Monroe, or the Relax Centre Glamour, where their Euros would guarantee what they had come for.

Vronsky pushed through the crowd to a table in the corner where Vladimir Petrov and Sergei Zadonov, leaders of the planned demonstration, were already sitting, tall glasses of golden Labietis beer in front of them. They too ordered food and beer and then talked through the arrangements for the next day, the raucous cacophony of competing languages, delivered at full volume and overlaid with the music from the band in the corner of the bar, drowning out what they were saying.

Vronsky did not see anyone watching the two Russian-Latvian activists, but that did not mean they were not being observed right now. Back in Russia, he would certainly have any subversives, like these two, under close surveillance and nobody had ever said that the Constitution Protection Bureau, the Latvian domestic intelligence service, was anything other than highly efficient. But efficient or not, nobody was going to listen in on them here. Vronsky was even struggling to make himself heard.

When he was happy with their plans, Vronsky reached into his daysack and handed over a large, padded envelope stuffed with cash to Petrov, who moved to look inside it.

'Not now!' Vronsky snapped. 'You never know who might be watching.'

Petrov, duly chastened, put it in his briefcase.

'Right, time for you to go,' Vronsky said, dismissing them. 'But there's plenty more of that. If you get this right. Understood?'

Both Russian speakers nodded their agreement and left.

As they did so, Vronsky made a quick call into his mobile phone. As Petrov and Zadonov emerged from the bar, four men appeared from a side street and followed them.

0945 hours, Tuesday, 16 May 2017
Ādaži Training Camp, Latvia

'A MUCH BETTER EFFORT, guys. Fast, aggressive – you still need to work on the fire control orders. But you're heading in the right direction.'

Captain Tom Morland, leader of a five-man training team from 1st Battalion, the Mercian Regiment, sent by Britain to provide training support to Latvia, was debriefing a section of sweating Special Tasks Unit soldiers, Latvian Army Special Forces, who had just completed a 'live' section attack exercise on the firing range.

Morland had been in Ādaži, surrounded by nothing but endless miles of virgin pine forest and training areas, for three weeks now, and he was enjoying himself. The training was tough, realistic and fun; the Latvians were eager students and great guys to work with and to cap it all, he had the weekends off to explore Latvia and Riga, which was only forty minutes away.

Morland, 6 feet 2 inches, dark-haired and lean, was now a self-disciplined, tough professional but, if it had not been for Oxford and the Army, he knew he might now be one of those noisy, drunk Brits in Moloney's Bar, hoovering down too much Latvian Labietis beer and chasing the girls on a stag weekend away. In fact, it was already his team's favourite Riga bar and he had soon been informed that it was now official Team HQ.

The son of a butcher from Bridgnorth, in the West Midlands,

he'd first found an outlet for his over-abundance of energy and natural aggression as a fanatical Wolverhampton Wanderers fan, by picking fights with other fans after Wolves games at Molyneux Stadium. All that had changed when Ted Hunter, a grizzled former Para corporal who lived in his street and knew the family, had decided there was more to Morland than street fighting and, probably in time, prison. One Saturday evening, soon after the start of the new football season, Hunter had spotted the fifteen-year-old coming home, sporting a black eye. He had started chatting. Without any lecturing or sermonising, Hunter soon had the young Morland captivated with stories from Northern Ireland and the Falklands War.

In his spare time Hunter coached at a local boxing club so, one day, he took Morland along. There Morland found an outlet for his physicality and aggression and he quickly became an accomplished boxer. While he still went to football matches, he increasingly stayed out of trouble. Boxing taught him that a man doesn't need to fight; unless in self-defence or to protect others.

The second great influence on him was Mr Midgeley, his history teacher at Oldbury Wells Comprehensive. A red-haired Lancastrian with an acerbic wit who was deeply proud of his Rochdale roots, Midgeley recognised the intellectual potential in the young man. Giving him extra tuition, he inspired in him such a passion for history that he ended up getting into Oxford, the first in his family to gain a place at any university.

After Oxford he'd worked in the family business for a year, out of loyalty to his parents, before life as a small-town butcher palled and he'd been accepted by the Army – much to Hunter's delight, who took to calling him 'Sir' and pretending to salute whenever they saw one another. A year of officer training at the Royal Military Academy Sandhurst had followed and he had been commissioned in front of his proud parents into the Mercians, his local regiment; a tough, experienced, no-nonsense line infantry regiment, with an impressive operational record in Afghanistan.

Two years as a platoon commander came next and then eighteen months at a Training Regiment, teaching those hard-learned infantry skills back to young recruits. Then he found himself back at 1st Battalion, the Mercians, commanding Recce Platoon, the most coveted job for a young officer in the battalion. But, try and remain enthusiastic as he might, there was a growing sense of 'same old, same old' creeping in.

But at least this training team in Latvia was fun, or had been until a few moments ago when, exercise over, Sergeant Danny Wild – his number two and a tough veteran of Afghanistan and Iraq, with a Military Cross to his name – had announced he'd just received an email from the Battalion confirming his application to sign off had been accepted.

'You're what?' Morland asked in astonishment, when Wild had told him he was leaving the Army. 'But you can't leave. You . . .' And even as he said it, he realized how stupid he sounded. Of course Wild could and would leave the Army, just like so many of the best officers and NCOs in the battalion were doing in ever-increasing numbers these days.

It was the ones with brains and initiative who left, Morland thought, *those who knew they could use their training and skills to make a success of civvie life.* It was either the truly dedicated or the ones who lacked initiative and drive, all too often, who were the ones that stayed. He wondered where that put him.

'Why?' he asked lamely, realising that he should have known and should have at least tried to talk his sergeant out of it.

'Why? Come on, Sir. This is brilliant out here. But back in barracks . . . there's just not the buzz any more. Anyway, the missus has had enough of putting up with an army quarter managed by a bunch of useless civvies, who couldn't give a stuff about anyone in uniform. And now they're doing away with what few perks and allowances once made life tolerable. Quit while you're still ahead is my motto.'

The trouble was he found it hard to disagree with anything

Wild had just said. However, just as he realised he had run out of any arguments to stay, he saw the base commander walking up the path towards him. 'Tom. You're wanted in Riga. The Director of the Constitution Protection Bureau, Juris Bērziņš, wants to see you. My car will take you.'

The statement came as a total surprise to Morland, as he had not considered himself important enough to have a one-on-one meeting with the head of the Latvian secret intelligence service. 'Of course, Sir,' he replied and signalled to Wild to carry on without him.

As he signed his weapon in at the armoury, he wondered whether this might have something to do with the crisis in Ukraine. Certainly, the Special Forces Latvians he was working with were convinced that the Russians were coming for them, sooner or later. The gloomy view in the All Ranks Mess where they ate, and the near single topic of conversation the previous night at dinner, was that this latest Ukraine attack was just a distraction for a more general attack on the Baltics.

Asked for his opinion, Morland had been careful not to insult his hosts by disagreeing outright, but he had counselled against overreacting. After only three weeks in country, he was already very aware that living next to this resurgent and belligerent Russia would induce paranoia in any Western-looking, democratic neighbour; especially one with a deeply discontented Russian-speaking population. But as far as Russia attacking a NATO country was concerned, that was something altogether different.

The received wisdom across the British Army, and repeated by most middle-ranking officers he had spoken to ever since, was that this was the talk of old Cold War warriors, nostalgically harking back to those dark and dangerous days when the enemy was obvious and military budgets and organisations were secure. The world had moved on and was now a very much smaller place. Even Russia had to find a way of living within the current world order, if it were to succeed and grow as a nation state.

But Morland also remembered the ever-cynical Mr Midgeley and his thought-provoking lessons at school. 'Listen, lad,' he would say in his broad Rochdale accent. 'What does history continually teach us? That when everyone is convinced one thing is going to happen, you can bet your house and dog that the exact opposite is going to happen. Oh, and never listen to a politician. Not enough of them are historians.'

An hour later he was sitting in an anonymous government office in Riga. Bērziņš, in his early sixties, craggy faced and with a shock of white hair, leaned forward. 'Very good of you to drop in, old boy; do have a brew . . . I get Twinings to keep me supplied with English Breakfast tea.' Bērziņš, the son of Latvian refugees and UK born and raised, spoke perfect English with a crisp Sandhurst accent, the product of his time as a senior officer in the British Army. He had moved to Latvia following the collapse of the Soviet Union in 1991. He was now Director of the Constitution Protection Bureau, Latvia's counter-espionage and internal security service, and Morland could see he was measuring him as he spoke.

'We've got a puzzling case here and I need some help from the Brits. I know you're here to advise our Special Tasks Unit, but you have access to other agencies in the UK, and time is short. The police found the bodies of the two leaders of the Latvian Russian Union, Petrov and Zadonov, by the Monument of Freedom in the early hours this morning. It seemed that there'd been in a drunken fight; there were smashed beer and vodka bottles lying around and their throats had been slashed. But on closer inspection, both their necks had been broken. And, I have to say, most professionally. But what is really interesting is that when they were examined properly in the mortuary, they found the insignia of the Latvian Legion – those were the two SS divisions recruited in Latvia by the Nazis to fight the Russians during the last war – cut into their chests above their hearts.'

'OK . . .' said Morland, not yet sure what was required from him. For an infantry recce platoon commander, he was way out of his comfort zone.

'It's pretty clear the Russians are behind this. We've been watching them applying the usual propaganda and disinformation operations to undermine and discredit Latvia for some time now. And my colleagues in Lithuania and Estonia report the same. So far, so normal. Or at least, our version of normal. But in the last week, the leaders of the Latvian Russian Union have stepped up their activity in advance of tomorrow's demonstration. We know they've been talking to a Russian who's recently arrived in country. He's new and we've been watching him, of course. However, we could do with your team's support in monitoring tomorrow's demonstration. All indications are that it will get out of control. I'm appointing a liaison officer from my service to work with you. She's outside waiting. I'll introduce you now and you can get to work straight away.'

Bērziņš pressed a switch on his intercom. 'Please ask Marina to come in.'

The door opened and a stunning woman walked in.

Morland looked her in the eye as coolly as he could. She was a couple of inches short of six foot, long ash-blonde hair, high cheekbones and radiating physical fitness. He'd have put money on her being a distance runner or a cross-country skier. Or both.

Her eyes held his gaze in turn; greeny blue, steady and appraising him without any hint of embarrassment.

Morland looked away and caught the humour in Bērziņš's eyes. The old fox knew full well the effect Marina would have. But Morland was not going to give him the satisfaction of a reaction.

'Marina Krauja, meet Captain Tom Morland. Tom, I've told the Service to give you all the support you need. Miss Krauja is your point of contact and will work with you while you are in Latvia.'

She extended her hand. 'Delighted to meet you,' she said, in perfect English.

'Tom Morland. How do you do.' He shook hands with her before turning back to Bērziņš. 'Sir, we'll head back to Ādaži now. I'll brief the Permanent Joint Headquarters from there and we'll put together a plan.' He turned to Krauja. 'Shall we get going?'

'Captain, can I suggest we take my car?' said Krauja. 'That way we can talk. And we'll need to be independent.'

'Good call,' agreed Morland, aware that honours were currently even and that neither of them had acceded command to the other. If Bērziņš was enjoying the duel, he kept his face impassive as he turned back to the pile of paperwork on his desk.

Morland quizzed Krauja on the way back to Ādaži. If they were to work together, he wanted to know something about her. He quickly discovered that her English was the result of a degree in English Literature at Durham, where she'd won a scholarship. She'd then worked for Goldman Sachs in London for a couple of years, before tiring of the City and heading back to Riga to serve her country.

Morland asked her about Ukraine, Russia and the threat to the Baltic states. Again, he got the same line. 'There's no question,' she replied. 'The President is working up to something. All the indicators are there.'

Morland was surprised by how emphatic she was, but after only three weeks in country, he was also developing an uneasy feeling that when highly intelligent and cosmopolitan Latvians like Bērziņš and Krauja were so convinced of the President's bad faith, then they might just be right.

'Our history has made us deeply suspicious of Russian intentions,' she continued. 'Another time you should visit the Museum of Occupation in Riga. Then you'll understand that there's not a family in Latvia which wasn't affected in some way by the Russian occupation of Latvia during World War Two, or the Soviet occupation that followed. My mother was born in a Siberian labour camp after my grandparents were deported in the 1950s. They were eventually released, but my grandparents never recovered . . . and tens of thousands never came back.'

Morland was humbled into silence as he realised that as a Brit, he could not begin to understand what the Latvians had been through in the not-so-distant past.

She paused to reflect. 'You'll never have a better friend than a Russian. And I have a number. They'll give you their last kopek if you need it. They'll laugh with you, cry with you and drink with you to the end of time. But as a nation . . . as a neighbour . . . they're horrible.'

They drove into Ādaži. Morland pointed her to the training wing where the Mercian team had been given an office. As they walked in, Wild looked up from the laptop on which he was recording that day's training data. 'Hi, Sir. How was Riga? Pick up any useful info?'

The three other team members looked up at Krauja as she entered. She, in turn, appraised them coolly.

'Guys, we've got a new task. Meet Marina Krauja, our Latvian security service LO.' Morland was relaxed, inclusive and very much part of the team. But he was also determined to keep this focused and professional.

He updated them while the INMARSAT secure VTC was removed from its case and set up. The team signaller Corporal Steve Bradley, a giant New Zealander with a Maori mother, who had travelled across the world to join the British Army, adjusted the frequency and the Ops Room at the Permanent Joint Headquarters in Northwood appeared on the screen. Wild and the other two team members, Corporals Paddy Archer and Jezza Watson, sat at the back to listen in.

'You're on, Sir,' said Bradley and Morland took a seat in front of the 6.4 inch colour screen. 'Evening, Jerry,' he said as Major Jerry Dingley, the PJHQ desk officer responsible for supporting training teams in the Baltic states, sat down in front of the camera and asked Morland to start.

Morland told him the team training was going well and the Special Tasks Unit was making good progress with their hostage rescue skills. Next week the focus was to shift to long-range reconnaissance and patrol work, but given the innate toughness of the Latvians and their familiarity with their specific forest environment, Morland didn't think they could add much to improve their capability. In fact, he thought the Latvians could teach his team a trick or three to bring back home. Then he backbriefed Dingley on Bērziņš's request.

'On the face of it the murders were carried out by Latvian nationalists. But the view here is that it is too clinical for them; they're pretty crude at the best of times and this isn't their style. The carving of Latvian Legion insignia and cleanly snapped necks all point to the guys who do these things best, the Russians; FSB or Spetsnaz. The Latvian security service has some leads but needs support in pinning down the network. We're also concerned about threats to a big pro-Russia demonstration planned for tomorrow. We think Latvian nationalists may attempt to disrupt it. It's politically difficult for the Latvians to follow up on their own people. Doing so may cause further tensions. They've asked if we can do it for them.'

'Roger, Tom,' came Dingley's reply. 'We've been warned off about this from J2 Intelligence here at PJHQ. I've got our GCHQ liaison officer with me. She'll brief you on what the Government Communications Headquarters can do.'

And then on the small screen came a face Morland once knew better than his own. He hadn't seen Nicola Allenby since leaving Oxford. Brilliant – she'd left Oxford with the best First in Computer Science and Philosophy of her year – intriguing, funny and with the sporty good looks you'd expect from a former head girl of Cheltenham Ladies College, she was also a talented linguist; fluent in Russian, Polish and German from her upbringing as a diplomat's daughter. One of the many girls attracted by the physical challenge of the Oxford University Officer Training Corps, she had fallen for the rough diamond from the West Midlands. Inevitably, and as their relationship deepened, she had started smoothing off his many rough edges and in no time he was utterly devoted to her and she, it seemed, to him.

Then, at a May Ball, Morland had done something he had instantly regretted. He had thumped the brother of one of Allenby's friends; a chinless land agent from Cirencester, up for the party, who'd all too easily wound up Morland with disparaging remarks about 'chavs' from the Midlands. The fact that the guy had clearly fancied Nicola had a lot to do with his reaction, but something had changed in her in the instant that he had stepped in to protect her. For the next few days she was unusually unavailable. Then she had texted and asked to meet him for coffee in Brown's. She had not even started to drink the cappuccino he had just bought her before she had announced that they had no future together and walked out of the café.

'Meet our new GCHQ liaison officer, Tom,' said Dingley on the VTC. 'Over to you, Nicky.'

'We've met before . . . at Oxford. Good to see you again, Tom. Although the VTC picture is a bit hazy.'

Morland could hear the cool professionalism in her voice. 'I've got a clear enough picture of you from here. All that matters is that we can hear each other. Can you help us?' Morland was brisk and giving away nothing.

'Give me as much detail as you can and we'll start tracking down the network.'

Morland handed over to Krauja who briefed in detail on the extent of Russian infiltration of the Latvian Russian Union, together with what was known about plans for the next day's pro-Russian speakers demonstration. She also highlighted Latvian concerns about a counter-demonstration by Latvian nationalists. 'We think the Russians are winding each side up to cause civil disturbances and give them an excuse to intervene to protect their own people. Just as they did in Crimea and now in eastern Ukraine.'

'I understand.' Allenby was matter of fact and was clearly not going to give anything away about the British position on Latvia's concerns. 'I'll talk to my team at GCHQ and ensure my senior people are fully in the picture.'

'We'll also ask the guys at Vauxhall Cross, Tom,' added Dingley, referring to the British Secret Intelligence Service, MI6, head-quarters, based on the south side of the River Thames in Vauxhall. 'See if they're picking anything up. We've agreed the Latvian request for you and the team to get into a position to observe the demonstration and relay back what is happening.'

'The demo is due to kick off at midday tomorrow,' Morland replied. 'Let me know if you find out anything before then. We're heading into Riga tonight to recce the demo route and find OPs to monitor events.'

The update finished and the faces in Northwood disappeared as the screen went blank.

'So, Tom, as we're going to be working together pretty closely . . . You don't mind me calling you Tom?' asked Krauja.

'As long as I can call you Marina,' Morland answered, flattered that she had been the one to relax the formality.

'Of course.' She smiled. 'You know that girl?'

'I used to . . . but we've got work to do, Marina.'

Morland looked her in the eye, but he sensed that she already knew; beautiful *and* intuitive.

Morland turned to his team. 'Time to get into Riga and find out where we can best see things tomorrow. Without being seen.'

'I'll show you. Come,' said Krauja.

0800 hours, Wednesday, 17 May 2017
Riga, Latvia

THAT WEDNESDAY DAWNED brighter. The grey clouds and cold northerly wind had disappeared and the day promised to be fine. Despite that, there was a sense of foreboding in Riga, a feeling entirely foreign to the city. News of the murders of Petrov and Zadonov, the Russian Latvian Union leaders, had spread quickly through the large Russian population and their sense of shock and outrage was everywhere.

Vronsky was up early to capitalise on the events of the previous night. Leaving Brezhneva to first report back to Moscow and then maintain a steady stream of Twitter and other social media feeds to fearful Russian speakers desperate for news, he met the organising committee of the demonstration and a new leader was soon appointed. He then sat down with the RNZS commander and his subordinates to plan the course of the demonstration from start to finish.

The killings were having exactly the desired effect. As the news spread by word of mouth, by Twitter, Facebook and other social media – Brezhneva no doubt doing her part – so the anger mounted among ethnic Russians.

From early in the morning large numbers of Russian speakers walked, biked, bused or travelled by the ubiquitous trams to the designated assembly area for the demonstration, watched by Vronsky from a café where he sat drinking endless cups of coffee. Others came by bus and car, particularly from Daugavpils and other Russian majority areas in the east, beside the border with Russia. Some Russian speakers were Latvian citizens, but most were the so-called 'non citizens', denied Latvian citizenship because they refused to take the Latvian 'citizenship test' on a point of principle.

While there had remained a deeply discontented minority ever since the final withdrawal of Soviet troops in 1994, most 'non-citizens' accepted the status quo and were happy with their 'Western' style of life in Latvia. But now, and ever since the invasion of Crimea and Ukraine, they were exposed to a constant stream of Russian TV broadcasts and social media highlighting the discrimination, the lack of employment opportunities and the laws against speaking Russian. Every day they were told how much better things would be under the paternal protection of the President.

And in recent months, following a highly provocative petition organised by Latvian nationalists calling for ethnic Russians to be put into concentration camps, there had been a more direct message broadcast by the entertaining and thoroughly believable Kremlin TV, telling people to get onto the streets and demonstrate for their civic rights as ethnic Russians. And, if necessary, to be prepared to fight for those rights.

As ethnic Russians flooded into Riga that May morning, doubling if not tripling the population of the city, so the rumours swirled and began to take on a life of their own. On Vronsky's instruction, Brezhneva put out more feeds on social media calling for Russia, the Motherland, to protect her children, *all* her children.

She repeated the President's words from three years ago and they were re-tweeted and favourited, again and again: *95% of the Russian population think that Russia should protect the interests of Russians.*

And then the message changed: *The Latvians will never change. Russia must protect us. We call upon the President for protection.*

Meanwhile Morland and his team, dressed in nondescript civilian clothes and guided by Marina Krauja, took up covert positions in pairs, high up in the art deco Europa Royale Hotel on Krišjāņa Barona Street, directly on the planned route of the demonstration. From their positions they watched the hundreds of riot police lining the route, with more police held in groups in reserve. In the city centre, shops and offices closed, windows were boarded up and most headed home before the demonstration began.

The march began in the early afternoon. Urged on by RNZS members, identified by their march organisers' armbands, tens of thousands of demonstrators started to move towards the centre of the old city. Deep, rhythmic chants of 'Rossiya, Rossiya' filled the air. Banners with photographs of the President inscribed in Russian and English to ensure the watching world understood – *Россия слава, Rossiya slava, Russia Glory* – bobbed above the heads of the crowd as it moved in a mass phalanx. On the flanks, young men, faces covered in masks and with rucksacks full of stones, taunted the police who stood solid in full riot gear with shields raised and batons drawn. As they passed a liquor store a brick was hurled through the window. With a roar a mass of wildly yelling looters, urged on by the RNZS, grabbed bottles of vodka and devoured the contents.

The police formed a base line, fired baton guns into the rioters and then charged. Several went down and were grabbed by snatch squads, and bundled into the backs of police vans. Soon the steady, purposeful mass had become an enraged animal; vengeful, vicious, ever more intoxicated and looking for blood. More shops were looted, cars overturned and set on fire. As smoke billowed across the city, international TV crews, alerted to the impending carnage by Vronsky, rushed to get close-up shots of the crowd surging forward against the lines of police, hurling Molotov cocktails, which exploded with a 'whoosh' of flame against the lines of riot shields. Here and there the lines were penetrated and policemen went down, desperately beating their protective clothes to extinguish the flames.

And in the heart of it all was Vronsky, directing the RNZS militia leadership, who passed on his instructions to their lieutenants within the crowd by mobile phone.

As the crowds neared the Vermanes Gardens, the usually peaceful green square with its outdoor theatre at the heart of the elegant city, Morland and his team were able to observe, film and record from their vantage points above Krišjāņa Barona Street, as the crowd surged beneath them. Krauja was pointing out the leaders to Morland.

'Tom, that guy surrounded by RNZS organizers; medium height, early thirties, close-cropped dark hair, black zip-fronted fleece jacket over a white T-shirt. Got him?'

'Seen,' Tom replied.

'He seems to be in charge and he's new. He's the Russian we've been watching. We're pretty certain he met Petrov and Zadonov the night they were killed, but we lost him in the Old Town. We reckon he's been sent by Moscow to stir things up.'

Morland pressed the shutter on his Canon digital SLR camera with its zoom lens. There, face filling the lens and frozen in his viewfinder, was the dark-haired Russian that Krauja had pointed out to him.

'Got you . . . you bastard,' muttered Morland to himself.

Then, as the head of the crowd filled the Vermanes Gardens, there was a guttural roar as the mass of marchers were charged by a counter-demonstration of hundreds of nationalists from behind the university buildings.

The police lines were overwhelmed, caught between two masses of humanity hell-bent on killing each other. Nationalists hurled Molotov cocktails and bricks at the ethnic Russians, who fought back with bricks, glass shards from smashed windows and batons hidden under jackets. More cars burned and running fights flowed up and down side streets, as the pent-up anger and bitterness of the ethnic Russians exploded.

Morland looked back at the leaders and, through his binoculars, saw the Russian speak into his mobile phone; brief, to the point. He was giving an order.

A moment later, from the roof of the university, came three deliberate, aimed shots: the unmistakable sound of a sniper. Morland realised he had heard that sound before on the range only a week earlier, when the Latvians had given his team a demonstration of Russian infantry small arms. In fact, he had been allowed to fire it himself and its high-pitched crack was distinctive, as was the weapon itself, the special sniper rifle developed for the Spetsnaz: the VSS, also called the Vintorez or 'thread cutter'. It fired a subsonic, 9 millimetre, armour-piercing cartridge, tipped with tungsten, and was capable of penetrating a 6 millimetre high-density steel plate at 100 metres.

Morland remembered joking how he hoped he never got on the wrong end of one of these and here he was now, a week later, and some bastard was using one to fire into the crowd below.

Then, a second later, there was a haphazard burst of half a magazine on automatic. 'That's a bog standard AK 47M,' Morland muttered to himself. Now the shooting sounded as if it was the work of a lone lunatic and no longer a trained professional.

Morland saw the crowd part and start to run and, unable to see exactly where the shots had come from, he switched his binoculars there. On the ground, gushing blood, writhing and twitching in their death throes were the targets.

A TV crew from Russia Today, conveniently close by, rushed to get their close-up shots: three young, ethnic Russian girls murdered by a crazed, doubtless 'nationalist', gunman. But shot, Morland would swear, by one or more Spetsnaz snipers from the top of the university building. Those terrible images would be circulating the globe in moments.

Any more victims? No. That extra burst had definitely been for deception and had been aimed to miss. But Morland knew that the black-fleeced Russian with the mobile phone, the man whose picture he had in his camera, was the man who had planned this atrocity; the man who had given the kill order and who had as good as pulled the trigger.

'One day I'll get you, you bastard,' he vowed.

0700 hours, Wednesday, 18 May 2017
National Defence Control Centre, Moscow

FYODOR FYODOROVICH KOMAROV arrived early that morning at the National Defence Control Centre, the NDCC, where the War Cabinet meeting was to be held. The news from Riga had been phoned through to him on Tuesday evening, just as he arrived back at his apartment behind Tverskaya Street. He'd been at the gym working out on the judo mat with the President. Komarov had checked again the arrangements for this morning's meeting and was drinking tea in the office of the Commander, Lieutenant General Mikhail Filatov, as he waited for the President to arrive.

In the corner of the office, Russia Today was running and re-running the story of the killing of the three ethnic Russian girls on its 24-hour news bulletin. The open, smiling faces of the three girls, all promising students at the University of Riga, stared out from the TV screen.

Komarov raised his glass of tea in silent salute to Major Vronsky. He had chosen the victims well. They were beautiful. That alone would cause maximum impact and outrage and reinforce the messages being broadcast by Olga Bataman, the highly photogenic, articulate presenter on the morning news. Outrage that young, hard-working, well-educated Russian girls, their lives ahead of them callously snuffed out by a fanatic's bullets. And all the while peacefully exercising their democratic right to protest against the discrimination imposed on them by the fascist Latvian state. Followed by desperate pleas from the Latvian Russian Union for Russian protection. Russian mothers in tears, fury on their faces, demanding protection for their children. The outrage of a sniper allowed to escape by the Latvian police. Who would be next?

Meanwhile, Filatov sat nervously at his desk. The youthful-looking Commander of the NDCC who, with his perfectly coiffed hair and full lips, seemed more like a fashionable hairdresser than a Russian general, clearly knew that this was a big day for him. But it was also a dangerous day. It was rare for the War Cabinet to meet here and that meant he and his staff had to get everything exactly right.

Opened in December 2014 and built on the banks of the Moscow River, the vast, neo-Stalinist classic edifice sent a powerful message about the new power of the reinvigorated Russian state, after the chaos and weakness following the collapse of the Soviet Union in the 1990s. The President, like the early Romanovs after the 'time of troubles' of the early seventeenth century, saw himself as a new Peter the Great. It was his destiny to regenerate the greatness of the Russian Empire. The new top-security, fortified facility, with its imposing war rooms, brand new supercomputer in the heart of a state-of-the-art data processing centre, secret transport routes for emergency evacuation and helicopter landing site, was a visible manifestation of his intent. It had better work perfectly now the time had come to use it as it was always intended or in this new, reinvigorated Russia, it would be very much more than Filatov's job on the line.

'Sir,' Filatov's Military Assistant interrupted, 'all the members of the War Cabinet are assembled and the President's helicopter is due in ten minutes.'

Shortly afterwards, Komarov and Filatov, as the headquarters commander, stood at the edge of the NDCC helicopter landing site while the bulbous shape of the President's preferred helicopter, an updated version of the tried-and-trusted Russian rotary-wing workhorse, the Mi-8 'Hip', landed in a tornado of wind, roar of engines and clatter of rotors.

The side door slid open. Ignoring the steps rushed forward by the attentive ground crew, the President jumped nimbly out, his eyes hidden by wraparound sunglasses despite the overcast Moscow day.

The President gave Filatov a perfunctory acknowledgement of his smart salute. 'Take me to the War Cabinet Room,' he ordered.

Filatov anxiously led the President past the Guard of Honour, not a man shorter than six foot three, with burnished, gleaming jackboots, all presenting arms with the standard ceremonial firearm, the old SKS Soviet semi-automatic carbine.

Then it was into the building with doors opening as if automatically, into the lift and down to the ballistically protected basement and the principal War Room, with its concentric rings of desks and banks of computers. Around the walls were interactive screens showing maps complete with icons indicating the positions of Russian formations and those of the enemy during the rapid advance through Ukraine to Crimea, together with satellite photographs of the destroyed town of Mariupol in south-east Ukraine. Other TV screens showed live 24-hour news: Russia Today, Al Jazeera, BBC News 24 and CNN.

As he walked onto the bridge overlooking the War Room, the President was greeted by General Mikhail Gareyev, Chief of the Russian General Staff; the high-cheekboned, muscular Tatar, very much the tough-looking, twenty-first-century Russian general, in bizarre contrast to the coiffured Filatov. Gareyev quickly updated the President on the ease with which Russian forces were cutting through to Crimea.

'We estimate we'll have the route to Crimea secured within twenty-four hours, Vladimir Vladimirovich.'

'I am satisfied, Mikhail Nikolayevich,' the President responded curtly. 'Now for the War Cabinet.'

A door at the back of the bridge opened and there, standing around a circular table, stood the other members of the War Cabinet. On the walls were smaller screens showing the same maps and satellite images as in the main War Room. Flanking the screens were the same green curtains as in the President's office in the Kremlin, also tied back with the same gold ropes. Behind the President's chair there was only one decoration: the gold double-headed eagle of Russia on a red shield.

There was little need for discussion. The President turned to the Director of the FSB, Merkulov. As a former FSB head and KGB operative himself, the President never made a move without ensuring he was not underestimating his enemy.

'Lavrentiy Pavlovich, I am interested in two things. First, is the ground now prepared in Latvia? Second, can NATO respond?'

Komarov noted with approval how Merkulov came to the point immediately.

'Vladimir Vladimirovich, the answer to your first question is yes. The riots in Riga yesterday were the culmination of a long-running operation. The Latvian economy has been crippled over the past two years by a series of strikes. Our propaganda has sharpened discontent most satisfactorily among the Russian-speaking minority and polarised opinion among the Latvians themselves. The RNZS militia is trained, organised and ready. And, of course, yesterday's killing of the three girls has led to strident calls by Russian speakers for Russian protection. The integrity of Latvia as a state has been thoroughly undermined. My judgement is that the time is now ripe for the next phase of the operation.'

'And the answer to my second question? What about the

brigade the Americans have stationed across Eastern Europe on a rotational basis? I recall being briefed that this year we can expect a second brigade's worth of vehicles? And, of course, Prime Minister Spencer of the UK surprised us a couple of years ago by committing Britain to two per cent of GDP spent on defence. Has that made a difference?'

'With respect, Vladimir Vladimirovich, while you are correct on both counts, the FSB's assessment is that these are both little more than political posturing. At present. A timely headline in their newspapers and no more. While the Americans have a brigade spread from Estonia to Bulgaria, that hardly counts as a military capability. Only when the brigade is assembled together, and properly trained with the nations it is to operate alongside, can it possibly become effective. And that has not happened. Nor can it happen in less than a week and we will have achieved our objectives well within that timeframe. As for the second brigade's worth of vehicles kept in storage, that is hardly relevant. Only when the vehicles are fully crewed and it, too, is concentrated will it be an effective force. So while NATO can do little at present, there remains the danger of a continued build-up of forces by the West, which could well threaten us in time.'

'And the British?'

'Good fighters and still, for their size, the most capable armed forces in Europe, even if some of their generals are keener to tell their politicians what they want to hear than command as soldiers. Nevertheless, man for man, they are still a match for anyone in the world.'

General Gareyev nodded his agreement.

Komarov saw the President's momentary flash of irritation at the acknowledgement of the fighting qualities of the British, quickly subside at the criticism of British generalship.

Merkulov continued. 'Extra spending? It is all show. More headlines. The British government is playing political smoke and mirrors with its defence budget by now including not only the costs of the intelligence agencies, but also civil service pensions, to get them over the two per cent of GDP line. The military spending cuts of the past decade will take years to put right and would cost much, much more than they plan to spend. After all, Vladimir Vladimirovich, it is costing us a forty-per-cent annual increase in defence spending just to start putting right the neglect of those traitors Gorbachev and Yeltsin.'

'What are their vulnerabilities, Lavrentiy Pavlovich?' persisted the President.

'The list is long and responsibility for much of it lies with Defence Secretary Everage. He made millions in the processed-meat business. But knowing how to make a margin on sausages does not necessarily give you any understanding of geostrategy or war. How could it? That requires people with a sense of history and experience of war.' Merkulov allowed himself the hint of a smile.

The President nodded for him to continue, clearly enjoying the insult.

'What is more, he is at loggerheads with many of his senior military, because he succeeded magnificently in his cost-cutting task. He slashed their regular army manpower by nearly twenty per cent and said he would replace them with reserves. His generals told him they could never be adequately recruited or trained and he ignored them. The generals turned out to be right. Only a man focused on saving money at almost any cost, and with no understanding of the strategic consequences, would have taken such a risky gamble.' Merkulov paused, unsure what level of detail the President wanted him to go into.

But Komarov knew the President was loving this.

'Go on.'

'Their Prime Minister needed to save money quickly to reduce the deficit and he appointed this businessman to do it. He did as he was asked and certainly, their Prime Minister thinks he was a success. But now they are about to receive their dividend: bad decisions, taken in haste, for which they will pay the blood price.'

'*And* the money price,' the President interjected.

'*That* is the true genius of your plan, Vladimir Vladimirovich. NATO and the West will think this is all about protecting Russian speakers, but it is also about the balance of power in Europe. When NATO fails to react to our seizure of the Baltic states it will have failed, been defeated, and probably collapse. At that moment it will cease to pose a threat to Russia. Without NATO, Europe will be forced to beg us not to go any further. And apart from eastern Poland, which has historically been part of Russia, we probably won't. We'd all be happy to visit Paris as a tourist. But there will be a price to pay for our forbearance. We will demand that these criminal sanctions are lifted immediately, and with our victorious armies on their borders and our nuclear missiles pointed at them, will they refuse? I think not.

'The G7 will become the G8 once again and Russia will again be a leading player. Will the International Monetary Fund dare not grant us soft loans? I doubt it. And here's an amusing thought one of my staffers came up with. As we will once again own the Baltics and all three are members of the European Union, surely that will make us members of the EU? With three votes even . . .'

There were loud guffaws of laughter from the others at the joke but, behind his wintry smile, Komarov could see that Merkulov was deadly serious.

He waited for the conversation to die down before continuing. 'Because Russia has always been part of Europe and as EU members, we would be entitled to receive massive EU Structural and Investment Funds. Refuse and they will risk our missiles. And there will be no NATO to resist us.'

The President gave a tight smile. 'Boris Mikhailovich, our

much-esteemed but always very concerned Finance Minister, will be delighted to learn this. But then again,' he shrugged, 'I feel sure he will find something to worry about.'

'That is why businessmen and accountants should not be allowed anywhere near the business of war,' Merkulov replied.

'Exactly.' The President nodded. 'Now, tell me more about the problems the British face.'

Komarov knew how the President enjoyed being told in front of his generals how short-sighted and foolish his enemies were. Not only did it reassure the President that his plans would work, but it also let the generals know how lucky they were to have him as their commander-in-chief. Two birds knocked from the sky with one stone, as the British would say.

'As for their once-formidable navy, they have yet to replace the escort ships they scrapped, while the aircraft carriers they built have no aircraft to fly off them. Nor, despite the decision to procure them in 2015, will they have any anti-submarine, maritime patrol aircraft for at least another two years. Quite unbelievable for an island nation. You would think they would understand the sea, as we understand the land. But this British government? Apparently not.

'And as for their once-famous army? Our assessment is that they are now so weak that the deployment of a brigade, let alone a division, would be a major challenge. Indeed, when they deployed a small armoured battlegroup to Poland to take part in a flagship NATO exercise last November, our agents in the UK were picking up unconfirmed rumours that they were talking about bringing tanks over from their training fleet in Canada, because the serviceability and spares situation in their UK tank fleet was so dire.'

'What happened?' the President demanded.

'They ended up cannibalising what tanks they had in Britain and Germany, just to get half a tank battalion operational. It was all about saving face.'

'And did they succeed in saving face?'

'No.' Merkulov allowed himself to smile again. 'Although the other nations involved were too polite to comment. We have it on very good authority that the British military were deeply embarrassed, but their politicians did not want to notice.'

'We are indeed fortunate that this Defence Minister inflicted such lasting damage. What about NATO's ability to reinforce Latvia?' asked the President.

'All the indications are that NATO's celebrated Very High Readiness Joint Task Force is also a hollow force. For a start, it is only planned at being a brigade-sized force of five thousand men. It would struggle to deploy any heavy equipment in any meaningful timeframe. It has no permanent command structure and is dependent on bringing together units who have never worked together from across the Alliance, all the way from Albania to Norway. As for the rest of the NATO Response Force? The same applies. Only worse. And anyway, its deployment depends on all twenty-eight members agreeing the decision in the North Atlantic Council. Our friends in some of the capitals assure us that there is unlikely to ever be any such agreement. And, even if there were, by the time a decision is made it is likely to be too late,' Merkulov concluded.

'So we have an open goal in the Baltic states?' asked the President, looking around the table.

All present nodded assent.

'Comrades, as the universal poet and playwright William Shakespeare said, "There is a tide in the affairs of men which taken at the flood leads on to fortune." This is our tide and we must take it. History will not be kind to us if we fail to seize the moment to pre-empt any further encirclement and aggression from NATO. We must take this opportunity to destroy the Alliance while it is still weak.'

The President paused for effect and then said very quietly, but with menace, 'Let the attack on the Baltic states begin.'

TOM MORLAND, ALONG with the Latvian Intelligence Service Liaison Officer, Marina Krauja, was in their temporary office in the Training Wing at Ādaži as Corporal Steve Bradley, the six-foot-four-inch Kiwi, established comms with PJHQ over the INMARSAT secure VTC; a delicate operation conducted with an incongruously soft touch by such a giant of a man.

This time, as the Conference Room in PJHQ came into view, with the Joint Services eagle, crossed swords and anchor badge in the background, it seemed to reflect the overnight change in the world order because the picture on the monitor was very much sharper. Morland saw that the PJHQ Baltic team leader, Lieutenant Colonel Nicholas Graham, a balding, heavily bespectacled Gunner whom Morland had briefly met on his pre-deployment briefing, sat beside Major Jerry Dingley. Despite the small screen, he could also make out Nicky Allenby off to the side.

Graham led the session. Initially he was jovial. 'Morning, Tom. So much for your cushy team task in lovely Latvia. You've certainly stirred things up since you've been there!'

Then he became brisk and to the point. 'Thanks for your initial report on yesterday's events; very helpful. We've distributed it widely around PJHQ and in Whitehall. There's a lot on the wires about what happened yesterday and we're picking up some worrying developments on the Russian side of the border. But first, fill me in on some of the detail behind your sitrep and give me a feel for the atmospherics. And the question I want to get to the bottom of is the extent to which this whole thing was fomented by agents provocateurs, Russian or otherwise.'

Morland quickly summarised what he and the team had witnessed yesterday, then focused on the Baltics team leader's question.

'Sir, there's no question that what happened yesterday was orchestrated. The way the demo boiled over was certainly the result of a carefully planned and professional operation. I'm as certain as I can be that those marshalling the demo are part of some sort of self-protection militia set up by the ethnic Russians. I'm also pretty sure that, thanks to Marina and the Latvian Intelligence Service, we know the individual who is behind it.'

'Go on,' said Graham.

'I'm talking about the guy Marina pointed out to me – he's the man the Latvians have been watching – the fellow in the photo we sent through last night on the data link; black fleece, dark hair. A tough-looking bastard. I suspect he's Special Forces, possibly FSB. I'm as certain as I can be that I watched him give the order on his mobile for the snipers to take out the Russian girls. And I'm also pretty certain that what I heard was a VSS sniper rifle, followed by a burst of AK47 as cover or deception. I fired a VSS on the range only last week when the Latvians gave us a demo of Russian weapons.'

'Roger that, Tom. We've got the J2 intel analysts working on the image now. We've also got our people crawling through the TV footage of the shooting as that might help confirm your analysis. That was good work.'

'I assume GCHQ are trying to track down his mobile number. I'll bet there's a link with the numbers we gave you earlier. He made the call around ten minutes after I took his picture and the time is recorded on the photo.' Morland looked at Allenby on the screen enquiringly.

'Don't worry, Tom. We're on the case.'

'We'll check that, too. I'll give you some direction in a second. Now, we've got some stuff on the strategic picture which you need to hear.' Graham turned to Dingley. 'Over to you, Jerry.'

Dingley spoke into the microphone. 'Tom, the Russians have pretty much closed the Ukrainians down in the south-east and it is as good as game over down there. However, we've had reports that they've called another of their snap exercises, but this time they're concentrating on the Western Military District and the Baltic Fleet. It also looks like the Northern Fleet, based in Severomorsk, just north of Murmansk and with access to the Barents Sea, has been ordered to sea with a carrier battle group, together with a number of strategic nuclear submarines.'

He paused to allow Morland to note the key points.

'On land, 6th Army, headquartered in St Petersburg, has deployed all its formations out of barracks into concentration areas on the Estonian and Latvian borders, while we're seeing indications that 1st Guards Tank Army from Moscow Military District is deploying by rail and road to reinforce 6th Army. That's important, because it gives 6th Army the ability to sustain combat operations for some time. Most worrying is the move of 2nd and 16th Spetsnaz Brigades to Pskov, base of 76th Guards Assault Landing Division. They're in the middle of a deployment exercise at the moment. Oh, and you'll be well aware that Pskov is only fifty minutes' flying time to Riga.'

Morland was only too aware of the fact. His Latvian Special Forces friends had told him that the Russians could land an airborne brigade in Riga in less than four hours. And what, they had asked Tom, could NATO do about that? He had had no answer. Certainly not one they would want to hear.

'What about air?' Morland questioned, pushing aside thoughts about how vulnerable they all now were in the face of such a massive Russian force build-up.

'I was coming to that, Tom. Their 16th Air Army is in easy flying distance of the Baltic states and appears to be at, or near, full combat readiness. It's just been reinforced with two regiments of the advanced Su-34 Fullback fighter-bombers on top of the MiG-29SMT Fulcrum fighters, the newer variant which replaced the standard MiG-29s. They also have modernised Su-25 Frogfoot close-support fighter-bombers. It's an old aircraft, but it's had a good record in a number of recent Russian operations, particularly Chechnya and Georgia.'

'Thanks, Jerry. I've got that,' said Morland.

The Baltics team leader cut in. 'Tom, I want you to be aware of the strategic picture because you've got a new job. So, here's my direction. Your team task is finished. You're now our PJHQ liaison officer to Latvia. Your team stays with you, but apart from them, you're on your own. As you know, our dedicated military attaché was removed in the last round of defence cuts. It's now down to you to be our ears and eyes.'

'Got that, Sir.' Morland felt a sense of rising excitement, mixed with extreme trepidation; he might just be about to find himself at ground zero of the next big conflict.

'What we could be seeing, Tom, are all the ingredients of ambiguous or deniable warfare; what Russia did in Crimea and eastern Ukraine. This could be all about undermining the integrity of Latvia from within, without having to deploy overt military force. Or it could be something far more heavy handed. We have no idea at the moment. It could go either way, or it could be a storm in a teacup and there are plenty here who tend towards that conclusion, which is why I still have operational control of you for the time being.

'I happen not to agree with the optimists. So, I want you to get everywhere and to update us every time you have something useful to report. I want you to base yourself in the embassy, where we've got better comms, and you'll have some security and life support. But I particularly want you to get alongside the Latvian Chief of Defence, General Raimonds Balderis. He's a good man. He came to PJHQ last year. We've been in touch with his office and he's expecting you this afternoon. Also, get yourself known in the National Armed Forces Joint HQ and, above all, stay in close touch with their Special Forces.'

'Roger, Sir.'

'Have you any questions for me right now?'

'Nothing immediate, Sir.'

'Good man. Jerry will pick up any questions and provide all the usual reach-back support. We'll come back on the analysis of your picture of the man in the riot. Nicky will come back to you with GCHQ input, once they've had a chance to analyse the mobile traffic. Good luck.'

As before, the screen went black. 'Well, Sir,' commented Wild laconically, 'we've got our work cut out now.'

1400 hours, Thursday, 18 May 2017
NATO Headquarters, Brussels

A S A ROYAL Marine who had spent much of his early career at sea, waiting on a ship for things to happen, McKinlay had reserves of patience that rarely ran dry. But today was really testing him. He was back, for the third time since Sunday's meeting, in the NAC Council Chamber sitting at the great round table. His immediate boss, the SACEUR, had, yet again, been called across the Atlantic to testify before the Senate Armed Forces Committee, which is why he was representing him today.

The second meeting that week had followed the same pattern as Sunday's meeting, with nothing to show from it except a series of self-serving statements from ambassadors of NATO nations whose countries had little in the way of armed forces worth speaking of in any event, and whose commitment to the cause of collective defence appeared to be measured anywhere between paper thin and non-existent. But McKinlay also knew that, however irritating the tortuous process of the NAC, it had proved in the past to be remarkably statesmanlike in its decision making. And once a decision had been made, the need for consensus meant that the nations were usually prepared to stick with it. Shame at being seen as a backslider was a great motivator.

He never ceased to be impressed by Secretary General Kostilek, the former Polish prime minister, for the way he steered the NAC's meetings. True, many ambassadors complained that he did not allow them enough time to fully explain their nations' positions.

But at least, thought McKinlay, *he kept things moving.*

When ambassadors began to repeat the same platitudes, he cut them short and asked them to focus on the issues at hand. As for the Chairman of the Military Committee, the Danish general, Knud Vahr, if anything McKinlay admired him more. Not only did he have to sit through endless NAC meetings listening to the ambassadors, he also had to put up with the dead weight and disinterest of the Military Committee, that group of senior military representatives from each of the Allied nations who were meant to add value to the NAC, but who seldom could be prevailed upon to say anything. Many were at the end of their, usually, distinguished careers, and were more focused on enjoying the Brussels diplomatic dinner-party circuit and the excellent networking opportunities it offered for future consultancy opportunities.

Today's meeting had been called following the chaos in Riga yesterday. The decision-making body of NATO was debating the issue that underpinned the Alliance's very existence: whether recent events in Latvia warranted the declaration of Article 5, the founding principle of the North Atlantic Treaty. This stated that an attack on one member state was an attack on all. It bound all members to come to the aid of the victim – as if they themselves were under attack. The motion before the NAC was whether to declare an Article 5 emergency on behalf of the three members who had called for it: Latvia, Estonia and Lithuania.

This was first time since the 9/11 attacks, and only the second time in history, that an Article 5 emergency had ever been called and that, McKinlay knew, made this meeting deadly serious.

But what seemed to be making it particularly serious for some of those seated around that circular table was that the meeting had been called over lunchtime, because of difficulties in programming the Secretary General's attendance. Some ambassadors were already showing irritation at missing out on their daily, all-expenses-paid lunch. Despite the seriousness of the world situation, McKinlay couldn't help chuckling to himself as he watched the emergency solution to the developing culinary crisis; a couple of Belgian waiters, in white shirts, black bow ties and waistcoats, entered and began to circulate minibars of extra-dark Cote d'Or chocolate to help quell the growing pangs of ambassadorial hunger.

Chocolate safely dispensed and waiters removed, the Secretary General opened the meeting. He invited the Latvian ambassador, as the representative of the principal nation under threat, to open the discussion.

'Secretary General, my fellow ambassadors, generals, dear colleagues and friends, only once in its sixty-eight-year history has NATO agreed the declaration of Article Five, and that was after the unprecedented attack on the USA on the eleventh of September 2001. A day of infamy we will all remember only too well. Today the motion before you is to declare an Article Five emergency at the request of my country and our close friends and neighbours, Estonia and Lithuania. I will leave it to the Estonian and Lithuanian ambassadors to explain their countries' positions. But from the Latvian perspective, what we have seen in the past few months, and most graphically in the rioting in Riga yesterday, is the progressive application of the new Russian techniques of warfare designed to undermine the integrity of Latvia before there is any need to cross our boundaries with an invasion force.

'The very rules of war have changed and what we are witnessing in Latvia is the role of non-military means of achieving political and strategic goals; war, as it were, by other means.

The advantages we in Latvia enjoy as a result of NATO's unconditional guarantee of collective defence are being nullified by
the sophisticated application of hybrid or asymmetric techniques
by Russia, techniques we saw most recently in the invasion of
eastern Ukraine and Crimea three years ago. In essence, to
paraphrase General Gareyev, the Russian Chief of the General
Staff, what we are seeing is the use of special operations forces
and internal opposition to create a permanently operating front
through the entire territory of what Russia has deemed to be
an enemy state; my peaceful, democratic, freedom-loving Latvia.'

He stopped for a sip of water in order to control his emotions.

'And if this were not enough, we have seen unprecedented
military activity on the borders of Latvia and our Baltic neighbours. Our history tells us never to trust Russia. It was Count
Shuvalov, a Russian who was Governor General of what were
then the Baltic Provinces in the Tsarist Empire one hundred
and fifty years ago, who said, and I quote: "The historical
mission of the Baltic provinces is to serve as a battlefield for
the problems of the highest politics in Europe." Please, my
fellow ambassadors, we have no desire to be Russia's battlefield
once again!'

He stopped, overcome with emotion. He had the attention
of all.

'Our memories are long. Latvia has only existed as a sovereign state for two decades between the world wars of the last
century and once again since 1991. So, we are all too aware of
the fate which is in store for us if we fail to deter the Russians
this time. We firmly believe that, unless NATO declares an
Article Five emergency and provides immediate military, diplomatic and political support to Latvia, Estonia and Lithuania,
then Russia will attempt to take over the Baltic states. Secretary
General, I call upon the allies to accept that an attack is taking
place on Latvia right now and therefore to agree to implement
Article Five.'

He stopped, sighed, took off his spectacles and sat back. Silence reigned in the NAC Chamber. After a pause, Secretary General Kostilek called upon the Estonian and then the Lithuanian ambassadors to speak. Both spoke in turn, equally eloquently and equally persuasively.

Kostilek turned to the Chairman of the Military Committee. 'General Vahr, can I ask for the advice of the NATO military authorities, please.'

'Secretary General, I regret that the Military Committee is unable to agree a common line due to different views among nations. I therefore propose we ask DSACEUR for his military advice.'

Kostilek nodded and turned to McKinlay. 'General, the floor is yours.'

McKinlay cleared his throat. 'Thank you, Secretary General. In line with the direction of the NAC, the NATO military authorities have spent much time considering the nature of Article Five in the twenty-first century. We recognise the dangers of viewing it through Cold War spectacles. So, ladies and gentlemen, we must no longer think of an attack on a NATO member in terms of massed Soviet tanks invading across the Inner German Border, or biting off a chunk of northern Norway, as we did back in the Cold War days. This means the Latvian ambassador is right. The military assessment is that what we are seeing is a new form of state-on-state war in which, gradually, the Russians will ramp up the pressure on the target state, in this case Latvia, while remaining under the threshold of what would traditionally generate an Article Five response from NATO. The best way to stop this crisis from getting out of control is to meet the Russians with strength.'

He looked around the table. This was clearly not what the majority of ambassadors wanted to hear.

He continued. 'I have, of course, discussed this with SACEUR in Washington and his view is unequivocal. This is the gravest situation that has faced NATO in recent years. SACEUR and I believe that we are closer to war than at any stage in its history. Some might say, "What about the Cuban missile crisis?" My response would be that, even at the height of that crisis, Soviet Politburo decisions were coloured by memories of their twenty-six million war-dead from the Great Patriotic War. There is a new generation in the Kremlin who have not learned these lessons the hard way. We are now up against an adversary which integrates nuclear weapons into every aspect of its war-fighting doctrine and is prepared to use them. Any miscalculation could lead to an outbreak of fighting between NATO forces and the Russians. And because Russia will be able to concentrate stronger conventional forces than NATO, that increases the risk that once Russia has defeated us in the Baltic states, the President will resort to what he calls "nuclear de-escalation".'

McKinlay stopped for a moment, conscious of the confusion on the faces of some ambassadors. 'Ladies and gentlemen, you're right. There's a nasty paradox here. What the Russians call nuclear de-escalation, we call nuclear blackmail. It's no more than the President saying to us, "Try and retake the Baltic states and I'll nuke you." We stop and he calls it de-escalation.

'So, to avoid getting to this, we must deter any aggression in the first place and that means demonstrating strength and resolve in the Baltic states. You will recall that we already have the Standing NATO Mine Countermeasures Group operating in the Baltic and it will be in Riga shortly for a long-planned port visit; that is fortunate timing. However, we need to demonstrate NATO's absolute commitment to collective defence by the immediate deployment of the Very High Readiness Joint Task Force to the three Baltic states. That deployment should be followed by the sea, land and air components of the NATO Response Force. Meanwhile, ACTORD – for the uninitiated among you and in NATO acronyms, "Activation Order" – should be declared by SACEUR in order to initiate the deployment of NATO headquarters and forces. You should be aware that this will also release the necessary NATO common funding to pay for the deployment.

'SACEUR's and my unequivocal advice is that, by sending a strong signal of NATO resolve right now, we may force the Russians to think twice before proceeding further against the Baltics. NATO would, emphatically, not be attacking Russia by doing this. But by stationing multinational NATO forces in these countries, Russia will be in no doubt that an attack on one would truly be an attack on all. I know I must avoid making any political comment but let me finish by telling you what any soldier who has studied his profession will tell you . . . Wars are caused by weakness. History teaches us that, time and time again, aggressors attack when they think they can get one over their adversary. Russia is militarily stronger than it has been for a long time. NATO weaker. Our conclusion is that this is one such moment. That is why we give the advice we do.'

Secretary General Kostilek then gave the floor to the ambassadors. Successively, the US, UK, Poland, Norway and Denmark supported the proposal. France came to the support of its old ally Poland. Most of the southern Europeans stayed silent; unwilling to support the proposal, but equally unwilling to cross the USA.

More encouraging than I had hoped for, thought McKinlay. *We may even get a positive decision pretty quickly.*

Then the bulky German ambassador, appetite for lunch entirely unsatisfied by a small bar of chocolate, took the floor; bombastic, loud and aggressive.

'Germany cannot accept this military advice under any circumstances. Not only have the NATO Military Authorities broken procedure by not declaring Activation Warning before Activation Order, but we also believe that such a deployment by NATO will be seen as a provocation by Russia and lead to precisely the situation we are seeking to avoid. No. There can be no deployment of the Very High Readiness Joint Task Force and certainly no deployment of the NATO Response Force, yet. Germany insists that all the political means of defusing this crisis must be brought to bear before going down a path which could lead to a major war in Europe.'

McKinlay could now see from the relief on the faces around the table that the German view had many supporters, and not only from the southern Europeans. The Greek ambassador was next. Unshaven in his leather jacket, McKinlay noted he was today sporting a gold earring, along with the gold medallion visible above his T-shirt.

'After the saga of the Euro and Germany's overbearing attitude and lack of understanding for the problems faced by Greece, I am surprised to find myself in agreement with the German ambassador.'

He nodded to the German ambassador, who looked back as if the Greek was something unsavoury the restaurant cat had brought in.

'Greece has always been a loyal member of the Alliance but, on this occasion, we find that our ties of Orthodox brotherhood and the support we have been given by Russia in our recent troubles must take precedence. Greece believes it would be totally unjustified to provoke the situation further by any form of NATO deployment. Greece cannot accept that recent events . . . and my government sends its condolences to the families of those students murdered by this lone madman . . . constitute an attack on Latvia or any of the Baltic states. What we have heard is a totally unjustified and hysterical overreaction by these warmongering generals. The NATO Military Authorities over-reach themselves. There must be no declaration of Article Five.'

McKinlay saw Kostilek begin to drum his fingers on the table.

And then the Hungarian spoke – or rather read his statement.

'Hungary recognises no threat from Russia to any NATO country. Hungary cannot support any declaration of Article Five.'

Kostilek held his hand up. 'I regret that I have to exercise my prerogative as Secretary General to intervene.' His voice was even and carefully modulated, but he was clearly angry. 'The bedrock assumption of this Alliance is collective defence . . . What we have just heard from Germany, Greece and Hungary strikes right at the very heart of that assumption. There is a clear and present danger facing one, if not three NATO allies. The fact that the solidarity of NATO is being undermined by three nations who are only too ready to accept that American taxpayers should continue to underwrite their defence, without being prepared to pay their way, only adds insult to injury. Worse than that, I detect a degree of posturing to domestic politics in these statements.'

He got no further. The German ambassador erupted with a roar of anger, stood up, gathered up his papers and stormed out of the chamber. The Greek followed, knocking over his chair as he did so. The Hungarian sat there, mouth open like a fish gasping for air, gesturing for one of his aides to tell him what had been said, for his English was not up to understanding the Secretary General's words.

There was stunned silence in the chamber. This was unprecedented.

Kostilek took the floor again. 'I suggest we adjourn for thirty minutes and then return in ambassador-only format.'

Relieved, the remaining ambassadors concurred.

'I see there are no objections. We return in thirty minutes.'

1600 hours, Thursday, 18 May 2017
National Armed Forces Joint HQ, Riga, Latvia

LIEUTENANT GENERAL BALDERIS, the Chief of Defence, kept a small, functional office manned by a PA in the National Armed Forces Joint HQ and had just arrived for a briefing. 'I'm glad to see you, Captain Morland,' said the general, shaking hands.

Lieutenant General Raimonds Balderis was a former Special Forces officer; robust and exceptionally fit for a man in his late fifties. He spoke good, albeit accented English, the product of a year spent at the US Army War College in Carlisle, after the collapse of the Soviet Union. 'I've always enjoyed my dealings with the Brits, so it's good to have you with us. These are dangerous times and we need all the help we can get. The Prime Minister and Cabinet have this morning ordered the mobilisation of our National Armed Forces, including the National Guard, as a precautionary measure after yesterday's events in Riga and the Latvian Russian Union's call for Russian protection. I'm about to start a briefing in the Joint Command Centre. I'd like you to sit in. And Miss Krauja, it's important that you are there too. We need to maintain the closest links with your Service.'

Here, Morland could see, was a man who would remain steady under pressure. Latvia was going to need such hands on the tiller in the days to come.

Shortly afterwards he was sitting with Krauja and just behind Balderis in the newly completed, high-tech briefing room, a product of Latvia's recent modernisation as a result of NATO membership.

The Joint HQ Chief of Staff, an impressively sharp, young-looking colonel, started his briefing. Morland asked Krauja why the colonel was speaking in English and she pointed out the staff and liaison officers from Latvia's Baltic neighbours, Estonia and Lithuania, as well as two non-NATO neighbours, Finland and Sweden. English, she explained, was the only language that they all readily understood. And it was, of course, NATO's *lingua franca*.

The Chief of Staff described the build-up of Russian forces on Latvia and Estonia's borders under the guise of a 'snap exercise', with concentrations of armour from the lead elements of 1st Guards Tank Army now arriving in assembly areas west of Opochka and Velikeye Luki, near the Latvian border. He then confirmed the information Morland had heard from PJHQ, that two Spetsnaz brigades had arrived in Pskov, the base of 76th Guards Assault Landing Division.

He also confirmed that the Division's lead regiment, 23rd Air Assault Regiment, had just completed an airborne exercise in the area of Nevel on the Belarus border, around fifty minutes' flying time south of Pskov, sixty kilometres east of the Latvian border, making it a similar distance to Riga. Even more ominously, despite returning to its base at the end of the exercise, the Division was being maintained at high readiness and satellite surveillance was picking up signs of the outloading of ammunition and other logistic preparations.

During the initial phase of the exercise it had dropped its paratroopers, together with their newly issued BMD-4 amphibious infantry fighting vehicles. These were armed with the powerful 100-millimetre, low-pressure rifled gun; a 30-millimetre co-axial auto cannon, capable of firing high-explosive fragmentation rounds; and laser-guided anti-tank missiles, as well as its 7.62-millimetre PKT coaxial machine gun.

'That's an impressive bit of kit,' said Balderis, turning to Morland. 'I did two years as a conscript with Soviet airborne troops and the Russian airborne troops are good. Never forget, the Russians invented airborne forces. They're the only airborne troops in the world equipped with integral armoured vehicles. The BMD-4 can be parachuted direct from an Il-76 transport plane with the entire crew and passengers sitting inside the vehicle as they float down. That allows for instant target engagement after landing. They literally hit the ground moving and firing. And if that's not enough, they've recently added a company of T-14 Armata tanks to the division to give it extra firepower.'

'And we shouldn't forget,' added Balderis, raising his voice to the room generally, '76th Guards Assault Landing Division is battle hardened and well led. Its current commander, Major General Aleksei Naumets, was my platoon commander when I was a Soviet conscript and he was a mean bastard even then. It took part in the invasion of Ukraine in 2014 and fought in the Donbass. They took casualties. All buried in Ukraine to avoid negative publicity back home. After Afghanistan and Chechnya, the Russians liked the sight of returning body-bags no more than the Americans. But these guys are good soldiers. And tough as hell . . . They know what they are doing.'

He turned back to Morland. 'We've been seeing regular incursions by fifteen to twenty Ilyushin Il-76, four-engine, heavy lift "Candid" aircraft flying out of Pskov. That's easily a battalion's worth of airborne troops with light armoured vehicles. They fly up to the border, alert our radars, and then fly north along the border before heading back to Pskov. They might do that three or four times just to rattle us. It doesn't. But it shows just how quickly they could get significant numbers of troops on the ground if they wanted to. And, of course, they monitor our response times and positions of our radars.'

'Don't the Baltic air-policing fighters intercept them?' asked Morland. 'I know the NATO nations provide them on a rotational basis to help protect your airspace.'

'If only . . .' Balderis grunted. 'It depends which nation is providing it. The Brits, Americans, Danes, Norwegians and French are pretty good. But much depends on the duty officer at Ramstein, in Germany, where they are commanded from. If he's feeling punchy then they intercept. But all too often, the Russians are allowed to get away with it. So they think NATO is a soft touch. And who is to say that one day they don't turn right at our border and just keep coming. By the time the aircraft have been scrambled it will be too late. Anyway, it's pretty academic. You can't do much against a division with only four fighters.'

'That's correct, Sir,' the Chief of Staff confirmed. 'We've seen a massive increase in Russian air incursions in the last week, both across the border and into our airspace above the Baltic. Up three hundred per cent on the previous period last month. As well as that, the Navy have been tracking Russian Baltic Fleet ships en route to Kaliningrad. They are routinely sailing into Latvian coastal waters.'

Balderis pondered. 'I know how the Russians think. They'll be convinced they've softened us up with their Special Forces, propaganda and civic disturbances. They'll strike when they're confident we'll offer no resistance. But they still don't understand us. We let them in without a fight in 1939. But not this time . . . This time we know what it's like to live under them. This time we'll fight those bastards to the death,' he exclaimed with feeling.

He composed himself and turned back to the Chief of Staff. 'So much for the good news from Russia. What about the internal threat?'

The briefing continued. 'Sir, the Constitution Protection Bureau liaison officer here has confirmed the extent of RNZS, Russian People's Protection Force, participation in yesterday's riot.' He looked at Krauja, who nodded her head in agreement.

'The RNZS continue to call on Russia for the President to protect them. We estimate that the RNZS is stood by in all majority Russian-speaking communities and will be mobilised quickly if Russia gives the order. We're also watching carefully in case it's mobilised as a nominal self-protection force following our call-out of the National Guard.'

'Yes, we'll need to watch that. The sooner the mobilisation can be completed the better,' responded Balderis. 'But it's going to take a couple of days before we're completely ready.'

'Correct, Sir,' said the Chief of Staff. 'I was coming to that. The regular Land Forces infantry brigade is at full readiness now and moving to occupy its pre-recced wartime positions. The Naval Flotilla is patrolling the coastline of the Baltic and the Gulf of Riga. As for the Air Force, the aviation squadron is deploying with the infantry brigade, while the air surveillance squadron maintains overwatch on all likely border crossing sites.'

'Air defence?' questioned Balderis.

'The air defence wing is deployed to cover pre-recced landing sites around Riga. War stocks of logistics are being outloaded and the Training Schools have adopted their wartime roles. The National Guard mobilisation is going well and we've had an impressive turnout of reservists. We estimate that the first to be fully ready will be the Third Defence District in Riga; probably by midday on the twentieth of May.'

'What about the Second Defence District in Rezekne?' questioned Balderis. 'If the Russians roll in across the border, they'll be first in contact. They'll be heavily outnumbered. I know they'll put up a good fight, but they can't hope to stop them.'

'The National Guard in Rezekne should be ready by midnight on the twentieth.'

'Do what you can to speed things up.' Balderis turned to the Land Forces commander next to him. 'I'm taking nothing for granted.'

He looked at the Chief of Staff. 'And our Special Forces, the Special Tasks Unit? I want them ready in Ādaži as my special reserve. They're to be prepared for immediate tasking, whether we're faced with a landing in Riga or an invasion across the border – or both. Make sure they've got some helicopter lift if they're needed.'

He looked at Morland again. 'And it's important you maintain close contact with them. They may also need your help.'

Morland clocked that. If it all went to hell in a handcart that's where his team needed to be. Any professional soldier always needs to think through the 'what if' question, even if the 'what if' sounds far-fetched. These men and women were in deadly earnest, even if the rest of the world was downplaying events up here. Morland decided they'd keep their large 'bergen' rucksacks packed and weapons handy; as they might, after all, end up spending more time in the forests than they had expected to. Just as well that he and the team had spent the last three weeks in Ādaži getting acclimatised.

'Sir, I'm sorry to disturb you.' It was Balderis's MA, his Military Assistant, at his shoulder. 'Admiral Howard, the SACEUR, is on the line from Washington. He's about to see the President and is keen to talk to you before he does.'

'Hold the briefing,' said Balderis. 'I'll be back in twenty minutes. This is important.'

He left the room for his office, signalling Morland and Krauja to join him.

He entered the outer office and turned to his MA. 'Put the call through to me and then listen in on speaker. I want Captain Morland and Miss Krauja to listen in as well.'

He then went through to his inner office to take the phone call, but was back out again in moments as there was no call. The phone was dead.

They checked the other phones. Dead too. On the MA's computer screen a document he had been working on started to devour itself. Then the screen went black. As did all the computer screens.

They tested the connections. Switched off the machines, unplugged and switched them on again. Nothing.

Five minutes later the Commander of the Joint Forces HQ burst in looking worried. He spotted the General and gave him a quick salute. 'Sir, all computers and phones in the HQ have crashed. We suspect a cyber-attack. We're implementing the cyber defence plan and reversionary modes. We'll also send an advance party to open the reserve HQ in the old Soviet bunker at Ligatne.'

'You get on with that and get the message out to push on with the mobilisation with all speed. I'm heading back to the Ministry of Defence.' He looked next at Morland. 'Have you got comms?'

'Yes, General. Inmarsat VTC and secure phone, to anywhere in the world. Back at the embassy.'

'Come with me now to the MOD. You'll get a picture of what is happening and then I want you to get the message to the UK and the US. At this moment you may be our best link with the outside world.' Balderis strode out of the building to his waiting car.

Two hours later they were in the Ministry of Defence in Valdemara Street in the centre of Riga, a few blocks from the scene of yesterday's rioting and still littered with burnt-out cars and the smashed windows of looted shops. Everywhere there was chaos. None of the traffic lights were functioning and, as cars blocked every intersection, they had left the vehicles and walked the last couple of miles through streets crowded with confused and worried people trying to get home.

In the Defence Ministry, there was a sense of order and purpose – despite the blank computers and silent phones. Balderis called on the Defence Minister and after updating him, returned to his office. Reports came in by any means possible; bike, runner, or walked by messenger across the city from other ministries and key national infrastructure. What was becoming ever clearer was that this was a cyber-attack on a massive scale and all national infrastructure had crashed. The electricity grid had shut down, the flow of natural gas had stopped, financial transactions rerouted or ceased altogether, telecommunications disrupted, air-traffic-control radars blank and the airport shut down. In the streets there was a sense of resignation. And anyway, people were still in shock from the unexpected violence of yesterday's riot.

Calmly, Balderis took it all in, then turned to Morland.

'Captain, I think you have the general picture? Now, please be so good as to send a detailed report to your country and ask them to pass it on to NATO and the United States of America. There can be no question. Latvia is under attack and we need immediate NATO support.'

SERGEANT TAFF JONES of the Royal Logistics Corps eased the armoured BMW into the purpose-built garage – the so-called 'bat cave' – at the back of the large, grey 1960s building housing NATO's Strategic HQ. McKinlay pulled himself out of the back seat, where he'd been working on a stack of papers. As he stood, he felt the usual sharp pain where his lower leg had been.

'It could be another long session in the office, Sergeant Jones.'

'No problem, Sir,' responded Jones. 'I'll be stood by whenever you want to head home.'

It had already been a long haul in Brussels. After the walkout by the German and Greek ambassadors in the NAC, there had been a cooling-off session. The NAC had met for an hour and a half in 'ambassador-only' mode – with no officials present – during which the Secretary General had apologised for his remarks.

Diplomatic niceties satisfied, the NAC had then reconvened in full session to reconsider the declaration of Article 5, which would trigger the deployment of the Very High Readiness Joint Task Force to Latvia. But the three ambassadors were unmoved and did not consider that events in Latvia warranted the declaration of Article 5. Moreover, such a move, they argued, would be an unnecessary provocation. Before any consideration of military measures, there would have to be a concentrated effort to resolve the crisis by political and diplomatic means.

Without full consensus, Kostilek had been able to do no more than state that he would continue to monitor the situation and confirm they would all meet again tomorrow.

The German ambassador had begun to ask whether even that were necessary, but an angry intervention by the US ambassador led him to withdraw his question.

It was pretty clear to McKinlay that the White House would be leaning heavily tonight on the Chancellor's office in Berlin, the Bundeskanzleramt – that grandiose piece of modern architecture, ten times the size of the White House, and known with deadpan Berliner humour as the 'Elefantenklo' or elephant's crapper.

McKinlay, again attending in SACEUR's place, had sat on through the inclusive debate. He needed to brief SACEUR on the nuances of the politics at play, even if he, as DSACEUR, was only responsible for the military implementation of any decisions.

When it had finally finished, he was a worried man. Every professional fibre in his body screamed that unless NATO took immediate action, it would almost certainly be too late. All the indicators pointed to an imminent Russian attack on Latvia and quite possibly Estonia and Lithuania, too. Unless Article 5 was declared right now, NATO would have failed in the one mission for which it had been set up: to come to the aid of a fellow member under attack. Once the Russians were in country they would be almost impossible to dislodge. NATO had to stop the attack happening in the first place and that meant declaring Article 5. Unless NATO started getting credible forces on the ground, it would be game over before it had even started.

With multinational NATO troops in Latvia, the Russians

would have to know that firing on Latvian forces would also mean firing on other NATO forces. That might – just might – make them reconsider where this was going to end. Even an Article 5 declaration might not be enough to deter them, although in a saner world and with a different president in charge, it would be. But of one thing McKinlay was now convinced: if it was just Latvians defending Latvia, the Russians would not hesitate. Crimea and Ukraine in 2014 had shown that, as did this new attack on Ukraine right now.

Dammit, he had wanted to shout, as he listened to the ambassadors grandstanding, if anybody here cares to think back to the Russian invasion of Georgia in the 'friendly' days of 2008, when the world was swearing peace, brotherhood and the end of war at the Beijing Olympic Games, then that would tell any doubters exactly how the President thought. And what the President planned to do next.

After the meeting he had a one-to-one session with General Vahr, the Danish Chairman of the Military Committee, in the corridor outside.

'Knud, NATO is staring at disaster unless we get things moving. Right now. And yet, without NAC authority, we're stuck. I'm going back to SHAPE and I'll call up SACEUR. He needs to know how bad things are. I'll also call up the Chiefs of Defence of the main contributors to the VJTF and ask them to reduce notice to move bilaterally, on a national basis and not a NATO basis. That way, if . . . and when, the NAC agree Article Five, we can get it moving to the Baltic states as quickly as possible.'

'It's a clever move talking to the nations, David.' Vahr was supportive but wary. 'However, it'll backfire if it is seen as an initiative by SACEUR. And it'll be even worse if it is seen as your initiative. I've no doubt the US will be working on the Germans overnight, so I'm confident we'll eventually get agreement. But the NAC is very sticky about the military getting ahead of the game. Any change of readiness must look as if it has come from the nations themselves. We have to play the long game on this.'

McKinlay opened his mouth to speak, but Vahr held up his hand to stop him. 'Before you say anything, I know, David. It may well be far too late by then. But wasn't it ever so?'

Now back in SHAPE and reflecting on events in Brussels, McKinlay walked up the stairs that took him direct to his office door, entered, and was greeted by Group Captain Jamie Swinton, his Principal Staff Officer. The rest of his front office team of three Military Assistants (German, French and British), his Flag Lieutenant and his PA all stood.

'Sit down, guys,' said McKinlay. 'I keep telling you there's no need to stand when I come into the office.'

'Evening, Sir,' said Swinton, ignoring him and still standing. 'The only thing to add to the news of the cyber-attack on Latvia is that the NATO Communications and Information Agency and the Cyber Centre of Excellence in Tallinn are all over it at the moment. The boffins are working the wiggly amps to help the Latvians get their systems back up and running. And, by pure chance, I've just managed to get a call through to General Balderis's MA in Riga on my mobile. He's a chum of mine and I happen to know he has an American mobile and number from his time at Staff College in the States. I tried him on that on the off-chance and got him. You probably want to speak to him before SACEUR?'

'That's good – well done, Jamie. Put me through.' He went through to his office and sat down.

Swinton followed, handed him his iPhone and pulled up a chair so that he could listen in.

'Raimonds, how're things? You're having a tough time.'

Balderis's voice was clear, albeit he sounded a long way away. He was calm and measured.

'David, my friend. Things are very dangerous here. All our

command and control systems are down, but we're working to get things under control. I feel that we are living through that exercise you ran in Riga last year, Steadfast Pyramid, when we war-gamed an attack on Estonia and its reinforcement by NATO under Article Five. But this time it's for real. And it's us and not Estonia. Yet.'

Balderis paused to gather his thoughts and McKinlay guessed his friend was not really as calm underneath as he was showing on the surface. He doubted he would be under similar circumstances.

'Russia has already attacked Latvia by indirect means. Now we must expect something more direct. I think it will come in a very short time. This is the time we need that unconditional support from our NATO friends and allies. If anything warrants a declaration of Article Five, it is this. Where is it?'

McKinlay felt that he was personally letting his friend down. Balderis had looked after him so well when he had spent a couple of weeks in Latvia last year, running the war game. Then, as scripted, NATO had of course declared Article 5. Now it was for real and NATO had not.

'Raimonds, I am not going to raise false hopes. Today's NAC was a disaster. The Germans insist on an attempted political solution before there can be any declaration of Article Five, or any question of military deployment. I'm about to talk to SACEUR in the States and then I'll be on the line to the UK, France and Denmark to see if they can't get things moving unilaterally, on a national basis.'

Balderis allowed himself a touch of irony. 'Our grandparents would never have believed that the mighty Fatherland – Germany – would one day be the most pacifist nation in Europe.' He gave a bitter laugh. 'To paraphrase Bismarck, they clearly think the Baltic states are not worth the bones of a single Pomeranian Grenadier. Thanks, David. I know you'll do what you can.' And with that the line went dead.

'SACEUR's coming on to your Tandberg secure video link now, Sir.' Sergeant Lorna Bevin placed on his desk a mug, resplendent with the Globe and Laurel badge of the Royal Marines, and brimming with steaming, strong tea. 'And seeing as you missed lunch, here's a couple of biscuits.'

'Thanks, Lorna, you're a star.'

'Hi, Dave.' SACEUR came through on the Tandberg from Washington. 'I've heard about the NAC. What a mess. I'm about to head over to the White House. The National Security Advisor has called me over to talk to the President. What can I tell her?'

McKinlay was blunt. NATO was about to fail to protect one of its members and a number of European members appeared more worried about political process than recognising that, for the first time since 1945, they were on the edge of a major war in Europe; two NATO members, Greece and Hungary, seemed almost pro-Russia and even if they hadn't yet invaded, which looked imminent, the Russians were effectively attacking Latvia right now. McKinlay then concluded with a bald statement: if the Alliance were not to fail catastrophically, and thus be rendered redundant in one stroke, Article 5 had to be declared.

'OK, Dave. That's clear. Let me reassure you, wearing my US hat as Commander European Command, and *emphatically* not as SACEUR, I'm going to ask for an immediate deployment by land, sea and air to reinforce Latvia. That though is strictly between you and me, until I have confirmation. If I do not get it, I never said this to you. I never asked the President. Do we understand each other?'

'Fully,' said McKinlay, keenly aware of the degree of trust his boss had just placed in him.

'Good. What you've just told me should help me persuade the President to give the final executive order. Meanwhile, on the NATO side, we've somehow got to get the Very High Readiness Joint Task Force moving. Frankly, I'll do it without

NAC approval if I have to, so can you work the nations and let me know when I get back where we stand with force generation? I'm flying back tonight, just as soon as I've seen the President. See you tomorrow sometime.'

Howard disconnected, was momentarily frozen on screen, and then the Tandberg closed down.

McKinlay sat back in his chair and sipped his tea. It seemed a long time since he'd been out with his black-and-white working springer in the forest behind his residence, La Belle Alliance, early that morning. It had been a long day, but there was a lot to do yet before he could even think of heading home. He hoped his wife had walked Megan that afternoon, otherwise he'd have a very disgruntled dog when he finally got home.

Two phone calls later, to the French and Danish Chiefs of Defence, and he had mixed success. The French were prepared to support the Latvians unilaterally, but only if a French general took command of the Allied effort if, and when, it became a NATO operation. McKinlay, as the man responsible for allocating the flags to post, assured him that he was happy with this, but only if the French provided the majority of troops in the force. That sensible stipulation did not sit well with the French, who made it clear that they did not yet have an agreement.

After him, the Danish Chief of Defence was typically direct and to the point. Denmark had a bilateral agreement with the Latvians and was in the process of sending a battalion of mechanised infantry and a tank company to Latvia. It would be there within five days.

'If only everyone was like the Danes,' commented McKinlay to his PSO, Swinton. 'We'd better try the Brits now, Jamie. What do your spies tell you?'

'Not good news, I fear. The MOD is pretty forward leaning and, naturally, the Army, Navy and Air Force elements of the VJTF are gagging to go. But there's a real blockage in Number Ten.'

'Well,' mused McKinlay, 'better get me Vice Chief on the secure Brent phone. He at least understands NATO, unlike the Chief of Defence Staff. I'll see what he says.'

He knew Air Chief Marshal Sir Tony Wilson, the Vice Chief of Defence, well. They'd worked together when he'd been a young, newly promoted lieutenant colonel. Wilson, a serious-minded, upwardly mobile RAF navigator with some NATO experience in Germany, had been a fellow planner in the Ministry of Defence. Sharp, inclined to being abrasive, he nevertheless had a good feel for the Alliance dimension. He was also straight-talking and would tell McKinlay how it looked from the UK perspective.

The Brent phone call was put through, McKinlay heard the familiar bleeps telling him his conversation was secure, then Wilson came on the line.

McKinlay got straight to the point. He outlined the situation in Latvia as NATO saw it and debriefed Wilson on today's NAC.

'So there's no immediate prospect of a declaration of Article Five for the moment, Tony. If the Americans decide to do something unilaterally to reinforce Latvia, is there any chance of UK joining them with units you've already got declared to the VJTF?'

Wilson confirmed what Swinton's spies had told him.

'We're up for it in the MOD. The problem is the PM.'

'The usual issue?' questioned McKinlay.

'Afraid so,' replied Wilson. 'He's surrounded by acolytes to whom the use of force, especially any mention of "boots on the ground", is anathema at the best of times. But faced with an Article Five crisis, Number Ten has gone into meltdown. The prospect of telling the British people that our soldiers may have to fight and die to defend the Latvians is too much for him. Word has it that it was discussed in Cabinet this morning and his considered contribution was that Britain spends far too much money on Latvia – stag-party beer money – and the Brits who spend it are unlikely to be the sort who would vote for him anyway. His bag carriers thought that was hilarious. On top of that, as we saw with the decision to launch air strikes over Syria, the PM refuses to do anything involving guns and body-bags without a clear House of Commons majority.'

'But he's got a majority,' McKinlay said.

'Sure, but it's pretty narrow, notwithstanding that Labour have gone into meltdown since Corbyn was elected leader. The problem is that many of the Tory backbenchers, especially the younger generation, aren't prepared to back Article Five. All that stuff about Chamberlain in 1938, and why should our boys fight and, if necessary, die for a faraway country about which they know little and care even less.'

'Look how that ended up,' McKinlay muttered, as much to himself as to Wilson. This was no longer the country he had joined the Royal Marines to serve.

'Would a call from Washington help?' he asked finally.

'Maybe. But it would have to come from the White House.'

'Leave it with me. I'll keep you posted, Tony. Speak to you soon. And stay well.'

Then he called to Swinton in the next door office. 'Jamie, can you get SACEUR on the line? I need to speak to him before he gets to the White House.'

2200 hours, Thursday, 18 May 2017,
Central European Time 1600 hours,
Eastern Standard Time
The White House, Washington, D.C.

'So, madam president,' concluded MacWhite, 'we're as certain as we can be that the Russians are on the point of moving into Latvia. And very likely Estonia and Lithuania, too.'

Bear Smythson paused from his note taking – one of his more menial, but nevertheless important jobs as Executive Assistant to Abe MacWhite, the US National Security Advisor – and looked around the walls of the Situation Room, known among the National Security Council staff as the 'woodshed'. It had been refurbished fairly recently and the original wooden panelling had been removed, because the acoustics made it hard to hear for those listening in via video or telephone. Certainly the new 'whisper wall' fabric lining the walls was having its effect. The silence was oppressive, as the president of the most powerful nation on earth digested the facts that had just been briefed to her. Nobody moved.

President Lynn Turner Dillon looked around the table. Concentrated in that single room, where so many decisions about war and peace had been made, were the generals and admirals who controlled America's war machine. She looked at MacWhite, the former Special Forces general, at Admiral

Howard, the SACEUR, and at the Chairman of the Joint Chiefs. All were men who had seen the brutality of combat and its consequences. These were not the warmongers of popular fiction. To a man, they found the reality of war abhorrent. But these were also men who knew that there are times when countries need to fight to protect themselves and their values.

She made up her mind, then spoke slowly and deliberately, looking each man in the eye in turn. 'There is no question that what the Russians are conducting is an attack on Latvia. Latvia is a NATO member, an ally of America, and a country America has always stood by and recognised, even when others accepted its occupation by the Soviet Union. The propaganda barrage, the orchestration of yesterday's riot and the cyber-attack you've just updated me on, are all part of this attack. The President is set on bringing Latvia back under Russia. We've got to stop him. Set up a call to him as soon as possible, please. Meanwhile, we should be prepared to use the military.'

She turned to MacWhite, the rock on whom she increasingly relied for his judgement. 'What do you recommend, Abe?'

MacWhite turned a pencil over in his hands. 'Ma'am, I think you're right. You need to talk to the President in Moscow. Make sure that we are not misreading this in some way. We'll get that set up now.'

Bear caught the eye of one of the NSC staffers, who left the room to set up the call.

MacWhite continued. 'But we've also got to show the President that we're determined to protect Latvia. We've heard that the Germans and others have stopped NATO declaring Article Five. You've talked to the Chancellor and she's made it clear that the Bundestag and the Constitutional Court, to say nothing of her coalition partners SPD, the Social Democrats, will have to have their say before she can support the implementation of collective defence.' He looked at Admiral Howard.

SACEUR nodded his agreement.

'I think we need to get troops on the ground, reinforcement to the Baltic Air Policing mission, and ships into the eastern Baltic. If NATO won't do it, we'll have to do it bilaterally and with other willing allies.'

'With what – and with whom?' asked the President, turning to the Chairman of the Joint Chiefs, General Marty McCann, a sandy-haired Bostonian of Irish extraction. A former tank commander, he was also well known for his fine singing voice and tendency to burst into song. But this was not a time for Irish ballads.

'Madam President, in line with your direction, from last Saturday we reduced notice to move timings of 6th Fleet, 18th Airborne Corps, Special Operations Command and US Air Force Europe to twenty-four hours, with follow-up elements at between three and seven days. So in terms of immediate support, we could get six F-16s and roughly three hundred airmen from the 31st Fighter Wing at Aviano Airforce Base in north Italy, into Lielvārde Air Base, south-east of Riga.'

'How quickly?'

'The first transport planes from the Contingency Response Group can be there in twenty-four hours to set things up for the F-16s. Once they've got things ready on the ground, say another twenty-four hours, the fighters will follow. So, we'll get the first fighters into Latvia around forty-eight hours from now.'

'And what else?'

'On the navy side, 6th Fleet has two destroyers conducting a port visit in Hamburg at the moment. They could be in the Gulf of Latvia in twenty-four hours. Land forces are more of a problem. It'll take five days to get the personnel to man the brigade's worth of vehicles we've got warehoused in Eastern Europe into the various countries the equipment is stored in. Then add at least another ten days to concentrate them in one place, as they're spread real wide. So there's not much we can do with them. My recommendation is to deploy the 82nd Airborne Division Global Response Force. That's a Combat Team of around four hundred and fifty soldiers with the combat support and logistics to be able to operate on their own for several days. We can deploy the lead elements in eighteen hours.'

'Why can't they operate for longer?' the President questioned.

'Airborne forces have to fight using what they land with, until they can link up with other ground troops or be resupplied by air. That means limits on their heavy weapons, mobility, logistics and stores. Once we've got them in, we'll follow up with a brigade of air-landed ground troops, that's around five thousand men, to reinforce them within a few days. But until the second wave are on the ground, the Global Response Force will be on its own. But that's what they're trained for.'

Satisfied, Dillon turned back to MacWhite. 'What about other allies?'

MacWhite looked at his old friend McCann, a comrade whom he'd fought alongside in many campaigns. 'Where do you think the Brits will stand, Marty? You know them well.'

'We're getting close again after they messed up in Iraq. In actual fact, 82nd Airborne have been doing good work with the Brit 16th Air Assault Brigade. They put together a damn good exercise earlier this year – 900 Brits from '3 Para Battlegroup dropping to secure an airfield alongside the All-Americans,' McCann replied, referring to the famous nickname of 82nd Airborne Division.

'That sounds like just what we need to make this a coalition operation,' interjected the President with interest. 'We need our two closest allies in there with us and it's worth slowing down a bit to achieve that. The question is: will the British political leadership will have the stomach for this . . . ? And the French?'

'Ma'am, no question that the French military will be up for this. The worry is that their army is totally fixed on internal security. They've got ten thousand soldiers deployed guarding schools and supermarkets against the jihadi terrorist threat, so readiness will be an issue. And, of course, we can't be sure of the politicians. It's much the same for the Brits, although thankfully they're not committed to internal security in the same way. You can be sure that their military will be more than keen to get involved and their soldiers are still pretty good. The challenge will be the political leadership.'

'Leave the British PM to me.' Dillon was firm.

'Madam President, if I may.' SACEUR spoke. 'I've just spoken to my Brit deputy who briefed me on today's North Atlantic Council meeting. He told me that Number Ten is pretty well in meltdown at the prospect of declaring Article Five and having to deploy British soldiers to defend Latvia. The military may be up for it, but the Prime Minister seems determined to go to Parliament and there's no certainty that he'll get a majority. In fact, and on past form, even a small majority may not be enough to persuade him.'

'Sounds like I need a personal call with the Prime Minister . . . Remind me, Marty, how quickly can you get the 82nd Airborne into Latvia?' quizzed Dillon.

'If you give me the green light now, we'll get the Global Response Force into Riga in eighteen hours. And if the airport is still closed as a result of the cyber-attack, we'll drop them in. Straight out of Fort Bragg, non-stop across the Atlantic, like they did last year on Exercise Anakonda in Poland. It's the airborne way.'

'And if the Brits were able to join you?'

'No problem, but it would slow things down. We'd arrange a link-up on the ground in the UK with their lead airborne company. We've checked with the Brits and it's 3 Para. As I told you, they've trained alongside our lead battalion. That means they know each other well, have all the comms and other details squared away, and they've practised precisely this sort of operation. But to get all of that organised would mean it would take about thirty-six hours before they were all on the ground in Riga.'

'Marty, you've got that green light. Please get them all moving. Now, I've got some calls to make. The President, the PM and then the French. I'll do them from the Oval Office.'

Thirty minutes later, Bear was in the Oval Office. President Dillon was at her desk, made from the timbers of HMS *Resolute*, which Bear knew had been a gift to the US president from Queen Victoria in 1880, a memorial of 'the courtesy and loving kindness' shown to the UK by the American people. That desk, and the fact that she still sat at it when she and her many distinguished predecessors could have sat at almost any other desk, epitomised the Special Relationship that had long existed between the two countries. But now, sitting opposite MacWhite on one of the two olive-green sofas that faced each other on the cream carpet, Bear wondered just what Queen Victoria would think of this present British prime minister. Not much, was his opinion. By contrast, it was fortunate that Dillon was already showing the inner steel needed for the brutal nature of geopolitics; not unlike that long-dead Queen.

Then a Presidential aide entered, looking flustered. Rather than use the hotline – not the red telephone of popular mythology, but a data link known formally as the Washington–Moscow Direct Communications Link and located in the Pentagon, at the National Military Command Centre – Dillon had wanted to talk to the President direct, albeit through an interpreter. The initial contact had already been made to the Kremlin and the White House had been assured that the President was in his office and waiting.

'How are we getting on fixing that call?' questioned Dillon.

'I'm sorry, Madam President. We've spoken to the President's office in Moscow. We had it all set up, but he's decided he won't take your call after all. You won't believe this but, since they gave us the green light, the President has apparently just left the office. He's pre-booked to do a freefall jump with the Russian airborne forces parachute display team, at an air show early tomorrow morning. Apparently he regrets not being able to talk to you, but it's midnight in Moscow now and apparently he needs his sleep so that he can demonstrate his strength and courage to the Russian people tomorrow morning. He hopes you will understand.'

Dillon breathed out slowly. This was not a time to show that she was furious at being so obviously snubbed. MacWhite looked at Bear and both men looked away; this was also not the moment to comment on the humiliation of the President of the United States at the hands of the President of Russia. But Bear noted, staring hard at his notebook, of one thing there was now no doubt: the President had no interest in trying to resolve this crisis.

'Bear, why don't you go and check personally that the Brit prime minister can take the President's call?'

Bear went into the outer office and took the phone the President's aide handed to him. 'It's ringing in the Prime Minister's office at Chequers. You're secure.'

'Chequers . . . Where the hell's that?' demanded Bear, himself furious at what he had just witnessed in the Oval Office. To him checkers was a board game.

'The country residence of the Prime Minister of the United Kingdom,' came the response. 'The Prime Minister likes to start his weekends early as he enjoys his family time. He can be very chilled.'

Then the phone was picked up. Bear heard an English voice speaking, in what he later discovered was a south London accent.

'Hello. Trev Walker, the PM's Director of Communications.'

Bear was courteous. 'I'm sorry, Sir. I guess there's been a misunderstanding. I'm calling from the White House. I'd hoped to talk to the PM's aide to set up a call with President Dillon. This is not a media issue.'

'Don't worry, mate,' came the retort. 'I'm on the inside track with the PM. And anyway, he likes to keep the staff to a minimum while he's at Chequers. I'll handle it. What's the call about?'

'Russia, NATO, Latvia and the way ahead.' Bear was surprised to find himself talking to the Brit PM's media guy and not his Military Assistant, but guessed that was the way they did things over there. Nevertheless, Bear felt his irritation rising at the Brit's obviously false friendliness and doubtless feigned ignorance. After all, what else would the President of the United States of America be ringing the British Prime Minister about at this exact moment in time, other than the crisis in Latvia. But, as was his custom, he took people as he found them. He knew no other way.

'Hi, Trev. Bear here,' he replied, trying to keep his voice friendly. 'Can you get the Prime Minister on the line, please.'

'No, mate. You put the President on first, then I'll get the PM.' Walker was quick to try and take advantage of the American's courtesy.

There was a strict protocol for arranging such phone calls and Bear knew it full well: the junior waits for the senior. And there was no question who was the senior leader here. Which meant that Bear was having none of this. What was more, he hadn't grown up on the wrong side of the tracks in Atlanta without developing a sixth sense for a chancer. 'Thank you, Sir. But no. I'll wait for the Prime Minister.'

Walker obviously knew when he was not going to win, because there was a pause and next moment there was a different voice on the line. However, Bear noted that Walker clearly did not like coming second; his failure to tell him who he was going to speak to next was another clear breach of protocol and designed to wrong-foot him.

'Prime Minister here,' a slightly high-pitched, nasal voice speaking in what Bear recognised as the Queen's English came on the line.

'Hold on, Sir. I'll put you through to the President.' Bear waited for Dillon to pick up and greet the Prime Minister and then flicked to 'monitor call'.

'My dear Lynn.' It was the PM speaking. 'How wonderful to hear you. How are you?'

'Good thanks, William.' Dillon was big enough not to be rattled at being stood up by the sky-diving machismo of the President, but she still had to talk to the French and small talk had never been her strongest suite. Quickly she ran through her thinking and then announced her decision to deter the Russians from further aggression against Latvia with a rapid deployment by sea, land and air.

'But to be effective, William, the United States needs allies in this. I've worked on the Chancellor in Berlin and I'm reasonably confident we'll get Germany to sign up to Article Five, but it will take time. And we haven't got time. I don't anticipate a problem with the French, but I really need the UK to join us and quickly. When all's said and done, no other armed forces are as close to us as yours . . . And we trust you. Our two nations have been through a lot together and I'm told your airborne troops have been working closely with ours, practising just this sort of operation. Can I count you in?'

The Prime Minister hesitated and then blustered. 'Ah well, Lynn. Of course I understand where you're coming from and I *do* agree that the Russians are playing a seriously dodgy game. But as for sending troops to Latvia . . . I'm really not sure. We'd be awfully concerned at winding up the Russians even more and there's really not a lot we can do. After all, it's very much their backyard . . . Don't you think?'

'Prime Minister.' Dillon dropped the 'William' and her voice turned cold. 'Are you *seriously* telling me that the UK is not prepared to stand up and defend the freedom of a NATO ally, facing the most egregious aggression from a resurgent Russia, determined to defend Russian speakers, wherever they are, and by invasion if necessary?'

'Well, no. Of course not, Lynn.' The Prime Minister was squirming now. 'But you have to understand. My hands are tied. I really can do nothing with the military without first putting it to Parliament. Besides, we don't need to worry about Russia and any reductions in our conventional forces, because we're well covered with our Trident independent nuclear deterrent.'

'Prime Minister,' President Dillon's voice was withering, 'your complacency stuns me. You clearly do not understand the most basic principle of deterrence: that it needs to be matched at every level, whether conventional or nuclear, if it is to be effective. Let me make it crystal clear to you in words of one syllable. If we don't stop the Russians right now, this means war in Europe . . . and that will escalate into nuclear war, as surely as night follows day. Your generals *have* explained that much to you?'

The Prime Minister tried to be firmer. 'Now come on, Lynn. I'm sure it's not that bad, yet. Nobody has attacked anybody . . . and,' he sounded almost petulant, 'well, my people are telling me that there's no way we can commit British service personnel to a war in the Baltic states. As you know, we're in a bit of a transition period here and we don't have our usual forces equipped and ready to go. My generals assure me it's only a temporary blip and—'

He got no further as the President interrupted. 'Are you telling me that you want to go down in history as the first UK prime minister not prepared to stand by a NATO ally in its hour of need? What happened to a thousand years of history? To Britain's finest hour? As . . . as far as I am concerned, such a capitulation would be the end of any so-called special relationship.'

Bear imagined he could hear the Prime Minister gulp. 'I'll . . . I'll see what I can do, Lynn.'

The phone clicked and went silent.

1735 hours, Saturday, 20 May 2017
Lielvārde Air Base, Latvia

IT HAD TAKEN him only two hours and twenty minutes, flying at a cruising speed of 435 knots in his F-16C multi-role fighter aircraft to cover the 900 miles from Aviano Air Base, north of Venice, to Latvia, but Major Philip Bertinetti, US Air Force, was still looking forward to landing and stretching his legs. In line with his instructions from US Air Force air traffic control at Lielvārde, part of the advance party sent ahead to receive the American fighter aircraft, he descended with the second F-16 piloted by Mike Ryan, his new wingman, flying in formation to the rear and left of him. As he banked right he saw, 3,000 feet below him, the gentle curve of the Gulf of Riga, with its miles of yellow, pristine sandy beach fringed by green forest. Then he picked out the beach resort of Jurmala, with its attractive art nouveau wooden houses, the summer playground for the Russian aristocracy in the days of the Tsar and, in Soviet days, a favourite of the Communist Party leadership.

Reminding himself to return one day for a visit with his wife and family when this was all over, Bertinetti started going through his pre-landing checks until there, in front of him, was the runway at Lielvārde. He lowered the landing gear, opened his airbrake and reduced airspeed. Checking his glideslope was within the 2.5–3 degree bracket, he ensured the FPM, the flight path marker, on his heads-up display was over the threshold of the runway and pulled his throttle rearwards. Soon he was closing with the runway and dropping. Within seconds of landing he flared the aircraft gently, decreasing power to idle as he pulled back on the stick.

Touchdown! The F-16 ran true and straight along the runway. But as his instructor always used to tell him, you're only as good as your last landing – and that one was pretty good. Especially, some would say, in the circumstances. However, for Bertinetti, the past was the past and he had to be perfect right now, because anything less than perfect and he suspected that he would be on the next flight home, but in a passenger seat and no longer the driving seat; the only place he was ever happy in any airplane.

It had been quite a week. Shot down only seven days ago over eastern Ukraine, while providing top cover for US Army trainers working with the Ukrainian Army, he had been swiftly picked up by a Combat Search and Rescue helicopter and repatriated to his home base at Aviano for medical checks and debriefing. He'd been judged in perfect health by the Medical Group and lost no time in persuading the Brigadier General commanding 31st Fighter Wing that he needed to return to duty, to ensure that his recent combat experience against the latest Russian fighters could be passed on to other pilots. Normally, he would have been grounded and kept under observation, but times were definitely not normal and the general had finally relented. Bertinetti had managed a few days at home with his long-suffering wife Diane and their two daughters, before the call came to deploy eight F-16s to Latvia.

The two F-16s were guided onto the pan by ground crew wearing US uniforms; a C-17 and two C-130 transport aircraft from 435th Contingency Response Group had flown to Lielvārde the day before, to prepare the way for them. His canopy opened,

Bertinetti removed his oxygen mask, unstrapped himself and stepped out of the cockpit. Then he stretched, took off his helmet and sucked in a lungful of fresh air, before climbing down from the aircraft on the ladder put in place by the ground crew. They hooked the aircraft up to a tractor, which would pull it into a hardened shelter. In minutes, the maintenance crews would be all over it.

'Welcome to Lielvārde, Major! I am Colonel Teteris, the base commander.' As he stepped onto the rain-streaked pan, Bertinetti was greeted by a stocky Latvian officer, who was evidently waiting for him.

'It's a pleasure to be here, Sir. Phil Bertinetti.' The dark-haired Coloradan first saluted smartly and then shook the proffered hand.

'Everything is ready for the arrival of the remaining F-16s. Your Contingency Response Group landed yesterday and has set up the necessary support. We Latvians will continue to secure the outer perimeter and provide other host-nation support, although we have had some difficulties, which I will brief you about shortly. Meanwhile, 435th CRG is now set up to provide airfield operations, command and control of air operating out of here, weather support, close protection and defence of your aircraft and personnel, maintenance and everything you need.'

'Sounds like them,' said Bertinetti. 'They don't waste any time getting things organised.' It was good to know that the well-oiled machine that was the US Air Force was in place. That would send an important message of reassurance to the Latvians, but after his experiences in Ukraine, he doubted it would deter the Russians, as many were hoping it might.

Teteris looked preoccupied. 'Major, I have to tell you that things are very bad here. Latvia suffered a catastrophic cyber-attack two days ago. We have some communications, but much of our national infrastructure has been badly affected. We are doing all we can to fix things, but we can offer you only limited support.'

Shortly afterwards, after a much-needed cup of strong, black coffee, Bertinetti had linked up with his kit – flown in by C-130 the day before – and found the room and bunk he'd been allocated in the transit accommodation. He and Teteris then met up with the CRG commander, discovered that the remaining four F-16s were expected that night, and talked through the way they were going to operate, while Mike Ryan, his wingman, checked reception arrangements for the remainder of the squadron.

Bertinetti was conscious that he was going to have to step carefully. Both Teteris and the CRG commander were colonels and he was a major. Although they were merely there to provide support for him and his men – the ones who would be doing the flying, the fighting and, quite possibly, the dying – he still had to follow their commands. He was going to have to find a way of telling them what needed to be done, even though he was their junior.

'Sir, I suggest we establish contact with the Latvian National Armed Forces Joint Headquarters. They probably need to know what we can bring to the party and I'm sure they'll want to know when we reckon we can declare full operating capability.'

'Good idea, Phil,' replied the CRG Commander. 'Why don't you take a car and head into Riga? I want to stay here and make sure everything is set up for the incoming aircraft.'

'I'll take you,' said Teteris. 'They would very much like to see you at Joint HQ. I'll get a message through to say you are coming. We've now got enough communications for that.'

Two hours later, with Bertinetti still in his aviator's flying suit but, given that he was now in an operational theatre, carrying his grab-bag and issue 9 millimetre Beretta pistol, the car entered the compound of the Joint HQ in Riga.

Teteris led him into the building and, much to Bertinetti's surprise, immediately took him to the Chief of Defence's office, where he was personally welcomed by Lieutenant General Raimonds Balderis, a measure of the importance the Latvians placed on the deployment of the American F-16s. Bertinetti briefed him on the ETA, the estimated time of arrival, of the remaining F-16s.

'That's very good news, Major,' said Balderis. 'Now you need to tie down the details of command and control and how you are going to operate alongside the NATO Baltic Air Police mission. It is not straightforward, as they are not operating from Latvia. Correct, Colonel Teteris?'

'Correct, Sir,' responded Teteris. 'The mission is currently operating out of Siauliai Air Base in Lithuania. We need to talk to the Operations Centre to work out the details.' He then turned to Bertinetti. 'Come, I will take you.' They saluted and left Balderis's office.

As Bertinetti entered the Operations Centre, he couldn't help but notice a tall, dark-haired young man, wearing what looked like British combat uniform, sitting apart from the Latvian officers and talking to a slim, blonde-haired girl.

The young man saw Bertinetti's flying suit with its US flag on the shoulder and stood up.

'I'm Tom Morland, UK Liaison Officer to the Latvians. You must be here with the first F-16s?'

'Sure thing, Tom. Good to meet you.' Bertinetti extended his hand and introduced himself. He glanced enquiringly at the blonde girl.

Krauja looked him in the eye. 'Marina Krauja. I'm with the Latvian Interior Ministry.'

Teteris led them all into the Operations Centre, on the wall of which was a digital map showing Latvia and its borders. On the Latvian side of the Russian border, blue icons indicated Latvian army positions. Further east, inside Russia, Bertinetti could see the concentration of red icons around Pskov, with more to the south around Opochka and Ostrov.

'All part of the snap exercise the Russians have been conducting,' commented Teteris.

In front of the map, staff officers and watch keepers sat at rows of desks in front of computer terminals. Headsets on and speaking quietly into remote microphones, they issued orders, digested and passed on situation reports. As subordinate units reported locations, icons were automatically updated on the digital map.

'I see you've got over the cyber problems,' said Bertinetti.

'We have been expecting such problems – they are as much a part of modern warfare as close air support or an artillery fire plan before an attack. We've learned from the experience of our Estonian friends. They established a cyber home guard, manned by civilian computer experts. Most of them are hackers and teenagers. Our people were able to get most of our key systems back up and running. They're still working on the problems. But at least Joint HQ can still operate from here.'

'Come,' he said to Bertinetti, 'I'll show you the air operations centre where we coordinate with the Baltic air policing mission.'

He took Bertinetti and Morland into a side room, where they sat down with the Air Planners and he worked through the coordination with the NATO mission while the Brit officer watched and listened. Once completed, Teteris led them into the main Air Operations Coordination Centre, along the wall of which was a radar screen showing the recognised air picture; flashing radar icons indicating the listing of all aircraft in flight within Latvian airspace and that of her neighbours. As in the main Operations Centre next door, watch keepers sat at desks with their computers, headsets and microphones – plotting, observing, controlling, recording and reporting.

Teteris explained how each aircraft was identified as friendly or potentially hostile, with the information drawn from a number of different sources, including the integrated Latvian military radar system, civilian air traffic control and NATO's central Air Operations Centre at Kalkar in Germany, which integrated all airspace control in the north and east of Europe.

Bertinetti nodded. This was second nature to him, but it was good to see the Latvians were so well-organised. 'That all figures. I see you've got our F-16s linked into this already.'

'We watched you all the way from Aviano,' said Teteris with a smile. 'And we're watching your other F-16s on their way, too.' Then the smile disappeared. 'As are, no doubt, the Russians . . . Also, this is where we pick up *their* incursions into our airspace. Every day now, without fail.'

He pointed to the concentration of winking radar returns around Pskov, 175 miles east of Riga and inside Russia. 'That's where they usually take off from. Ten or so Il-76 Candids, their medium-range military transport aircraft. They fly west to our border, then track north along it, before circling round to repeat the manoeuvre. They often take off about now, so they'll be up to our border after dark. They do it to intimidate us.'

'And they may be setting a pattern. Get you used to seeing them there at a specific time,' Morland suggested.

Bertinetti looked at the Brit again; tough looking for certain, and clearly intelligent as well.

Then Teteris stared at the radar returns. Hard.

Bertinetti heard him say something in Latvian to the watch keeper nearest him, who replied, then spoke quickly into his microphone.

Teteris turned to Bertinetti and Morland and pointed. 'That concentration around Pskov. It's significantly larger than usual. We need to watch that. The watch keeper is sending out a warning to the Baltic Air Policing detachment. I think we'd better get back to Lielvārde, Major, right away.'

Bertinetti nodded agreement. 'Let's roll.'

'And I'm heading back to link up with my guys at the

embassy. Good luck and I hope we meet again,' he said to Bertinetti, who watched as he turned and walked out of the Operations Centre with the striking blonde girl. He anticipated that the other F-16s would be landing soon. Given the new sense of palpable concern in the Operations Centre, his gut instinct told him that they couldn't come fast enough.

At that moment the radar picture in the Air Operations Coordination Centre, the digital map image in the Operations Centre and all the computers flickered, faded and then went black. The watch keeper spoke into his microphone. But there was nothing. He tried his telephone. Again nothing. The hackers had struck again.

The lights flickered and went out. In the dark they heard a generator kick in somewhere and a faint wall light slowly pierced the darkness. 'Let's go,' exclaimed Bertinetti. 'NOW!'

0100 hours, Sunday, 21 May 2017
Lielvārde Air Base, Latvia

IT HAD BEEN a tortuous drive from Riga thanks to the chaos caused by the latest cyber-attack. Bertinetti had left the Latvian Armed Forces Joint Command HQ with Teteris, the Lielvārde Air Base commander, in a desperate hurry to get back to the airfield. The radar picture they'd seen in the Air Operations Command Ops Room, before it had gone blank, was ominous. It had shown a major concentration of radar icons around Pskov, the Russian aviation base 175 kilometres east of Riga, and Bertinetti wanted to reassure himself that the remainder of his F-16s – which were expected any minute now – were refuelled, armed and ready to go in the event of a surprise Russian attack. As they finally drove through the main gate of the air base at one o'clock in the morning, the loud wailing of sirens shattered the quiet of the night.

'That's the attack signal! I've got to get to my command post!' Teteris was already accelerating past the gate guard who, recognising him, waved him through, a look of near panic on his face as he clearly wondered what on earth was happening. Screeching to a halt and not bothering to shut the car door, Teteris ran into the Station HQ.

Bertinetti followed him, mind racing. If the base was under imminent Russian attack, he had to get himself and his jets airborne and out of Latvia. Much as it galled him to cut and run, he'd had it drummed into him on being tasked to this assignment that his mission was to deter an attack, and if Russian and American pilots went head-to-head in combat, then a potential world war might follow.

One look in the Ops Room was enough for Bertinetti. The picture, remoted in from the Contingency Response Group's field radar outside and unaffected by the cyber-attack, showed a series of red dots winking fifty kilometres to the east of the runway perimeter; given their slow speed and numbers, they were most likely Russian helicopters en masse. Ominously, and closing in on the air base, were several rapidly moving dots. They could only be high-speed aircraft, probably ground-attack jets, whose task would be to destroy the air defences before the airborne assault.

A figure in US Air Force combat uniform wearing the silver eagle of a colonel appeared at his elbow. It was the commander of the 435th Contingency Response Group and he spoke urgently. 'In case you're wondering where your buddies are, Bertinetti, your F-16s were turned back when we picked up the attack warning.'

Bertinetti turned to him, aghast.

'Orders direct from US Air Force Europe, Ramstein. The President doesn't want to start World War Three. We were sent here to stop the bastards coming over the border . . and it's too late for that now.'

Bertinetti protested. 'But, Sir. Latvia's coming under attack, so we're all being attacked. I thought that was what NATO was all about. What kind of signal does it send to the world if Americans are seen to be running away, when we should be protecting an ally?'

'Steady, Bertinetti,' responded the colonel as calmly as he could. 'Don't say anything you'll regret. I've had my orders and the others have been turned around. And that's that. You're to get airborne as quickly as you can . . . And *that's* an order. I ordered your wingman to head back without you. He refused and I respected that decision, as I know you fly in pairs and you would be very much more vulnerable on your own, so I let him stay. But Ramstein want you back in Aviano ASAP . . . In one piece. Understood?'

Bertinetti heard the roar of a fast jet starting up, but said nothing.

'That's Mike Ryan getting ready to leave,' said the colonel, changing the subject. 'There's a vehicle waiting to take you to the hardened shelter and your aircraft is already prepped. That radar picture gives you all the briefing you need . . . Now go!'

'And what about you, Sir?' Bertinetti asked.

'We'll take our chances.'

Bertinetti saluted. Next, he stepped forward to where Teteris was standing in front of the digital map issuing orders in Latvian. He quietly thanked him and wished him luck. Teteris gave him a grim smile and a nod of thanks and turned back to the job at hand.

Five minutes later, he was beside his F-16 being greeted by the Crew Chief. 'All ready to go, Sir. I've connected ground power. The Data Transfer Cartridge weapons info is all set and ready to go. Panels, weapon racks, pneumatic pressures and oil are also checked and good to go. Let's get you into your G-suit.'

Quickly Bertinetti struggled into his G-suit, climbed the ladder and lowered himself into the familiar cockpit. The Crew Chief expertly strapped him into his seat, hooked up the G-suit hose and parachute harness, then climbed down and removed the ladder.

Alone in the cockpit, his heart thumping as adrenalin coursed through his body, Bertinetti forced himself to calm down and run through the standard pre-start routine, as if this were just another training flight. He positioned his switches rapidly and glanced around the cockpit. Satisfied that all was in order, he put on his helmet, then hooked up the oxygen hose and attached it to his harness, before plugging it into his Combat Edge vest. As the flow of oxygen kicked in, he relaxed and breathed deeply. Above him he heard the hum of the canopy closing and locking.

Ready, he radioed the tower for start clearance. Then he heard the Crew Chief's voice: 'Clear aft and front. Chocks in. Fire-guard posted. Go for start when you are ready.'

'JFS – Jet Fuel Starter – ON,' he replied and heard the whine of the jet fuel starter engine. He looked down and noted the dial of the Revs per Minute gauge, near his right kneecap, beginning to gently wind up. Above and beside him the strobe and navigation lights began to flash.

'Twenty per cent – check'. Bertinetti lifted the throttle up and clunked it forwards through the gate to allow the high-pressure fuel to start flowing to the main engine. The plane came to life; once again a living, flame-snorting creature.

'Forty per cent. Shut down JFS.'

The whine turned to a scream. 'Seventy per cent – main engine start complete. Avionics on, inertial navigation system aligned, aircraft systems check. Ready for departure.'

The aircraft began to move and Bertinetti pulled out towards the runway. A moment later there was a voice from the control tower in his headset: 'Apollo, hold position. Bandits incoming!'

Bertinetti thought fast; it was too late to stop now and, anyway, he would be a stationary target out here on the tarmac. 'Cobra Two, I'm rolling now. I'll take my chances.' No time for a normal take-off. Just get into the air as quickly as possible.

Not a moment too soon either, as ahead of him, alongside the perimeter fence, he saw flashes of gunfire as four Bofors, 40-millimetre cannons of the Latvian Air Force air defence, desperately tried to engage a pair of Su-25SM Frogfoot fighter-bombers as they hurtled past, loosing their rocket pods as they did so. Explosions seared into the night sky as multiple rockets found their targets and the base's heavy air defences fell silent.

'Focus on take-off. Nothing else matters. You can deal with them when you're airborne.' Bertinetti was back at Nellis Air Force Base in the southern Nevada desert and he heard the voice of his instructor on the Red Flag exercises.

His brain remained on auto as he released the throttle, while the F-16 bucked forward like a bronco in a Western rodeo. Ahead of him the other F-16 was taking off, piloted by his wingman Captain Mike Ryan, the flames from its engines flaring in a series of concentric rings, repeated deep red then lighter in the darkness, from shockwaves caused by supersonic efflux from the jet pipe coming into immediate contact with the subsonic air just behind the aircraft. As his own aircraft gathered speed, he was conscious of the runway bumping beneath him and the forest flashing by. Then he saw a necklace of tracer as 30-millimetre cannon rounds from an Su-25, passing low over the runway, blasted past his canopy at high velocity, before immediately overshooting him.

Not a chance, brother. You were just a bit too keen, Bertinetti thought to himself, elated at his lucky escape.

In less than twenty seconds he had reached take-off speed of 180 knots and, as he applied gentle aft pressure to the stick, the bumping from the runway ceased. He was airborne.

'Keep the stick back' – his flight instructor's voice from Nellis was once again in his ear. He sensed the power of the after-burner beneath him as the nose of the F-16 reached near vertical and surged higher, ever higher. He felt the G-forces dragging him back and the G-suit compress around his limbs, to restrict the flow of blood to his lower body and ensure his brain continued to function. In another twenty seconds his altimeter registered 15,000 feet and the tracer was left far below him. He was now high above the clouds. Away to the east the first glimmers of dawn were reaching over the far horizon, while to the west, and towards home, it was still pitch black. He banked towards the light.

For a moment he was alone, all was peaceful and he felt the familiar, but always exhilarating, sensation of being airborne. Now he could think: first, and foremost, where the hell are those bandits? Until he was at full power and height they had the advantage.

Next link up with Mike. What could they do to help protect the air base from attack? Any restrictions placed on him by his rules of engagement were now irrelevant as he had been fired upon by a Russian plane.

Decision made. He'd first do what he could to protect the Latvians and Americans in the base from attack and then he'd head home, as ordered. Besides, he had a score to settle with the Russians.

'Apollo, this is Ghost One. Are you airborne?' A voice crackled urgently in Bertinetti's headphones. It was Mike Ryan.

'Affirmative, Ghost One. Airborne and spoiling for the fight. We gotta go after those Su-25 Frogfoots. Those are our guys on the ground down there and they're getting hammered.'

'Roger, Apollo. Glad to hear you're with me. It's been kinda lonely waiting for you.' Ryan's relief was palpable.

And then Bertinetti heard another, more urgent, American voice in his headset.

'Apollo, Apollo, this is Lielvārde. We're under attack.' It was ground control. 'Two Bandits. One eight zero, closing on the airfield at fifteen thousand feet.'

'Copy that, ground. I've got them on radar. Ghost One. We're attacking . . . Ghost One. Keep me covered. Datalinking the targets now.'

Bertinetti banked in the direction of the red icons in the multifunction displays in the cockpit, one beside each knee, which were the Russian aircraft out there in the darkness, and opened up the throttle. He felt the surge of power as the engine kicked in. This time there would be no ambush. He was the ambusher.

On his multifunction display he picked up the tell-tale icons of another two Su-25 Frogfoot fighter-bombers lining up to bomb the air base.

'Apollo, Fox Three,' said Bertinetti, indicating that he was engaging the closest with an AIM-120 Advanced Medium-Range Air-to-Air Missile, known to all as the AMRAAM.

In the cockpit he felt a momentary shudder, as the two under-slung missiles were launched.

The missiles seemed to pause, then their rocket motors flared and they suddenly surged forward, their flaming burners disappearing into bright red dots as they accelerated towards their target.

Then it was time to concentrate on the second Su-25. As his head-up display indicated that the weapon system had locked onto the second aircraft, he stabbed the weapon release with his right thumb.

In his head-up display he saw both targets manoeuvre violently to evade the missiles, banking into a steep dive, left and right. There was a flash as the first missile exploded harmlessly. Then, from his cockpit, Bertinetti saw the yellow-and-red flash of a second, much bigger explosion, as one of the aircraft erupted into a fireball that continued billowing forwards for a second or so, before starting to float towards the earth.

Another explosion and another fireball told Bertinetti the second aircraft had also been hit. The sequence had been too quick for either pilot to have had a chance to pull the ejection handle and escape; exactly as had happened to his wingman and friend, Leroy, back in Ukraine. 'Those were for you, Leroy,' Bertinetti muttered to himself.

'Ground, splash two,' said Bertinetti into his microphone. 'Time for us to head for Aviano. But we'll be back.'

There was no response from Lielvārde Air Base.

2330 hours, Sunday, 21 May 2017
Camp David, Catoctin Mountains, Maryland

THE VIP BLACKHAWK helicopter of the US Army's 12th Aviation Battalion, the unit responsible for transporting the Washington power elite, circled over the forest in the dark, turned into the wind and then hovered before settling on the 'H' of the landing site set high in the Catoctin Mountains of north Maryland, at Camp David, the presidential retreat.

As the rotors slowed and the engine closed down, General Abe MacWhite, sitting in the comfortable airline seat in the passenger compartment, spoke into the fixed microphone that went with the headsets he wore. 'Thanks, Chief. Great flight . . . and sorry to disturb your weekend.'

'No problem, Sir,' came the response from the pilot. 'That's what we're here for. We'll be ready to take you back to DC when you're done.'

Typical of the boss, thought Colonel Bear Smythson. *He never forgets to thank the troops for what they do for him.* That pilot would never have guessed the gravity of the news he was carrying to the President.

Even during the Cuban Missile Crisis of 1962, when the world had stood on the verge of nuclear Armageddon, the Soviets had pulled back at the eleventh hour. Today, however, the Russians had thrown caution and common sense to the winds and attacked three NATO countries without warning. It was going to take cool heads to ensure that nuclear missiles did not start flying and mutually assured destruction became a reality.

Bear had no doubt that MacWhite was the right man in the right place. Perhaps the only man who could extract America and the world from this horror. But what if the President disagreed? On such small matters as how the pair of them presented and explained the crisis to the President would such decisions be made. Unless she had absolute trust in MacWhite and his team, the President would not feel comfortable working with him. It would be difficult to overstate how much was going to depend on this meeting.

The side door slid open and MacWhite unbuckled his straps, then leaped out with the agility of a twenty-five-year-old, acknowledging as he did so the smart salute from the loadmaster.

Bear followed him into the waiting people carrier, driven by an immaculately turned out female US Marine Corps Lance Corporal, who took them up the front drive of Aspen Lodge. There, in the moonlight, sitting on top of a hill in a three-acre forest clearing, Bear saw the rambling single-storey wooden cabin used by US presidents since Franklin D. Roosevelt had converted a camp built for federal civil servants and their families into a presidential retreat and refuge from the rigours of Washington.

The two men were shown into the living room where President Dillon sat chatting with Pete Chiarini, her Senior Executive Assistant, who invariably travelled with her to ensure the umbilical cord back to the White House remained unbroken. Both men knew Chiarini well and shook hands as he came forward to greet them.

It was Bear's first visit to this room, the President's inner sanctum, and he took in the atmosphere of relaxed, informal warmth and comfort: wooden walls decorated with paintings by classic American landscape artists, beamed rafters under the low roof, a glowing log fire in the grate to ward off the chill of a spring night in the mountains, deep-cushioned sofas and low table lights around a rustic, wooden coffee table. Large, picture windows, which in daytime would doubtless provide panoramic mountain views, were hidden by well-chosen check curtains.

Dillon, in jeans, a plaid lumberjack shirt and deck shoes, greeted them. 'Welcome, gentlemen. I'm very glad to see you,' she said in her warm, vibrant voice, which Bear was beginning to recognise as a key element of the charisma she radiated.

'Madam President,' began MacWhite. 'Good evening . . . or should I say good morning. It's good of you to see us. I'm sorry we've had to disturb you at this time of night, but there've been some important developments I need to brief you on in person.'

'Of course, Abe. I appreciate that,' Dillon replied. 'Now, you gentlemen have come a long way and it's late. Please sit down. What can we get you to eat and drink?' She gestured at the sofa opposite where she'd been sitting.

MacWhite, the tall, rangy ex-Special Forces soldier, whose eccentric passion for sea buckthorn and ginger tea was well known, declined food and asked for his usual herbal tea. With some regret – it was going to be a long night and he could have murdered a Danish, but he did not want to be the only one with a mouth full of food while the others were talking strategy – Bear contented himself with strong black coffee.

'I understand you've been talking to SACEUR?' With the immediate needs of the men in her team satisfied, she was now all business.

'Yes, ma'am,' said MacWhite. 'We've also got some satellite photos to show you.' He nodded at Bear, who unpacked his laptop, placed it on the table where Dillon could see it and switched it on. MacWhite then leaned forward to brief her on his recent Tandberg VTC conversation with Admiral Howard. The latter's report had been devastating in its implications.

'Madam President, Admiral Howard was talking in his capacity as COM EUCOM . . . forgive me, ma'am.' MacWhite apologised for his free use of acronyms. 'That's Commander European Command. SACEUR is double-hatted as a national, as well as a NATO commander. He reports that USAFE, that's US Air Force Europe, have managed to get a pair of F-16s out of Riga. They were the advance flight of the eight due to land last night, following your approval of the mission on Thursday. They took off from Lielvārde Air Base in Latvia as it was being attacked by Russian aircraft, as a prelude to what we must assume will be an airborne assault to seize the airfield.'

'What happened to the other F-16s we ordered to Latvia?' Dillon looked anxious, obviously expecting bad news.

'We turned them around in mid-air when we picked up the first intel reports of an imminent Russian attack. There was no point in risking them when any deterrent effect had already been lost.'

Dillon nodded.

'The F-16 flight commander, Major Bertinetti, was ordered to return to his base at Aviano to prevent the Russians capturing any US fast jets, but shortly after take-off he destroyed two Russian aircraft, probably Su-25 Frogfoots. He was attacked as he was on the runway. So it was self-defence. But the really bad news is that we had around three hundred men from the Four-Thirty-Fifth Contingency Response Group on the ground at Lielvārde. We've lost contact with them and we have had to assume they're either dead or prisoners.'

Dillon looked puzzled and MacWhite explained. 'We had to send them there to set up the operating base before the F-16s could land.'

'But the F-16s are no longer there,' Dillon exclaimed in annoyance.

No-one had thought to explain the logistical complexities of the operation to her and Bear guessed from her frown that she must have assumed the fighter planes could just fly in and bug out, as and when required.

'Exactly . . .'

Bear could see that MacWhite had decided to bludgeon through this issue as they had discussed in the helicopter. The President was the Commander-in-Chief and it was MacWhite's duty to brief and advise her, but she also had to take some responsibility for learning the basics of the way things worked on the ground. This crisis was already developing a dynamic of its own; a dynamic that was speeding up, and MacWhite did not have the time to explain every detail of what was planned and the consequences. That way nothing would get done.

'We weren't able to pull them out in time. They will inevitably have been involved in defending the air base alongside the Latvians. So it is highly probable that American military personnel have either been, or are currently, in ground combat with the Russians. There's no way they would have been able to put up more than a token resistance, as they were only carrying their personal weapons. I guess we can expect to see the survivors paraded on Russian TV pretty soon.'

MacWhite paused to let the words sink in.

'So, on top of the US aircraft shot down over eastern Ukraine, we've now had US aircraft in combat and shooting down Russians, and US military personnel are on the ground in Latvia and probably also in combat with Russians.' Dillon had recovered her poise. 'Sounds to me like we're in it . . . like it or not.'

'Dead right, ma'am. But don't forget one thing . . . in each case the Russians fired on us first. But it's not only Latvia, ma'am,' continued MacWhite, as Bear brought up a different file of satellite pictures on his laptop. 'The Russians have also attacked the international airports at Tallin in Estonia and Vilnius in Lithuania. As you will see, the intelligence picture we are building suggests that we may well be witnessing a full-scale invasion of the Baltic states. Put bluntly, it makes no strategic sense for Russia to bite off chunks of these small countries. The President has always made it plain that he wants the Baltics back and I fear that is what we're seeing here.'

MacWhite, who could also see the screen, paused to let Dillon study the pictures on Bear's laptop. As he scrolled through the grainy, indistinct images of Russian troops and aircraft, Dillon looked at the screen intently, saying nothing.

'Next photo please, Bear.'

Bear clicked the mouse.

'We're pretty sure that this is an amphibious task force en route out of St Petersburg. Most likely destination? The west coast of Estonia or the Gulf of Riga to reinforce the land invasion. The Russians will be keeping their options open, depending on where they enjoy most success or where they meet resistance. So far, and be under no illusions,' concluded MacWhite in his characteristic drawl, 'it's slam dunk to the President.'

Even though he had already been through the photographs and discussed what they meant with MacWhite on the helicopter to Camp David, Bear still found it hard to believe the reality of what the President was now looking at on the screen. It was as if he was back at Leavenworth, at the School of Advanced Military Studies, playing a part in 'The Strategic War Game', the concluding exercise of the course.

But this was for real, and yet these remote pictures, detached and distant, conveyed no hint of the drama unfolding on the ground and at sea. The contrast between the mountain calm and peace of Camp David and the grim events MacWhite was describing was almost inconceivable. Then again, Bear tried to console himself, these old walls had seen it all and heard it all before, from Pearl Harbor and the grimmest days of the Second World War, through the Cuban Missile Crisis and into his own times; dark days and desperate deeds planned in the rustic comfort of this very room.

As President Dillon looked up from the screen, Bear could see the shock and concern in her eyes. Nothing she had experienced up to this moment could have prepared her for news such as this. However, she had not become President of the United States of America without being able to hide her emotions when necessary. And it was necessary now.

MacWhite continued talking, Bear sensed, in order to give her time to better control her inner turmoil, as she came to terms with the full implications of what she had just heard and seen.

'The next question, Madam President, is whether the NATO nations will now be prepared to activate collective defence under Article Five. If they fail to do so we will be on our own and our people might well conclude that, if Europe does not have the will to help us in this undertaking, it is not for our people to die helping them. If we step back, Russia will dominate Europe, and strategically the world will have become a very much more dangerous place.'

Dillon paused for a moment and then answered, her voice full of resolve. 'This is not the first time in history that the freedom of Europe depends on the resolution of the US president . . . You can depend on me. But NATO *must* step up to the mark, too. What is Admiral Howard's view?'

In that moment, Bear felt once again the leadership that the West was going to need so desperately.

'He'd just seen Kostilek, the Secretary General, before he talked to me,' MacWhite answered. 'Kostilek is one of the good guys, but he's pretty gloomy. He'll try his damnedest, but he doubts whether he can get full NAC consensus about Article Five.'

The President raised an eyebrow, but MacWhite anticipated her next question. 'An Article Five event cannot be declared without full consensus from the North Atlantic Council, the decision-making body of NATO. And we know there's more than one nation that will not sign up to confronting Russia.'

The President nodded her understanding. 'Continue.'

'The NAC is due to meet in a couple of hours. That's eight a.m. Brussels time. Admiral Howard tells me the general view is one of defeatism, but pragmatism: if the Russians have taken the Baltics, there's nothing anyone can do but accept it. But if that happens, NATO is dead in the water. NATO exists to defend its fellow members and a failure to do so negates its very purpose. It becomes a talking shop and no longer a military alliance. And there's no shortage of talking shops in Europe.'

The President gave a small smile at MacWhite's well-aimed jibe.

He continued, 'It's easy to be wise after the event but if NATO had stationed permanent, well-equipped forces in the Baltic states, it's highly unlikely that the Russians would have chanced it as they have.'

'Too right . . . but too late now,' responded Dillon. 'What about the Brits and French?'

'The Brits are beginning to make the right noises, especially now their Special Forces are secretly working up a joint plan with us to infiltrate into the Baltics to support the insurgents. But we still need them to go public that they are with us militarily. As for the French, the military are as gung-ho as ever, but the politicians are still making contradictory noises. That, ma'am, is one I will have to leave to you.'

Bear could almost see Dillon's mind working as she sat and digested the news. Twice in the previous century America had stepped in to help save her allies in Europe. Bear knew his history; throughout his childhood America had under-written European peace and freedom and helped prevent the Cold War turning hot. Now, nearly thirty years after the end of the Cold War, Americans were again fighting and dying in Europe. Meanwhile, some Europeans, even though they were facing an existential threat to their survival as Western democracies, were not only trying to avoid picking up their share of the burden, but were actively preventing others from doing so.

'Hell,' she said, 'we'll just have to persuade them, won't we?'

Bear could see from the glint in Dillon's eyes and the jut of her jaw that she was a fighter . . . and a leader.

'It's one hundred years since America first defended European freedom and I don't intend to duck the issue on my watch. So let's start working those phones. Starting with the Prime Minister. This time he's going to get a pat on the back for looking after the Global Response Force. I was told before you arrived that they'd already landed in Britain.'

'How did you know, ma'am?' MacWhite asked in surprise.

'CNN, General. I know, it's an upside-down world we live in when the internet and TV news has information and live footage before even you get a chance to brief me. By the way, getting the Global Response Force moving was a good call. Thank you for that.' She looked at MacWhite with a smile.

'I'm going to thank the Prime Minister for the fact that, once again, Britain is standing shoulder to shoulder with us. And I'm expecting him to get stuck into the fight. If I read him right, he won't be able to resist that.'

The Chief of Staff spoke. 'Madam President, may I suggest we set up your calls from the bunker?'

0330 hours, Sunday, 21 May 2107
British Embassy, 5, J.Alunana Street, Riga, Latvia

SUNRISE COMES EARLY in Latvia in May, but with a sky thick with cloud, it was still dark at 3.30 a.m. when Marina Krauja woke Morland.

'Wake up, Tom . . . It's happening. Russian airborne landings at the airport and east of the city.'

Morland was instantly awake. It had been all too short a night. By the time he had got back from the Latvian National Armed Forces Joint HQ to their base in the British Embassy it had been around midnight. He had briefed his team about the cyber-attack on communications he'd witnessed at the Joint HQ and, assuming the worst, had told them to be prepared for a quick move out. They needed to ensure their bergen rucksacks, radios and personal weapons – the standard British infantryman's SA80 A2 LA85 assault rifles – were ready and their belt order webbing held at least four magazines of 5.56 millimetre rounds and enough food for the next 24 hours. He'd then grabbed some sleep, now interrupted.

'We may have to leave Riga in a hurry, Tom,' Krauja said. 'We'll need to be able to move fast and be self-sufficient.'

'Shouldn't you be looking after yourself, Marina?' Tom had been determined not to drag Krauja into peril on his account.

'No, Tom. I will do what I was ordered to do. My boss told

me to stay with you and your team. It's important. You and your radios may be the only way we can get the full story to the outside world.' Dressed in trekking trousers, hiking boots and a T-shirt with a fleece top, she had placed her rucksack on the floor beside Morland's bergen.

Her blonde hair was tied back, her face flushed from the fresh night air, and Morland noticed a new light in her blue eyes. Keeping her voice calm, she brought him up to date on the night's events so far. 'I've just called in at the Constitution Protection Bureau office. They're getting reports that Russian airborne troops have been landing by parachute onto the international airport and there's a second landing somewhere to the east of the city, as we can hear gunfire from that direction. The Latvian battalion and the National Guard protecting the airport are fighting back, but Russian troop-carrying helicopters are now landing more men and vehicles. It looks as if it will only be a matter of time before we are overwhelmed.'

Morland thought fast. *Better get the news to PJHQ to alert them. And then get 'eyes on' to confirm what was happening.*

Krauja read his mind. 'We need to get this news out quickly, Tom.'

Once again, Corporal Steve Bradley set up the Inmarsat VTC. From his steady and practised movements, Morland would not have known this was not another drill, instead of preparing to report the start of a war.

Major Jerry Dingley, from the Baltic desk at PJHQ in Northwood, came into the picture and was quickly joined by Lieutenant Colonel Nicholas Graham, the bespectacled Baltic team leader.

Without any preamble or formality, Morland briefed him on what he knew.

In return, Graham told him that PJHQ were getting reports that the Russian Baltic fleet had left St Petersburg and signal traffic indicated submarine activity off Riga, Tallin, Helsinki and Stockholm. 'We need to know what is happening in Riga, Tom,' the colonel continued. 'Chief of Joint Operations is briefing Chief of the Defence Staff before he heads into COBRA, the Cabinet Office Briefing Rooms, in a couple of hours. Things are likely to move pretty quickly now. Your mission is for you and your team to report back what is happening. You guys are our only eyes on the ground. We need to get confirmation – photos, that sort of thing – that the Russians have landed. Once you have hard proof that it is Russian regular forces, you are to send it here ASAP and then get out. Without getting involved. Do you understand me?'

Morland nodded, but did not speak. He felt diminished, agreeing these instructions in front of Marina. Here she was, willing to put her life on the line to help them. And here he was, obeying orders to get some incriminating photos prior to escaping.

'No heroics,' stated Graham. 'The government doesn't want dead or captured British soldiers in Latvia. That would tie their hands politically. . .'

Graham stared at Morland down the screen, clearly unconvinced he had accepted his orders. 'There's nothing you can do to help Latvia except get those photos. Do you understand? Proof. Out. That simple.'

'Yes, Sir.'

The colonel continued, 'The minehunter HMS *Padstow* arrived in Riga yesterday with the NATO Standing Mine Counter Measures Group. She's been told to take you out. But she's getting ready to leave in a couple of hours, so you'll need to get your skates on. Head out to Riga International Airport and see what's happening. We need hard evidence that the Russians are on the ground and that it's an invasion, before we can properly protest what is happening. Then get back to *Padstow.*'

'We'll do our best, Sir. I'll report back once we're on *Padstow.*'

Morland checked his watch: 0355. He thought quickly. The streets were empty so, if Krauja was prepared to drive them, it wouldn't take more than 45 minutes to get into a place where they could observe the international airport. Then 25 minutes back to the quayside where *Padstow* was tied up. Add a fudge factor of 30 minutes . . . and round it up. He looked at Krauja enquiringly. He didn't need to ask.

She nodded. 'Of course I'll drive you.'

Morland looked back at the screen. 'Can you tell the Captain of *Padstow* we'll aim to be with him by 0630 latest. Any later than that and something will have gone wrong. But don't worry, we'll stay out of trouble. We're recce. We observe without being spotted.'

'Will do. Good luck.' The Baltic Team faded from the screen and the Inmarsat was quickly packed away.

'Come with me, guys.' Krauja was being as decisive as ever. 'I've picked up a Land Cruiser from the office. There's plenty of room for us all and our equipment. I know the back roads to the airport. We'll take a look and I'll get you to your ship . . . then I'll need to get back to my office. Some of us will have a war to fight.'

Morland said nothing, stung by the barb. He would shortly be returning to safety in England, and despite his direct orders to the contrary, he felt that he would be deserting Krauja.

He suppressed a momentary, idiotic thought, that he could persuade her to join him on the ship and so keep her out of harm's way. But one look at the determined tilt of her jaw and he knew that to even hint at such a suggestion would be deemed a grave insult. And in that moment, and contrary to all his training, he realised that he was thinking of her as a woman and no longer as a fellow professional.

'The ambassador . . . ,' he almost stammered in his confusion, needing something to say. 'I'd . . . I'd better brief him.'

While the team shouldered bergens, picked up weapons and

their other kit and clattered downstairs to Krauja's car, Morland found the ambassador in his office. He and his staff were gathering files for incineration. Morland quickly explained his new orders, bid him farewell and good luck, then joined the team outside.

'Let's go, Marina.'

Krauja needed no urging. Ignoring the now-working traffic lights, she drove the packed Toyota Land Cruiser fast through the empty streets, before crossing the bridge over the swollen River Daugava in the growing light of near dawn.

Twenty minutes later, Krauja halted amid a group of high-rise flats on the edge of the western suburbs of Riga and Morland wound his window down. Ahead of them he heard explosions, while occasional flashes and tracer rounds arced into the air. He checked his map. The airport was still several kilometres away to the west, but it was clear that there was a major firefight going on out there.

'I can get closer, Tom.' Krauja showed no fear.

'As long as we can keep under cover, that's OK,' replied Morland. 'We don't want to get into the open.'

'We'll take the Jurmala cycle path. That's the way we bike to the beach in summer. It's wide enough for this vehicle and it skirts the airport perimeter. It goes through the forest, so we won't be seen.'

Fifteen minutes later, they were driving smoothly along the cycle path running through the forest. Finally Krauja stopped, reversed off the track into the trees and cut the engine. She pointed, but did not need to. The firefight was very close now and it was light enough for Morland to see the high, iron-link perimeter fence.

'Through the trees and you'll see the airport.'

'De-bus!' Morland ordered.

The team jumped out of the Land Cruiser, shook out into a V formation to ensure all-round observation and moved the short distance to the edge of the forest from which, just as promised, they overlooked the northern perimeter of the airport. Krauja stayed with the vehicle, guarded by Corporal Paddy Archer, ready for a quick getaway.

Morland dropped to the ground, leopard-crawled to the edge of the forest and lay prone. He listened and looked around. No immediate threat. He pulled out his mini-binoculars from his breast pocket. The rest of the team took up positions in all-round defence, rifles pointing in a 360-degree circle. He looked through his binoculars. 'Oh, shit!' he exclaimed, despite himself.

From the safety of his cover, Morland looked down the length of the runway. It was a scene of horror. Smoke billowed from lime-green-liveried AirBaltic passenger planes lined up on the hard-standing a kilometre away. In front of the modern, glass-fronted passenger terminal, a vast Russian Mi-26 Halo helicopter, capable of lifting ninety troops, lay on its side, burning fiercely. Curtains of machine-gun fire snaked across the runway and abandoned parachutes billowed on the grass. A full-scale assault on the international airport was under way.

However, despite the carnage on the tarmac, things were obviously not going well for the defenders, because yet more airborne soldiers were de-bussing from the cavernous bellies of other, intact, Mi-26 Halos and, as their feet touched the ground, they started skirmishing towards the buildings. Morland was impressed despite himself; these were highly trained and very brave troops, who were assaulting into murderous and well-aimed fire. However, with the sort of numbers being deployed, there was only going to be one outcome here this morning.

Then there was a heavier volley of fire from the far side of the runway and shells smacked into the terminal buildings, ripping chunks out of the walls and doing God knows what damage to the defenders inside.

Morland trained his binoculars on the vehicles doing the

firing, and in one muzzle flash, saw what he had expected and feared: Russian BMD-4 armoured vehicles. They would have been dropped with the initial parachute landings. There was no doubt about what he was witnessing; this was the cream of the Russian airborne, with the latest equipment, at work here.

The problem was that he was not close enough to get the quality of photographs the colonel had demanded; the unambiguous evidence that these were Russian regular forces and not some proxies, or some militia, as the Russians would doubtless claim – a game the Russians had played so cleverly and for so long in Ukraine.

Next moment he switched back to the terminal, as he saw flashes and heard the unmistakable crump of mortar rounds exploding among the advancing Russians. As the rounds fell on the hard tarmac, they blew the troops over, scythed down, just like the toy plastic soldiers Morland had played with as a child and knocked over with his finger to signify they were dead.

'Those Latvians sure know how to use their mortars.' Morland heard Sergeant Wild's voice in his PRR, personal role radio, in his ear. 'They're giving the Russians something to think about . . . There'll be a good few less in the queue for coffee and doughnuts when they finally get to the cafeteria.'

Morland could almost feel himself smile at the sergeant's grim, gallows humour. But the happy thought that the Latvians were fighting back so effectively was destroyed moments later by a loud roar just above their heads. It was a flight of four Mi-24 Hind helicopter gunships, which opened fire on the airport buildings. Smoke from 80-millimetre rockets snaked from weapon stations mounted on their stub wings, while 23-millimetre nose-mounted cannons sent burst after burst into the Latvian infantry fire positions.

The roar and clatter of huge helicopters did not stop as four more Hinds roared low to replace the first flight, which turned for home, ammunition exhausted. Soon there was a regular taxi rank of gunships pouring fire onto the hapless Latvians from a mere 200 feet above the heads of Morland and his team.

Ghastly though it was to watch, Morland knew that this was his proof and this was his moment. He raised his camera and took photograph after photograph of the Hinds in action above him; switching every so often to record the devastation they were creating. They were so low and moving so slowly and with such confidence that he was even able to ensure that he captured their registration numbers; the Int boys back home would love those shots. They would probably be able to name the pilots. This was the proof the colonel had demanded. This was Russian airborne forces at work. No ifs. No buts. No militias or proxies.

It was, though, now time to get out before they were spotted. Morland could see this was now the endgame of the defence and he noted there had been no more mortar strikes since the Hinds had started their deadly pounding. The Russians would soon move in and finish off the survivors and then they would be moving to their secondary targets. He wanted to be gone by then.

He spoke quietly into his PRR to tell the other two that it was time to move back to the car. Morland and Watson began to move back, covered by Wild, making the most of the cover provided by the trees.

Then Morland heard the roar and clatter of another two Hinds approaching. However, these were not firing rockets or shells. He found himself frozen in appalled fascination as they flew overhead, almost knowing what was going to happen next, but somehow unable to not watch it. He raised his camera again as the Hinds flew over the passenger terminal. Two large drums dropped, one from the back of each Hind. They could only be one thing.

The 250-kilogram, fuel-air explosive bombs landed on the building.

There was a roar as the terminal erupted and, even from over a kilometre distance and lying prone on the edge of the forest, Morland felt the intense heat and blast hit his face. There would be no Latvian survivors for the Russian soldiers to finish off after all. In fact, Morland wondered whether that massive explosion might not have taken more than a few Russians with it.

And now there was silence from the buildings; silence everywhere in fact, a shocked silence. Then vehicles appeared, supported by infantry, which closed on the building. The fight for the airport was over. The Russians would next spread out to secure the perimeter. He spoke into his microphone.

'Move now. Fast.'

The team quickly retraced its steps to where Krauja and Archer were waiting with the Land Cruiser under cover and mounted up.

One look at Krauja's eyes told Morland of her desperate need to know what was happening at the airport and to its defenders. He guessed that she would have friends in that Riga-recruited National Guard Battalion, which had defended the airport so bravely. But he knew, too, that this was not a moment for emotion.

Instead, he reverted to the professionalism of a soldier giving a situation report. After the trauma of what he had seen, it was the only way. Anything more than an emotionless statement of the bare facts would be in danger of wrecking Krauja. And he was suddenly unsure how he would handle that.

'Major Russian airborne assault on the airport. I'd estimate it at least a battalion-plus strength; supported by Mi-24 Hind attack helicopters and BMD-4 airborne armoured vehicles. Defenders put up a strong fight, but have now been neutralised. The airport is now in enemy hands. I have photographic evidence of Russian helicopters attacking. Our task now is to get those pictures back to the UK as quickly as possible. We need to get to *Padstow* ASAP.'

Krauja took a deep breath and exhaled slowly. 'My younger brother was a reservist in that battalion. He was in his first year studying law at the University of Riga.'

Morland was lost for words. Her quiet dignity somehow made the situation even worse. He nodded in acknowledgement of what she had just told him and then pointed at the car. Without saying another word she strode to the driver's door, got into the seat, turned the key and, once the last door had slammed shut, accelerated hard back down the narrow cycle path towards Riga.

Soon they were through back streets lined with old wooden buildings and back down to the Daugava again. As they drove, they kept the windows down and rifle barrels facing out, all the while keeping a sharp lookout for more Russians. From the scale of what they had witnessed back at the airport, they could be landing more troops anywhere.

Krauja turned right and made her way through the narrow streets of the old port quarter and then joined the main highway. Finally they drove onto the 600-metre length of the Vansu bridge, high above the Daugava River.

'There's your ship. Down on the left,' said Krauja, pointing.

Morland looked left as Krauja indicated and there, his view partially obscured by the metal guardrails that ran alongside the bridge, were three small battleship-grey mine countermeasure ships, alongside the dockside on the other side of the river; all that NATO had been able to agree among themselves to send to Latvia in its hour of need. And now, from the activity on the deck, he could see they were preparing to leave.

HMS Padstow *wasn't much to look at*, thought Morland, *and she carried no weapons worth mentioning. But thank God, the Royal Navy was here.* Further alongside the dock, at the stern of the next ship, he could see the black, red and gold flag of Germany.

Now that escape was at hand, he wasn't quite sure how he

was going to say goodbye to Krauja. Something told him that when he said farewell, as he knew he must, he would not be seeing her again. Krauja had unfinished business with the Russian airborne and he doubted she would survive. And then, as they reached the centre of the bridge and Morland was about to start saying his goodbyes, it happened.

High above them, too high to hear the roar of their jet engines, Morland spotted the tiny silhouettes of two Su-25KM Scorpions – Russia's state-of-the-art ground-attack aircraft – as they banked below the clouds. He leaned out of the window to get a better view and saw them straighten for a moment and then, from each of them, came tell-tale twin streaks: laser-guided bombs. Morland had only ever seen them fired in news clips from Ukraine, but he was in no doubt about what he was witnessing and what would happen next.

Improbably and shockingly, the bombs began to snake down, heading directly towards the bridge and the Land Cruiser. He instinctively ducked, as if they were meant for him. But in the split second as the bombs streaked over the bridge, he knew he was being ridiculous. Those bombs were designed to destroy something very much larger and more valuable than him and his camera.

Next moment the bombs hit two of the ships on their left.

Nevertheless, Morland forced himself to glance back up. He saw the aircraft circle, bank again and, fearing nothing and nobody, let loose more bombs.

As Morland again looked left, the two ships erupted in a ballooning yellow fireball – intensely red at the centre. He clearly saw chunks of molten material spin high into the air, before falling back into the water with a hiss of steam. A wave of heat engulfed them through the open windows and the car rocked wildly when the blast wave hit it. As they drove off the bridge, slowly now, the fireball subsided and he saw the two closest ships in flames. Then there was another, deeper roar as the ammunition and explosives on board each vessel erupted in an even bigger fireball. HMS *Padstow* and FGS *Eckernförde* turned turtle, broke up and began to sink.

Krauja drove into a side street, then halted. 'What now, Tom? That's your way home gone.' She was pale, angry at what she had witnessed and now struggling to control her emotions in the face of what the Russians were doing in her beloved Riga.

Morland looked around at his team, all of them in shock. Only moments ago he had not known what to say to Krauja after watching her countrymen being massacred at the airport and learning about the probable fate of her brother. Now he, too, was a witness to the death of fellow Britons.

Morland felt he was looking at a film playing in slow motion. He thought with perfect clarity, staring out of the window as he spoke, saying what he felt, exactly as he felt it; not something he would normally do with his soldiers. But then he had never witnessed anything like this before. 'Those fucking bastards have just sunk a British and a German ship. That means we must now be at war with Russia . . .'

Krauja glanced at him expectantly, evidently wondering what he was going to say next.

He turned to look at his team and they looked back at him. He saw the expression on their faces that said: What the fuck now, boss? But he also saw the stubborn determination of British infantrymen, now really pissed off and more than ready to fight against the odds. Whatever it took.

'OK, that part of the job's done and dusted. Nobody needs those bloody photos now. The proof about the Russians' intentions is sinking right there, in the harbour . . . We're staying to fight with the Latvians.'

'Well, that didn't take the brains of an archbishop, Sir,' Wild said. 'Unless someone has got a magic, bleeding carpet, they've sunk our only way home. I reckon we should head back to

Ādaži and link up with our special forces mates. Just think, guys, we'll get to do that forest-training phase after all.'

'Good call, sarge.' Morland looked at Krauja, grateful for the sergeant's attempt at a joke, however small it might be. 'Can you drop us back at Ādaži, Marina? Once you've done that I suppose you'll be heading back to Riga?'

'I'm taking you to Ādaži, but I'm staying with you. You need me now more than ever. And we'll need that radio of yours before this is over. Ādaži will be where the fightback will begin. Not here in Riga. Not after this morning.'

Krauja looked at Morland. Their eyes met.

Morland's heart missed a beat. He felt immensely protective. He knew he'd go to the ends of the earth for her. At that moment in time, fighting for Latvia meant fighting for Marina Krauja. But she must never know.

'What are you waiting for, then?' he ordered. 'Let's go.'

1230 hours, Sunday, 21 May 2017
The Russell Arms, Butler's Cross, Buckinghamshire

TREV WALKER SIPPED morosely at a Diet Coke and checked the emails on his iPhone. He was sitting in the open-plan bar of the Russell Arms, a rambling, quirky pub just under a mile north of the Prime Minister's official residence at Chequers, in the green and leafy Buckinghamshire countryside on the edge of the Chiltern Hills. Normally he'd be quite happy to spend Sunday lunchtime in a pub, but surrounded as he was by boot-clad hikers and check-trousered Sunday golfers, fresh from eighteen holes on the nearby Ellesborough club course, he felt uncomfortably out of place. In his ill-fitting and crumpled off-the-peg suit and scuffed black shoes, he knew he looked like it, too.

Walker was happiest in the Red Lion, halfway down Whitehall and almost opposite the entrance to Downing Street. That was where he could meet, network and extend his influence. A country pub full of newly countrified people relaxing on a Sunday was well outside his comfort zone.

He looked across at the lunch table in the corner of the dining room where the Prime Minister sat with his family. It had clearly been a good morning for him. He sat, like any other forty-something father, focused on his pretty wife and young children, completely happy. Walker accepted that the

PM was reasonably conscientious at dealing with his ministerial boxes, usually before breakfast, but sometimes, thought Walker, the PM overdid the relaxing. Photos of him with his family might sit well with middle-class, female voters – one of the PM's fixations – but one result was that he could end up reacting to events, rather than driving them, like that latest telephone call from President Dillon of the United States.

Walker had no time for the British defence establishment at the best of times. In fact, he enjoyed treating them with undisguised contempt and revelled in the knowledge that his suits and unpolished shoes drove some of them into a fury, before he even started to talk down to them. But even he had to admit that the government's approach to defence was too much smoke and mirrors and that Dillon's criticisms had been exactly on the mark.

Walker knew full well that there was precious little proper strategic thinking going on in 10 Downing Street. He knew also from this morning's telephone call with President Dillon in Washington that she knew that, too. But he had to give her credit for the way she'd flattered the PM and asked him to stand alongside the US. But again, it was all about creating the right perception for the focus groups on which so many government decisions were based. For the PM to be seen as new best friends with the charismatic new US female president would be good for his image with women voters and with the media. Tough and statesmanlike, it was just what the PM needed with all his ongoing EU issues.

Walker felt a tap on his shoulder and turned to see one of the PM's close protection team. 'You're wanted outside, Trev,' he said, signalling Walker to follow him out.

Outside the pub, even Walker had to admit that the warm, spring sun shining on the translucent green of the surrounding trees was uplifting. But that was only a momentary thought as the officer pointed out a silver Mercedes E-Class, beside which

Kate Bowler, the PM's Private Secretary, was standing. Tall and slim, with brown hair tied back, she was usually enigmatically relaxed. But today Walker could see that she was grim faced and looking positively shocked, despite making an effort to compose herself.

She strode towards him as soon as she spotted him. 'I need to see the PM, Trev. He's got to get back to Downing Street. Now.'

Normally, he would have demanded to know what was going on, but not today. He had never seen Bowler like this before and now was not the moment to aggravate her. Walker turned and went back into the pub. He sidled up behind the PM's chair.

'Sorry to interrupt, boss,' he muttered, 'Kate's outside. She says you've got to get straight back to Number Ten. Something important has come up.'

'Can't it wait, Trev?' the PM said irritably. 'Our food hasn't arrived yet.'

'No, boss. You need to speak to her now.' Walker was not putting up with any argument.

The PM apologised to his wife, kissed her goodbye and ruffled his children's hair, then reluctantly followed Walker into the Russell Arms car park.

'Couldn't it wait, Kate? I was enjoying a brief down moment with my family,' the PM said sulkily.

Bowler was firm. 'You need to get in, Prime Minister. I'll brief you on the way to Downing Street.'

A personal protection officer opened the rear left door for the PM, who got in obediently and sat next to Bowler. Walker quickly got into the front, before any of Bowler's team tried to take the seat. The PM's two chase cars pulled out in front and behind, switched on their sirens and headed south for the M40 and London.

'It's bad news, Prime Minister. Brace yourself for a shock.'

Bowler faced the PM, who nodded for her to speak, all attention now.

'It's HMS *Padstow*, the minehunter with the NATO mine countermeasures group. She's been sunk with all hands in Riga. She was bombed early this morning by the Russians. They also sank a German ship. They're invading Latvia. It's war.'

The white-faced Prime Minister crumpled in deep shock on the seat behind him. Walker knew it was best to say nothing and leave him to feel sorry for himself. Better to spend the time thinking through the ramifications of this news and how best to spin it. But try as he might on the journey back, he could not see one good thing about what Bowler had told them. It was an unmitigated disaster and the press were going to eat them alive.

Tomorrow's headlines didn't bear thinking about – and as soon as he could, he'd get onto the editors to do as much damage control as possible. What that ship was even doing there, in the middle of a war zone, he could not imagine, but he would find out. He suspected that the admirals and generals had allowed this to happen. But there was no point tearing into them as they so richly deserved. At least not yet.

An hour and a quarter later, the Prime Minister was still looking pale with the shock of realising that his career and reputation were on the line as a result of the sinking of HMS *Padstow*, when Walker led him from the front door of Number 10, down the long corridor to the Cabinet Room, through the double doors and into the cramped office known as the 'Den.'

'CDS will be here shortly. He's the one who set you up for this,' said Walker. 'You need to show him who's boss.'

Shortly afterwards there was a knock on the door. Walker opened it and there stood General Sir Jim Mainwaring, Chief of the Defence Staff, grey-haired, short and inclined to stoutness. A man whom Walker had initially thought of as a down-to-earth West Countryman – 'a soldier's soldier' as the press had reported his appointment with evident delight – but whom he had quickly come to respect as a canny Whitehall insider, in his own way as Machiavellian as himself.

Walker had made it his business to seek out Mainwaring's vulnerable points, so knew that he had only made his way up the greasy pole as a staff officer and had never commanded in combat. And much to Mainwaring's chagrin, despite his chest full of medals, he had never heard a shot fired in anger. Nevertheless, Walker rather approved of the way Mainwaring had got to the top by telling politicians what they wanted to hear. That was very much the Walker way, only with a difference. He prided himself on ensuring that what politicians, especially the PM, thought they wanted, was what Walker wanted and believed was right.

Which meant that when things went wrong, he was prepared to stand behind those decisions; more than could be said for the queasy-looking general now standing outside the door, waiting to be invited to enter. Normally he just blustered straight in, as if by right. But not today. Walker had long suspected that Mainwaring could not possibly believe even half the things he had been telling the PM for the past two years. His almost sheepish demeanour now told him that he had called Mainwaring right.

Nevertheless, he puffed out his chest before he spoke. 'I've come to brief you before you attend COBRA, Prime Minister,' he announced portentously in a strong Bristol accent.

It was enough for the Prime Minister to recover his composure. Walker had told the PM it was time to put him in his place and he did not disappoint. He spoke with withering sarcasm. 'So . . . CDS. Sending a bunch of NATO minesweepers was going to deter the Russians, was it? Wasn't that what you told me?'

Mainwaring knew better than to reply. Instead, he stood silent.

'Thanks to your military advice, we're in a hell of a mess. Trev tells me this is the worst British naval disaster since the Falklands War. "Sunk with all hands" will be the headlines tomorrow . . . How the hell do you propose getting us out of it?'

As the Prime Minister spoke he lost his control for a moment. However, instead of exploding in rage, as many a prime minister before him had done in similar circumstances, he choked. Tears welled up in his eyes and his cheeks reddened with anger. With an effort he controlled himself.

'CDS, let's be clear. I accepted your professional military advice that the presence of the NATO group, with *Padstow* as part of it, would send a strong signal to the Russians. And now . . . and now the ship is sunk and most of the crew are dead or missing.' The Prime Minister's voice then went ominously quiet. 'Kindly explain.'

Now it was Mainwaring's turn to look shocked. He knew he owed his place as the Head of the Armed Forces to his ability to work the Whitehall machine and ingratiate himself with politicians. Now he was facing a personal disaster. He had been looking forward to his imminent retirement and taking his place in the House of Lords, but that had to be in jeopardy. For the first time in his carefully constructed career he had got it badly wrong. And what his wife would say when she heard was a different level of disaster altogether.

'Prime Minister.' He pushed such considerations aside and forced himself to speak calmly and authoritatively. 'The Chiefs have just met and we've considered the position. We believe that the UK needs to show strength at a time like this. We've had a disaster . . . but we've faced disasters as a nation before and always come out of it.'

The Prime Minister looked at him. 'What do you propose?'

'Prime Minister,' replied Mainwaring, 'we have to accept that the sinking of HMS *Padstow* is an act of war by Russia and the invasion of Latvia means we are bound under Article Five of the Washington Treaty to come to their assistance. It is too late to send land forces, although we've given orders for them to go to immediate readiness to move. We're concerned that a deployment of air forces – ours and theirs shooting each other down – might commit us earlier than we necessarily want to be committed. The recommendation of your Chiefs of Staff Committee, which I am authorised to pass on to you as your government's principal military adviser . . .'

Walker could see the Prime Minister's irritation at this pompous and long-winded soldier who had, on an instant, stopped using the word 'I' and was already manoeuvring to a position of joint blame and responsibility by using the words 'we' and 'committee'. But the Prime Minister also played this game and played it a lot better than this already failed general.

'Do get to the point, CDS,' he said tersely.

Mainwaring continued, 'As I was saying, Prime Minister, the recommendation of your Chiefs of Staff is to deploy a strong naval force to the Baltic. It will be a demonstration of our solidarity with Latvia and the other Baltic states; it shows that we are a good NATO ally, but by poising ourselves at sea, we can remain uncommitted.'

'And what will this force consist of?'

'We propose to send a Task Group based on HMS *Queen Elizabeth*, Prime Minister.'

Walker knew that *Queen Elizabeth*, an aircraft carrier and the biggest ship ever to enter service in the Royal Navy, had just been commissioned. But he'd also noted in his daily scrutiny of the newspapers that various retired admirals, generals, and even air chief marshals had long been fulminating that the F-35 aircraft meant to fly off her decks had not yet been declared fit for operations. It was rare, in his considerable experience of Whitehall, for all three branches of the Services to agree on anything, but this seemed something they were all of one mind on, which was worrying.

'Boss, you might want to know if she has any aircraft yet?' Walker interrupted.

The Prime Minister raised a questioning eyebrow.

'Well . . .' Mainwaring paused. 'It is correct that it will be some years before the F-35 Joint Strike Fighters we're buying from the Americans will be operational. However, our considered military advice is that we can still have an important deterrent effect by embarking a Royal Marines Commando unit of around seven hundred men on board *Queen Elizabeth*, together with the Merlin and Chinook support helicopters needed to lift them. Also, the Task Group will have an amphibious ship in support – and that's got landing craft, so that we can put the troops ashore if we need to.'

'And what do you suppose the Commando will do?' The Prime Minister was perplexed.

'Well, that's the point, Prime Minister,' replied Mainwaring, his West Country burr moderating as he began to regain the initiative. 'We retain great flexibility. If we need to put them ashore, we can. On the other hand, by poising off shore they'll keep the Russians guessing as to our intentions.'

'And the Russians? How will they react?'

'It is our considered view that they would not dare attack the *Queen Elizabeth*. By sending the Task Force we would be saying, "Thus far maybe, but no further".'

The Prime Minister looked at Walker.

'It'll play well on the front pages, boss. Show we're not being pushed about. Just like Maggie T . . . If in doubt, assemble a Task Force.'

'Then go for it, CDS.' The Prime Minister squared his shoulders and tried to look Churchillian. He thought, *Perhaps I might be remembered as a war leader after all.*

1500 hours, Monday, 22 May 2017
HMS Queen Elizabeth
Middle Slip Jetty, HM Naval Base, Portsmouth

COMMANDER JAMES BUSH RN took one last look around the flight deck before heading into the forward island of the aircraft carrier to update the Captain in his cabin under the bridge. As Executive Officer of HMS *Queen Elizabeth* he was second in command and, as such, responsible for the day-to-day running of the ship and the efficiency of its crew. And today he had more than enough to think about. He'd been asleep in his married quarter on the edge of Portsdown Hill, overlooking the Royal Navy dockyard at Portsmouth, when the call had come through from the ship's Duty Officer at 2.35 a.m.: *Queen Elizabeth* was to deploy to sea in three days time as lead ship of a British amphibious Task Force.

Twenty years in the Royal Navy, much of it spent at sea, meant that Bush was used to coming awake in an instant, accepting and digesting new and sometimes worrisome information and then acting decisively on it. But even he had felt compelled to ask the Duty Officer to repeat what he had just said, as his brain tried to absorb the enormity of it.

'In response to the Russian invasion of Latvia and the sinking of the mine countermeasures vessel HMS *Padstow*, is what it says here, Sir.'

Bush caught himself before he swore. He did not want anybody knowing his reaction to such news and anyway, it was important that he displayed no concern to the young duty officer who had just phoned him. That would come later when he saw his Captain. But he was, quite simply, aghast. Sending *Queen Elizabeth* to war without its fighter aircraft to protect it would be much like sending a tank into battle without shells; it might very much look the part, but without its offensive fire power, it would be as much use as a chocolate fireguard against other tanks. Aircraft carriers were floating airfields, no more, no less. Without aircraft to defend it, the carrier would risk becoming a vulnerable, high-prestige target; a very large, not very fast, and certainly not very manoeuvrable high-prestige target. And he was second in command of it.

At least, he thought to himself as he turned on the bedside light, realising that he was going to have to wake his wife as he put on his uniform, *the ship had been delivered on time and they had managed to do the majority of their work-up training*. Which is why, he supposed, some idiot had decided they must be ready to fight.

There was a discreet cough from the other end of the phone and Bush realised he had been so shocked by this message that he had forgotten that the Duty Officer was now waiting for him to issue orders.

Bush was instantly the naval officer once again. 'Thanks for the call. Now I want you to get the message out to the ship's company. Initiate the emergency recall system and put out a warning order to the O Group, that's all Heads of Departments. I want them all in the Ops Centre at 0800 with a report on their preparations for departure for sea and where the problems are. Got that?'

'Aye aye, Sir,' responded the Duty Officer.

Bush put down the phone by his bedside and pulled on his working rig of dark-blue cotton, flame-retardant trousers, and

shirt with the three gold rings of a commander on his epau-
lettes. Kissing his still-drowsy wife farewell, with the promise
that he'd be back to sort out his kit, he'd turned off the light
and yet hesitated for a moment until he saw her roll over and,
doubtless, go straight back to sleep – like him, she had long
ago learned to put up with these late-night interruptions and
frequent absences.

Thank God for Jacky, he thought to himself with a deep surge
of love and affection. She had not volunteered for the Navy,
but without her long-suffering selflessness and countless others
like her, where would the Navy be? He let himself out of the
front door of their small, three-bedroomed, semi-detached
married quarter without disturbing the sleeping boys and got
into the ancient VW Polo they were just able to afford as a
second car, before driving the twenty minutes into Portsmouth
Naval Base.

And now, as he surveyed the deck of *Queen Elizabeth* – 'longer
than the Houses of Parliament' as the official blurb liked to
emphasise, and the pride of the Royal Navy – Bush was satisfied that preparations for putting to sea were under way as
effectively as they could be. 'Lucky we were preparing to deploy
to sea next week anyway,' he muttered to himself, as he watched
dockside cranes lifting palleted loads of supplies, ammunition
and all the materiel of war onto trailers on the flight deck.
From there they were pulled by small tractors onto the elevators and lowered to the hangar below to be stowed.

Quite where some of this war materiel should be stowed,
and in what order it would be needed, would require guess-
work, experience and common sense. However, Bush knew
that nearly all the more senior officers, and certainly all the
senior ratings, would have had some experience of war-fighting
conditions in Britain's many adventures in the Middle East,
which meant there was no shortage of the latter two on board
the vast ship.

He glanced down to the quayside where soldiers of the Royal Artillery's Commando regiment, tough, hard-looking men in their famous green berets, shouldering massive bergen rucksacks and encumbered with the full armoury of their personal weapons, were waiting to climb the gangways before disappearing into the maw of the ship. A Chinook helicopter hovered as it deposited one of the Gunners' 105-millimetre light guns on the flight deck in a roar of engine noise.

A hard-headed realist, who'd joined the Senior Service as a junior seaman, Bush was a thirty-eight-year-old whose qualities had been quickly recognised. He'd flourished in the meritocracy that is the Royal Navy. Initially noticed as a Navy First XI footballer, he had applied that same determination to be the best he could be to his job and been commissioned from the lower deck, working his way up the hard way. His father, a veteran petty officer of the old school, who'd survived the sinking of HMS *Coventry* by Argentine bombs in the Falklands War of 1982, had drilled the importance of ruthless professionalism into him – it was only sheer professionalism that had led to so many surviving that horrific sinking in the lonely wastes of the Southern Ocean.

Bush was now applying the same professionalism to ensure *Queen Elizabeth* could put to sea in time. Bush was anything but sentimental, but even he allowed himself a moment of pride as he looked at the purposeful activity everywhere on the vast flight deck. He could see that this crew might be newly formed, but they would be OK. To be Executive Officer and second in command of the largest ship ever built for the Royal Navy was a fine thing. Not for the first time, Bush wished his father, who'd died five years before, could see him now.

But then the chill of concern hit him again in the pit of his stomach; an aircraft carrier without aircraft. It was a contradiction in terms. His Captain had briefed him early that morning before he'd assembled the O Group. *Queen Elizabeth* had been ordered to deploy as the flagship in command of a Littoral Manoeuvre Group with the Royal Marines and an eclectic mix of helicopters – RAF Chinooks and Navy Merlins, Army Apaches and the new Navy Wildcat Lynx – and all without any helicopter work-up training to iron out any problems; some as basic as whether the RN, RAF and Army helicopters would even be able to talk to each other, let alone the ship. But that was a minor wrinkle compared to his second major concern: Bush knew without being told that the Task Group would be deploying without a strong-enough escort screen. Aircraft carriers do not sail on their own, they need to be protected by rings of escorts: anti-submarine frigates, anti-aircraft destroyers and hunter-killer submarines. But, thanks to the government defence cuts of 2010 and earlier, there simply were not enough fighting ships available and within reach to meet the needs of this new emergency.

This is going to be the mother of 'Come As You Are' parties, thought Bush.

Still, they managed it on no-days' notice with the Task Force in 1982. But then he could hear his father's voice: 'We only did that because, back in Maggie's day, we had a proper navy – before the latest lot of bloody Tory politicians chopped it to pieces. Maggie Thatcher would be turning in her grave if she could see what this shower has gone and done . . .'

As he clattered down the companionway to the Captain's cabin, Bush could not help reflecting that his father was right – as usual. *Queen Elizabeth* was a fine ship and he wouldn't have wanted to be anywhere else, but cutting the number of escort ships in the Royal Navy to find the cash to pay for the two shiny new carriers, particularly when there were doubts about whether the second ship could even be properly manned, was barking mad; more about saving shipbuilders' jobs and political posturing than attempting to give the Royal Navy the balance of ships it needed for the future. A point, Bush remembered with a grin, that even his father – a hard-line Labour supporter all his life – had been forced to concede. The last lot might have ballsed things up in 2010 but, as he had liked to point out to the old, militant class warrior, it had been Labour before them who had ordered the carriers and started cutting escorts in the first place.

Pushing all thoughts of his father aside, he drew back his shoulders and knocked on the door that led to the Captain's office cabin, through his Secretary's miniscule outer office.

'Hello, Sir. The Captain's just finished on the phone to Fleet HQ. You're to go straight in,' said the Secretary, an earnest, bespectacled officer wearing the two-and-a-half rings of a Lieutenant Commander, who had stood up as Bush walked in.

'Enter,' came a drawled command from the half-open door of the Captain's office.

Bush went into the cabin and closed the door behind him, saluting as he did so.

Commodore Tony Narborough pointed at the hardbacked seat in front of his desk. A tall officer in his early forties, with a receding chin and hair brushed straight back from his forehead, like a 1950s film star, he affected (ridiculously, thought Bush) a primrose-yellow, silk paisley-pattern cravat with his navy-blue, working-rig shirt. The grandson of an Admiral, his father had been a Lloyd's 'name' who had been declared bankrupt following the Lloyd's crash of the early 1990s. Destined for Eton, Narborough had instead been sent to the local comprehensive, where he had been hardened by the insults and fists of the other boys.

Disgusted by what the City had done to his father, he had joined the Navy, driven by an ambition to restore the family's good name and become an Admiral. And he'd done all the right things so far: he'd been Flag Lieutenant to a high-flying admiral, played cricket for the Navy, commanded a dashing frigate and then a helicopter carrier ahead of his peers, before heading up the Ministry of Defence branch responsible for planning the size and shape of the Royal Navy. Knowing that his future promotion depended on it and that to show any dissent was career suicide in a political world of harsh financial cuts and military restraint, Narborough had delivered exactly as his masters had demanded.

He'd helped push through the cuts in escort frigates and destroyers, in order to find the money to finish building the over-budget and much-delayed carriers. The last government had concluded that it was politically more acceptable to scrap small surface ships than declare the carriers to be 'white elephants' and scrap them. Bush had a certain sympathy for Narborough on that near impossible call; any naval officer formally advising the scrapping of the iconic carriers would be dead Navy meat.

It was therefore no surprise when he was rewarded with the command of *Queen Elizabeth*, the most prestigious command the Royal Navy had to offer.

'What ho, Number One,' said Narborough. 'How are things going?'

Bush sat down in the proffered chair and pulled out his notebook.

'I'll give you a detailed state of play at this evening's O Group, Sir, when the Heads of Department will also brief. Right now, Warfare, Supply and Marine Engineering are on track. I'll be happier when Weapons Engineering sort out the problems with the Phalanx anti-missile system. But the big issue is aircraft.'

'Continue,' said Narborough.

'Sir.' Bush took a deep breath. 'You're not going to like what I have to say, but I'll say it anyway.' This would not be the first time he had spoken bluntly to a senior officer, hence, despite his highly successful command tour on a frigate, his reduced chances of commanding anything else. 'But to take a carrier to sea to fight the Russians, without the aircraft which are its principal weapons system, is asking for trouble.'

Bush was a seaman to his core, but he'd kept a watchful eye on the F35B Lightning II joint-strike programme, was well briefed on the cost overruns and delays to the programme, and was aware of the technical glitches with both software and hardware that had delayed their introduction into service.

'Now listen, Number One.' Narborough smoothed back his hair. 'I told you this morning that we're deploying as the flagship of a Littoral Manoeuvre Group. Our task is to sail for the Baltic and be ready to poise off shore to demonstrate the resolve and determination of the British government and the NATO Alliance to face down the Russians and, above all, to stop them trying anything else on. Our masters accept they've got the Baltic states by the short and curlies and there's not a lot anyone can do about it. But we can stop them going any further. We may not have any Lightning IIs, but we'll have an impressive mix of helicopters and be able to pack quite a punch ashore with the Marines if needs be . . . and let's get this straight, nobody has said anything about actually fighting the Russians.'

Bush knew that to push the issue any further would amount to insubordination. He'd expressed his concern with the mission they'd been given and he now had two basic choices. Turn to the right and get on with it, or resign his commission in protest. But to do the latter on the verge of a possible war would be tantamount to cowardice.

However, he tried one more tack. With just nineteen frigates and destroyers left in the Royal Navy after the last round of defence cuts, Bush knew that the Task Group would be lucky to get more than a handful of escorts to provide the all-important anti-submarine and anti-aircraft defence systems needed to ensure the protection of *Queen Elizabeth*. Some were in long-term, planned refit, others in dock for servicing and repairs, yet others in far-flung parts of the world, and while they might be making best speed to return, they would not be back in time to join the Task Group before it sailed. Back when the Royal Navy had a fleet of some size they had always been able to make do when a crisis unexpectedly erupted. Now the navy was so small – 'lean' was a favourite expression spouted by politicians trying to sell a negative as a positive – there was no longer anything to spare in the cupboard.

'Sir, are you happy with the makeup of the Task Group?' he asked Narborough.

The Captain narrowed his eyes. 'What's bugging you, Number One?' he demanded in his high-pitched, nasal voice. 'We'll have the amphibious ship *Bulwark* with a Royal Marine Commando on board along with us. I'd hoped for the second amphibious ship, *Albion*, as well, but sadly . . . well . . . you know how it is. After the last round of cuts we can't man both of them as well as the carrier any longer. As for escorts, Fleet HQ has promised two Type 45s: *Daring* and *Dauntless*. They're the most capable destroyers ever launched, as well as the world's best air-defence ships. Our anti-submarine protection will be provided by the hunter-killer sub *Astute* – and there's no better way to defend against subs than with another sub. Our anti-sub escorts will be two Type 23s: *Kent* and *Lancaster*. So, together with our two Royal Fleet Auxiliaries for logistic support, I reckon we'll be quite a punchy Task Group.' Narborough looked pleased.

Bush knew his time was running out but decided to press on, although he knew when to concede a point.

'I get the point about the Type 45s and *Astute*, Sir. Nevertheless, however good the Type 45 anti-aircraft capabilities are, there are only two of them – and let's not forget that they can only ever be a backstop at best. It's the Lightnings we haven't yet got which are meant to be our first line of air defence. So we're cutting it very fine. As for the Type 23s: only two anti-submarine frigates is taking a real risk with the depth and balance of our anti-submarine protection screen, particularly as we'll be up against the Russian Kilos. They've got plenty of them and the new generation is top class. If they send a few of those after us, we will have real problems trying to track them all, especially without maritime patrol aircraft and only one hunter-killer sub. The Nimrods may have been old, but they did the job.'

'What are you trying to say, Number One?' Narborough was on the verge of getting cross, but Bush also knew that the Captain had a grudging respect for him. While unlikely to translate into an unambiguous recommendation for command, he knew that the canny, upwards-thrusting Commodore listened to him.

'You're commanding the Navy's biggest-ever ship. We'll have over two thousand on board with our crew and the commandos. You and this ship are the pride of the Navy. But if we went to the bottom, it would be as big a disaster as *Repulse* and *Prince of Wales* being sunk by the Japanese in 1941 . . . You'll be remembered forever as the unlucky captain. And the name Narborough—'

'Enough.' The Captain held up his hand and smiled and Bush knew he had got away with it as Narborough, with his typical arrogance, assumed that it was his own good name he was worried about, rather than the safety of the ship and its crew. In fact, Bush realised in a moment of grim humour, he had probably just done what was needed to get an 'outstanding' on his next Annual Report. Next moment his guess was confirmed.

'But don't think I don't appreciate your concern, Number One. It's been noted. Relax. It's not going to happen. The Russian navy has never recovered from the rusting hulks in Murmansk after the Cold War. It's manned by conscripts. They'd never dare come near us. Now, I'll see you at the O Group at 1900 hours.'

Bush had said what needed to be said and knew he could go no further. He stood up and saluted.

'Aye aye, Sir.'

Bush left the Captain's day cabin. *Fat lot of good that did*, he thought, *but someone had to say it*.

Bush decided to walk the ship again, talk to the sailors who were making things happen and get a feel for the atmosphere. As he emerged into the huge space of the hangar deck, a scene of frantic activity met him. Pallets of stores were being unloaded from trailers by working parties of sailors, while the Viking armoured vehicles, Land Rovers and light guns of the Army's commando gunners were being parked along the sides of the hangar to make space for incoming helicopters. At the heart of it all, directing, cajoling and gripping any slackers, Bush saw Executive Warrant Officer Geordie Rae, the senior Warrant Officer on board and a man who knew better than anyone how the lower deck ticked. I'll get the truth from him, Bush said to himself, making his way through the chaos.

Rae was a forthright Mancunian, who had known Bush since they were both junior Able Seamen seventeen years earlier, and the close bond of friendship, formed as young men, had lasted after Bush was commissioned. Rae spotted Bush and immediately grinned, braced up and saluted. They might be old shipmates, but now Bush carried the Queen's Commission the usual formalities applied.

'Morning, Sir. Good to see you . . . Come to see how the troops are getting on?'

'Exactly, Geordie.' Bush was not one to stand on ceremony. 'How are the vibes?'

'Where do you want to start?' Rae wiped the sweat from his face with the back of his hand and gestured to the working party he'd been directing to carry on with their task.

'You've no need to worry about the quality of the crew or the ship. They'll be more than up to the mark . . .' Rae dropped his voice, clearly anxious not to be overheard being anything but positive. 'But don't kid yourself that all is well. The guys and girls are seriously worried. We're pushed to man the ship properly, so each watch is light on people; it's criminal that, to save money, the amphib *Bulwark* hasn't got any hangar space for helicopters, so we've got to keep her helicopters on board here. The Lord alone knows how that will work out at the sharp end, when the bootnecks on *Bulwark* need urgent transport. A midshipman on his first day at sea could tell you that bit of bean-counter-inspired ship design is a lethal cock-up just waiting to happen. Then, to cap it all, one of the Type 23 anti-sub escorts is on its last legs. Apart from that, it's all peachy . . . Sorry to whinge, but you did ask.'

'What's the score on the Type 23?' Bush asked.

'*Kent* is only fit for the knacker's yard,' replied Rae. 'My mate is her Executive Warrant Officer and he tells me she's fucked; that she's well overdue a full refit. Strictly between us, and it would be his arse on the line if this went any further, when she put into Portsmouth at the end of her last trip her skipper was no longer willing to risk going to Full Ahead in case she blew something. The chances of her generators and turbines lasting around the North Foreland are pretty much zero. Then we'll be down to one anti-sub escort . . . and what if one of the Type 45s decides to blow its generator? Then we'd be right royally buggered. I'd have hoped for four Type 23s; two might just have sufficed, but not if things go tits up out there. One can't begin to do the job.'

'Thanks, Geordie,' said Bush quietly. He knew that this was a coded signal that morale was more than fragile and that the Navy was being asked too much of this time. 'There's no getting around it. The cupboard's bare. Something like this wasn't meant to happen and certainly not in Europe. We still haven't recovered from that crazy assumption in the 2010 Defence Review that we'd never have to go to war again, so the clever dicks in the MOD never thought we'd have to assemble another Task Group in double-quick time. Trouble is, as you know, the other anti-sub escorts are either spread to the wind doing other stuff or they're in refit. We've just got to do the best we can, Geordie, God help us.'

Three days later, with the Rear Admiral commanding the Task Group embarked, together with his staff, HMS *Queen Elizabeth* left Portsmouth Harbour to go to war. Blue-jacketed sailors in their best rig lined the decks, while emotional crowds gathered on Southsea Common to wave off the Task Group. As Bush stood on the bridge, he felt a lump in his throat and a flush of pride as the mighty warship moved slowly into the waters of Spithead, before heading out past the Martello forts built to protect Portsmouth from the French, and into the English Channel, following the course so many great warships had taken before.

Yet, despite this sense of pride in being part of the golden thread of excellence exemplified by the Royal Navy, a premonition of dread gripped him. He only hoped that the politicians and admirals and pundits were right and Russia would not come out and fight them, lest it provoke a wider European war and an almost inevitable nuclear exchange. History might indicate otherwise, though. Back in 1982 the experts predicted the Argentinians would buckle as soon as they saw the Task Force heading towards them. But that had not happened, had it?

1900 hours, Monday, 22 May 2017
National Defence Control Centre, Moscow

STANDING ON THE bridge overlooking the War Room in the National Defence Control Centre, Fyodor Komarov, the President's Chief of Staff, could see that the man chosen to set up and run it, Lieutenant General Mikhail Filatov, was looking anxious.

Well he might in front of this lot, but he'd better get used to it or he'll end up commanding a camp in Siberia, thought Komarov, standing behind the President, who was flanked by his key cohort of advisors; the men who ran Russia's war machine.

Below them a host of staff officers, all too conscious that they were being watched by the man who could determine their fate at a word, sat at the concentric rings of desks, quietly working the banks of computers and secure telephones. Around the walls the interactive screens now showed detailed maps of the Baltic states and Sea, together with those of north-west Europe, the North Sea and English Channel. The TV screens were showing multiple live 24-hour news feeds. Had the sound been turned up, they would have heard a cacophony of anxious presenters and frantic journalists.

Instead, in complete silence, clips of film showed Russian vehicles and soldiers moving purposefully through the streets of cities in Estonia, Latvia and Lithuania, watched by shocked and sullen crowds of civilians. Although, in stark contrast, some Russian TV feeds were showing scenes of Russian flag-waving locals – doubtless the Russian-speaking minority – throwing flowers and kissing the victorious Russian soldiers. On one screen, marked as showing Russia Today, clips of Russian soldiers in their camouflage uniforms were interspersed with grainy black-and-white footage of advancing Soviet troops from the Great Patriotic War.

The President's eyes narrowed in satisfaction and he nodded to Filatov. 'What are you waiting for? I came here for an update and I haven't got all day.'

Filatov took a deep breath, smoothed back his well-coiffed hair and started.

'Vladimir Vladimirovich, I am pleased to tell you that Russian armed forces have enjoyed complete success. Thanks to the very effective *maskirovka* operation and the efforts of the RNZS, the Russian People's Protection Force in Latvia, as well as the cyber operation, the integrity of the state collapsed like a discarded balloon. Latvia is almost completely in Russian hands. Seventy-Sixth Guards Assault Landing Division has secured the international airport and the air base at Lielvārde. We have just heard from the divisional commander that his most battle-hardened formation, Twenty-Three Air Assault Regiment – you'll remember how well they did in the recovery of Ukraine three years ago – is now effectively in control of Riga. Meanwhile, First Guards Tank Army is making good progress and estimates it will be in Riga in four hours.'

'What about opposition, Mikhail Nikolayevich?' asked the President, ignoring Filatov and turning instead to his Chief of the General Staff, Gareyev, dressed today in a simple soldier's combat fatigues.

'The Latvians fought hard, but their army was only five thousand full timers and twenty thousand reservists, many of whom never even deployed in time. They didn't stand a chance.

We're lucky NATO hadn't stationed any well-armed, permanent forces there. That could have changed things completely.'

'So, there was no NATO involvement?' persisted the President.

'Well, not quite, Vladimir Vladimirovich. The Americans sent a large detachment to Lielvārde Air Base to set things up for their F-16 force. The F-16s got out just in time, but the detachment of airmen joined the Latvians in the defence of the air base. They fought bravely. The survivors are now prisoners of war.'

'Make sure they're properly treated. They'll be useful bargaining chips if we have to negotiate . . . as we may have to, if this triggers NATO into reacting.' The President looked thoughtful, doubtless trying to ponder the consequences of this unexpected and unwelcome bit of news. Then he changed the topic. 'You said they fought bravely. What about our losses?'

The Defence Minister, once again in his heavily bemedalled uniform, decided to push himself forward, doubtless keen to share in the glory of the moment. 'Insignificant among the airborne infantry, Vladimir Vladimirovich,' he asserted.

An interesting statement, thought Komarov, because just before coming up to the bridge, he had heard that there had been significant losses among the attackers, both at Lielvārde and the international airport at Riga.

'What exactly do you mean by insignificant, Alexandr Borisovich?' asked the President.

The Defence Minister opened his mouth, but it was clear he did not know the answer, so Gareyev stepped back in.

'First reports indicate at least ten-per-cent casualties, which is heavy. Around forty killed in action and over two hundred and fifty wounded. Although overwhelmed, the Latvians fought like devils,' he said, with a soldier's respect for a tough adversary.

'Anything else?'

This time the Defence Minister did have his facts to hand as he spoke again. 'The Air Force lost two Su-25 Frogfoots, shot down by a US-piloted F-16 over Lielvārde.'

Komarov noted that the President looked angry at this news and he knew just why. Although a veteran of Soviet times, so by no means a state-of-the-art aircraft, the Frogfoot was a highly capable machine and they could ill afford to lose any this early in the game.

'Tell me the American was shot down.'

'No, Vladimir Vladimirovich. He got away.'

'Two of our best fighters for none of theirs. You told me that our planes were every bit as good as theirs . . .'

'They are, Vladimir Vladimirovich. But when planes are matched it comes down to the individual skills and war-fighting experience of the pilots. This man is an ace and—'

'You know him?' the President demanded.

'Our people intercepted his radio transmissions. We believe he is the same pilot that knocked down our plane over Donbass—'

The President held up his hand for silence and turned to look over the War Room below, the only sign of his anger the whiteness of his knuckles as his hands gripped the wooden balustrade.

Calmed, he turned. 'The next time I hear about this pilot you will report his death. Whether in the air or in his bed, I don't care which, or how. See to it.' He glared at his generals, not expecting a reply. 'With regard to our infantry losses, I suppose that was foreseeable. These Latvians are no better than German peasants and never learn when they are beaten. Make sure it's kept quiet and ensure the bodies are returned to their families in the usual way. That will keep the mothers of the soldiers off my back . . . And, if you want to keep your post,' he pointed at the Defence Minister, who blushed with embarrassment, 'you'll be sure of *all* your facts before you next open your mouth.'

Komarov knew exactly what the President was referring to. Just as during the Soviet fighting in Afghanistan, after the invasion of Ukraine, the bodies of soldiers killed in action had been returned to their families with no ceremony; in cheap plywood coffins dumped outside their apartments in the middle of the night to avoid any adverse publicity. The families were told to put up and shut up or face the consequences. Not for Russia the mawkish, morale-sapping practice of western countries: the Fallen returning with ceremony in flag-draped coffins and reported on by TV crews.

During this ill-tempered exchange Filatov had held back, but was now almost hopping from one foot to another, like a child desperate to interrupt a conversation. Finally, judging that the worst of the President's temper was dissipated, he summoned up the courage and burst out, 'Excuse me, Vladimir Vladimirovitch. Forgive me for interrupting, but I failed to give you a key detail about the damage done to the opposition.'

The President, who had turned about to walk to the War Room, stopped suddenly. 'Tell me more, General,' he asked, his voice like ice.

'The other news just in is that two Su-25 Scorpions sank two NATO ships in Riga Harbour, tied up alongside,' Filatov announced, not sure whether to smile at the good news or keep his face grave, in case the President was not happy with this unexpected development. 'The aircraft had orders to sink Latvian Navy ships, but initial battle-damage reports indicate that they were British and German.'

Komarov saw the Foreign Minister stiffen beside the President. 'Vladimir Vladimirovitch, so much for your policy of divide and rule that you ordered me to pursue among the NATO allies,' he said, with the smooth sarcasm of a diplomat presented with the most egregious example of military incompetence. 'It would be difficult to think of anything more likely to get Germany to sign up to Article Five than sinking one of her naval vessels. And to compound it, sinking a British ship as well is almost unbelievable. At one stroke the all-conquering Russian Air Force has effectively united NATO against us.

Congratulations, Mikhail Nikolayevich.' He looked derisively at the Chief of the Russian General Staff, who glared back at him in fury.

The President turned to Gareyev in a rage. 'I want a full report on why this happened on my desk tonight. And, if this is true, the Commander-in-Chief of the Air Force is not only relieved of his command, but he's to be in Lefortovo Prison within the next hour. Is that clear?'

Gareyev wanted to point out that at 20,000 feet identification was not straightforward, but he also knew that the FSB had told the Air Force that the NATO ships were due in port, so he could do nothing but nod his head. 'It will be done, Vladimir Vladimirovich,' he said.

'Right.' The President turned abruptly and walked towards the War Cabinet room. 'Enough about Latvia and the Air Force's efforts to unite NATO against me. I want an update on the other Baltic states and likely reactions from the Americans and NATO.'

Once seated at the cabinet table, a series of staff officers briefed the President in detail on the success of operations in Estonia and Lithuania, both now effectively under Russian control after a series of lightning strikes by airborne forces, now being backed up by amphibious landings by the Baltic Fleet on the coast of Estonia.

'And now, Viktor Anatolyevich,' said the President, turning to his deputy, 'it's over to you to reintegrate them into Russia. I want a referendum held in each country within ten days. The question you put to them is simple: do they, or do they not, want to become part of the Russian Federation. Meanwhile, their armed forces are to be disbanded. Russian speakers must, of course, stay and are to be the basis of their new security forces. Any – and that includes Russian speakers – not prepared to swear the oath of allegiance to me as President are to be deported to the gulags.'

'With pleasure, Vladimir Vladimirovich,' the urbane former Ambassador to NATO replied with a smirk. 'The result will be a foregone conclusion. As Comrade Stalin used to say: "It's not the voting that counts. It's the counting that counts".'

The President ignored the attempt at humour and turned to Merkulov, head of the intelligence service, the FSB. 'What should we expect America's next move to be, Lavrentiy Pavlovich?'

Komarov could see Merkulov choose his words with care. After all, he was known for owing his survival and promotion both in the KGB and the FSB to his well-judged ability to think ahead and, above all, to avoid boxing himself into a corner.

'With their military losses in Latvia, America is now probably locked in, like it or not, Vladimir Vladimirovich,' he replied. 'The new President, Turner Dillon, is a relatively unknown quantity, but the character picture we have been building up suggests she will be cautious about committing herself any further. Although she was very critical about Obama's foreign policy weakness during the election campaign, the reality is that America has never regained the face lost when Obama stepped back from his so-called red line over chemical weapons in Syria, or when you checkmated him, again in Syria two years ago, by attacking American-backed rebel forces and so helped stabilise Assad's position. That was the moment for America to show its resolve and face us down. They did nothing except complain. However, as with any unknown quantity, and as we both know from harsh experience, Vladimir Vladimirovich, Dillon may yet surprise us. She already has with her decision to send those troops to Latvia. A foolish decision, but an unexpected one nevertheless. And one, I fear, with consequences . . .'

The President looked troubled, but Komarov knew he was too reliant on Merkulov's unwavering loyalty, and that of his feared FSB, to press him further. 'What about NATO . . . Now that we've sunk two NATO ships?'

'On the face of it, Vladimir Vladimirovich, these sinkings are indeed unfortunate. It is now as certain as it can be that Germany will sign up to Article Five and be joined by the other wobblers, particularly France, which usually follows Germany. UK has been weak and irresolute in its foreign policy under Prime Minister Spencer for some years now, but it is likely that the sinking of a British ship will force him to present a bold front. As for Greece, it remains dependent on German support to underwrite its loans, so the Greeks probably feel obliged to follow Germany. Much as they hate it, they cannot afford not to. Nevertheless, let me reassure you. You have completely wrong-footed NATO and demonstrated conclusively the Alliance's failure to take the necessary measures to defend the Baltic states. The simple fact is that, even if all the nations now agree on Article Five, you are in complete possession of the Baltic states. NATO can do nothing except invade and they are hardly likely to risk a general war in Europe to do that. Even if they had the forces, which they do not. You have effectively outmanoeuvred them.'

Merkulov looked at the President, who nodded back for him to continue. And he did not disappoint. 'The reality is that by letting us take the Baltics without intervening to stop us when they clearly had the chance, NATO has effectively ceased to exist as a military alliance. It has lost three member states and cannot recover them. NATO has been put to the test and failed.'

The President reflected for a moment and then smiled, baring his teeth. He looked around at his advisors before striking the table with his fist. This was his moment to show that he was a man of both will and destiny.

'The way ahead is clear.' He looked at his Foreign Minister. 'Yevgeney Sergeyevich, you are to continue to work away at the minor nations of the Alliance to wean them away from

American influence; to divide and rule, make sure they do not rediscover their balls. But at the same time, remember that there is only one principle of war which matters. And that is concentration of force. You are to make it *very* clear to America and NATO through your diplomatic channels that any attempt to recapture the Baltic states will be judged an attack on Russia. An attack on Russia will invite the *most* extreme response. Never forget, America is a bully and, like all bullies, will back off when confronted. There is only one way to deal with America . . . and that is to show strength.'

'Meaning?' Everyone knew precisely what the President meant, but the donnish Foreign Minister wanted to hear him say it in front of everyone.

The President looked around the room again, clearly aware of the enormity of what he had just been asked. Then, eyes cold, voice deadpan and betraying no hint of emotion or stress, he replied, 'I am ready to use tactical nuclear weapons, exactly as we have practised in all our recent exercises, in order to stop any counter-attack by NATO. What I like to call nuclear "de-escalation", because it is the surest way to get the West to step back from the brink of a nuclear exchange. And there is no way America will risk the destruction of Europe or its own cities by replying in kind.'

The room was silent. Komarov looked at the faces around the table. No-one dared show any emotion, but even he, who had rehearsed this moment with the President earlier that morning, felt the sense of occasion at the President's carefully considered words. It was one thing to integrate the use of nuclear weapons into every aspect of military doctrine. It was quite another to hear the President unambiguously risk nuclear Armageddon and the eradication of life in Europe.

'And another thing,' continued the President, 'I judge that one more hard, knockout blow will force our adversaries back into their corner and leave us master of the battlefield. So, whether it is against America or another NATO nation, if the opportunity presents itself, you are to seize it. A few western deaths now will save many deaths in the future.' He turned to Gareyev, the Chief of the Russian General Staff, as he said this.

The general sat formally to attention, arms rigid by his sides, before responding. 'Yes, Vladimir Vladimirovich. This is a sound military doctrine. We must seize our opportunity when we are presented with it.'

At that moment a staff officer came in, spoke quietly to Gareyev and placed a piece of paper in front of him. He read it and gave a small smile.

The President raised his eyebrows. 'Tell us, Mikhail Nikolayevich . . .'

'Vladimir Vladimirovich, the new British super carrier, *Queen Elizabeth*, is preparing to leave Portsmouth. She will sail east up the English Channel with an amphibious task force. Our information is that she will be heading for the Baltic Sea. The task force is unsupported by maritime patrol aircraft and has woefully inadequate anti-submarine protection.'

The President grinned wolfishly and stood up.

'Watch them carefully and keep me updated. This may be our opportunity.'

'I SEE THERE ARE no objections,' concluded NATO Secretary General Kostilek, looking round the North Atlantic Council table as he concluded yet another session called to consider the declaration of Article 5 in support of the Baltic states, the third meeting that day.

'The communiqué we have agreed activating Article Five in defence of the Baltic states will be released shortly. This has been a difficult process and I congratulate all members on the considered and statesmanlike way you have finally reached agreement, but in the face of the outrageous aggression against our Baltic states members, together with the direct attacks on the US Air Force in Latvia and the sinking of *Eckernförde* and *Padstow*, I would have expected no less. The Alliance now faces the test of conflict. While we have reached agreement on the fundamental principle of collective defence, that unity is now about to be tested as it has never been tested before. In the dark days which will no doubt lie ahead, I ask you all to remember that Alliance cohesion is the source of our strength and therefore critical to the successful resolution of this crisis. Not only will the survival of NATO depend on it, but peace in Europe will never be achieved without a strong alliance. Only if we remain resolutely united, will we liberate those member states whose sovereignty has been so brutally abused by the aggression of Russia. Our purpose is clear: the expulsion of Russia from the Baltic states.'

General Sir David McKinlay, sitting in the VTC room in the CCOMC from where he had taken part in the NAC, leaned back in his chair and watched on the screen as Kostilek stood up and left the chamber, followed by SACEUR, Admiral Max Howard. *At last,* he thought, *common sense has prevailed.*

Major General Skip Williams, the hawk-faced American Deputy Chief of Staff Operations at SHAPE, looked at McKinlay.

'Too bad they couldn't have reached that conclusion a week ago, Sir.'

'Aye, Skip. And the tragedy is that it took our two ships to be sunk and a lot of American, German and British lives lost before they could get their act together,' replied McKinlay, relapsing into his broadest Falkirk accent. As a proud member of the Naval Service, he felt deeply for the sailors who had been lost in the air attack on Riga.

He stood up, wincing as his weight bore down on the stump of his amputated leg. When he was tired, as he was now, the dull ache of the phantom pains always seemed worse. This was no time for feeling sorry for himself, though. 'It's too late to help the Baltics . . . and God alone knows how we'll ever push the Russians out. But at least the Russians haven't prevailed over the wobblers in NATO – as no doubt they've been trying to do behind our backs. They overplayed their hand. That simple. If they'd contented themselves with only attacking local forces, the usual suspects would have had the perfect excuse to stay out. But even the Germans are angry and that really is saying something. I can imagine the President kicking a few butts in Moscow,' he said, with a grim smile.

Group Captain Jamie Swinton appeared at his elbow. 'The

Force Generation team are in your office now, Sir. And Lorna's fixed you a brew.'

Shortly afterwards, McKinlay, mug of tea in hand, looked around his conference table at the team. Headed up by Colonel Fritz Hansen, a former panzer battalion commander of the Bundeswehr, the multinational team of Norwegians, Americans, Italians and British was responsible for the detailed engagement with the member nations to deliver the forces required for NATO operations.

I couldn't ask for a better bunch, McKinlay thought to himself. But NATO could only be as good as the nations wanted it to be and too often the political rhetoric did not match the military reality.

'It's looking really bad, Sir,' said Hansen, getting straight to the point. 'We're struggling with the Very High Readiness Joint Task Force. The lead battalion group is some way from being ready to deploy. Hardly surprising since it's a composite battalion of three different nations and they have never trained together properly. As well as that, the British tell me that most of the reserves they depend on are some way off being ready.'

He looked at McKinlay and shrugged his shoulders in regret. McKinlay knew how much he would hate having to say such a thing. Criticising another nation in public was a no-go area in multinational, hypersensitive NATO. But right now he was having to censure his own boss's nation, even if McKinlay was a NATO, rather than a British commander. But Hansen was a good man and said it regardless and McKinlay respected him for it.

Hansen was right: what sort of cake-and-arse party was this? NATO's much-vaunted VJTF, established with a great fanfare at the NATO Summit in Wales in September 2014, was proving to be a political fudge rather than a credible military force. It now looked as if it was going to fail at the first hurdle because, while nations had delegated command and control to SACEUR immediately Article 5 was declared, the time it would take to deploy the force meant it would not be ready for at least another twenty-eight days. Not only that, Britain was so dependent on reservists after the catastrophic Defence Review of 2010 that the sinews of the force, particularly command elements and logistics units, were incapable of rapid deployment.

'I can't say I'm surprised, Fritz,' he said, letting him know that he was not offended by his comment. 'I know from my own experience that it takes weeks, if not months, to get a reservist called up and processed, let alone trained to a suitable level to fight alongside a regular, and that is time we just do not have. And don't get me going on our inability to recruit even half enough reservists in the first place. Anyway, why don't you run through the gaps and where we are with the NATO Response Force preparations? We reduced its readiness to move four days ago. It should be pretty much ready to deploy . . . So, how quickly can we deploy those forty thousand troops "anywhere in the world", as the Alliance has told the world it can do?' McKinlay's voice was now heavy with irony. Everyone in the room knew full well that these 40,000 troops were pure fantasy.

Hansen gave a small smile. 'First, the good news. The maritime component of the NRF, NATO Response Force – that's five frigates and destroyers, one each from Portugal, Canada, Norway and two from France – is currently on an exercise in the eastern Mediterranean. It'll take them eight days to steam to the Baltic. They've put some valuable training time under their belts and they're good to go. Tom has also heard some more good news.' Here he looked at the Royal Navy Commander, who was part of his team of force generators.

'That's right, Sir,' continued Tom Black, recently captain of a Royal Navy Type 23 frigate and now a key player in Hansen's team. 'The UK is deploying an amphibious task group to the Baltic led by our new carrier, *Queen Elizabeth*. It's expected to deploy on Wednesday. That means it could link up with the NRF maritime component in due course. If the UK is prepared to wait for it to catch up, that is.'

'Why would they wait?' asked the Turkish Air Force lieutenant colonel, who had recently joined his team from an operational tour on the Syrian border. He spoke excellent English, unlike his Greek army counterpart, who had so far refused to even accept his arrival. The two men from the traditionally belligerent countries were continuing, in customary NATO style, to score points off each other at every opportunity.

'Good question, Erol. Explain please, Tom.'

'Simple. Command and control. For starters, the NRF is commanded by a French admiral, who happens to be senior to the British admiral on *Queen Elizabeth*. That means there will be questions to sort out about who will command the Task Group when it joins up. Call that one wrong and you can imagine how that will play with the Brits . . . or the French for that matter.' Black shrugged his shoulders.

The others in the room nodded back in understanding. Anyone who had spent any time at NATO knew that, with certain nations at least, the needs of the 'flags to post' plot – which nation had which generals in which job – frequently meant messy compromises that made little operational sense.

'The bigger problem, though, is that we need a command-and-control structure in the Baltic as NATO maritime forces arrive and come on-line up there, and STRIKFORNATO – Naval Striking and Support Forces NATO – is the obvious HQ to send. *Queen Elizabeth* may not have its designated fighters on deck, maritime-patrol aircraft, or enough naval escorts running dedicated, integrated defence, but that does not mean there are no NATO assets right on hand in the Baltic. Because there are. Plenty of them. Aircraft out of Germany, Poland and Denmark – to say nothing of our partners, Sweden and Finland.

The same for anti-sub maritime-patrol aircraft and naval escorts. The Baltic is a positive hive of NATO activity at this very moment. But unless *Queen Elizabeth*, or a NATO HQ, is getting and controlling all that information they are sending back, and in real time, it is uncoordinated and may count for little.'

Now it was the Greek logistics lieutenant colonel who looked confused, although whether it was lack of understanding of the English language, or naval tactics, McKinlay could not be sure. But instead of getting angry, McKinlay reined himself in. With Greece so unexpectedly falling into line behind Germany and signing up for Article 5, he was going to have to be extra diplomatic and keep the Greeks well on side. The time-honoured NATO 'two-step' – the time-and-energy sapping diplomatic waltz, anathema to a fighting soldier like him – was just beginning.

'The point is this.' He held up his hand to Black to show he would explain. 'Only a headquarters can properly control information and order action. So, if a German maritime aircraft or a Danish frigate detects a Russian submarine in the area, they will report it back to their own national headquarters. That information should then find its way to the *Queen Elizabeth* and other NATO shipping, but,' he shrugged for effect, 'how long will that take? An hour? A day? *Queen Elizabeth* needs that information instantly, if she is to be able to act on it straight away.

'Conversely, if one of *Queen Elizabeth*'s escorts spots a Russian sub anywhere in the area, she needs aircraft up, or escorts over it, to scare it away or sink it. That order will need to be actioned in seconds. At this moment, a request could easily take hours to be received and actioned through the different national head-quarters, by which time it will be too late. There's no point in having all the depth charges and missiles in the world, if they are pointing in the wrong direction, or not ready to fire when they are needed, where they're needed. So the answer is simple: all maritime assets need to be under NATO command and that includes the *Queen Elizabeth* Task Group.'

The Greek nodded his understanding, while the Turk shook his head in mock bewilderment that he had even needed something so basic explaining to him. Heads were going to need to be cracked together, McKinlay decided, as he waved to Fritz to continue.

'The bad news is that the land component is in trouble. As you'll recall, Sir, we had serious problems filling the gaps in the force structure at the recent Global Force Generation Conference back in March.'

McKinlay nodded. He remembered that tortuous conference only too well.

'The nations have not forgotten you being very blunt, Sir,' added Hansen. 'You were very clear that if the NRF was to be credible as a NATO reserve, the nations would have to step up to the mark with properly trained forces . . .'

'Right.' McKinlay could see where the colonel was going with this and interrupted him. 'There's no point in crying over spilt milk. Take me through the detail. I want to know the status of each unit, the nation concerned, and what we need to do about it. I'll then talk to the Defence Chiefs of the nations facing the biggest challenges and brief SACEUR so that he understands the art of the possible.'

Two hours later, after an exhaustive session with his staff and a couple of difficult telephone conversations with the Defence Chiefs of France and Spain, McKinlay was sitting in SACEUR's palatial office. Both men could not help but keep glancing at the silent CNN picture on the flat-screen TV, set between the multiple books arranged in shelves next to it. It was showing shots of Russian troops setting up road blocks in the cities of the Baltic states.

McKinlay came to the point. 'Bad news first, SACEUR. The land element of the NRF is not fit for purpose. As you know, NATO is meant to be able to deploy forty thousand all-up, with the lead element being the VJTF brigade of five thousand. But, that's awa' wi' th' fairies.' He momentarily relapsed into Scots in his irritation. 'We can't even deploy five thousand from the VJTF, let alone forty thousand from the follow-up NRF and, for a change, it's not the force generation which is the problem; it's moving units across Europe and into position.'

'I'm not sure I'm following you on this one, Dave.'

'We're seeing the unintended consequences of closing internal European borders as a result of the migrant crisis. To give you an idea . . . The VJTF is running into all sorts of problems moving equipment and ammunition across borders. For example, I'm hearing that it could take up to fifteen days to get the diplomatic clearances to move ammunition from Germany into Poland, all the result of efforts to counter jihadi terrorists moving freely about Europe after the Paris attacks. More than that, we've just heard that the Albanian and Croatian units, which are inbound from the Balkans, are stuck on the Hungarian border, because the border police are are not letting them cross as a result of the measures put in place to control refugees.'

SACEUR now nodded, but looked angry. The failure of the EU and NATO to work together as a result of the politics of the eastern Mediterranean never failed to irritate him.

'Anyway, I've talked to Frontex, the EU agency responsible for coordinating border management, but it's been next to useless. To cap it all, the Turks are vetoing any parallel work with the EU because Cyprus was admitted to the EU without resolution of the issue of Turkish-occupied North Cyprus. Conclusion: we're not going to get anything quickly and some not at all. The Russians may have done a brilliant job of forcing the shirkers into agreeing Article Five by sinking the two NATO ships and slaughtering the US Air Force detachment at Lielvārde, but be under no illusions, putting their names to an agreement and actually sending forces to fight the Russians are two very different matters.'

Admiral Max Howard rubbed his chin reflectively. 'Hmm, from what you've just told me, I'm not sure we'd want some of them anyway . . .'

McKinlay nodded his agreement. 'Exactly. A brigade made up of fourteen nations who've never trained together properly is a pretty flaky force to put into a fight.'

'OK, Dave, let's look on the bright side,' SACEUR continued. 'I'm not sure we're in the business of fast reaction with land forces anyway. As you say, it's too late to save the Baltics. The President has won this round. But we are in the business of pulling in the allies to demonstrate our readiness to respond to any more aggression. Stop them heading for, say, Poland. All we've got at the moment is maritime forces and even then, although Article Five has been declared, some nations will have to go to their parliaments before they can ratify it.' Howard was clearly referring, obliquely, to the British prime minister's dependence on the support of the House of Commons, while in Germany the Bundestag and Constitutional Court would doubtless demand to have their say.

McKinlay watched SACEUR look out of the window, as he considered the gravity of the situation that he faced as NATO's strategic commander. Decision made, he turned to face him again.

'Dave, I'm thinking about my enemy . . . about the President, holed up in the Kremlin, surrounded by his small clique of advisors, paranoid about an attack from NATO. He thinks he can control the dynamic of what he has started. He believes, and the others will be telling him, that now that he's got the Baltics he'll be able to hunker down . . . that the threat of his S400 and nuclear Iskander missiles in Kaliningrad is more than enough to ensure we won't dare to try to recover the Baltic states.'

'He might hunker down, which would be the clever thing to do,' responded McKinlay. 'But, just like Hitler, he may think it was too easy and that may encourage him to keep going while he can.'

'Good analogy, Dave. Hitler initially had no intentions of occupying France or planning an invasion of Britain, but when it came to it, he found it much easier than he'd expected. Then he realised that if he inflicted a crushing defeat on his enemies, they'd never be able to come back at him. The President is not only paranoid with his fear of NATO, but he's also paranoid because he knows that the only way he'll leave the Kremlin is feet first . . . either as a result of old age, or with a bullet in the back of his head. If he's to make it the former, he's got to stay in power, come what may, and that means he's got to keep going. If he's found it so easy to take the Baltics, what is to stop him marching into Warsaw? Or even Berlin? He's making the age-old mistake of thinking that war has a logic and that he can control it. But no-one can control the dynamic of war once Pandora's box is open. He'd have done well to have studied Clausewitz.'

McKinlay, recalling his Commandant's paper on Carl von Clausewitz at Camberley, quoted from the Prussian philosopher of war: 'War has its own grammar, but not its own logic.' Then he added, 'And he's also forgotten that strategy has a human dimension.'

'That'll be our opportunity, Dave,' continued Howard. 'In his quest for dominion. What do the Russians call it . . . *Derzhava*. He's failed to take account of the reality of war; that there will always be completely unexpected turns of events that mean his intention to settle for one thing will become unrealistic and he'll have to settle for something else. He thinks he can apply his professed A2/AD – anti-access/area denial – strategy to lock us out of the Baltics. But he's not thought through the second- and third-order implications of that. Not least the fact that people in the Baltics won't settle for it. And it's my guess that most of the Russian speakers there will be outraged by what he's done and join the opposition. They may have been getting hot under the collar with the internal politics of some of what was going on over there. But that's the very point. It's politics, and when push comes to shove, I'll wager they much prefer living in an imperfect Western democracy than under the President's boot. Look at the numbers of Russian-speaking Ukrainians who've been fighting the Russians there.'

Admiral Howard nodded to himself as he spoke, the Ivy League professor considering an intriguing hypothesis. 'That'll be our opportunity. We'll find a way to unlock the door rather than try and bash it down. And I'll tell you right now, my thinking is that we should start considering an attack somewhere other than the Baltics . . . like Kaliningrad. That's what he'll least expect. And that's the way to ensure that the President's hubris turns inexorably to nemesis.'

McKinlay nodded. He was also instinctively in favour of getting onto the front foot with offensive action, and Kaliningrad, the old, East Prussian port city on the eastern Baltic – once called Königsberg and now a tiny Russian territorial enclave, sandwiched between Lithuania and Poland – was a tempting target, particularly if the Russians became bogged down in the Baltics. Indeed, Kaliningrad was the key to the Baltics.

'I like that idea, SACEUR,' said McKinlay, 'and you'll remember that when we war-gamed a Russian attack on the Baltic states, we concluded that the most effective NATO response was to kick the Russians hard between the legs in Kaliningrad. Losing a bit of Russian territory will make the President look very stupid. If we can do that, we might just persuade him to pull out of the Baltics. Rather than go head to head against the Russians and almost certainly start a nuclear war, it would be much better to look for the indirect approach

. . . and it could offer the politicians the option of a land swap down the line.'

Howard nodded in agreement and McKinlay continued, 'The good news is that the maritime element of the NRF is in a position to respond. We're only talking about five frigates and destroyers and they're in the Mediterranean, so it'll take eight days to get to the Baltic. On top of that, the Brits are getting *Queen Elizabeth* and an amphibious task group ready to deploy to the Baltic.'

'Now that's more like it!' Howard was instantly enthused. 'That will tie in well. If the Brits wait for the NATO force to arrive, we'll have a useful package. It would be even better if they came together and waited for the US. We've got a carrier group based on the *Theodore Roosevelt* heading across from Norfolk, Virginia. They'll be off Copenhagen by the first of June. 6th Fleet is making best speed from the Red Sea and will be on station in the southern Baltic by the fifth of June.'

'OK, Sir. Are you happy to give the executive order to get them moving? As for an attack on Kaliningrad, we'd better get the staff thinking about it right now, even though it will take time to put sufficient forces together. I'll talk to the Chief of Staff and ask him to start framing the problem.'

'Go for it, Dave. Do it now.'

0440 hours, Friday, 26 May 2017
Somewhere in the forest, Gauja National Park, Latvia

MORLAND STRETCHED HIS cramped legs and wiggled his toes in his boots in an attempt to get the blood circulating in his chilled feet. He was lying prone under a camouflaged waterproof poncho, which covered his shallow trench overlooking a track that led down the slope to a rickety hunter's footbridge over the River Gauja. Another poncho beneath him gave minimal protection from the damp and cold seeping from the earth up into his body. He lay behind a Latvian 7.62 General Purpose Machine Gun – known universally as the GPMG, or more familiarly as the 'gimpy'. It was Belgian-made, but exactly the same weapon Morland had been trained on as a cadet at Sandhurst and still, after fifty years, the main British infantry section heavy machine gun. The GMPG was made ready with the first round of a belt of 200 in the breach. The remainder of the belt was coiled neatly on the poncho to the left of the gun.

Just like being on stag, on sentry duty, back in the forest blocks at Sennybridge in Wales, he thought. *Only difference is, it's not raining . . . yet.*

Normally he would have a number two beside him to feed the belt smoothly into the breach – they might be fearsome bits of kit, but they were also temperamental and prone to

238

jamming, if not operated correctly – but right now Morland was alone. He was on guard while the rest of the team slept in the bunker behind him. He liked taking the last stag before dawn 'stand to'. It meant he was awake before the rest of his team and able to think through and reflect on what the day ahead would bring. It had been bitter overnight, but around him the forest was coming to life. The dawn chorus of song-birds was sounding as the first grey light began to filter through the fresh green of the new leaf cover. In front of him, the river tumbled over stones into pools of clear water. A red deer stag grazed on the far side of the river, blissfully unaware of his presence.

However, try as he might, he could not expunge from his mind's eye the blinding flash and roar as HMS *Padstow* had been blown apart five days earlier. Since then events seemed to have gone into uncontrolled overdrive. During the drive to Ādaži, Krauja remained silent at the wheel, stunned by the violence she had witnessed and the probable death of her brother at Riga Airport, but staying focused and determined as she drove the Toyota at speed through Riga and back to the Latvian Special Tasks Unit training camp. They had arrived not a moment too soon, as the Latvians were preparing to deploy into the forest; going underground to fight. Ādaži would be a key military target for the Russians as soon as they were established in Riga. They had to get out and fast.

'The rest of the unit is on the border. We've only got twenty guys and we could really use reinforcement – if you're happy to work with us, Tom,' said Major Jānis Krastiņš, the Special Tasks Unit commander. 'Why don't you check back with the UK and then we need to get you kitted out fast. Just tell me what you need.'

They'd set up the satellite link and called PJHQ, who'd agreed Morland's suggestion that he and his team should remain with the Special Tasks Unit. However, they were only to coordinate with the Latvians so as to be able to observe and monitor the situation. Morland was under specific orders to avoid confrontation with the Russians, until it became clear what action NATO was to take. Killing Russians, or being caught or killed himself, might well limit the government's ability to manoeuvre. When he reminded PJHQ of his description of the sinking of *Padstow* and suggested that must change his mission, he was abruptly told to follow orders.

Helping pack away the satellite Morland saw that, at this stage, no-one back in the UK had the first idea as to how to react to the Russian attack. But the situation was stark to him; he and his team were trapped in Latvia, *Padstow* had been sunk, and like it or not, the UK was at war with Russia and that was that – even if they had not realised it yet. He'd do what he was told and lie low, but if the opportunity came to have a crack at the Russians, he would grab it. Meanwhile, Morland was to set up a twice-weekly prearranged radio 'sked' to brief back and to receive orders.

It had not taken long to prepare themselves. Their bergen rucksacks were already packed with minimal personal kit. The Latvians gave the team a spare GPMG to supplement their SA80 rifles and as much ammunition as they wanted from the armoury. The rest was already being driven off to be buried in the forests.

Their Inmarsat satellite system was too heavy and bulky for a patrol moving fast and light, so the Latvians gave them a spare Harris secure manpack radio. Not only would it enable them to talk to the Latvians in the forest, but its satellite capability would also allow them to link up securely with PJHQ in the UK. Bradley, the team signaller, spent half an hour with the Latvians testing it, checked he could speak to PJQH and pronounced himself more than satisfied, but with one concern.

'What about batteries, Sir?' he asked. 'Where are we going to get a replen?'

Major Krastiņš reassured him. 'Don't worry, we've been preparing for this. We'll be using an old Forest Brothers bunker as our safe haven. It's deep in the forest and it's been well stocked with batteries, ammunition, rations and everything we might need for a prolonged stay.'

Morland had heard about the Forest Brothers while they'd been training the Special Tasks Unit; it was the name for the thousands of partisans who had taken to the massive forests of the Baltic states to fight a guerrilla war against the Soviet occupation of their countries from the late 1940s, well into the 1950s. Unbelievably, the last Forest Brother had only emerged from the forest in 1995, a full four years after Latvia had gained its independence from the Soviet Union. A fact that had at first astonished Morland who, up until then, had thought it was only the Japanese who had a monopoly on fanatical soldiers refusing to accept defeat. However, his all-too-brief time training the Latvian Special Tasks Unit already had him rethinking that assumption. He would not want these people as his enemy.

Meanwhile, Krauja went outside to call her office on her mobile phone to explain what had happened. She returned looking visibly upset.

'They've given me clearance to stay with you, Tom . . . but things are really bad in Riga. The Russians have taken over all the key buildings; there are Russian army road blocks on all the main junctions. They've declared a curfew after six p.m., they say they'll shoot anyone found outside after that time, and they've started to round up all the ministers and senior government figures. They've taken my boss, Juris Bērziņš.'

'That's bad,' said Morland awkwardly. 'He's a good man.' He waited a respectful moment before asking about General Balderis, an impressive man who had left a lasting impression on him.

'Last heard of fighting at his Joint HQ . . . apparently nobody got out. If anyone resists they're not taking prisoners. He told me he had no intention of ending up in Siberia and it sounds as if he won't be . . . ,' Krauja paused and took a deep breath, getting her emotions back under control. 'Now give me a rifle. I'm a Nordic skier and I do the biathlon. I hunt boar and deer with my father, so I can shoot straight.'

Soon they were ready and the team had set out from Ādaži in civilian vehicles, alone or in pairs to avoid attracting undue attention. Not long after, they had turned off the main road at Sigulda, with its attractive, white clapboard, wooden church and houses. Here they headed on forest tracks to Ligatne, site of a former Soviet command bunker built deep in the forest, where they hid their vehicles so they were impossible to see from the air and difficult to see from the ground, unless, that is, you as good as walked into one. Thereafter, it was bergens on, and into the trees. Led by a Special Tasks Unit soldier who knew the forest intimately, they had finally, after several gruelling hours, stopped in a clearing deep in the thickest part of the forest, close to the Gauja river. Ahead of them was a well-camouflaged entrance.

'Welcome to your new home, Tom,' said Krastiņš cheerfully. 'This is one of the Forest Brothers' lairs. The Russians never found it and not even the locals know about it.'

Morland lowered his bergen and took a swig from his water bottle. 'How're you doing, Marina? Feet alright?'

Krauja looked at him. 'I'm fine Tom, thanks. I'll walk you off your feet before this is over.'

Krastiņš overheard the exchange and laughed. 'She will, you know. As will the rest of my team. I told them to go easy with you during training . . .'

Morland looked round. All the Latvians were smiling.

He grinned back. It was a good start. The Latvians were joshing with them, which meant they were willing to accept them as part of their team.

The next couple of days passed quickly. A routine was established in the well-stocked bunker. To avoid giving away their position, radio transmissions were limited to prearranged data-burst skeds only, conducted some distance away and never from the same spot; otherwise the Russians would locate them in no time. They listened in to Latvian State Radio, LVRTC, from which they were able to build up a picture of the Russian occupation. Standing patrols of a couple of soldiers were established around the bunker as close protection and regular foot patrols went further out every day to check for any sign of Russian activity. At night, sentries were posted covering potential approaches to the bunker and patrols brought in. They all took their turn on stag.

Morland, lying in his shell scrape, looked at his watch. Dawn 'stand to' had just finished and the day routine was about to begin. He crawled from under his poncho with the GPMG and returned to the bunker.

Inside, it was warm, dry and comfortable and reminded him of Badger's den from *Wind in the Willows*. The steps descended into an underground room. One side wall was taken up by a large map of Latvia, a table and radios; another by a table, upon which sat a two-ringed, camping-gas cooker. A low door led to another room lined by bunks. A generator hummed quietly, providing power to run an air-conditioning system, the radios and a battery charger. In another cramped space off the bunk-room were a chemical toilet and metal camp basin.

Twenty yards across the clearing in the forest was a second bunker set up as a store facility. One room was lined with shelves on which were stacked Latvian Army 24-hour ration packs, batteries, ammunition, claymore mines and explosives. A second, bigger room contained Stinger hand-held SAMs, old Carl Gustav anti-tank weapons with their still highly effective HEAT ammunition, and six motocross motorbikes together with fuel and spares.

All very comfy, but it's not going to win the war, thought Morland, *we've got to find a way to get the Russians onto the back foot. I'm not going to hang around here indefinitely playing Hansel and Gretel.*

Sergeant Danny Wild handed him a mug of tea. Morland took a sip. It was strong and sweetened, Latvian-style, with honey. 'Thanks sarge, just what was needed. It was getting pretty chilly out there.'

'Brad's just received a message by data burst from PJHQ,' said Wild quietly. 'They've picked up SigInt and from Russian soldiers tweeting that a senior Russian general and an unnamed high-profile VIP could be flying into Riga by helicopter in the next couple of days. They want to talk to you at greater length.'

'Let's run it past these guys,' replied Morland, moving over to where Krastiņš and Krauja were conferring urgently in Latvian.

Krauja turned to Morland. 'The Russians have announced on Latvian State Radio that any partisans hiding in the forest will be treated as traitors, uniform or no uniform, and shot. They've promised to trawl through the forests and flush out any guerrillas.'

'That's hardly a surprise,' said Morland. Then he explained what Bradley had just picked up from PJHQ and that they wanted a longer conversation. 'We'll need to get at least twenty kilometres away from here, as they'll zero in on our broadcast location once we start talking. That will be followed by an air strike, probably followed by a company of paras within about thirty to forty minutes. Although they won't know what we're saying as it is encrypted.'

'That might give us just the opportunity we're looking for. To hit them hard and where they least expect it,' Krauja said, with a steely look in her eye.

Krastiņš joined in. 'We can use your call, Tom, as a come-on and set up an anti-aircraft ambush. We've got the Stingers here in the store and I've been itching to use them.'

'Who knows, this may even create an opportunity to have a go at this high-profile VIP,' added Krauja.

'A perfect come-on,' Morland said. He knew all about come-ons from his training and had listened to the veterans of Iraq and Afghanistan describe how everything the enemy did had to be viewed as a possible come-on; the initial incident being the lure to draw you in for the main attack. And, of course, as far as the Russians were concerned, he and the Forest Brothers were no more than terrorists. Which meant he had to start thinking like one, if he was going to survive. Krastiņš was right, once the Russians realised it was an encrypted trans-mission, they'd have to investigate and in this terrain, that had to mean by air.

'OK, Jānis, we've got a sked, a pre-planned radio call, in six hours, so we need to get moving. Where do you suggest we do it from?'

'Let's get close to Ligatne, the old Soviet underground command bunker where we left our vehicles. That's bound to wind up the Russians. No-one knows the forest tracks here better than my guys. Your team can ride pillion. Let's go.'

Later, after a short but exhilarating high-speed motocross journey along forest tracks, on the backs of six high-performance bikes ridden by the Latvian Special Forces, Morland, Krauja and the team, together with two Stinger anti-aircraft missile launchers, were in all-round defence in a harbour area, five kilometres from the old underground bunker at Ligatne. Bradley had set up the Harris Falcon satellite link to PJHQ.

Morland slipped the headset over his ears and adjusted the throat microphone, then had a sudden thought.

'What's my call sign, Brad?' he asked the giant Kiwi.

'Penda One, boss.'

'Who the hell's Penda?' asked Morland.

'Come on, boss. You should know. He was a seventh-century king of the Mercians. A real heathen bastard,' grinned Bradley.

Morland had no time to reply for, at that moment, he heard the voice of Lieutenant Colonel Nicholas Graham, the PJHQ

Baltic team leader, in his ears, punctuated by the regular background bleep indicating that the transmission was secure.

'Penda One, this is Zero, radio check, over.'

'Penda One, send, over.'

No time was wasted. After receiving Morland's updated situation report, Graham said: 'Critical information. I have GCHQ liaison officer Allenby sitting with me now. She reports that GCHQ are intercepting comms between the Kremlin and Russia Today TV. Senior Russian general expected in Riga accompanied by mega-important VIP, identity as yet unknown, within next twelve hours. Russia Today will film visit live. Number Ten looking for some sort of spectacular attack as retaliation for sinking of *Padstow*. Over.'

'Penda One, Roger.' Morland was momentarily nonplussed by what he was being asked to do. However, with Allenby at the other end of the transmission and perhaps behind the interception, he did not want to sound hesitant. Then he pushed any thought of her to one side and focused on the task he was being given. 'I'm well established with the Latvian Forest Brothers. We are using this sked as a come-on to attract Russian air assets into the area. We'll hit them with an anti-aircraft ambush.'

'Zero, Roger,' said Graham. 'However, we need you out of there ASAP as this senior general and VVIP are now your priority targets. A spectacular, live on Russian TV, will send a message to the Russians and encourage everyone in the Baltics that they are not getting it all their own way. This is now your only mission. Confirm, over.'

'Penda One, Roger,' replied Morland. 'But we'll need a lot more information and very quickly if we are to be able to mount any sort of attack in this timeframe. We are a couple of hours' travel time from Riga at best and with no hold-ups. Our information is that Riga is currently very high risk as mass round-ups are being conducted.'

'Zero, wait out,' said Graham.

About three minutes later, PJHQ were back on air. 'Intercepts indicate that general and VVIP will visit forward positions with film crews. That may present a better opportunity if they come to your area. Over.'

'Penda One, Roger. Pass to GCHQ liaison officer that we need any useful info the moment she gets it, if we are to be able to act on it in time. Over.'

'Zero, Roger,' came back Graham's voice. 'We'll send data burst to alert you to the need for next call. Meanwhile, we'll continue to work on the interception link. Over.'

'Penda One. Roger, out.' And that was it. PJHQ, Graham and Allenby had disappeared again.

Quickly the radio was packed up, motorbikes mounted, and the team left for the rendezvous point some five kilometres away. Meanwhile, about one kilometre from the ambush site, two teams peeled off on their motorcycles. Krastiņš had calculated that, if the Russians did attack the transmission location, they were likely to use the tracks into the Soviet bunker as a convenient fly line. Accordingly the two Stinger teams, each of two Special Forces soldiers, were placed on either side of the most likely fly line for the Russian Hind attack helicopters. As ordered, the rest of them drove on. If this went wrong, there was no point in them all being killed or captured.

Afterwards, Morland still found it difficult to believe how quickly the Russians had arrived. Thirty-five minutes later, he picked up the distant noise of helicopter engines. And then the sound of explosions, as what had to be Mi-24 Hind gunships opened fire on the empty forest from where he had made the call to PJHQ. 80-millimetre rockets snaked from weapon stations mounted on their stub wings and pulverised the trees, while 23-millimetre, nose-mounted cannons hosed down what the Russians doubtless thought was a Forest Brother hideout.

Morland looked at Krauja. 'Well, that much has gone to plan.'

A few moments later there was a lull in the Russian attack, almost as if the helicopters had either run out of ammunition, or were closing in to inspect the damage. Next instant there was a sharp crack, followed by a stream of smoke as a Stinger anti-aircraft missile rose into the sky in the far distance. It must have latched on to a Hind because there was a fireball above the tree line, followed a good couple of seconds later by a dull thump. And then silence.

'Now the Russians are going to really get stuck in. They're going to flood the area with troops. Definitely time for us to thin out,' said Krauja tersely.

The Stinger teams appeared at the RV shortly afterwards and, a couple of hours later, after another crazy motorbike ride through the forest on a different and very much longer route, in case they were somehow being tailed or monitored, they were back in the hidden bunker. As they entered, Krastiņš greeted them. 'Mission accomplished. Well done. Losing a Hind to a Stinger will bring back unhappy memories of the Mujahedeen in Afghanistan in the 1980s. As expected, the Russians came back pretty quickly and gave Ligatne a good malleting.'

He stopped and looked troubled. 'The bad news is that we've also picked up that a National Guard contingent, which was hiding out in the forest nearby, was attracted in by the shooting and caught the full force of Russian revenge. The Russians will think they were responsible, so that's probably let us off the hook. However . . . those poor bastards . . .'

There was silence in the bunker. All knew that when the Russians exacted revenge, they did so with total ferocity.

There was a cough and Morland looked round to see that Bradley, the New Zealander, had entered the bunker unnoticed. For a big man, he moved with the agility of a gymnast.

'Boss, I've just picked up another data-burst transmission from PJHQ.'

The informal greeting in public like this was usually frowned upon in the Mercians, but somehow, here in the forest, it didn't seem to matter. However, still shocked by what he had just heard, Morland was not in the mood for pleasantries. 'And?'

'Message reads: GCHQ intercept of email from Russia Today states that Commander Western Military District accompanied by unnamed VVIP – possibly even the President – to visit Ligatne, site of recent success against Latvian insurgents. TV crews to be in position for arrival 270930 local May. VVIP party expected 271000 local May.'

'Got him!' said Krauja, her fists clenched. 'That's the President coming to gloat over the murder of another bunch of Latvians. If it's him, they'll want TV shots of him at the front line on Russia Today. Probably waving a rifle. They want to broadcast Russia's victory to the world. Fucking bastards . . .'

Nobody said anything, while Krauja recovered from her outburst. She paused and then continued, her voice calmer. 'Great work by your friend at GCHQ, Tom. The Russian General Staff forbid any use of email by their soldiers in case it's hacked. But I'm guessing they've been caught out by their obsession with favourable propaganda, as Russia Today only use email, text and mobiles. All easily hackable. Appropriate somehow.'

'Right,' said Krastiņš, interrupting. 'That's 0930 tomorrow morning. We need to get to work. We've got to make a plan, give orders, rehearse, and infiltrate into position before first light.'

He spoke in Latvian to a Special Forces sergeant in the bunker. Then he turned to Morland. 'Let's meet in thirty minutes to start planning. We'll need all the good ideas you can muster. And we need your people giving us any updates they can as to what the Russians are planning.'

The rest of the day passed in a maelstrom of planning, orders and rehearsals. The Mercian team, together with Krauja, Krastiņš and the Stinger teams, were to infiltrate back through the forest to set up another anti-helicopter ambush. Krastiņš was emphatic that the aim was not to kill the VVIP or Commander Western Military District, no matter how tempting.

'If he's killed, he'll become a martyr to the cause of glorious Russia,' explained Krastiņš. 'Much better to humiliate him on TV. We'll shoot down another helicopter and we've got to try to make sure he's in the picture when it happens. Failing that, we'll blow something up behind him and in camera shot. That way they won't be able to edit it out. It'll go viral in seconds and he'll be humiliated in Russia. What's more, we'll have demonstrated that we can pick and choose what we do to him and that will encourage our people to keep resisting. This is all about perception and not actual sabotage.'

The sentiment was fully endorsed by PJHQ when Morland backbriefed them on the plan via the planned sked, followed by a direct order from the PM that neither the President nor the General were to be targeted.

The PM and CDS are doubtless terrified of a Russian revenge attack, Morland thought to himself. Left to his own devices and in the mood he was in, he would have given it to the President or whoever, and with both barrels. But Krastiņš was probably right. It was said that the President was almost a pussy-cat compared to other more extreme nationalists lurking and manipulating well out of the media limelight. A dead martyr President, killed live on TV, might bring them to the fore and that would be a catastrophe.

By dawn the next morning, the ambush was set. Four Latvian Special Forces Stinger teams, two men wearing night vision goggles to each motorbike, had infiltrated through the forest close to Ligatne during the night. They had taken up positions in a circle around the base, one team at each point of the compass. They were under strict instructions to leave the troop-carrying Mi-8 Hip helicopters to fly into Ligatne unmolested, as it seemed logical that the VVIP party and TV crews would arrive that way. Targeting members of the press, even by accident, was not their intention and would backfire badly. Their task was to shoot down one of the distinctive Mi-24 Hind gunships, which were bound to fly continuous protective top cover while the VVIP was being interviewed on the ground below. Knock down one or more of those Hinds and there had to be a very good chance it would be in full view of at least one TV crew, and that would be a PR coup worth risking their lives for. Certainly, the Forest Brother ambush crews thought so.

Morland and his team had crawled in close to support the Stinger teams by setting up an ambush; to cover the teams' escape route if they were pursued as they bugged out after the missiles had been fired. Morland was now lying in the prone position with his SA80 rifle made ready next to him. He reflected on the plan and, as he had first thought, it was about as high risk as it could be. But it would also be about as spectacular as it could be, *if* they could pull it off. Anyway, there was no point worrying. The ambush was set and it would be up to training and chance now. Once the Stinger teams fired on the top-cover attack Hinds, there was bound to be instant retribution from the latter, but the plan needed the TV crews to keep filming the mayhem – as any half-competent cameraman would, given this would be the scoop of a lifetime. Then, as it was most probably being filmed live, the shots would go viral within seconds. And as a fall-back, there were bound to be people there with mobiles filming the scene. In fact, given modern technology, they'd be very unlucky not to get some live film of the ambush from somewhere.

In a perfect world, they'd get two or three helos down and the Russians running around in panic, focusing on protecting the VIPs, while they slipped away to the ERV – the emergency rendezvous point.

He looked left and right at his team's ambush position. They'd rehearsed their drills until everyone knew their tasks and positions instinctively. Krauja lay five metres away, equally watchful behind her borrowed Latvian Army–issue G36 assault rifle, face smeared with black-and-green stripes of cam cream, blonde hair tied back. The remainder of the team was in position on either side of him, ready to hit any Russians coming up the narrow forest path to their front. Archer was cut off. Watson was on Morland's right with, beyond him, Bradley behind the GPMG, covering the ambush killing area right in front of them. Wild lay further along, ready to initiate the claymore anti-personnel mines and turn the track into a mass of high-velocity ball-bearings. They were all linked by their personal radios, but in the event of the inevitable confusion and any loss of comms, the signal to bug out to the ERV was the firing of a red Schermuly flare by Watson. Morland noted that it now lay beside him, prepped and ready to fire.

All too slowly, the hands on his watch moved towards H Hour. And then, at 0920, he heard the sound of multiple helicopters from the west, the direction of Riga. *That'll be the first troop-carrying choppers with the TV crews and their Hind escorts*, he thought to himself. *They'll need to set up before the VIPs arrive.* Then he felt the pit of his stomach tighten with nerves. *This is unreal . . . it can't be happening to me*, and he knew at that moment what fear was.

'Get a grip, Mr Morland,' he heard Colour Sergeant Carty of the Welsh Guards, his old instructor at Sandhurst, say. 'Just think what the others are thinking.'

Meanwhile, above him, the first Mi-24 Hind gunship flew overhead as it started to fly circuits as top cover. They can't possibly see us down here, he told himself, so keep focused and be ready for a clearance patrol on the ground. If the Russians are any good, they'll have them everywhere.

Then his watch showed ten o'clock and he heard the deeper, slower noise of a pair of Mi-8s. *That'll be him*, thought Morland, *it won't be long before he lands now.*

The next five minutes seemed to last an hour and still the Mi-24s circled. Then they pulled in tighter to Ligatne, leaving them undisturbed. That had to mean the VVIP was on the ground and the gunships were now providing close-in top cover.

Another ten minutes passed. Just as Morland was beginning to wonder if the fact that the Mi-24s had closed in on the VIPs meant the operation had somehow been compromised, there was the unmistakable crack of a Stinger, followed by a second. Through the canopy above him Morland saw two flashes of light, followed by two snaking smoke trails. He lost sight of the heat-seeking missiles, but there was no doubt about the two loud explosions.

'Splash two Hinds . . . Yes. Got the bastards!' Morland wanted to punch the air in triumph.

0830 hours, Saturday, 27 May 2017
10 Downing Street, Whitehall, London

FOURTEEN HUNDRED MILES away in the PM's 'den' in Number 10, Trev Walker sat with the Prime Minister, William Spencer, in front of a TV carrying breaking BBC News reporting on a live link, helpfully subtitled into English, from Russia Today. They watched as the President landed by helicopter at a bunker-like building at Ligatne, deep in the Latvian forests. Escorted by the burly, jowly Commander of Western Military District, the two men walked over to where the bodies of the Latvian so-called terrorists responsible for shooting down a Russian Mi-24 Hind were on display.

Neither man said anything as the camera panned along the bodies, laid out in a row, a selection of the weapons that they had been captured with piled up behind them.

Then the camera switched to the President, who eyed them coldly, unmoved by the twisted, bloodied corpses.

For a moment, Walker thought he was going to kick one of them to display his contempt. If he had intended to, the President controlled himself and instead, he prepared to speak to the film crews; eyes narrowed, face furious.

Next moment there were two loud explosions in the sky behind the President. As if hypnotised, the live feed from the TV cameras first found and then focused on the two fireballs and then began to track the pieces of burning helicopter as they fell to the ground.

Then the camera turned back to the President, as if looking for his reaction to the shock attack that had just taken place above them.

What they filmed instead was the natural reaction of close-protection officers anywhere. Two beefy bodyguards leapt on the President, pushing him to the ground, before covering him with their bodies to protect him as best they could.

The camera continued to run and it was as if the world stood still for long seconds. Soldiers cocked their assault rifles and turned, ready to repulse an attack that failed to come; journalists lay on the ground, in the mud, unsure what to do next. Finally, pistols still cocked and ready, the bodyguards got up, followed by a furious President; now covered with mud and swearing at them, pushing one of them away, as he still tried to do his duty and shield him with his body.

Walker looked at the Prime Minister with a huge grin on his face. 'You've done it, PM. You've bloody pulled it off . . . Congratulations.'

The Prime Minister smiled back. 'We have, haven't we? That'll show that bastard who is boss. Now, let's see how the media react . . .'

Meanwhile, Walker and Spencer watched, first in astonishment and then in growing amusement as the mud-splattered, angry President continued to shout and swear at his protectors on live TV, before screaming at the camera to stop filming. It took almost a minute before terrified aides led him off towards a waiting armoured vehicle and out of camera shot.

Instead of stopping, the camera turned back to the humiliation and horror of two helicopters burning in the forest behind them, smoke rising from their funeral pyres and the sound of ammunition cooking off in the intense heat, making it sound as if there was an intense firefight taking place among the trees.

'Well, PM,' said Walker finally. 'You asked for a spectacular and you certainly got one. What do you think? A Military Cross for our man in charge out there? Or perhaps even a Conspicuous Gallantry Cross. That would cheer everyone up and show them that Britain means business.'

'I thought the idea was not to let the Russians know we were behind this, Trev. Remember what they did to Litvinenko? He'll get his gong, but we'll keep it well under wraps. I'll tell you what, though. I'll have another chat to the Americans. Ask what they have done to stop the Russians lately.'

THE REPEATED CLANG of the electronic bell, with the disem-
bodied voice announcing, 'This is not a drill. This is not
a drill. General Quarters. General Quarters. All hands man
your battle stations. All hands man your battle stations,' sounded
over the carrier's PA system. Unless already in position, the
men and women of the ship's crew immediately stopped whatever they were doing and moved swiftly to their designated
action stations. Commander James Bush RN, Executive Officer
of HMS *Queen Elizabeth*, stood on the bridge, receiving calls
from each department as it reported ready for action, and took
keen note of how the crew were making themselves ready for
war. *Getting better*, he thought to himself grudgingly, *but I'm
not giving these buggers an inch. There's still a long way to go before
this crew is as slick as it needs to be.*

Three days out from Portsmouth and *Queen Elizabeth* had
passed through the narrow confines of the Skagerrak, entered
the Baltic, and was now twenty-five nautical miles north of the
Polish port of Świnoujście, the port of Szczecin, situated just
east of the German border to their south. Once out of the
English Channel, the order had come from the Prime Minister
to sail into the Baltic Sea, where the Amphibious Task Force
was to poise off shore to demonstrate UK resolve, before linking

up with the five frigates and destroyers of the NATO Response Force Maritime Component; themselves inbound from the eastern Mediterranean, but not expected in the Baltic for several days yet. Once they were all together, he would feel a lot less concerned.

Usually the most positive of men, Bush nevertheless thought back to the warning from his old shipmate Executive Warrant Officer Geordie Rae, before they had left Portsmouth. HMS *Kent*, the Type 23 anti-submarine frigate, had in fact defied expectations and lasted a full day after rounding North Foreland, but, ordered to take part in a high-speed anti-submarine drill, had broken down and been forced to limp back to Portsmouth for a new generator and a replacement for its shattered propeller shaft. That left the Task Group with only her sister ship, HMS *Lancaster*, as an anti-submarine escort.

The chickens are really coming home to roost, thought Bush. When will the MOD bean counters ever get the message that running ships beyond their sell-by date makes no sense, operationally or financially. He was reminded of Admiral Beattie's bitter comment at Jutland in 1916: 'There seems to be something wrong with our bloody ships today.'

Yes, they had HMS *Astute*, the hunter-killer submarine, operating independently ahead of the Task Group, but she was probably sneaking around off the coast of Kaliningrad – two hundred nautical miles to the east – keeping an eye on what was coming out of Baltiysk, the main base of Russia's Baltic Sea Fleet. That left only one anti-sub escort covering the whole Task Group, which was taking one hell of a gamble, like placing all your chips on one number at roulette, and Bush was not a betting man. That said, he had to assume that the politicians, advised by the spooks and the admirals, knew what they were doing.

Queen Elizabeth was at the very western end of the Baltic, enough to show a presence but not to show aggression. And, he had to admit, ever since the Russians had grabbed the Baltic states they had gone quiet. Like a python swallowing a pig, they were now trying to digest their meal. And it was a very angry pig indeed. Reports said that the invaders were having to deploy ever greater quantities of men and materiel to control the enraged populations of the Baltic states. These Baltic nations had anticipated the problem and planned accordingly. Fearing just this invasion, the Baltics had pre-stocked forest hideouts with sophisticated weaponry. And, it transpired, they were not only extremely well trained and quick to learn, but the vast forests of their homelands were giving them plenty of places to hide.

TV news bulletins – and the Russians were rapidly discovering the hard way that if you opted for TV propaganda then you could not necessarily control the story – were reporting with admiration how effective the guerrillas were: most single shots resulted in a dead or injured Russian. Moreover, Russian helicopters, forced to fly low over the forests to stand any chance of spotting or pursuing guerrilla fighters, were taking one hell of a hammering from surface-to-air missiles. Even back in Russia, excepting state-controlled media, there were already parallels being drawn with the bloody horror of Chechnya.

Finally, to add insult to injury, there had been the very public humiliation of the President, who had arrived to triumph over his dead enemies and, doubtless, warn of what was to come to those who resisted. Instead, the world had watched on live TV as he shouted and swore at his guards, while burning helicopters fell from the sky behind him.

Bush allowed himself a grim smile at that thought. Yesterday, seeing a bunch of sailors leaning over an iPad and laughing, he had gone to investigate. They had shown him how some wag had superimposed the screaming President's curses as recorded on live TV –dubbed in English – over the picture of Hitler ranting in the bunker from the film *Downfall*. Apparently the spoof had gone viral and multilingual. Even as Bush laughed and then told the sailors to get back to work, it had struck him how it made a refreshing change from incessant images of the President as all-conquering warrior and sportsman.

In fact, and just as important, even serious TV journalists and commentators were now suggesting that the President's very public humiliation might have been the moment that the Baltics started to fight back. First they had laughed. Then they began to take heart. Although Bush doubted the President saw the joke. He could well imagine that the President – not a man known for his sense of humour – now had a score to settle with those who had carried out the attack.

While he was delighted that things were not all going the Russians' way in the Baltics, his overriding concern remained the *Queen Elizabeth* and her lack of dedicated escorts. He had voiced that issue to the Captain back in Portsmouth. He had listened and told him to get on with it. Now, like any sailor under orders, he was reconciled to having to put up and shut up. These few ships were all the Navy had been able to deploy at short notice to accompany the Task Group. No amount of worrying was going to magic up new escort ships and subs, let alone air cover from maritime patrol aircraft, in the next couple of days.

Certainly, there was no shortage of friendly assets in the vicinity but, as an ex-Warfare officer himself, he knew there was a massive difference in having a British Nimrod aircraft – scrapped by the last government – flying top cover and was able, at the push of a radio pressel 'send' switch, to instantly update the Captain in the Command Centre as to the location of any enemy assets; as opposed to the veteran, but nevertheless very capable, German maritime patrol Lockheed P-3C Orion aircraft, which had waggled its wings at them as it flew past half an hour ago, but was still not able to communicate securely with the *Queen Elizabeth*.

Help, however, was sailing towards them. It would be another couple of days before NATO was able to take command of the operation and the Amphibious Task Group became integrated into a coherent force with the five frigates and destroyers of the NATO Response Force Maritime Component. Meanwhile, he hoped that the Russians were fully preoccupied trying to subdue the Baltics and did not need to further antagonise NATO by having a poke at them. The last thing they needed was to be stalked by a Kilo Class submarine – their highly capable and very quiet diesel-electric attack boat, optimised for anti-shipping and anti-submarine operations in relatively shallow waters like these.

If that were not enough, today had brought a brand new problem. The Admiral was commanding the Task Group from his flagship, *Queen Elizabeth*. He had ordered them to carry out a practice amphibious landing on the Griefswalder Bodden, the sheltered bay between the island of Ruggen and the north German coastline. This would not only be a useful work-up for the Task Group, which was still learning to operate with the new carrier, but would allow for plenty of media pictures of tough-looking Royal Marines dashing ashore across pristine sandy beaches. The politicians believed that would send a message to the Russians that Britain meant business.

The Admiral's plan was straightforward. The amphibious ship *Bulwark* would close in on the coastline, protected by a pair of escort ships operating as a team: the state-of-the-art Type 45 anti-aircraft destroyer *Dauntless*, and the remaining Type 23 anti-submarine frigate, *Lancaster*. Meanwhile, the carrier would remain out at sea, together with the anti-aircraft destroyer *Daring*, acting as picket ship, forward defence, and the two Royal Fleet Auxiliary logistic support ships, which provided first line supplies – and the *Queen Elizabeth*'s greedy gas turbines would need refuelling every two days to keep the tanks topped up.

The Task Group commander faced a classic dilemma, similar

to that faced by Admiral Sandy Woodward while retaking the Falklands: how to protect his all-important carrier, while at the same time protecting his amphibious force as it closed with the land. The commander had gone for a trade-off, protecting his amphibious ship with the only pair of escorts he could muster, and standing out at sea; thus improving the radar picture, which got ever more cluttered the closer to land a ship got. To reduce the vulnerability of the carrier from a submarine attack, he had the remaining Type 45 destroyer *Daring*, which was principally a state-of-the-art anti-aircraft platform, but still had a credible anti-submarine capability with its sonar and Merlin helicopter.

Finally, far out in the eastern Baltic, HMS *Astute*, the hunter-killer sub, was searching for any movement of the Russian Baltic Fleet by conducting a continuous all-sensor underwater search. Occasionally she would stick up her periscope to suck in the electronic picture, all the while being ready to attack any submarine posing a threat to the Task Group. The trouble was, as Bush knew all too well, the Task Group really needed more killer subs, to say nothing of additional escorts. The sea, even at the western, 'friendly' edge of the Baltic, was a very big space and a well-operated enemy submarine a very small object.

On top of this, to be conducting a demonstration amphibious landing when the Royal Navy was at war with Russia – because that is what he understood by Britain signing up to Article 5 – offended Bush's common sense. Close with the enemy in the finest Nelsonian traditions by all means, or stay well back and out of trouble until you are ready to take the fight to them. But do not 'poise' and present a target for no clear strategic gain.

On the flight deck below, Bush watched the organised chaos as men, guns and equipment of the Commando Artillery Regiment and the Commando engineers cross-decked to the amphibious ship in order to take part in the landing. Brightly coloured figures, jackets coloured and coded according to their role on the flight deck, controlled and guided Merlin troop carriers as other long lines of commandos in full battle gear, laden with bergens, body armour and all the paraphernalia of war, stood patiently on the elevators, waiting to be called forward to board them. Larger, twin-rotored Chinooks hovered low as they picked up guns and Viking lightly armoured tracked vehicles and transported them forward to the beaches. Film crews filmed it all and, to the watching world, this was a magnificent projection of Royal Navy sea power by the pride of its battle fleet.

Clad in white flash hood and gloves, he stepped into the darkened calm of the Ops Room, the nerve centre of the ship. It was here that the ship's radars and the weapons systems that protected the ship were operated from; kept separate from the flight operations, which were conducted from the control tower, as on any airfield. As Bush's eyes adjusted to the low light, he saw banks of computers manned by masked operators, on whom the blue light from radar screens and other monitors cast an eerie glow.

In the centre of the Ops Room stood the tall figure of Commodore Tony Narborough, the ship's captain, flanked by his Principal Weapons Officer, the conductor of the complex orchestra that defended the ship.

'Hello, Number One. We've got a bit of a flap on,' said Narborough, trying to appear calm. '*Daring* has just signalled that she's picked up a sonar trace. Possibly a Kilo.'

'Any indication of the direction she's heading in, Sir?' asked Bush, his voice muffled by the flash hood everyone wore when at 'action stations' to reduce the risk of the catastrophic burns that, after drowning, were the greatest risk in warships.

'Looks like she's heading in the general direction of the Amphib group, to our south,' replied Narborough. *Lancaster* and *Dauntless* are covering the Amphib group with an active sonar search, while *Daring* is covering us to the north.'

'Shouldn't we delay the landing until we've dealt with the sub threat?' suggested Bush.

'Fair point, Number One, but the Admiral's made it clear that the landing exercise goes on. The world is watching and filming and we don't want them to see us turn and run at the first bit of bother. Anyway, the Int boys fully expected the Russians to test our defences, but no-one thinks they are going to actually attack. That said, we'll assume they might, so we've got to be ready for anything. Trouble is, we've yet to get clearance to move from passive to active ROEs – our Rules of Engagement – so, until they change, all we can do right now is monitor, track and observe . . . Unless, of course, we need to apply self-defence.'

While Bush could admire Narborough as a highly competent sea captain, he also knew that he was not a man inclined to question the decision of his immediate superior, lest it impact on his career. That meant, in effect, that while a ship could always move from passive ROE to active in the event of an attack, it would in fact be too late. Once missiles, bombs or torpedoes were heading in their direction, the ROE state was entirely academic. As far as Bush was concerned, given that a Royal Navy ship had already been sunk by the Russians, if any enemy vessel or aircraft came within striking range, then it should be deemed a legitimate target and engaged. And if the situation was so fraught that London deemed it too provocative to go to active ROE, then what on earth were they doing at the entrance of the Russians' backyard in the first place?

This, though, was not a sentiment that would endear him to his Captain were he to share it in public. 'Then shouldn't we close up with the amphibs?' Bush asked instead.

'That way we're presenting a nice, neat package for the Russian sub captain. No, Number One, we're staying dispersed. Besides, we're safer in the open sea, as the proximity of land

and shallower water would constrain us and prevent us manoeuvring.' Behind his flash hood, Narborough's voice was sharp, almost petulant.

Bush knew that detection of submarines in shallow water was especially difficult. Moreover, the changing temperature and salinity layers at different depths made detection in the Baltic even more challenging, which meant the submarine had the advantage over them. Narborough knew that every bit as well as he did, so this was not a discussion worth prolonging.

Then the voice of the Principal Warfare Officer rang out urgently in the muted Ops Room: '*Daring* reports possible Kilo Class sub at longitude 54 degrees, 25 minutes, 23.898 seconds north; latitude 14 degrees, 24 minutes, 35.280 seconds East. Contact is bearing 26.75 degrees, distance 10.234 nautical miles.'

'Find out what she's doing about it,' ordered Narborough.

'I've just spoken to her. She's got her Merlin anti-submarine helicopter up, sonar is active and she's searching for it.'

Bush thought quickly. The submerged speed of a Kilo Class was 17 knots. The range of her UGST wake-homing torpedoes, with their 200 kilogram explosive charge, was 22 nautical miles. So the Kilo was already in a position to launch a torpedo at *Queen Elizabeth*. However, if the Russian sub captain was any good, and he would be good, he'd want to get eyes on his target before launching a torpedo; probably within 10,000 yards, or five nautical miles. That meant *Queen Elizabeth* could expect an attack in about thirty-five minutes, if that was the Russian's intent.

How the hell did the sub manage to creep up so close without being spotted? The alarm bells might be sounding in Bush's head, but the answer was blindingly obvious: *We've handed ourselves to him on a plate by not having enough anti-sub escorts!*

He looked at Narborough. In the narrow gap in his white flash mask between nose and forehead, Bush saw a moment of fear in the Captain's pale blue eyes. And then it was gone.

Grabbing a microphone, the Captain spoke urgently to the bridge. 'Officer of the watch, order damage control state One, condition Zulu. Helmsman, commence zigzagging at maximum speed. That'll make it more difficult for him to stay with us. Then slow down at random – down to five knots, which will make it more difficult for him to hear us. Get a Merlin with sonar buoy airborne between us and the sub. Now . . . Number One, I'm staying here to fight the ship. I want you on the bridge.'

'Aye, aye, Sir.' Bush saluted briefly and left the Ops Room at speed.

0935 hours, Saturday, 27 May 2017
Control Room, Kilo Class submarine Krasnokamensk, Baltic Sea

CAPTAIN OF THE Second Rank, Alexander Ivanovich Chernavin of the Russian Navy stood in the cramped, darkened control room of Kilo Class submarine *Krasnokamensk*. To his left, in the confined space, faces illuminated by their plasma screens, was the Ship Control Panel manned by the planesmen, who steered, submerged and surfaced the boat under the close supervision of the Diving Officer of the Watch. Behind them stood the Chief of the Watch. On his right were the sonar operators, who were operating both active and passive sonar. They were keeping a close track of the contact they were following from the sound of its propellers and the noise of its hull as it moved through the water. Beside him stood the Executive Officer, his second in command.

It was warm inside the control room and there was an overriding smell of men's sweat, usual in a submarine that had been at sea for days. In common with all the crew, Chernavin wore blue, flashproof cotton trousers, trainers and a faded, sweat-stained, blue-and-white striped *telnyashka*, the long-sleeved undershirt, a legacy of the Tsarist navy; beloved by the submariners of the Russian Navy and considered the mark of elite forces.

The control room was silent and Chernavin suppressed the adrenalin that coursed through his body. Drilled into him as a submariner at a moment like this was the need to stay ruthlessly calm, to calculate the odds like a mathematician or a five-dimensional chess player. There was no other way, if he and his crew were to first succeed and then survive. In a moment he would chance a look through the smaller attack periscope, but now was the time to compute and anticipate the surface picture, to visualise what was happening on the sea above them and to prioritise what he needed to see. Then, when he raised the periscope above the surface, he would know in advance what he wanted to look at. Minimising the time the periscope poked its tiny head above the waves was the best way of limiting the chance of being spotted by the radars, or the keen eyes of the enemy lookouts.

If he was now hesitating, it was because *Krasnokamensk* was within close torpedo range of something very much larger than anything Chernavin had ever contacted before, even in training against the biggest ships in the Russian fleet. A well-trained Russian submarine sonar operator would usually have added the type and class of ship, perhaps even its name, logged as a result of the detailed data built up over many years of monitoring NATO exercises and studying the specific noise signatures of different ships. But *Queen Elizabeth* was so new on the scene that no-one had yet logged her characteristics.

If I screw up now, the Navy won't forgive me after all the time and effort they've spent on training me.

Chernavin was a realist, a product of his upbringing as the son of an agricultural worker on a collective farm near Moscow. However, for a moment, he felt a sense of destiny. It was as he had read in novels; that everything in his life had somehow been designed to bring him to this point. Chernavin had excelled at school, particularly at mathematics and physics, and been selected for officer training in the Russian Navy in the dark days after the collapse of the Soviet Union. He had first served in the Northern Fleet, when Murmansk had been full of rusting submarine hulks, the detritus of a once-proud navy and a source of shame to those who operated them. However, times had thankfully changed and Russia had rediscovered her pride under the President, under whose personal direction her navy was being re-equipped.

Meanwhile, through persistence, hard work and skill, Chernavin had demonstrated his competence in the black arts of the submariner and been rewarded with the *Krasnokamensk*. After two years in command, she was a tight ship with a well-trained crew and now was his time. He'd monitored many NATO exercises, followed the UK's Trident nuclear submarines close into Faslane – particularly after the demise of Britain's maritime patrol aircraft had allowed the Russian submarine fleet to go where they had never been able to before – but he had never come up against anything like the contact the sonar operator had been tracking for the past hour. It was huge and he knew he had to get eyes on it, however fleetingly.

The nearest he had come to it, sonar and acoustics-wise, were the vast cruise liners so beloved of elderly Westerners. So, before proceeding, he first needed to see his target. He also knew that the golden rule for submariners was 'don't be counter-detected'. If the enemy found *Krasnokamensk*, they would be meat for the crabs, crushed to death by the pressure of multiple underwater explosions as vengeful escort frigates rained down depth charges on them.

But Chernavin was now worrying about those escorts. *Krasnokamensk*'s sonar had indicated that they had come close to a destroyer, almost certainly one of the Royal Navy's new Type 45s, operating a sonar buoy with its anti-submarine helicopter. But they'd dived and applied a sprint-and-drift manoeuvre to give it the slip, running deep at maximum speed of 17 knots for fifteen to twenty minutes before drifting at five knots to minimise the sound of the submarine's engines, in order to throw the British sonar off the trail.

But the enemy escorts had to be near. Any large, capital ship would have them in profusion, particularly the flagship of an amphibious group. In the Russian Navy, it would be deemed criminal negligence to put to sea without proper defence in depth, so the others must be out there somewhere. But there appeared to be nothing.

Surely, it can't be so easy? Chernavin thought to himself. *It must be a trap.*

The orders from HQ Baltic Fleet operations on the last occasion he had surfaced and picked up a radio signal were unambiguous. A British amphibious task group was expected in the western Baltic. He was to get close enough to track it. Furthermore, it was the direction of the President himself, repeated so there could be no mistake, that if the opportunity for a hard, killer blow against the NATO aggressors presented itself, it was his duty to take it. To Chernavin, the President's order could not be clearer: if he had the chance, it was his duty to sink the new British super carrier *Queen Elizabeth*.

The silence in the control room was broken by one of the sonar operators: 'Range of unidentified contact now 10,000 metres. Contact appears to be zigzagging at speed.'

Meanwhile, the monotonous tone of the planesman started to call the depth as the submarine surfaced steadily from its operating depth of 200 metres: 'Fifty, forty, thirty, twenty . . . Approaching periscope depth. Periscope depth . . . Now.'

'Hold her there,' ordered Chernavin. 'Up periscope.' And, leaning down, he grabbed the handles of the periscope as it slid up to him. Before it had even reached knee level he was down, squatting on his haunches, anxious to get his eyes to the viewfinder and so make the most of every precious second to look at the contact.

He was too experienced a submariner to need to waste any

time adjusting his eyes to the lenses of the viewfinder, so he saw her instantly: HMS *Queen Elizabeth*, with her vast deck, the ski jump in the bow and the twin islands on the starboard side. Despite being five nautical miles away, she was magnified by the powerful lenses of the periscope and the great ship seemed to fill the viewfinder.

'Down periscope. Flood torpedo tubes one to three. Stand by to fire,' ordered Chernavin. There was a whoosh as the periscope disappeared into its mast well in the deck of the control room.

Then he turned and looked at his Executive Officer, still standing behind him. 'Confirm visual sighting of British carrier, *Queen Elizabeth*,' Chernavin said.

The Executive Officer stepped forward. 'Up periscope.'

Like his captain, he squatted as it rose so that he could gain maximum time at the viewfinder. A five-second look was enough. 'Down periscope.'

Chernavin looked enquiringly at him.

'Confirmed,' came the response.

The tension in the submarine was touchable. Chernavin took a deep breath and, for a moment, he felt a deep calm as time seemed to stand still. Then the reality of the moment hit him. What he was about to do would go down as an event of the magnitude of the sinking of HMS *Royal Oak*, the pride of the Royal Navy's Home Fleet, by a German U-boat in Scapa Flow in October 1939. Or the sinking of the mighty battleships *Repulse* and *Prince of Wales* by Japanese dive bombers in 1941, an event that changed the course of the war in the Far East. And now, HMS *Queen Elizabeth*, the largest ship ever built for the Royal Navy, was about to join them and he, Captain of the Second Rank, Alexander Ivanovich Chernavin of the Russian Navy, would be the man responsible.

For a moment he paused, keenly aware that he would be sending hundreds of unsuspecting British sailors to a watery grave. A student of history himself, he understood full well that this attack was on the personal order of the President, but against a country that he was not even sure was yet at war with Russia. The British mine countermeasures ship sunk in Riga was different. It had been collateral damage and should not have been there in the first place. This was a deliberate and, some might say, unprovoked attack. Chernavin's indecision was only momentary, though. He looked at his Executive Officer and knew that, if he had wanted to hold off, then he should not have ordered him to confirm it was the British carrier. If he ducked this decision now, the President's wrath would be implacable. He had little doubt he would end up against a wall and his extended family would never see the outside of the Gulag again.

'Bearing three–three–five. Range, nine thousand metres,' chanted the sonar operator, like a Russian Orthodox priest standing by the iconostasis in an incense-filled church.

'Identity confirmed. Stand by to fire,' Chernavin said to his Fire Controller.

Krasnokamensk continued to slide silently under the waves.

'Shoot.'

There was a perceptible thump throughout the submarine as the first torpedo left its tube; a pause, then another, and then a third.

'Torpedoes away . . . Ten degrees down on the planes! Hard a starboard!' ordered Chernavin. 'Take her down to one hundred metres,' he told the planesmen.

The submarine tilted steeply as it dived deep and right to avoid detection. Then, as it stabilised, there was silence again in the control room as they waited for the inevitable.

The sonar operators heard the rapid, rhythmical thud of *Queen Elizabeth*'s giant propellers change note as the torpedoes were spotted and she desperately began to take evasive action.

Too little and too late, Chernavin thought, as the sophisticated torpedoes latched on to their vast, slow turning target. It might evade one, but it stood no chance against three. Chernavin prayed silently. *Let there be no malfunctions*. The consequences of failure were more terrifying than the guilt that would come with success.

Then, audible to every crewmember of the submarine, was a muffled explosion. The first torpedo had struck home. Another pause, then another two explosions.

The sonar operator now chanted the litany of death: 'Explosion . . . Second explosion . . . Third explosion.'

In the earphones of the sonar operators, the thud of *Queen Elizabeth*'s propellers stopped, to be replaced by the screams of collapsing bulkheads.

PART TWO

Recovery

2230 Hours, Friday, 2 June 2017
Prime Minister's Office
House of Commons, London

TREV WALKER KNOCKED on the door of the functional, if cramped, office used by the Prime Minister in the Palace of Westminster and walked in. As he did so, that much-quoted line of Harold Wilson, a former Labour prime minister, came to mind: 'A week is a long time in politics.'

A lot had happened that past week. First had come the dreadful news of the sinking of HMS *Queen Elizabeth*, pride of the Royal Navy. The news had stunned the country, to be followed by an outpouring of anguish and fury, directed first at the Russians who had perpetrated this atrocity. Then, increasingly, at the politicians and top military brass who had allowed this to happen. Nearly 900 men and women, sailors and marine and army commandos – the commandos laden down with bergen rucksacks, body armour and weapons, as they were preparing to disembark – had died in minutes, when the ship went down.

It was a figure beyond the comprehension of a nation that knew only the flag-draped coffins of the comparatively few servicemen and women who had been repatriated from the wars in Afghanistan and Iraq. This was a casualty count not experienced since the Second World War. And for the first time ever, large numbers of young women sailors were included in the list of mass casualties. Nor were there many bodies to mourn. Most were entombed inside the carrier, deep beneath the Baltic Sea.

The Ministry of Defence Press Office had done its best to focus on the many acts of heroism; such as the ship's captain, Commodore Tony Narborough, who had gone down with his ship, and the Executive Officer, Commander James Bush, last seen desperately trying to rescue a young female sailor whose legs had been blown off when the first torpedo exploded under the ship's magazine. But nothing could stem the growing tide of anger felt by a traumatised nation, which gradually mutated into a stubborn determination to fight back and not to take this outrage lying down.

Of course, Walker reflected, it was inevitable that Prime Minister William Spencer, himself in an advanced state of shock, should be subjected to a sustained attack from the media at the state Britain's armed forces had been allowed to fall into under his leadership. It had not helped that the newspapers, with deliberate cruelty and despite Walker's efforts, kept referring to it happening 'on his watch'.

Armchair admirals pilloried his recklessness in dispatching ships into a war zone without adequate protection, especially when it became known that a couple more days would have seen a suitable NATO force arrive in theatre. The same newspapers that first encouraged and then praised his leadership in sending the *Queen Elizabeth* were the ones that most viciously condemned him.

Prime Minister Spencer, ever the consummate politician, had instinctively tried to hang on to power. First to be sacrificed had been Mainwaring, the Chief of Defence Staff and, as head of Britain's demoralised Armed Forces, an obvious and immediate bone to throw to his critics. He had been ignominiously sacked, without the consolation of a peerage, much to his humiliation and the fury of his wife.

However, the Prime Minister's attempt to put the blame on Mainwaring had not been enough to call off the baying hounds of the media and his increasingly outraged and vocal party, which had conveniently forgottten that they had been happy enough to sanction the various defence cuts when it had been their seats at risk in previous elections.

Walker had quickly seen the way the wind was blowing and tried to tell Spencer that resignation was the only honourable way out. But to no avail. Instead, recalling Churchill's victory in a confidence debate in the House of Commons in 1942, after the disasters of the fall of Singapore and Tobruk, Spencer had called for a confidence debate, too. Despite an impassioned plea for national unity at this moment of historic crisis, it had, predictably, been a disaster, with one hitherto loyal backbencher after another lining up to condemn the Prime Minister's leadership and call for his resignation.

Back in 'The Den' in Number 10 Downing Street, after the overwhelming vote of no confidence, Walker had rehearsed the traumatised Spencer in the resignation speech he had quickly scribbled for him, before leading the now wet-eyed Prime Minister to face the array of media microphones and TV cameras outside the front door of Number 10. Here, in full view of the world, first pink-faced and finally blubbering like a chastened schoolboy discovered doing something unspeakable, Spencer's glittering political career had ended in tongue-tied humiliation.

Walker, however, was not one to look back, for this was also an opportunity to further his own interests. He had always maintained close links with the Chancellor of the Exchequer, Oliver Little; tough, ruthless, sardonic, but also a masterly political operator, who had been extending his tentacles of influence across Whitehall to take advantage of the day when the Prime Minister eventually stepped down. That day had now come earlier than anticipated. Nevertheless, Walker was quick to see the opportunity to consolidate his own influence by supporting Little's leadership aspirations.

All it had taken was the merest of hints to the editor of the *Sun* and selected others that, while Little had an excellent relationship with the American president, the other leading candidate to take over as PM 'carried no weight in Washington'. Unsurprisingly, given the current crisis, the country needed a prime minister with clout inside the Washington beltway. Therefore, it was Little who had seen the Queen that morning to confirm his appointment as her new Prime Minister and head of Her Majesty's Government. He now sat at his desk; square-shouldered, gruff-voiced and pugnacious, glaring at a clearly unhappy Everage, still Defence Secretary.

'What the hell do you mean there's nothing that we can do to respond?' The Prime Minister was clearly furious; his jaw stuck out obstinately, as his eyes bore into the wilting Defence Secretary. 'Do you mean to tell me that your recommendation to me after the Russians have sunk *Queen Elizabeth*, with the loss of nearly nine hundred sailors and commandos, is that we sit back and do nothing? You cannot be serious!'

'Well, Prime Minister . . .' Everage said ingratiatingly in his Estuary accent. Walker was reminded of Dickens's *David Copperfield* and Uriah Heep, as Everage, hair flopping over his gaunt undertaker's face, wrung his hands together and tried to avoid eye contact with the irate Prime Minister.

There was a knock on the door and Walker went over and half-opened it, irritation at the interruption turning to approval when he saw who it was.

'Sorry to interrupt, Prime Minister,' said Walker, noting the relief on Everage's face at being let off the hook. 'It's the new Chief of the Defence Staff. The police refused to let him in without an escort. He insists on seeing you.'

'Show him in,' the Prime Minister ordered.

Walker fully opened and then stepped away from the door

to allow General Jock Kydd – despite accepting a knighthood from the Queen, he had made it known that he was never to be referred to as 'Sir' – to enter.

A sudden surge of physical energy, like an electric current, filled the room as Kydd stepped forward and looked around, as if checking where any potential threat could come from. Broad-shouldered, slightly hunched, he rocked gently from foot to foot, fists clenched at his sides, like a boxer sizing up his opponent.

Looking at him, Walker couldn't help thinking that the new CDS looked more like a bodyguard in a movie about the Kray brothers than the new, professional head of Britain's Armed Forces. He took in the shaven head, ill-fitting, black off-the-peg suit, white shirt with chest hair poking up above the fastened collar, stringy blue tie, and black, steel-toecapped, 'executive super safety' shoes, bought from the Bodyguard Workwear online shop.

On taking over as Prime Minister, Little had immediately appointed Kydd, whom he had first come across in Afghanistan where he had set up a programme to bring former Taliban into the political process, as his new CDS. Despite his eccentric manner, Little recognised Kydd's qualities and the importance of his evident credibility with the Americans. A phone call to Kydd had brought him out of very recent retirement.

Little dispensed with pleasantries. 'CDS, I am told by the Defence Secretary that there's nothing we can do.'

Kydd was in no mood for pleasantries either. 'Fucking bollocks, Prime Minister,' he growled. 'The shagging war's not over till the general says it is and this fucking general is not saying that. No fucking way.' He looked contemptuously at Everage, who squirmed and writhed like a demented octopus.

Walker rolled his eyes at the Prime Minister and muttered theatrically in Kydd's ear. 'Go easy on the effing and blinding, mate. We've got the point.'

Kydd continued, 'Sorry about the language, boss . . . Where was I? Oh yeah, the Russians may be in the Baltic states, but that doesn't mean we leave them be. There's no point in trying to push them out directly. Much better to whip up the insurgency to make them feel the heat, force them to move as many people and as much stuff in there as possible to try to contain it, and then punch for the jugular; somewhere they least expect it and where it'll hurt the most. Kaliningrad looks good to me . . . and my mate Dave McKinlay, the Deputy SACEUR in NATO, tells me that they've already war-gamed it.'

Walker had never heard of the place, so was glad when the CDS elaborated. 'That's the former East Prussia – Königsberg. It's a small chunk of Russia between Lithuania and Poland, surrounded by NATO territory; Poland to the south and Lithuania to its north. With Lithuania in flames and the Russians fully occupied trying to control the insurrection, that makes it much harder to defend and much more vulnerable to a surprise attack from Poland, the sea or through Lithuania.'

The Prime Minister leaned forward. 'This is more like it. Go on.'

Kydd outlined a possible course of action. The insurgency across the Baltic states was rapidly getting out of control with thousands of men and women now in the forests resisting the Russians, who were discovering they had bitten off very much more than they could easily chew. Britain should support the American lead by providing the support, equipment and training the Baltics needed to enmesh the Russians ever more tightly there. As it was, GCHQ was picking up indications from Russian soldiers on social media and other sources that they were thinning out their garrison in Kaliningrad, in order to reinforce their overstretched troops in Lithuania.

Britain just happened to have a small party of infantrymen working with the Forest Brothers in Latvia, so it might be possible to get eyes on the ground in Kaliningrad. Meanwhile, it was entirely possible for Britain, America and its NATO allies to assemble a force by land, sea and in the air to hit the Russians where it would cause the most trouble for the President with his own people: Russian-owned Kaliningrad.

'Lose Kaliningrad and he'll be seen as a failure and, in Russia, that makes him a dead man walking.'

'How long do you reckon it'll take to assemble the forces and what do we need?' asked the Prime Minister.

'It'll take a good month plus, Prime Minister,' replied Kydd. 'And we're talking about a one-corps, possibly two-corps operation. With three or four divisions on land. Say sixty thousand to eighty thousand personnel, plus a major amphibious effort to put it ashore. I reckon we could pull together a division with the French. The Germans and Poles may be able to combine. If that happened, we'd put it all under the Allied Rapid Reaction Corps. And the Americans have also got 82nd Airborne at immediate notice to move, plus a Marine Expeditionary Force already on its way across the Atlantic. So that's another corps-sized force. We'll need to regain command of the Baltic, but the Americans have got 6th Fleet inbound as well as a substantial air effort.'

Walker could see that the Prime Minister liked what he heard. Little questioned Kydd further. 'It's really important that we have a substantial British effort. After all, we've taken the biggest hit . . . Apart from the Baltics that is—'

'OK, Prime Minister. I get that. But the bottom line is that the Armed Forces are still reeling from the cuts made by the last government.'

'What are you implying?' Everage snarled.

Kydd looked down at him. 'Since you ask, you're more on the hook than anyone,' he said bluntly. Then, eyes boring into the hapless Defence Secretary and entirely forgetting Walker's plea to moderate his language, he added, 'And whichever stupid fucker thought they could cut the regular Army by a third and replace it with reserves needs their fucking head examining.'

The Prime Minister sighed and rolled his eyes. 'OK, CDS. I take the hit. But what could we, should we do now?'

Kydd thought. 'We've still got 20th Armoured Brigade stationed in Germany, which makes it a bloody sight easier to move it to Eastern Europe than a brigade stuck on Salisbury Plain and on the wrong side of the Channel. With a massive effort – and I'm talking wholesale cannibalisation of the rest of the Army – we could give them the manpower, equipment and logistic support to bring them to war establishment . . . That means *proper* fighting strength, not some fucking paper strength.

'And be under no illusions, when I say cannibalisation, I mean just that. Tank regiments without working tanks, artillery regiments without guns. If anything else blows up in the meantime – like a jihadi attack, Paris-style – we are entirely fucked, because that would mean putting soldiers from tank, gunner, helicopter and logistic regiments, as well as the infantry, outside supermarkets, schools and other potential targets right across the nation . . . as the French army has had to do. So all our military eggs, what few working ones we have left, will all be in this one basket.'

The PM looked up, stunned at Kydd's onslaught. 'Are you seriously telling me that it's got this bad, CDS?'

'Yes, and . . .'

'Rubbish,' Everage intervened, a triumphant look on his face. 'We've still got eighty-two thousand in the Army and you're seriously telling us that we're pushed to find a brigade of five thousand men. We've got lots of brigades . . .'

And now Kydd interrupted him in return. 'Every last one of them underequipped and undermanned. To bring them up to full war-fighting establishment we'll have to fill the gaps from across the rest of the Army. Not only that, many units, particularly logistic units – without which no army can fight – are now dependent on reserves. Great people reserves, salt of the earth, but not easily available in the time span we're talking about, and there's lots of gaps in key roles.

'Then there's equipment. Much of our heavy war-fighting kit, the stuff we'll need against the Russians, has been neglected as you've spent the money on the latest kit to fight the insurgencies in Iraq and Afghanistan – a very different type of war. To put heavy equipment into battle – tanks or mobile guns, for example – you need spare engines, generators and a host of other stuff which we don't have in our stores any longer. You lot decided to stop spending money on this boring stuff. But if a tank hasn't got a track pin to hold the track together, a part for the engine, or exactly the right nut to hold the gun in place, then all it's good for is a museum. You certainly cannot take it to war.

'And, finally, logistics. That's about gettting the fuel, bullets, water and everything else that's needed to where you need it. That requires a complex supply system from the factory to the front line. Above all, it has to be robust enough to stand the test of combat. And much of that thinking, capability and understanding had been lost.'

'Stop there, CDS.' It was Little who now interrupted. 'I'm with the Secretary of State on this. Surely we can send at least an army division and the paras as well. The marines, well, of course, now . . .'

'Sir.' Kydd now moderated his tone. 'The Paras are integrating with 82nd Airborne, as I said. Special Forces have, of course, been gearing up from the start. But a combined arms division? No . . .'

He gazed at the ceiling for a moment, thinking hard. 'Let me try to give you an example of what you,' he nodded at Everage, 'have done with your constant and ill-thought-through cost cutting . . . I take it you know what I mean by a Bailey Bridge?'

Both men nodded.

'A genius bit of kit. Invented in the Second World War and still used today. It's like man-sized Meccano. The girders bolt together and each girder is designed to be carried by six men. No more and certainly no less. Now, the bean counters ran a calculator over the Engineers and forced them to lose men. So, now there's only five regular soldiers left to carry each girder and five men are not enough. A few girders maybe, but not a bridge's worth. Worry not, says the chief bean counter to the press and parliament, the sixth will be a reservist and will be there when we need him. But while number six exists on paper, he does not necessarily exist in reality, as he has not been recruited. And even if he has been recruited, he's not going to be there in time for what's happening right now, because there's not been the time to process him and then train him to the level of the rest of the team. Which means that when we need a Bailey Bridge built to get our men across a river and into battle, the engineers cannot physically build it. Five men cannot lift lots and lots of girders designed to be lifted by six.

'So, what does the ever-resourceful Engineer colonel do? Knowing that it could be the genuine difference between life and death that there is a bridge built when and where it is needed, he begs, steals or borrows a number six from another regular unit. But they now have only four men per girder. Multiply that across the Army and you can see why I tell you we've been hollowed out. It *will* take all our resources just to put together one properly constituted, ready-for-war brigade. That will leave us with loads of cannibalised formations that will be good for casualty replacements, but little else.'

'That's the first I've heard of this,' snapped an angry Everage.

'Naturally,' Kydd replied. 'Do you think that a colonel or general is going to tell *you* he cannot build a Bailey Bridge? What do you think would happen? End of career for him for whingeing for starters. Keep protesting, and too loudly, and I wonder. Court martial? Complaining is not the military way. We improvise until we can improvise no longer. And that is where we are now.'

'And why are you whingeing now, General?' Everage's voice dripped sarcasm. 'I only mention it as you've just had the gall to lecture us on what is the military way.'

'Because someone has to tell you. And, if you hadn't noticed, I couldn't care a flying fuck. I'm retired anyway.'

'Enough!' The Prime Minister banged his hand flat on a table. 'Is there *any* good news?'

'Well, Third Division HQ has just done a useful exercise with a French brigade, so with some concentrated work-up training we could form a multinational division of two brigades, with an artillery brigade attached . . . Give me two weeks, Prime Minister, and I'll give you a force you can be proud of . . . But you need to engage right now with NATO Heads of State.'

'What do you need?'

'NATO has nearly three and a half million men and women under arms. That far outnumbers Russia's armed forces. But NATO needs to get its act together and that needs political leadership. Without that, the fucking Russians are going to walk all over us.'

'I'll get on the case,' the Prime Minister answered, looking at Walker who nodded in agreement.

'You're going to need to, Prime Minister,' retorted Kydd. 'I want you to be in no doubt what I'm talking about here. These are troops from different countries, who have never or only rarely trained together. They fire different-sized ammunition from different weapon systems; they've got radios which may or may not talk to one another, and they speak multiple different languages. None of which is exactly clever when you are trying to call down accurate artillery fire, while enemy rounds are killing the men around you, and one mistranslated number might result in a ton of so-called friendly fucking shells landing on you or your mates. There's nothing simple about this and . . .'

'General,' Everage interrupted, seeing his opportunity to defend himself. 'We've listened to you lecture us on our defence cuts, but *you* know perfectly well that NATO agreed to deliver a reinforced Response Force at the Cardiff Summit three years ago. Now you're telling us that you can't deliver what *you* promised.'

Kydd looked Everage up and down before replying. 'Wrong yet again, Secretary of State. You defence ministers sat round a table and then told us lot about the brave new world of multinational force projection and so-called agile fucking forces that you had invented, while you stuffed your faces with lobster and Chateau de Whatever. Who knows, it might even have worked. That is if you hadn't slashed the very forces you promised each other *and* removed the budgets that would have allowed us to train together so we could try to make it work.

'Well, congratulations. We emphatically don't have the forces or working equipment that you will doubtless tell me we have. And we certainly haven't trained for this. So this will be very touch and fucking go. And it's only because of the Americans that it might even be possible to pull it all together . . . and also because I have total respect for our fighting men and women and I believe in the extraordinary things they can achieve when asked to . . .'

Everage wilted for a moment in the face of the CDS's vehemence. Then, ever the politician, he drew a deep breath, ready again to argue his corner.

'I said, enough,' the Prime Minister snapped. 'Point taken, CDS . . . How will the Russians react?'

'That's easy,' replied Kydd. 'They'll threaten to nuke us. For starters, they've got Iskander tactical nukes deployed in Kaliningrad.'

'But haven't they've only got limited range and impact?' countered Little.

'Range, yes. Impact, no. Each one of those tactical nukes is many, many times more powerful than the bombs that flattened Hiroshima and Nagasaki. And you may think that is an acceptable risk sitting out of Iskander range in London,' Kydd gave both men a hard look. 'But if you're Polish, German or Danish, and well within Iskander range, you'd take a very different view. Besides, once tactical nukes start getting flung about, it's a very short step to an exchange of intercontinental ballistic missiles . . . the really big boys. And then it's welcome to Armageddon.'

'But surely, even if we're outmatched conventionally, we've still got Trident?'

'OK, Prime Minister,' sighed Kydd, 'let me take you through this from first principles. You ask what the Russians will do and I'll repeat. They'll do what they've done at the end of every snap exercise they've called recently. Launch an Iskander tactical nuke as what they call a de-escalatory measure to stop us dead in our tracks and stop us counter-attacking.'

'Hardly sounds to me like de-escalation. Surely them firing a nuke will lead to all-out nuclear war?' asked Little.

'That's precisely the point, Prime Minister. It's counter-intuitive . . . the President knows that there's no way you are going to risk the destruction of human life in the UK by launching a Trident at Russia in response to his tactical nuke when, by so doing, you can almost guarantee a retaliatory strike from an intercontinental ballistic missile in return.'

'So, how should we respond? We just have to take it on the chin?'

'Sadly, with the state of our Armed Forces as they are today . . . Yes. That would be my advice. Plenty of people told the last government that to be effective, deterrence needs to be matched at every level, conventional and nuclear. As I've just explained, you can't weaken conventional forces and expect Trident alone to protect you. Conversely, if we did have strong conventional forces, but no Trident, they could easily defeat us by threatening to nuke us and we would have no way of deterring them. By allowing our conventional forces to be run down as they have, our whole defence posture is now dangerously out of balance. When you're up against a ruthless predatory bastard like the President, that means we are now in a very dangerous place.'

'So those billions spent on Trident were a false insurance policy, CDS?'

'You've got it in one, Prime Minister . . . if they weren't matched by money spent on strong conventional forces. If you put all your money into Trident, you either accept defeat or you make mutually assured destruction – or MAD – more, not less, likely. Can you put your hand on your heart and say you'd order the captain of the at-sea Trident boat to launch when you know that, whatever happens, millions upon millions in Britain are going to die? I doubt it. When it gets to that point, you can forget the theology of nuclear deterrence. Second strikes and all that. It becomes a moral issue. Are you going to respond to one apocalyptic war crime with another?'

'You're saying we'd have been better putting our money into conventional defence?'

'Spot on again, Prime Minister, although backed up by Trident; conventional and nuclear deterrence are two sides of the same coin. As I've told you, one needs the other to work properly. But there's more to it than that. It's one thing to have capability, you've also got to communicate your determination to use it. That means telling the world, as your predecessor did, that your army isn't for fighting but is there for humanitarian relief, is not only downright dishonest, it's fucking dangerous. Our enemies have been watching and listening. Wars start when one side thinks the other side is so weak it can get one over it. Which is why we are where we now are . . .'

'So, where does that leave us, CDS?'

'We're going to have to be seriously clever, Prime Minister,' said Kydd, looking sombre. 'Either that or kiss goodbye, not only to the Baltics, but to human civilisation as we know it . . . Which is why, right now, I see a sneak attack on Kaliningrad as the only possible option. You need to speak to President Dillon and the NATO Sec General as soon as possible, if we are to begin to get this show on the road before next Christmas.'

Little looked at Walker. 'Trev, fix that. As soon as you can, please.'

Then he turned to Everage. 'And you're sacked!'

'But, Oliver,' Everage spluttered in indignation. 'You agreed those cuts. You were the one who demanded savings to deal with the deficit. Surely you—'

'Enough,' the Prime Minister interrupted. 'I agree. I did. But that was then and this is now. I've changed my mind, as I'm entitled to. The military clearly have no confidence in you and nor do I. Leave now. Your resignation speech will have to wait as well. CDS and I have got much bigger problems to deal with.'

1900 hours, Saturday, 3 June 2017
The Presidential Dacha
Barvikha, Odintsovsky District of Moscow Oblast

KOMAROV LEANED FORWARD from the bench in the pine-walled banya and ladled more cold water onto the red-hot coals. There was a hiss as a cloud of steam exploded, followed by a throat-catching surge of heat. The President lay stretched out, face down and naked on the towel-draped bench while Komarov, with only a towel wrapped around his waist, picked up a *venik,* the fragrant, leafy bundle of birch twigs, and vigorously worked it up and down the President's back, buttocks and the backs of his legs; the traditional way to boost blood circulation and relieve tension and stress.

'You're not in bad shape for a sixty-three-year-old, Vladimir Vladimirovich.' Even in the banya the usual formalities applied. 'Mind you, given everything that's going on at the moment, Russia needs to you stay fit and strong to lead the country through this war. I'll programme another game on the tennis court next week – plus a couple of sessions on the judo mat.'

The President grunted, sat up and wrapped his towel around his waist. Despite the elation felt throughout the nation at the dramatic sinking of HMS *Queen Elizabeth*, it had not been an easy week, largely due to the humiliation of becoming an international laughing stock. Komarov was pleased to see that the banya and birching had improved the President's mood. He looked at the hour-glass by the door; time for the cold plunge pool.

Thirty minutes later, the President, clad in a white, towel bathrobe, sat in the rest area while his live-in mistress, a thirty-five-year-old, willowy former Olympic gymnastics gold medallist, brought him a glass of *kvass*, the slightly fizzy, sweet-sour, banya recovery drink made from rye bread and flavoured with mint so beloved by Russians. Despite the war in the Baltic states, the declaration of Article 5 by NATO precipitating war with the Alliance, followed by the sinking of the *Queen Elizabeth* in the Baltic, the President's weekend routine in his dacha, forty-five minutes from the Kremlin to the west of Moscow, was sacrosanct. He'd left the Kremlin after lunch, spent a vigorous afternoon on the tennis court with Komarov, and was relaxing before enjoying dinner and the night with his mistress.

First, though, it was time for the President's evening VTC briefing from the National Defence Control Centre, the grandiose, recently completed, neo-Stalinist building from which Russia's war effort was directed. However, in place of Lieutenant General Filatov, who commanded the headquarters and usually gave these briefings, the Tatar features of General Mikhail Gareyev, the Chief of the General Staff, filled the VTC picture. Inset on the right of the screen were the impassive faces of the others in the War Cabinet: the Deputy President, Defence Minister, Foreign Minister and Director of the FSB, all patched in from their various offices in Moscow.

'Where's that general who looks like an Italian hairdresser?' demanded the President.

'Listening in, Vladimir Vladimirovich,' replied Gareyev. 'But I wanted to set the scene before he and his staff brief you in detail.'

Komarov was now concerned. His people were telling him that things were not going well in the Baltics, but the Presidential briefings back in the Kremlin this last week, while certainly not as upbeat as they had been the week before, had down-played any major problems. However, as it was Gareyev giving tonight's briefing, it could only mean he was about to give bad news. First, he was the only one prepared to talk to the President straight and, second, the War Cabinet must have waited for the President to be at his dacha to deliver this news. That must mean they were afraid to tell him in person. At the end of a TV link the President's menace was, inevitably, somewhat diminished.

Even as Gareyev began to speak, Komarov detected from the on-screen body language of his ministers and senior advisors that the President's position was no longer as absolute as it had been only a week before.

Gareyev continued. 'The strategic picture is still favourable and our adversaries in the West are fully aware that any attack on us will result in a nuclear response. To reassure you, Vladimir Vladimirovich, you reduced notice to fire in our operational submarines, five of which are deployed at sea with eighty missiles on board. Each missile has sixteen warheads. That means we have a total of three hundred and twenty sea-launched warheads, each capable of completely destroying a major city. We also have our strategic rocket forces with three hundred and five land-based, intercontinental missiles, carrying a total of one thousand, one hundred and sixty-six warheads. Finally, we have our smaller, battlefield systems, such as Iskander, designed to take out specific military targets, but which will still completely eradicate a small city. They are also on a reduced notice to fire. You can see why we are confident about the strategic picture.

'However . . .' and he paused for obvious effect before delivering what Komarov knew was going to be bad news. 'The situation in the Baltic states has changed and is giving ever more cause for concern.' Then, in the clipped unemotional tones of the professional soldier, Gareyev outlined how the

Baltic states were aflame with the spirit of resistance and the extent to which Russia had underestimated not only the fury and anger their liberation would generate, but also the level of preparation the three countries had undertaken in expectation of an invasion.

Then he confronted the event that had possibly inflamed the spirit of resistance even more than the brutality of the occupation: the President's embarrassment in the forest clearing at Ligatne, where he had been filmed on live TV ranting and raving at his security detachment against a backdrop of Russian helicopters being shot out of the sky in a well-planned aviation ambush.

'We have to recognise, Vladimir Vladimirovich,' continued Gareyev, 'that after the events at Ligatne, our propaganda line that we are in full control of the Baltics is faltering. Even the Russian speakers are coming out against us and many are joining the insurgents in the forest, so it's hardly surprising that our adversaries are able to tell a more compelling story. We need a two-pronged strategy in the Baltic states. While imposing the strictest security, we also need to apply economic and social effects to persuade the majority of the population that they will be better off in the Russian Federation. I believe . . .'

The President held up his hand for Gareyev to stop; he clearly needed to dominate the discussion, not let the general take control as he was beginning to. 'Before you go any further, Mikhail Nikolayevich, any more news on the names of who was responsible for the attacks against me and my soldiers last week?'

'Vladimir Vladimirovich,' replied Gareyev, slipping back into his role of tough but utterly loyal supporter. 'This was almost certainly a detachment of the Latvian Special Operations Forces supported, as you well know, by a small British military team. Our sources in UK are still working on their names, but it is getting ever more difficult for them to operate there. We know these terrorists are in the forests from a number of intercepts. But they're only using data-burst transmissions very sparingly and they change location immediately. There's one hell of a lot of forest out there to hide in.'

Komarov saw the President's neck flush and knew, from the way in which he held his right hand down on the desk with his left, that it was only with the greatest difficulty that the President was able to restrain himself from shouting at the irritatingly confident general, who was now making excuses for his failure to find the perpetrators.

'I want them captured. Is that clear, Mikhail Nikolayevich,' he said, his voice furious. 'I am not prepared to be made a fool of by the British, let alone British Special Forces. Is that clear?'

'We no longer believe these are Special Forces, Vladimir Vladirovich,' continued Gareyev in a measured tone. 'We are informed it is a five-man team of infantry under a captain. They were the only British trainers in Latvia at the time of the liberation and we now know they went into the forest with Latvian Special Forces.'

It would have been bad enough, but just about explainable, if the Presidential humiliation had been at the hands of Britain's elite Special Forces. But for this to have been the work of ordinary soldiers was doubly embarrassing. Komarov noted the other faces on the screen remained totally neutral, for fear of drawing the President's wrath.

'If they're not Special Forces they'll be easy to pick up. I want that captain, preferably alive. In fact—'

Komarov guessed that the tiger was about to bare his fangs and he was not disappointed.

'I am surprised, Mikhail Nikolayevich, that you dare face me and tell me that these ordinary infantry soldiers can attack your President with impunity and, a week later, you have failed to capture them.'

General Gareyev must have realised that he had overplayed

his hand because his tone became conciliatory. 'I agree, Vladimir Vladimirovich. It shall be so and this insult to you cannot stand. I'll put Vronsky, the Spetsnaz major responsible for planning the demonstration in Riga, on the case. He knows the Baltic states and his network is strong. This British captain will be his top priority.'

The President nodded, apparently appeased for the moment.

Gareyev went on to explain that the demands of suppressing the eruption of guerrilla activity across the Baltic states was soaking up Russian military manpower and resources. With estimates of tens of thousands of men and women taking to the forest to fight the Russians as guerrillas – emulating the Forest Brothers' campaigns of the 1950s in Estonia, Latvia and Lithuania – Russian generals were being forced to strip out manpower from other areas. Ukraine, the southern Caucasus and Crimea were being thinned out, but more were needed. Gareyev confronted the issue head on.

'If we are to crush this insurgency, I need every man I can get my hands on deployed across the Baltic states. Right now. These people are naturals at irregular warfare and unless I concentrate effort against them and crush them quickly, our hold on the three Baltic countries will be jeopardised. Every success just encourages them to think they can win, and pulls in more recruits . . .' Gareyev looked back at the President from the TV screen. 'And you cannot afford for that to happen, Vladimir Vladimirovich.'

His meaning to Komarov and the underlying threat it carried was very clear: the President had to get this right or his position as leader would become vulnerable. Having led the Russians to war, his vision of incorporating the former Soviet republics of the Baltic states into the Russian Federation had to work. If it failed, then those who had supported him in order to see national pride restored would desert him for the unforgivable crime of destroying that very pride.

Komarov could see that the inference was not lost on the President.

'What are you proposing, Mikhail Nikolayevich?' he asked Gareyev.

'I need to thin out our garrison in Kaliningrad,' he said bluntly. 'If we try to stay strong everywhere we will be strong nowhere. As I told you, we have thinned out in Ukraine, but I can only go so far. Any more and the "dubs" – dumb Ukrainian bastards – will be pushing our forces back and, if we suffer reverses there, that would be the ultimate humiliation. That said, the main threat comes from the Baltic states, so that is where the main effort should be. Kaliningrad is secure and I will leave sufficient forces there. The population is Russian and loyal, so that at least remains a secure base for us.'

'And NATO?' the President asked, as he did at every such briefing.

'No change. Any threat from NATO? Not a chance. First, it is still in disarray, so it will be unable to mount any credible threat against us. Second, even if they had the men, the Western Alliance would not dare undertake offensive operations against Russian soil.'

'To reinforce General Gerayev's point, does NATO understand that if they ever try to attack Russian soil I will use nuclear weapons, Yevgeney Sergeyevich?' the President asked the Foreign Minister.

'Certainly they do. It has been made quite clear through diplomatic channels that you would not hesitate to use them in the event of either a NATO attack on the Baltic states, or any attack on Russian soil,' the Foreign Minister replied, with all the smoothness of a man used to dealing with diplomats.

Alongside him on the screen, the Deputy President and Director of FSB nodded in support.

'In fact,' the Foreign Minister continued, 'just so we are clear,

Vladimir Vladimirovich, it has been made known that Russia considers that the Baltic states are once again Russia.'

'Very well, Mikhail Nikolayevich. You may take the increased risk in Kaliningrad . . . but I want the insurrection in the Baltic states crushed within the month. Is that clear?'

'Very clear,' said Gareyev.

'And that British captain brought to me in Moscow.'

Komarov flicked the switch on the remote control and the screen went blank. The President sat silent, deep in thought. Here, Komarov could see, was a man who had thought he controlled events, but was now beginning to recognise that the dynamic he had started was not so easily controlled. Obviously, the propaganda war was not going as planned. The two NATO ships sunk in Riga and the US airmen slaughtered at Lielvārde had been written off as an unfortunate error – collateral damage. But the sinking of the *Eckernförde* had so enraged Germany that it looked as if it had jolted them out of their traditional pacifism. Not only were the Germans rediscovering their balls, they were now ready to implement the collective defence guarantee.

The unexpected consequence of these errors was that NATO had agreed Article 5, but that meant little on its own. Certainly, none of the Europeans, except for the British – still under the illusion that they were a serious international player, despite shedding power quicker than a whore dropping her knickers – had looked to be preparing for offensive action. But the President's extraordinary humiliation at Ligatne had changed the whole dynamic and with it their plan.

Once Britain had signed up to Article 5, HMS *Queen Elizabeth* had become a legitimate target. However, there had been international TV crews and journalists on board and on nearby ships, some now dead. Footage had gone out to the world of the sudden and unexpected torpedo attack under a sunny blue sky; followed by the mass drownings recorded for posterity on film, with associated sounds. Westerners everywhere could imagine their sons and daughters aboard the stricken ship as it sank.

Now every NATO ship and every base everywhere in the world was on full alert against another Russian attack. Newspapers and TV shows were endlessly debating the legitimacy, or not, of the attack. People who had never even heard of NATO, let alone Article 5, were listening to rolling TV news and programmes where experts discussed the importance of signing up for it. And all because the President had taken the Ligatne attack personally and ordered the sinking to get his own back on the British.

Cold, pragmatic self-interest would have left the ship afloat and tolerated the British playing their delusional war games with their undersized and underfunded armed forces. Before long the outrage of the West over the Baltics would have fizzled out and Russia would have been left free to deal with her rebellious Baltic peoples. Instead, a new British prime minister had taken over – a man, it seemed, very unlike his predecessor and with the stomach for battle. The House of Commons vote to implement Article 5 to fight for the Baltic states, which would almost certainly have been knife edge or rejected before the sinking, had passed with a massive majority.

Now even the most cynical foreign observers of the British scene were remarking at the return of the 'Blitz' spirit of 1940. Even more unexpected had been the reaction of hitherto pacifist Germany, where the Bundestag and Constitutional Court had been almost bellicose in their support for Article 5. Meanwhile, it looked as if America under its new president, despite its much-heralded Asia–Pacific pivot, might be about to refocus on Europe and resume its infernal interference with European defence. This was despite the President's clever move in repatriating the American bodies and prisoners taken at Lielvārde air base in Latvia with due ceremony, in an effort to make some sort of amends, and try and draw a line under the matter. In Moscow and St Petersburg, word had it that the intelligentsia, hitherto uncritical supporters of the President, were whispering – very quietly – that all this had come about because the President had lost his temper and become a laughing stock.

And now, the President had just ordered General Gareyev to put Major Vronsky, his lead operative in Latvia and the man currently charged with hunting down the leaders of these Forest Brother terrorist cells, to finding a lowly British captain of infantry; a man so unimportant that he hardly even counted as a pawn in the deadly game of geopolitical chess they were now engaged in. That more than anything made Komarov wonder whether the whisperers might be right; that the President was losing his sense of perspective and with it his grip. He prayed he was wrong because, as the President's enabler, it would be a very exposed place to be if the President insisted on making any more poor decisions.

At that point the President's mistress entered the room. 'Darling,' she purred as she ruffled the President's sparse hair. 'Have a glass of champagne. Our dinner is nearly ready . . .'

Komarov promptly stood up and left the room. The fact that the War Cabinet had not warned him that Gareyev would give the President this very downbeat briefing meant that they were talking to one another, but no longer to him. The tectonic plates looked as if they might be shifting. It was time to start making some new alliances.

1345 hours, Monday, 5 June 2017
The White House, Washington, D.C.

Pᴇᴛᴇ ᴄʜɪᴀʀɪɴɪ, ᴛʜᴇ President's Executive Assistant, walked through the door and sat down in the easy chair by Colonel Bear Smythson's desk.

'Jeez, Bear,' he said to Smythson, who did the same job for General Abe MacWhite, the chief in-house advisor to the President of the United States on national security issues. 'There's been one hell of a change in British attitudes. The President has just come off the phone with Oliver Little, the new Prime Minister. What a change from that fag who was there before. This new guy's seriously on the war path. Whatever you say about the Brits – and their bullshitty *Downton Abbey* accents and stiff-upper-lip crap don't fool me – they take some time to get going. But when they decide to get serious, boy do they go for it.'

Bear leaned back in his chair. 'So, they're rethinking things after the *Queen Elizabeth*?'

'Too right, Bear. The President is pretty wound up about the *Queen Elizabeth*, specially coming on top of the killing of US Air Force troops in the attack on Lielvārde air base. She sees the return of the survivors and the bodies as rank cynicism by the President. Sort of damned if he did return them and damned if he didn't. And the fact that the Russians are hanging on to the Ukraine Four, as the press are now calling them, as they continue to insist they are Special Forces, has got her even more riled up.

'The Russians are playing this all wrong. Even if President Dillon wanted to find a way to avoid further conflict, she'd be hard pushed to. Don't forget, there were CNN and Fox News crews on board and a couple of journos . . . Some of them still missing, presumed drowned, like the rest of those poor bastards. Killing our boys and girls in Lielvārde was not clever. But killing fellow journalists? That's sacrilege. The press is talking about the Special Relationship and meaning it for once. Throw in the shared tragedy and the new empathy between her and the Brit prime minister and this is certainly rekindling our link with the Brits. She and Little are now totally aligned on the need to take the offensive against the Russians. The Brits are putting everything they can into the mix. The new UK Chief of Defence is pushing hard for an attack on Kaliningrad to unhinge the Russians and force them to swap the Baltics if they want it back. And the Prime Minister's right behind him. The President wants to discuss the idea with NSA at the two-thirty meeting.'

'Thanks for the fast ball, Pete!' exclaimed Bear. 'I'll brief the boss now, so he's warned off. But don't expect anything but first thoughts. The General is the most aggressive soldier I've ever served under, but only once he knows a plan will work. This is going to need some serious thinking and planning, but we'll have something for the President in the Woodshed shortly.'

There was no answer. Chiarini was already out of the office and Bear started firing up his computer.

Forty minutes later President Lynn Turner Dillon walked into the Situation Room, elegant and poised as ever, with not a hair out of place. As the door was closed behind her by the Secret Service agent on guard, she exuded the energy and freshness that a daily combination of gym and Pilates sessions ensured.

Standing up with all the others as she entered, Bear felt an almost physical sense of the power she gave off. The graver this crisis became, the more assured became her leadership.

I know how lonely command in war can be, he thought. *But, dammit, she's just thriving on it.* What was the saying? Cometh the hour, cometh the man? This time it was firmly cometh the woman . . . and what a woman.

With the President seated, MacWhite, the tall, lean former Special Forces general, who looked as if he'd be more at home riding the range somewhere out West than inside the Washington beltway, led the President through the agenda. They would start with the intelligence update before considering the strategic options.

MacWhite let the Int briefer run through a series of PowerPoint slides: the latest positions of the Russian Baltic Fleet at sea; Russian troop dispositions in Estonia, Latvia and Lithuania, calculated at upwards of 200,000 men and climbing; estimated strengths of the Forest Brothers – initially some thousands, but already rumoured to be climbing towards their 1950s apogee of about 50,000 men and women under arms, including many Russian speakers who had remained loyal to the Baltics and had been outraged by this assault on their much-prized freedom – and the latest digest of attacks against their Russian occupiers. This was followed by an analysis of Russian strength levels in Ukraine and Kaliningrad. For once, the Middle East was relegated to another meeting.

Briefing concluded, MacWhite leaned forward, elbows on the table, a thoughtful frown chiselling deep lines on his leathery, sunken cheeks. 'Ma'am, we're getting a strong sense that the Russians have bitten off far more than they can chew in the Baltic states. The people are responding magnificently and, by God, are refusing to roll over. Thousands, maybe even tens of thousands, have taken to the forests to pursue the fight and the Russians are having ever more problems each day that passes.

So it's interesting that we've picked up they may be on the point of thinning out in Kaliningrad, that's the little Russian enclave between Poland and Lithuania. Their Iskander nuclear armed missiles are there in force, but recent signal traffic plus a lot of vehicle movement from Kaliningrad into Lithuania that we're seeing on satellite imagery, all indicates that something odd is happening there. The only conclusion we can draw is that they're getting well and truly pulled in by the Baltic insurgency and they need reinforcements fast, if they are to stamp it out before it gets out of control. It's what I would do if I was the Russian commander: concentrate resources on the main effort while accepting risk elsewhere.'

'What can we do to support the insurgents?' asked Dillon.

'Simple, ma'am – weapons, equipment, training. We're preparing to insert liaison detachments of Special Operations Forces from European Command to coordinate support. With your permission, of course.'

'I'm happy with that,' replied Dillon crisply. 'Now, tell me what you think of the British idea of getting onto the offensive with an attack on Kaliningrad?'

MacWhite was cautious, the hallmark of a veteran with vast combat experience who knew that once embarked upon, war frequently developed a dynamic of its own; difficult to foresee, impossible to control.

'It's an interesting idea, ma'am. I gather the idea originated with SACEUR and his Brit deputy, a punchy so-and-so, I gather . . . a Marine,' he added approvingly. 'I gather the idea is that we snatch Kaliningrad and then offer it back to the Russians on the condition they get out of the Baltics?'

Dillon nodded. 'Correct.'

'OK, then I'll need to get the staff to look at the proposition in detail. We'd need to pull together the right force mix and set the political conditions with the NATO members if it is to have any chance of success . . . and it's a big ask for NATO to mount an offensive operation. But, no doubt about it, if we could pull it off, it would certainly unhinge the Russians strategically. It's the last thing they'd expect. But there are a couple of very important factors we need to consider. First, trying to evict the Russians from the Baltic states means taking them on where they are strongest. So, at first glance, that argues for a more indirect approach. *But*, if they're thinning out the Kaliningrad garrison, then that is definitely in our favour. The second issue, and by far my biggest concern, is that the Russian President has made it very clear that any attack on the Baltics, or on the soil of Russia, will result in the use of nuclear weapons. No ifs, no buts. And I for one believe him. Those Iskander nuclear missile batteries in Kaliningrad are within range of Berlin, Copenhagen and Warsaw. Which, of course, is exactly why they are there.'

He paused. 'That means we have to be clever. I'm hoping the National Security Agency will tell us that they can come up with something very clever on the cyber front – if they haven't done so already. Any cyber solution will need to cover all command and control systems, not just nuclear. Furthermore, it will need to be something they *know* will work. The consequences of calling this wrong when we are facing a nuclear response are beyond my imagination.'

'You take that up with them and I'll set the political conditions,' replied Dillon. 'But what are we going to need in the way of forces? What can we provide and what can our allies offer?'

'Ma'am, we're talking about one of the most heavily militarised regions of Europe here.'

In the short time he'd had to consider this idea before the meeting, Bear had pulled some figures off the Pentagon Intelligence website and handed them to MacWhite, who started reading them out.

'At full strength, and accepting that they might be thinning out, we estimate the Russians have got up to fourteen thousand troops in Kaliningrad, broken down into three fighting brigades, plus artillery, missiles and helicopters. Hardware-wise that works out at over eight hundred main battle tanks, twelve hundred other armoured vehicles and over three hundred artillery or rocket systems. That's a hell of a lot of hardware in a fairly small area. So, this can only work if the Russians significantly reduce those numbers to reinforce the Baltics.'

Dillon was silent as the scale of the Russian troops in Fortress Kaliningrad sunk in.

MacWhite added, 'We'd need at least a three-to-one advantage. So, assuming that large numbers of Russians are diverted to the Baltics, that takes us to an attack force of around fifty thousand, a minimum of a corps operation . . . With some serious anti-armour capability as a starter.'

'Where are they going to come from?' asked Dillon.

'Well, ma'am, following your decision to reduce notice to move on the eighteenth of May, 18th Airborne Corps is pretty much ready to move. The two airborne divisions, 82nd and 101st Air Assault are good to go, while the Global Response Force from 82nd has been in UK since we had to turn it back from landing in Latvia. We also took the precaution of starting to ship the two armoured brigades of 4th Infantry Division to Europe. They should be docking in Bremerhaven in the next few days. They'll link up with the two brigades we've moved to Germany, so that will give us a useful combined arms force with plenty of armoured clout.

'On top of that, we've got 2nd Marine Expeditionary Force out of Camp Lejeune, North Carolina embarked and moving across the Atlantic. Put alongside 18th Airborne Corps that becomes a punchy organisation, with all the amphibious capability needed to disembark a strong force. As for maritime, we've got 6th Fleet moving up through the Mediterranean at best speed right now and more ships on their way across the

Atlantic from Norfolk, Virginia to reinforce them. Air – all we need is in Europe already. So, depending on what the allies can produce, we've got the means to do what needs to be done to take down the Russians.'

He got no further as the President lifted up her hand. 'Whoa, General . . . You've lost me with all this detail. Take me through all that, one bit at a time.'

MacWhite grinned. 'Forgive me, ma'am. I guess my enthusiasm got the better of me. Sure. Bear . . . ?' and he looked across at Bear, sitting in the cheap seats behind the Situation Room conference table. 'Run the President through the slides you prepared for me before the meeting, will you.'

Bear systematically went through the make-up of the force, slide by slide. Dillon listened carefully, making occasional notes on a hard copy of the slides. She asked a number of perceptive questions of MacWhite and then looked at Bear.

'Thanks for that, Colonel . . . Excellent briefing. Now let me be sure I've got the troop numbers right.' She checked her notes and ran through the list she had made. 'That's around forty thousand for the 82nd and 101st Divisions. As well as that there's the 4th Infantry Division with two brigades, plus the two brigades in Germany, which amounts to close to thirty thousand. Then you mentioned the Marine Expeditionary Force, which you said had a division, an aircraft wing and a logistics group – all amounting to about twenty thousand personnel.' Dillon paused while she totted up the figures. 'I make that ninety thousand.'

While Bear was impressed at President Dillon's readiness to get stuck into the detail, he was slightly surprised at her fixation on numbers. A legacy of being a CEO he supposed, where the bottom line was paramount.

Then she turned to MacWhite, 'You said that the usual military planning figure for an offensive operation is three to one, so I can see we've got the force levels and, no doubt, the equipment which goes with it. But the challenge will be the execution, I guess?'

MacWhite nodded. 'We can deploy the manpower but we're going to have to outsmart the Russians at their own game. What we've shown you is the conventional capability that we can deliver. And assuming our allies can pull something together to fight alongside us, that's a powerful force by any standards. However, the key to success, and the only way we'll beat the Russians, will be by being cleverer than them. We have to neutralise their strength with our unconventional capability. And SOF, sorry, ma'am, that's Special Operations Forces, are going to be the key here. I'd rather do that off line with you, if you don't mind.'

Bear knew that, as an ex-Special Operations Forces commander, MacWhite was naturally reticent in discussing how SOF would approach such a challenge. As he'd once said to Bear, it was not a leak to the enemy he feared, but the inevitable political memoirs that would be bound to follow, which, in describing one solution to a problem, would limit the US from using the same solution in the future.

'Next, we'll need to wind up NATO to take this on. Although the bulk of the capability will be American, we need to multinationalise it in order to get the political buy-in. Let's face it, ma'am, if the Russians do go nuclear, we assess that it is most likely that they will initially use tactical nuclear weapons to destroy our attacking forces and defend themselves. So, while it will probably be Europe which will take the initial hit, we can take no comfort from that. The Russians will almost certainly escalate to the use of ICBMs, intercontinental ballistic missiles, to which we will be forced to respond, and that means a full nuclear exchange and the mass destruction of American cities . . .' He needed say no more. The consequences of an exchange of ICBMs was too awful to contemplate.

Dillon nodded, but did not react. Instead, she sat back in

her chair at the head of the table and took time out to think and study her notes.

Nobody said a word.

Then she looked MacWhite in the eye. 'Abe, we can do this and we must do this. Europe's defence and security is America's defence and security. We have taken too much risk and made too many assumptions about the world being a safer place just because it is a smaller place . . . and we've all been caught out. Now we've just got to do what needs to be done and let me be crystal clear,' and her voice hardened. 'If the Russians go nuclear, even with a tactical nuclear weapon, I'll have no hesitation in retaliating with ICBMs. So make sure that message is communicated loud and clear on every diplomatic channel. This is one issue we, and the world, cannot afford to have the Russians make any miscalculations about.'

She paused to let the implication of this message sink in then, voice softening slightly, she continued, 'Our allies in the Baltic states, freedom-loving, democratic countries, must be freed from Russian occupation and we'll do it. But, as you say, Abe, we'll do it cleverly. Now, Pete,' she caught Chiarini's eye. 'Set up a cabinet meeting today so that we can take this forward and then let's get working those phones. I want to start by reassuring London that America is up for the fight.'

1500 hours, Tuesday, 6 June 2017
NATO Headquarters, Brussels, Belgium

THE NORMAL BUSTLE and chatter of diplomats, military staff officers and note takers milling about before an NAC, North Atlantic Council, meeting was absent as McKinlay took his seat next to SACEUR in the conference room at NATO's Brussels headquarters. A deep sense of despondency hung over the room as Radek Kostilek, the Secretary General of NATO, walked swiftly into the chamber and sat down at the large round table at which the twenty-eight ambassadors of the member states were placed in alphabetical order, behind their name plates and individual national flags. NATO's failure to deter the Russian invasion of the Baltic states, the heavy casualties suffered by the US Air Force detachment at Lielvārde air base, the sinking of the two mine countermeasures vessels in Riga and, most catastrophic of all, the torpedoing of HMS *Queen Elizabeth*, had rocked the Western Alliance to its very foundations.

This had been a massive failure by the Alliance; a disaster unprecedented in the history of NATO and the military, political, social and economic consequences were at last sinking in, even in the countries most hostile to overt military action. The frontiers, as well as the balance of power in Europe, were about to change yet again and this time, unlike the end of the Cold War, the democratic West was going to be the clear loser.

Kostilek had confided to Howard and McKinlay before the meeting that he feared the Alliance was on the brink of collapse as a result. Whether NATO was to survive depended on how it reacted to these blows. He had to set the right tone from the start of the meeting, otherwise the naysayers would take control.

'Ladies and gentlemen!' Kostilek's voice, his Polish accent accentuated by emotion, was commanding. 'Please stand. We will first hold a minute of silence in memory of the many NATO soldiers and sailors who have only recently given their lives in defence of freedom.'

McKinlay pulled himself to his feet, as did everyone else around the table. As they stood in silence, the flags of member states that had suffered casualties were projected onto screens around the conference table in alphabetical order: Estonia, Germany, Latvia, Lithuania, United Kingdom, United States of America.

Then Kostilek sat down and addressed the Council. 'Ladies and gentlemen, the Alliance has suffered grievous blows in recent days as the result of naked Russian aggression against the Baltic states. While we are united in honouring our fallen comrades and in condemnation of Russia, we must also be under no illusions. The purpose of the Alliance since its foundation in 1949 has been collective defence, the rock on which it has been built for sixty-eight years. And yet, when the crisis came, collective defence meant nothing. The Alliance failed. You need no reminding that NATO is no more or less than the nations which make up the Alliance . . . That means the nations have failed.' He paused and looked slowly around the table, making it clear where he thought the responsibility for failure lay.

Point forcefully made, he resumed. 'Let me take you back to the Cold War. Yes, there were fewer member states back then. But our predecessors around this table understood that collective defence needs more than words. That words alone, unless backed by genuinely capable, strong defences, mean nothing to our enemies. What a contrast to where we are today! The Alliance has spoken loudly, has puffed up its capabilities, but has completely failed to deter Russia. Would Russia have dared to attack strong, resolute, well-equipped and truly ready armed forces . . . ? I say NO!' He spat out the word.

For a moment there were mutterings of disagreement and annoyance from around the table, exactly as Kostilek had predicted. NATO had faced the massed armies and aggression of the Warsaw Pact for forty years of the Cold War, but peace had prevailed. Why? Because the Warsaw Pact knew that NATO was ready and able to respond. Today's member states knew this. Hence the looks of shame, of guilt even, on the faces of some ambassadors at his words. It was this, Kostilek had explained to Howard and McKinlay earlier, that he would tap into when he spoke.

He banged the table with his hand and the room fell silent.

'And be under no illusions. The proof is that our brothers and sisters in Estonia, Latvia and Lithuania are now occupied by Russia and the President has decreed that they are to be incorporated into his empire of fear and terror.'

For a moment he softened his tone. 'Ambassadors of those countries, dear friends and colleagues, I extend our deepest sympathy . . . but rest assured,' again he struck the table to emphasise the point and his eyes flashed defiance. 'I speak for every nation in the Alliance when I say that we will not rest until you have regained your liberty.'

Kostilek stopped and again looked every ambassador in the eye. As a Pole, he understood far better than those from Western Europe the reality of life as part of the Russian Empire. Some looked down, but did not argue. Others looked back at him equally directly. Some even nodded their approval. The Secretary General had set the tone he was looking for.

He continued, 'Dear colleagues all. NATO is an alliance of three-and-three-quarter million men and women under arms. We far outnumber the Russians in men and equipment and resources. United we are terrifying; unstoppable. United, we can put together the means, not only to liberate our dear friends in the Baltic states, but also to defend the freedom, democracy and the rule of law we all cherish . . . The alternative is too terrible to contemplate. Will you too fall under Russian control? Will you find yourselves the next country in front of this Council, begging for help? Picked off one by one at the President's whim . . . Because, be under no illusions, that *is* what will happen next.'

And now, McKinlay saw, he really did have their attention. It was one thing for the Greeks to get loans from the Russians or on the international bond markets, but quite another to be informed that the interest on those loans now included the gift of a port for the Russian navy, or a base for their fighter aircraft. Even Greece could see that their independence was only possible because she was a vibrant democracy. Anybody who read a newpaper or watched a television had to be able to see that true democracy was anathema to the Russian President.

Kostilek concluded with a clarion call to action. 'Let me be clear. NATO has agreed Article Five and we are now at war with Russia. What I want from the North Atlantic Council today is a strong consensus that the end we are seeking is nothing less than the liberation of Estonia, Latvia and Lithuania and that you, the nations, will deliver the military means to achieve that. We must all be prepared to strain every nerve, every sinew in the fight to free the Baltic states.'

He paused to let his words sink in. Then he called upon the American ambassador to speak.

'Thank you, Secretary General. I am under instructions to pass on a direct message from the President of the United States of America to all NATO member states: the US will not abdicate from its responsibilities. Members can be assured that the US is, once again, coming to the support of Europe in its hour of need. We are in the process of deploying significant forces to Europe. The President is determined that NATO will do whatever needs to be done to expel Russia from the Baltic states. America *will* lead the force and provide whatever means are necessary to achieve victory. The President asks all the nations to live up to their obligations under Article Five and join us in this venture.'

Then came the challenge. 'But, if necessary, we will act alone.'

The UK ambassador spoke next. Dame Flora Montrose delivered the UK's message with her customary brevity. 'The UK's Baltic allies have been attacked and occupied. The Royal Navy has suffered unprovoked attacks on two ships, *Queen Elizabeth* and *Padstow*. Hundreds of our sailors, marines and soldiers have been killed. Britain will not stand by and watch this vicious aggression go unpunished. Britain therefore considers itself at war with Russia. Together with the United States and, we trust, all our NATO allies, Britain will do what needs to be done to re-establish peace and legitimacy in the Baltic region.'

There was a surprised murmur from the ambassadors around the table. Here, at last, was Britain stepping forward and taking a lead role in NATO – a welcome change from recent years.

The German ambassador, bulky and glowering, caught Secretary General Kostilek's eye and was given the floor.

'Secretary General, dear colleagues. Germany's history gives us a unique perspective and understanding of the impact of unprovoked aggression by a dictator unfettered by the need to conform to democratic institutions. What we have witnessed in the Baltic states is no different in tone from Nazi Germany's occupation of much of Europe in the Second World War. You will all be aware that the weight of history has continued to weigh heavily on Germany, hence our reluctance to participate in certain international missions where force has been used.

However, I cannot begin to express adequately the outrage and horror felt throughout my country at the sinking of FGS *Eckernförde* and the death of so many of its crew. This, as well as the attacks on our friends in the Baltic states and on the ships and soldiers of America and Britain, has totally changed attitudes in Germany. The Bundestag, the Constitutional Court, and the population as a whole are now overwhelmingly in favour of taking whatever action needs to be taken to expel Russia from the Baltic states. Germany stands by to play a full part in undertaking military action together, we hope, with our fellow NATO members. But without them if necessary.'

McKinlay was conscious that he was witnessing history. Germany, so long the most pacifist nation in NATO, was today sanctioning the use of force. Like so many of his senior military colleagues, he had the highest respect for the professionalism of German commanders and staff officers and the quality of its military hardware, but despaired of that country's consistent refusal to do anything meaningful with them. Now, once again, panzers marked with black crosses would be heading east. This time it would be in the cause of freedom and not of occupation.

'That's just what we needed to hear,' he muttered to Admiral Howard, next to him. Then he scribbled a note and gave it to his German MA, Commander Wolfgang Kretschmer of the German Navy, one of the three Military Assistants who looked after the wide span of DSACEUR's responsibilities and who had recently joined the office.

Kretschmer read it, nodded, and left the room to fix up calls to the Chiefs of Defence Staff of Germany and the UK.

McKinlay listened while a series of ambassadors reinforced the commitment of their countries to taking whatever military action might be needed to liberate the Baltic states, although Hungary and Greece remained silent, neither promising support but no longer – and just as importantly – refusing it either.

Judging the moment perfectly, Secretary General Kostilek intervened and summed up the mood of the meeting.

'Ambassadors, I congratulate you on your very positive statements. I see there is unanimity in support of taking whatever
action is necessary to liberate the Baltic states. If we get this
right, and there is no reason why we cannot, the future of the
Alliance is safe. I had no doubt that the nations would rise to
the challenge. The question now is what action can be taken.
For this we are in the hands of the NATO military authorities
. . . SACEUR, the floor is yours.'

'Thank you, Secretary General,' said Howard. 'You will all
be aware of the outline proposal we have circulated under
strictest security to each of you. I will not repeat what is in
that because it is of critical importance that the tightest operational security is maintained . . . and we can't do that in open
forum in the North Atlantic Council. I propose first that
DSACEUR outlines the general force generation requirement
so that you understand the scale of the challenge. Secondly, I
recommend that we arrange a Top Secret briefing for your
military representatives. They will then ensure that you understand what is planned. But, and most important, I now need
your authority to proceed with the detailed planning.'

Kostilek concurred. 'We all understand that secrecy is vital.
Can I take it that the Council approves the proposal that the
NATO military authorities take forward the planning of the
operation whose outline you have been briefed upon separately?'

There was silence. 'I see it does,' announced Kostilek before
anyone could disagree or ask questions. 'I therefore call upon
DSACEUR to discuss force generation.'

McKinlay looked around the table. In contrast to the previous
NACs, there was a sense of purpose and a determination he
had never felt before. In its blackest hour, this historic alliance,
the most successful the world had ever seen, had found the
will and determination to fight back.

'Ladies and gentlemen, I will not go into detail now. Suffice it to say that I will be engaging with each of your nations to discuss the detailed force generation requirement for the operation the Secretary General has referred to. Let me leave you with one point: the operation we are planning will require forces on a scale that NATO has not considered since the days of the Cold War. Unless your nations are prepared to support it properly, it will fail. Be in no doubt that the Alliance has the capability if it has the will. As the Secretary General said earlier, with millions of men and women under arms, NATO is more than a match for anything Russia can put into the fight. My staff are now engaging with each of your nations on what we need. I ask you to convey the message to your governments, that only if they are prepared to step up to the mark will NATO achieve success in liberating the Baltic states.'

He stopped and waited for questions. There were none and shortly afterwards the meeting was brought to a conclusion by Kostilek. Howard and McKinlay had their green light.

Admiral Howard leaned over to McKinlay when the last ambassador was well out of earshot. 'Now, as we discussed, we start preparing two plans. The deception plan and the real plan. You leave the bullshit one for me to sell to the ambassadors and their political masters. Once the information goes back to national capitals and it's been crawled over by every goddam civil servant, I'm banking on the Russians having a full copy on their desks a few hours after it has been circulated. Nevertheless, I'll only reveal details with huge reluctance and under enormous political pressure. That'll help allay inevitable Russian suspicions. You focus on the real plan. And keep it tight. Very, very tight. If the Russians get even a sniff of it. Well . . .'

An hour later, after yet another high-speed car ride through the Brussels traffic, McKinlay was at his desk in SHAPE, mug of tea in his hand, as the phone call on the secure Brent system was put through to General Reinhardt Jacobsen, the German Chief of Defence Staff, an old friend who had attended Staff College at Camberley with both McKinlay and Kydd, the new British Chief of Defence Staff.

If anyone can get the Germans to deliver something useful, Reinhardt will, thought McKinlay, as the call was being put through. Known throughout the German army as *die Lange* – or 'Lofty', on account of his great height – soldiering was in Jacobsen's DNA. His grandfather had parachuted into Crete in 1941 with the Luftwaffe's elite Ramcke Parachute Brigade and there had never been any question in Jacobsen's mind that he, too, would be a soldier. A panzer commander to the core, he assured McKinlay that 1st Panzer Division was being mobilised and that Germany had already agreed bilaterally with Poland that it would be reinforced by 10th Polish Armoured Cavalry Brigade – all up, around 15,000 men and 150 tanks.

'And David, if you can get the Brits to deploy HQ Allied Rapid Reaction Corps, we'd like to put First Panzer under command of it. That's an organisation which has kept the capability for commanding war-fighting operations and we trust it,' concluded Jacobsen.

The next call was to General Jock Kydd in London.

With the beeps on the Brent secure phone again indicating that speech was secure, Kydd greeted McKinlay as an old friend. 'Dave, you bastard. Good to speak. What a fucking shambles. Never mind, we'll sort it out.'

McKinlay briefed Kydd on the NAC decision to take forward the planning and asked what UK could offer. It was clear that there'd been a change of atmosphere in London with the new leadership after the disaster of HMS *Queen Elizabeth*. Kydd ran through the proposal; the armed forces had been put on a war footing and reserves had been called up, but would take time to be processed.

Kydd began to fulminate about the idiocy of replacing

battle-hardened professionals with theoretical reserves, but McKinlay cut him off. 'That horse has long bolted, Jock. Just do what you can with what you've got.'

'Sorry, Dave. It's just that, of all the stupid, fucking, irresponsible gambles, that one takes the shagging biscuit.' And so he moved on to the new Royal Navy task group that was being put together under HMS *Ocean* and the second amphibious ship, HMS *Albion*, with a Royal Marine commando embarked to support the American Second Marine Expeditionary Force. Meanwhile, every available RAF aircraft was now fully integrated into allied air operational planning. As for the Army, Kydd had put the British 16th Air Assault Brigade under command of the American 82nd Airborne Division, while the ARRC, Allied Rapid Reaction Corps, headquarters was preparing to deploy to Poland.

'But I tell you, Dave,' went on Kydd, reverting to his usual colourful language, 'it's a fucking unbelievable state of affairs here. When I look back at the Gulf War, it was a hell of a stretch, but we still managed to put together a properly constituted fighting division. Now, thanks to all these defence cuts, we're having to cannibalise every vehicle in the Army just to get one fighting armoured brigade ready for war. Frankly, it's fucking pathetic and, as you know only too well, Dave, you can do the square root of fuck all with a single brigade. OK, we've got a divisional HQ . . . Just. But we're going to have to go cap in hand to the French to reinforce us with a second brigade if we're going to put even a weak division into the field. We're working round the clock to get the brigade to Poland in the next ten days to start training.'

'That bad?' McKinlay asked, shocked in spite of the reports he had read of tanks and other armoured vehicles sitting in sheds minus engines, tracks and other key parts, but still counted as being 'on strength'.

'Yup, that bad, Dave. The only thing we've got going for us

is that we've still got 20th Armoured Brigade based in Germany. So at least we don't have to ship everything across the Channel. Nevertheless, the cuts and emphasis on Daesh and the Middle East have meant that they've been last in line for what little money has been available. It's going to be a guinea a minute getting them properly operational again.'

'But you reckon you can?'

'Just you watch. My size tens are going to start connecting with shiny MOD arses in the next few seconds.'

'I'd pay good money to see that!' McKinlay chuckled at the thought of the foul-mouthed Kydd kicking ministers and civil servants alike. Then he grew serious again. 'We haven't talked eyes on the ground. We're going to need our people in and soonest. NATO Special Operations Forces here in SHAPE are coordinating Allied support to the Forest Brothers in all three Baltics, but we need someone in Kaliningrad. Any thoughts on UK Special Forces?'

'Too fucking right, mate,' came the immediate response. 'We'll ensure they're properly coordinated with NATO SOF and we're working to get something in there ASAP. However, we've got a small team on the ground in Latvia right now . . . more by accident than design.' He explained how Morland and his team of Mercian soldiers were now operating underground with the Forest Brothers. 'But we've got to move them,' Kydd went on. 'GCHQ has picked up that the Russians are on to Morland and his guys. What's so fucking odd is that it sounds as if the President himself has ordered Morland's capture. Blames him for getting his face and arse rubbed in the mud by his security guys. They reckon it's got personal, because some dicky-bird has told us that Russia Today has a camera team on standby for when they bring Morland in. The President must be losing his fucking marbles to get so wound up about one young infantry captain.' He laughed sardonically. 'It's long been bloody obvious that he's a self-obsessed nutter. However, until he had this little hissy fit, I had rather assumed he was something of a cool operator.'

A thought occurred to McKinlay. 'Any chance of getting this Morland into Kaliningrad? These Forest Brothers are all interconnected and know the ground better than anyone else. They'll be our best chance of slipping him over the border undetected and, if necessary, they could pass him on down their chain. With luck, he'll be able to snurgle around with guys who really know the terrain. Then we could reinforce the deception by sending UK SOF to recce routes into the Baltics. The Russians are bound to focus on what they're up to.'

'Good idea, Dave. Director Special Forces was in my office earlier having heart failure as to how to get his guys into Kaliningrad. The border with Poland is out, as it is so short and heavily defended. The Shaky Boats★ think that going in by sea is suicide and I tend to agree. If they try HAHO'ing or HALO'ing in blind, the chances are they'll land on a Russian bayonet or at least a Russian. They are nearly all Russian there and they'll be reported in a moment. No . . . I like it, Dave. Coming in from the north and through Russian-occupied territory has to be the sneakiest way in. Consider it done.'

The phone went dead. Kydd's mind had clearly moved onto other things that needed chasing in London.

★Nickname given to the Special Boat Service.

0403 hours, Thursday, 8 June 2017
Gauja National Park Forest, Latvia

MAJOR ANATOLY NIKOLAYEVICH Vronsky, of 45th Guards Spetsnaz Regiment, checked his watch once again as he had done incessantly for the past hour. However, much as he wanted time to move on, it was refusing to do so and the luminous dials told him that it was still another twenty-eight minutes until 0431 and sunrise. That was when the attack on the camp was due to go in; a half-light to help his men see where they were going and distinguish between friend and enemy: dozy defenders doubtless awoken from a deep sleep and unable to react in time.

So far things had gone entirely according to plan, so now there was nothing to do but suppress his anxiety and wait. Even as he felt a drip of water find its way down the back of his neck he smiled: the light rain that had just started to fall was just what was needed. The soft pitter-patter of rain on the forest canopy would help mask any sound his team made as they moved in for the kill.

He stifled a yawn. The damp from the forest leaves he was lying on was soaking up into his body and his eyes felt heavy. It had been a long night's patrol through the forest to move into position without being detected, and that after a day silently closing in on their enemy. His body craved proper food and drink after a couple of days' hard routine; no cooking and only an occasional swallow from his water bottle, a couple of packets of dry crackers, and an unheated can of unidentifiable fish to sustain him. Enough of feeling sorry for yourself, this would soon be over, he told himself, and then it would be back to the barracks at Ādaži for a celebratory drink and a large steak; the Latvians had certainly known how to look after themselves and their Russian successors were enjoying the rations they had left behind.

Now it was time to focus. Once more he ran a mental check on the plan and the rapid pace of events that had brought him into the forest to attack this base, belonging, it appeared, to a particularly effective group of Latvian Forest Brothers. What still surprised him was the direct Presidential order he had received five days ago: to capture the British terrorists. Not for the first time, Vronsky questioned the wisdom of getting personal because, grateful as he was that the President had entrusted him with this mission, it smacked of the old-fashioned peasant vendetta. However, his orders could not have been clearer.

Certainly the Commander of the Western Group of Forces had taken the President's orders as his personal command and had stopped at nothing to locate them. Their communications specialists had only a few short intercepts of data-burst transmission to work on. However, despite the considerable efforts of whoever was transmitting to avoid creating a pattern, computer analysis allowed them to zero in on the deep forest in the northern, most remote part of the Guaja National Park, close to the Gauja River, an area almost unmapped and visited only by the occasional hunter.

Aerial searches by Zastava drones carrying full-motion video and multispectral imaging sensors, integrated with forward-looking infrared capable of detecting the radiation from a heat source beneath the forest canopy, next revealed a number of potential hiding places deep in the forest that suggested recent habitation. Although, whether by humans or bears was a moot point and required boots on the ground, rather than a heat-seeking lens in the air.

And then, four days ago, the searchers had struck lucky. A short text message from a mobile phone had been picked up from within a hundred metres of one of the possible forest hide locations. Surveillance drones had then revealed movement on both foot and by cross-country motorcycle. The link was made with the President's attackers two weeks ago – they had escaped on scramblers – and Vronsky had been ordered to mount the operation as a matter of urgency.

Time had been short and while Vronsky was confident of his Spetsnaz team's ability to find, attack and neutralise the insurgents, he was very much less confident of the profession-alism and combat experience of the battalion that would establish the all-important inner and outer cordons. But they were all that was immediately available.

At least the fact he had been personally selected by the President gave him the ultimate say in how the operation should be executed. Nevertheless, as a major, Vronsky still had to take account of the lieutenant colonel commanding the conscripts of the local Motor Rifle battalion, who would provide the cordons. Vronsky assumed that they must know the local area by now, but even on that count he had been disappointed; the nervous young soldiers had started off by patrolling into the woods, but as the numbers and effectiveness of the resist-ance increased, ever fewer came back out. Now they kept to the roads and their defended blockhouses as they were too few, and the forest too large, for them to be able to patrol in strength.

Had Vronsky known this from the outset, he would have insisted on being backed up by an airborne battalion or more Spetsnaz, but it was too late now. The Int and Comms boys had narrowed down the hide area to within a hundred metres and they had to attack before the murdering bastards moved, as was their habit. They were not proper soldiers, Vronsky mused; proper soldiers stood and fought. Terrorists bombed, shot and ran away, which is why a wall was awaiting all but this one man: Morland. Probably, Vronsky mused as he worked up his ambush plan, by the time the President had finished with him, he would have opted for the wall. Nobody had ever accused the President of being a forgiving man.

Vronsky had given his orders and the operation had been rehearsed several times; first by the companies individually and finally by the whole battalion working together, by day and then by night. They were as ready as they'd ever be, and so they had moved out. Now he was here and there was nothing for it but to hope that the young conscripts would not screw things up at the last minute.

This had meant keeping the plan as simple as possible. Without the President's demand for Morland intact, Vronsky would have slipped unseen into position and pinpointed the target with a laser designator at a set time. Some smart bombs dropped from a distance and there would have been nothing left to put against a wall. Instead, he had been forced to set up a camp attack. It would be launched from one side of the insurgent hideout with the simple aim of making the outnumbered and shocked Forest Brothers bug out in the other direction, straight into the ambush where Vronsky was now lying in wait.

The inner cordon, behind him, was the 'backstop' in case anyone got through his ambush position. There was also an outer cordon, which would prevent any interference from else-where in the forest. Very simple but very effective, and very much the plan he would have used even with an airborne battalion. But it was the quality of the individual soldiers that was worrying Vronsky. Once the rounds started flying, would the conscripts hold their position and shoot back? Would they shoot straight, or perhaps even shoot each other in the inevitable confusion? For that he had no answer and no solution. So he tried not to worry about it.

The message had come through at midnight that the cordons had been established, with heavy weapons even further behind and in support if required.

Vronsky and his team of ten Spetsnaz soldiers then moved noiselessly into their final ambush position. At H-Hour, the feint attack would be launched from the other side of the camp. In order to maximise surprise, it would be launched silently, meaning that if the Forest Brothers had not set guards, the attackers might even overrun the camp without Vronsky and his men getting involved. Not that Vronsky cared. He felt no need to shoot or to be shot at. All he wanted was the right result, regardless of how it was achieved or who achieved it. Unlike the President, he thought bitterly, he did not take things personally. Which was one reason he had continued to survive and thrive, while so many of his friends had become casualties in the various vicious conflicts in the Caucasus.

Vronsky looked again at his watch. The minutes were ticking by in the almost oppressive silence of the forest. And then, to his horror, Vronsky heard from behind him the sharp crack of two high-velocity shots: unmistakably an AK-74M, the standard Russian infantry assault rifle. That was followed a few seconds later by multiple bursts of automatic fire, swiftly followed by a short contact report from the outer-cordon company commander, broadcast into the personal radio clamped to his left ear.

Even as the company commander was reporting an attack on their position by unknown assailants, Vronsky was already raging to himself. 'The fools! The oldest mistake and attempted cover-up in the book . . . A negligent discharge by a bored soldier with an itchy trigger finger, followed by return fire and a spurious contact report.'

'Stand by for the enemy to bug out,' he ordered quietly into his microphone.

The trouble was that the Forest Brothers would now try to escape away from the firing and that meant away from their ambush position. Hopefully though, they would run straight into the assault group, even now preparing to attack. The plan might have cooked off completely arse about face, but it should achieve the same result. Although, whatever happened next, Vronsky mused as he checked the safety catch on his AS Val assault rifle, there was a soldier and his officer who were never going to forget their monumental balls-up today. But that would come later. First he had to destroy this rats' nest and capture this Englishman. He knew he could rely on his team to do the right thing, so right now, there was nothing to do but keep their heads down and wait for the attack.

And then it began.

Instead of catching them asleep as Vronsky had assumed, rounds launched from M19 60 millimetre American light mortars bought by the Latvian Army began to fall all around them, followed by long bursts from machine guns putting down deadly swathes of fire throughout the forest. And, in that moment, Vronsky realised that he had made the cardinal error of under-estimating his enemy. The Forest Brothers, alert and wary as wolves, must have realised that it was almost inevitable the Russians would find them one day, so had planned their counter-camp-attack plans carefully.

While Vronsky had assumed that the bunker itself would be protected by trip wires and claymore mines, he had not anticipated the machine guns mounted on fixed tripods in the sustained fire role, so they could fire long and accurate bursts down pre-recce'd approaches to the camp, or the light mortars, already set up to fire on likely forming-up points for any attack. Even as his ambush plan went to hell in a handcart around him, the professional soldier in Vronsky acknowledged that these Forest Brothers were good; very good. They could even teach him and his men a trick or two. If they survived. But they were not going to survive. The odds were still too heavily stacked against them.

That comforting thought was brutally interrupted as mortar rounds crashed through the trees and exploded above him, sending splinters of wood from broken branches flying like deadly arrows through the air. Next moment, machine-gun rounds scythed a deadly rain of copper-jacketed, high-velocity steel all around him, while the diabolical symphony of explosions and flashing tracer cracking overhead deafened him and made it almost impossible to think. Had he been standing, or up on one knee, he would now be dead.

'Fuck,' he almost screamed to himself as he forced his body as deep into the loamy earth as possible. They had even scouted out this ambush position and set it up as a pre-registered defensive fire location for their mortars. There could be no doubt now: these guys were professionals and they'd rehearsed this response until it was faultless.

Vronsky now knew something else. Unless he moved fast he'd lose his quarry. This first response was fully planned, and that meant the next phase – their escape – would be equally well planned and rehearsed. The GPMGs would soon run out of ammunition or overheat and then the escape phase would start. However, he could do nothing but stay alive until the storm of fire had passed.

Then, just as suddenly as they had begun, the mortar rounds ceased and the machine-gun fire stopped. He lifted his head and looked left and right. As far as he could see there were no casualties, but he wouldn't have expected any of his team to cry out if wounded anyway. Time to go.

'Prepare to move. Stand by to skirmish, then assault the camp on my order,' he spoke urgently into his radio, pausing to allow his men to ready themselves for the seventy-metre dash through the forest to the camp. 'Move now!' Vronsky yelled.

He pulled himself up, his cramped, stiff limbs resisting, and dashed forward as his wingman put down fire from his AS Val assault rifle. As he did so he was aware, left and right, of two or three others moving with him; not enough though. Some of his men must be down already.

Then it was time to dive forward, roll into a firing position, take aim, spot no target but, nevertheless, fire off a couple of rounds at the forest camp; then quickly roll over and put more bursts of fire down as his wingman ran forward. As he prepared himself to dash forward again, he heard the unmistakable, high-pitched whine of a motocross bike in high gear.

A number of 'pops' sounded nearby. Then white smoke started billowing up around him, obscuring the forest, making identifying anything impossible. *Bloody smoke grenades*, he thought, *all part of their escape plan.*

Next moment, and through a gap in the smoke, he spotted a Honda motocross bike roaring past. It had a Latvian driver but there was a differently dressed soldier riding pillion. For a moment his eyes locked with the passenger, who stared at him, frowned and then loosed off a couple of wildly aimed bursts of fire from what looked to be a British-issue rifle.

Before Vronsky could return fire, the bike careered around a corner further along the narrow track and, next instant, was lost to sight among the trees.

Vronsky's photographic memory kicked in, despite the mayhem all around him: dark-haired, bearded, late twenties, unfamiliar combat uniform, standard British army SA80 rifle; he must be British. Then disappointment and anger hit him like a double punch to the solar plexus.

That's my quarry and he's escaped . . . !

PART THREE

Riposte

1200 hours, Thursday, 5 July 2017
'The Tank', Pentagon, Washington, D.C.

THE JOINT CHIEFS' Conference Room, known universally as 'The Tank', was silent as the briefer outlined the detail of the plan to President Lynn Turner Dillon. Colonel Bear Smythson sat in his usual hardbacked chair, pushed up against the wall; not a main participant, but a silent observer. Flanking the President at the broad conference table in the utilitarian surroundings, much like any other conference room in a budget-conscious corporate office, sat the grey-suited Secretary of Defense, the National Security Advisor Abe MacWhite, together with General Marty McCann, Chairman of the Joint Chiefs and, finally the Chiefs of the Army, Navy, Air Force and US Marine Corps; the elite group of men who commanded and directed America's war machine.

Bear reflected on the events since the world had been turned upside down early on that May morning, two long and sleep-deprived months ago. Whatever the sacrifices demanded of him and his family as a result of his commitment to this job, he was all too conscious that, once again, he was in the extraordinary position of being a witness to history, as he listened to the briefer explain the plan to expel Russia from the Baltic states.

Next the briefer detailed the impressive forces that had been assembled, a testament to America's still vast military might: 6th Fleet and 2nd Marine Expeditionary Force were now poised at sea off eastern Denmark, and 4th Infantry Division had been transported across the Atlantic, disembarked at Bremerhaven, linked up with the armoured brigades from Germany and was in transit to the Polish training area at Drawsko Pomorskie. The 18th Airborne Corps, around 40,000 men and women in total, was now forward based in the UK, while Special Operations Forces Command had inserted a number of ODAs – Operational Detachment Alpha, the twelve-man basic unit of American SOF – into the three Baltic states, which were working closely with the Forest Brothers. As for air forces, an air armada had been assembled across Western Europe and was at full readiness.

'What are our allies putting into the fight?' asked Dillon.

McCann stepped in and answered the question. 'Ma'am, I'm pleased to say that our allies are stepping up to the mark. The British have put their 16th Air Assault Brigade under command of 82nd Airborne Division, which is now training in the UK. They've also managed to put together a small division using one of their armoured brigades and a French light-armoured brigade. It's undersized, but potent – and at least they're joining the party.

'As for the Germans, they've offered us 1st Panzer Division, which now includes a Polish brigade. All that has been taken under command of the Allied Rapid Reaction Corps, that's the British-led NATO high-readiness force, which brings in nineteen other allies. The bottom line is that these forces, together with a number of smaller units offered by different allies, amount to a useful contribution. We'll still need to underpin them and it's a hotchpotch of forces that have rarely worked together, let alone fought together, but we can't complain that our allies have not tried to deliver. And the fact that Europe is united over this is going to be very important for the political endgame.'

The President nodded. 'And what about the Russians. Have they thinned out in Kaliningrad?'

McCann nodded. 'Satellite images indicate they're maintaining strong defences along the Polish–Kaliningrad border and, as expected, the Iskander nuclear batteries are well defended by both ground and air defence. So no change there. However, the good news is that these formations are very localised. They've had to thin right out on the Lithuanian border in order to reinforce their troops in the Baltic states and they've stripped out their garrisons and equipment inside the country.'

'Does that present us with an opportunity? I'm thinking of that idea I heard about a few weeks ago, of snatching Kaliningrad and forcing the Russians to relinquish the Baltics to get it back.'

McCann looked back at his President. His blue eyes, usually alight with the sparkle of humour, were sombre. 'Ma'am, we've looked at the proposition in detail in line with the direction the National Security Advisor passed on.' He nodded at Bear's boss, Abe McWhite. 'The reality is that, although the Russians have thinned out in Kaliningrad, they've still got a significant force in place. If we were to attack conventionally, it would almost certainly result in a long and bloody battle with the Russians defending to the last man. We've concluded that the best way to succeed is to play the Russians at their own game.'

'OK – and how do you intend to do that?' questioned Dillon.

McCann stepped forward and took the laser pointer from the briefer. Here was a man who understood that it was the commander's responsibility to have the big idea and for the staff to implement it. Not for him a series of proposals created and driven by his staff, with him in the role of team manager. Unsurprisingly, thought Bear, his team respected and liked him for his no-nonsense, hands-on approach.

'I've talked through the detail with Admiral Howard, the SACEUR and his Brit number two, and we're agreed on the way ahead. Effectively, we're going to mount a massive deception by making the Russians think we're planning to invade the Baltic states in a huge envelopment operation. Because, after all, we've now got the manpower and equipment to do it and that's what we reckon the Russians would do in our place.'

The President nodded for him to continue, evidently fascinated to discover what the military had come up with.

'Ma'am, we intend to concentrate our conventional ground divisions in this area close to the Polish–Lithuanian border.' He pointed on the map to the town of Suwalki, in north-eastern Poland.

'Meanwhile, 6th Fleet will screen off the Russian's Baltic fleet in Baltiysk, their naval base in Kaliningrad. That will allow 2nd Marine Expeditionary Force to sail east towards the coast of Estonia. The aim is to make the Russians think we want to mount an amphibious landing here on the coast of the Gulf of Riga, south of Pärnu . . .' McCann pointed to the Estonian coast. 'It's the obvious place to land because of the long sandy beaches.'

Dillon nodded thoughtfully. 'This looks pretty conventional to me. So, where's the clever stuff?'

Bear smiled inwardly. Dillon was already getting the measure of her senior military advisors.

McCann grinned. 'With respect, Madam President, I haven't got to that yet.' He pointed way to the south now, at Kaliningrad. 'While we're massing force off the coast of Estonia and on the border with Lithuania, we'll mount the real operation . . . To secure and disrupt the nuclear-armed Iskander missiles in Kaliningrad.'

At the mention of the word 'nuclear', Bear noted President Dillon's eyes narrow and her face become expressionless. Like any sane person, she was clearly terrified of being responsible for the unleashing of even one nuclear weapon in heavily populated Europe.

McCann's voice was equally neutral now, as he pressed on before Dillon could interrupt him again. 'We know for a fact that the launch of tactical nuclear missiles like Iskander depends on release authority from the President, Defence Minister and Chief of the General Staff through their "Cheget" nuclear brief-cases – pretty much identical to any black, slimline attaché case, very like your own.' He nodded to the case on the desk. 'On the face of it, and in theory, all three have to agree and all three have their own suitcase,' explained McCann.

'But why are we only going after the tactical Iskanders?' Dillon asked.

'Can I stop you right there, ma'am.' McCann held his hand up, much to Bear's relief. He had been getting worried, too, that all this talk of different missile types – tactical versus strategic – was confusing the civilians in the room, including the President.

'Modern nuclear weapons are so powerful that it is almost academic whether a missile is deemed tactical or strategic if even one is launched. The consequences for Europe, the world, would be entirely catastrophic. If you aren't killed in the immediate blast, then fall-out will get you because, once one is launched, it is almost inevitable that the other side will respond with theirs . . . The consequence: MAD – Mutually Assured Destruction.'

The President nodded for him to continue.

'Iskander . . . or our Tomahawks for that matter, are tactical in that they can be moved around easily. The Iskanders in Kaliningrad are mounted on vehicles. You'll have seen shots of them driving past the saluting stand at their May Day Parade in Moscow. They are smaller and have a much shorter range than an ICBM, but as I said, it is pretty academic once they start flying. They can carry a normal warhead or a nuclear one – again like our Tomahawks. And, like our Tomahawks, they are extremely accurate and difficult to knock down. But the key thing to remember is that even the smallest one of these is many, many times more powerful than the ones we dropped on Hiroshima or Nagasaki. Just imagine that mushroom cloud, magnified many times over, exploding over the cities of Western Europe.'

McCann looked around him and, although Bear knew the horrendous statistics, he found himself almost unable to breathe with the magnitude of what was being described.

Satisfied that he had made his message clear, McCann continued, 'Now, the point for us here today is that the Russians moved *these* nuclear Iskanders to Kaliningrad to threaten NATO and destabilise the Baltics. Which they have certainly succeeded in doing. But that also means that, unlike their nuclear missile subs, which are hidden at sea, or their ICBMs, which are dug in far behind their borders where we cannot get to them, we could get at these. It is the fact that they are mobile that has made them potentially vulnerable to seizure. If we can first take down their command systems and stop them being launched. Which brings us back to Cheget . . .'

'So, how do they talk to each other?' asked Dillon, evidently guessing where this might be leading.

'By a number of means. The basis of the system is a two-way communications system called Signal A, with a sub-system known as V'yuga, all backed up by an emergency system: Perimetr. Signal A has a high degree of redundancy – that means back-up systems, in case the primary system fails – and is kept combat ready at all times. We know it is very reliable with several communications tracks, each with a different communications channel: radio, cable, satellite, tropospheric. V'yuga adds yet more backup with HF, VHF and a satellite link.'

'Sounds like they've thought things through,' commented Dillon.

'You're dead right, ma'am. These guys know what they're

doing. On top of which, Signal A and V'yuga are interfaced electronically and algorithmically, which again ensures a high degree of security for all the communications channels. And as if that's not enough, Perimetr – the back-up system – can transmit an order from the General Staff to the missile launchers direct, thus bypassing all intermediate command posts.'

McCann paused and the President gestured for him to continue.

'But there's more to it than that. Despite the President and the Defence Minister having their own suitcase for command and control, actual physical control of the unlock and launch authorisation codes resides with the military. In fact, the General Staff has direct access to these codes and can initiate a missile launch with or without permission of the political authorities.'

'So, if we captured the launch sites and the command posts, would we be able to take control of the missiles?'

'The million-dollar question, ma'am. We believe we can take control, but I will explain it at the end, so please bear with me. First though, while the Russians are focused on our main forces approaching the Baltics, 82nd Airborne will sneak in and secure the Kaliningrad launch sites. Meanwhile, our Special Forces will capture the command bunker from which all the sites are controlled. Once we've got them secured, we'll redirect the missiles at the Russians. They'll be bound to be threatening us once they realise what we've done, but we'll be able to threaten them back. And with their own missiles. I can't imagine the Russian people will exactly appreciate that scenario, especially once it's all over social media, which we will ensure it is the moment it happens.'

Dillon leaned back and as she thought through the consequences and how it would work out politically, she began to smile. 'If the President became a laughing stock after what the Latvians did to him in the forest, how much greater a humiliation this would be . . .'

Then her face hardened again. 'But how many launch sites are there? How many missiles? And what do we have to put on the ground to grab them?'

McCann was ready for these questions. 'We believe the Russians have got one hundred nuclear-armed Iskander missiles. Next slide please.' On the screen a high-resolution image of Kaliningrad appeared. 'They're on mobile launchers, but deployed at three protected launch sites.' And again, he directed his laser pointer at the screen. 'Here, at Pravdinsk, Yuzhnyy and Ozёrsk – with all the sites controlled from the command set-up at Pravdinksk – that's here, in the centre. As for numbers of our people. We'll need to insert Special Forces, specially trained to adjust the missiles electronically, but also to act as pathfinders for the main force. They'll be followed by an air assault force at each launch site to break in and secure the missiles.'

'How will you stop the Russians counter-attacking?' quizzed the President.

'Initially by the men on the ground – it takes time to plan and execute a major counter-attack – and then by holding them to ransom with their own missiles. But if it looks as if they're not going to listen to reason, the ARRC will be ready with three divisions to punch in to Kaliningrad to secure and protect the sites. But the bottom line is this . . . Once we have the missiles and the launch codes, that's when you politicians take over and tell the Russians to, first, back off or else and, second, get out of the Baltic states if they want Kaliningrad and their missiles back. And we believe they will have little choice but to comply.'

'That makes sense,' said Dillon.

'But we need one other key ingredient for this plan to work.'

'What's that?' Dillon demanded.

'We'll need to disrupt Russian command and control, both nuclear and conventional, for two reasons. First, we'll need to suppress what is probably the most effective integrated air-defence system anywhere in the world. Second, we have to stop them using the missiles against us as we go in to grab them. The Kremlin has made it very clear that if there's any threat against Russian territory, they'll go nuclear. And Kaliningrad, as I've said, is undoubtedly homeland. Don't forget either, they've told us outright that the Baltics now count as homeland as well. The only way this works is if they don't see us coming. If they do, then the missiles could be flying.'

Dillon frowned. 'So the risk is that they'll target 6th Fleet and 2nd MEF at sea and the divisions forming up under the ARRC in north-east Poland? Particularly if they think we're launching an invasion of Estonia and Lithuania?'

'Correct, ma'am,' replied McCann. 'That's why we have to disrupt those multiple nuclear communications channels I spoke about earlier: Signal A, V'yuga and Perimetr.'

'I get it,' said Dillon. 'Disrupt his command systems, seize his command posts and missile launch sites, turn the missiles back on them, and then invite them to come and have a chat. From a position of genuine strength.'

McCann agreed. 'That's what we figured, ma'am. Then all you've got to do is suggest he extracts from the Baltics and he can have Kaliningrad and his missiles back . . . without working warheads, I'd suggest, but I'll leave that to you. Meanwhile, we've got 2nd MEF and the ARRC with its three divisions ready to move into the Baltic states if the Russians show any reluctance to get out.' He paused. 'But we're still working on the cyber operation against the Russian communications channels.'

'Have NSA got an answer to that?' asked the President.

'Not yet, ma'am . . . but we're hearing that the Brits might have. They've got a team in Kaliningrad who have been feeding us the latest intel on those rocket sites. And because they and their Forest Brother mates have been doing such a good job of it, we've kept Special Forces out of Kaliningrad altogether. All part of the deception plan.'

Bear saw the President look confused, as did McCann, because he continued his explanation.

'If we send Special Forces into Kaliningrad now and that is detected, let alone they get caught, then the Russians are going to smell a very large rat and ramp up their defences. And it will be game over. So, for now, it's no special ops until it becomes essential, nor any NATO forces on the Kaliningrad border. CIA tell us that their Russian sources are convinced we wouldn't dare touch Russian soil. Which is why they are still thinning out their home garrisons and are using them to try and knock out the opposition in the Baltics. But this plan only works as long as this Brit keeps sending us high quality intel. If the team leader can do that and if we can drop our boys in and snatch the missiles without any being fired, well . . . the rest will be a slam dunk, ma'am.'

'I like the sound of this soldier, General McCann. Tell me more about him. What's his name?'

1600 hours, Tuesday, 6 July 2017
North Atlantic Council
NATO Headquarters, Brussels

'IN CONCLUSION, THE force generation process for this operation has been relatively successful and I would like to pass on my thanks to all nations for the excellent cooperation SHAPE has had from your Chiefs of Defence and Ministries of Defence. Secretary General, that concludes my briefing.'

And with that, General Sir David McKinlay closed his brief and sat back in his chair. By no means every formation and unit in the Combined Joint Statement of Requirement, or CJSOR in NATO jargon, had been provided. In particular, it was deeply regrettable that his own nation had faced such difficulties in putting together a force. Whether it was lack of Navy escorts and manpower or the Army's dependence on reserves to fill key gaps, the UK's defence capability was a shadow of what it once had been. Nevertheless, a number of critical deficiencies had been filled by the Americans, so he was able to brief the NAC that, in his professional military judgement, the force would be able to do the job it was being asked to take on.

Not only that, such had been the response from some nations that McKinlay had been called upon to exercise the wisdom of Solomon to avoid upsetting countries keen to offer what they could to the force being assembled to eject Russia from the Baltic states. He had even been happy to include contributions from non-NATO members, with Sweden, Finland, Australia and New Zealand figuring significantly. That said, there were other nations – the usual suspects – conspicuous for their lack of contribution and enthusiasm. That was a matter for another day, though.

'Thank you, DSACEUR,' said Secretary General Kostilek. 'Are there any more questions?' He paused momentarily, and then continued, 'I see there are none. SACEUR, the floor is yours.'

Admiral Max Howard got straight to the point. 'Secretary General, ladies and gentlemen. I want to add my thanks and congratulations to DSACEUR's. This has been a fine effort from the Alliance in generating the force levels we need for this operation. That's the good news . . . but there's bad news, too. It's one thing to pull together the force, but it's quite another to achieve victory. Sure, in line with your authority, we've been planning the detail of this very complex operation for the past five weeks. The Military Committee has been given a Top Secret briefing on the plan at SHAPE and your MILREPs – your Military Representatives – will have briefed you in detail. So you all know what is planned.'

He looked around the Council table at the twenty-eight ambassadors; most very capable diplomats but understandably, with very little comprehension of the complexities and mechanics of a military operation, particularly an operation on the scale of this one. He knew most of them personally and liked many of them as individuals. But he detected a certain smugness in the room; the knowledge that they were in the inner circle. They knew the plan and had the satisfaction of knowing that they were the ones who had given SACEUR authority to proceed. It was time to shake that self-satisfaction.

McKinlay knew that Admiral Howard had already cleared

his line with the Secretary General and the Chairman of the Military Committee, General Knud Vahr, so he was guaranteed support from those two, as well as the American and British ambassadors, who both knew what was about to happen.

'You will not like what I am going to say,' said Howard. 'But I have to. The bottom line is this. If the NAC continues to insist on retaining the right to give me the green light for each stage of what I need to do as your Supreme Commander, then I guarantee that NATO will fail in this endeavour. And if we fail to eject the Russians from the Baltic states, having assembled this impressive force, then the Alliance will have no future. And Europe will have no future. And Russia will have won. I don't need to once again spell out the political or military consequences of that horror scenario . . .'

McKinlay heard a perceptible intake of breath from around the table.

The German ambassador scowled and raised his hand.

Howard ignored the interruption and continued. 'If I had been sitting here thirty-five years ago, as your SACEUR, during the Cold War, I would have had the authority to deploy forces when I wanted if faced with Warsaw Pact aggression. I would not have had to turn to the NAC for the green light at each step on the way. Let me give you an example. My predecessors as SACEUR were able to order the deployment of the ACE, Allied Command Europe, Mobile Force – a multinational immediate response force – to meet any of its contingency plans once NATO's activation warning order ACTWARN had been declared. There was no requirement to go back to the NAC. As a result, NATO was able to make decisions with real agility and effectiveness.'

McKinlay could see the German ambassador muttering to himself and scribbling furiously.

'Contrast that with NATO's recent failure to deploy the Very High Readiness Joint Task Force, the successor to the ACE

Mobile Force, to the Baltic states quickly enough to deter the Russians from invading. Had I been able to do that without the authority of the NAC, I believe we would not be sitting here today, with Russia occupying three NATO countries. The irony is that many of the units were ready to deploy, but I had no authority to send them.'

Now the French and German ambassadors were whispering to each other.

Kostilek banged the table with his gavel. 'Please be good enough to let SACEUR finish.'

Howard continued, 'The NAC's insistence on clearing in advance any plan by the NATO Military Authorities is a product of an era that has now passed. I concede that it was politically expedient in Afghanistan, given the very different role of NATO out there. But I have to tell you . . . this creeping reduction in SACEUR's authority will guarantee military failure if it continues. You may think you are the only ones to have been briefed on my top secret plan. But I also have to tell you, that anything you are briefed upon will be on the President's desk in Moscow within hours.'

McKinlay looked around the table. Some faces were angry, others resigned, others curious as to where this was going. SACEUR had just had the bad manners to point to the ever-present elephant in the NATO room, something everyone present knew, but no-one ever referred to, at least in public: the fact that the information given to the NAC had a nasty habit of leaking straight back to Moscow. Many of the ambassadors were clearly unhappy at the insinuation and some were already demanding to speak.

Admiral Howard ignored the hubbub.

'Secretary General, it is right that the NAC should set the political end-state and I am quite clear what you want me to achieve. However, I have to be able to plan and execute the military strategy to achieve that without having to clear it every step of the way with the NAC . . . And without fearing for operational security. I therefore request the NAC give me full authority to proceed from here on to the end of this crisis without having to clear the details of the campaign with you. We can, of course, revisit this matter when Russia has been expelled from the Baltics.'

And now the muttering around the table was reaching a crescendo.

Kostilek banged his gavel again and called for order. 'My dear colleagues, I fully understand your concerns regarding this issue. I propose that we ask SACEUR and DSACEUR to step outside while we discuss it in closed, ambassador-only, session. The Chairman of the Military Committee, as the NAC's official military adviser, will of course remain.'

And with that, Howard nodded to McKinlay and the two men left the council chamber to be met by Captain Dan Rodowicz, the tall ex-professional basketball player who had joined up after 9/11 and was now part of SACEUR's forward liaison team in NATO HQ. 'Hi, Sirs. I suggest we head upstairs to the office and we'll fix you a coffee and something to eat.'

Two hours later, the call came through to the office requesting Howard and McKinlay to return to the chamber. As they entered, the room went quiet.

Kostilek welcomed them back. 'SACEUR, thank you for your patience. We have debated this issue in detail and I am pleased to say that, after considerable discussion, we have a consensus. We ask that you submit the usual daily update to the NAC and, in particular, that you keep the NAC appraised of any issues likely to have an impact at the grand strategic level. Furthermore, the NAC has agreed that, as Secretary General of NATO, you are to brief me in detail on your plan as it proceeds. Meanwhile, you have the green light to prosecute operations as you see fit.'

1030 hours, Friday, 7 July 2017
Government Communications Headquarters (GCHQ)
Cheltenham, England

CHELTENHAM, THE GENTEEL, quintessentially English spa town that sits at the base of the limestone escarpment marking the western edge of the Cotswold Hills, is dominated in the first two weeks of July by the music festival; this year, according to the *Daily Telegraph*, a 'shrewd mix of tradition and novelty, guaranteeing some very special musical experiences'.

This was utterly lost on Trevor Walker, the Prime Minister's Director of Communications, as he was driven through the suburbs of Cheltenham to meet Prime Minister Oliver Little. Not only was Walker totally uninterested in music, but with the country now effectively at war with Russia and a new Prime Minister in Number 10 Downing Street, he was preoccupied with ensuring his new boss's power base in the parliamentary party was secure.

The Toyota Hybrid Prius from the Whitehall car pool drew up at the gate of the Government Communications Headquarters and, after security checks, Walker was let in to the 176-acre site, dominated in the centre by the concentric-ringed, steel, aluminium and stone 'Doughnut', the largest building constructed for intelligence purposes outside the USA. Staffed by 5,500 employees, the purpose of GCHQ is to provide signals intelligence to the

British government, its various intelligence services and its armed forces. Soon he was at the helipad with the GCHQ Director, Ian Berry; breezy, early forties and fit, looking more like a rugby-playing, public-school housemaster than the head of one of the world's most pre-eminent spy agencies.

But thankfully, before he found himself having to make small talk about radios or the internet, or whatever these boffins liked to discuss, the clatter and then the roar of the red-and-white liveried AgustaWestland helicopter of 32 Squadron RAF obliterated any chance of a conversation as it landed. Moments later the Prime Minister was out and being buffeted by the fierce downdraught before being whisked away from the landing pad and into the principal conference room of the Doughnut.

Walker walked in behind his boss to see, as well as the GCHQ team brought together to brief the PM, the shaven-headed Chief of the Defence Staff, General Jock Kydd. He was dressed in his habitual, faded jungle-green combats without rank badges, sleeves rolled up high to reveal large, hairy biceps. As ever, Walker found he was unsure whether he was impressed or frightened by the man. Impressed because Kydd had immediately made things happen, unlike his Machiavellian predecessor. And frightened, not only because of the feral nature of the man, but also because he had an uneasy feeling that, if he said the wrong thing, the general would happily rip his head off.

'Prime Minister.' Infuriatingly, Kydd did not wait to be spoken to, but launched straight in. 'This is Dave McKinlay, the Deputy Supreme Allied Commander Europe. He's just flown in from NATO's strategic headquarters in Belgium for this briefing.' Walker noted a bulky, strong-looking, grey-haired general who, in his Royal Marines uniform and badges of rank, looked like another conventional soldier. However, a second glance revealed a steely look and the broken nose of a former rugby player and he realised that, although very different, the two generals were probably very much out of the same lethal mould.

'It's good to meet you, General,' said Little, shaking his hand. 'Where does NATO stand on this?'

'I'm here, Prime Minister, because nobody else, and that includes the Americans, can do what GCHQ have got planned and we fully support that plan. My role is to ensure the closest possible cooperation between what GCHQ can do and the NATO strategy. So, I'm here to listen in and take the plan back to SACEUR.'

'We really appreciate you finding time to visit us, Prime Minister,' said Berry, taking back control. 'We've got a plan which I think you'll find of interest. I've brought together the team who've been working this particular issue, so I'm going to leave it to them to tell you what they've achieved.'

'I hear you've found a way into Russia's nuclear command and control system,' said Little, imposing his authority in turn. 'If that's so, it's a potential war winner. But please continue.'

'Certainly, Prime Minister,' answered Berry. 'But without going into technical detail. Not because we think you won't understand it. More important, it's not something you need to know, so it's better left unsaid.'

'Look here, Ian,' said Little, 'I only managed to scrape a Physics with Chemistry 'O' Level. There's no chance of me letting any technical cats out of the bag!'

'Be that as it may, Prime Minister, but what I'm saying is, you may not want to know . . .' As he said this, Berry was looking hard at Walker, his meaning clear: he was not revealing any secrets to the Prime Minister's PR man, regardless of his top level of clearance.

The Prime Minister also looked at him, but instead of leaping to his defence as his predecessor would have done, he waved a hand as if to push the issue aside. 'Point taken. Continue.'

'Thank you, Prime Minister. In essence what we've done is

think through the problem as if we were terrorists hacking a nuclear command and control network. I'm going to leave it to Nicola Allenby, the team leader, to talk you through it. She's just back from PJHQ, where they are setting up this attack . . . If you authorise us to instigate it, that is.'

Berry indicated the four individuals sitting at the conference table opposite the two generals. Walker, sitting at the back and keen now to hide his resentment at the obvious put-down, took in the group, all in their late twenties. Two of the three men had half-grown beards, spiky hair and were ear-ringed and T-shirted: typical geeks. The third was bespectacled, wearing a tweed jacket and looked like a 1950s physics student. Allenby, the one woman, looked attractively self-confident, especially given her age and considering her audience. In fact, she looked positively sporty; more a young, high-flying corporate financier than someone who was planning an attack on Russia's nuclear systems.

Allenby was explaining how nuclear command and control covered everything required to maintain a nuclear weapons capability: personnel, equipment, facilities, organisations, procedures as well as the chain of command. 'Given the need for mobility, multiple launch platforms and redundancy – a back-up system in case the primary system fails – the Russian system is inherently vulnerable,' she went on in her clipped, precise tones, a legacy of what could only be an expensive education. 'We looked at the issue and decided we wanted two results. First, we looked at how we might take down the entire Russian General Staff communications system.'

Kydd, sitting opposite her, growled. 'Now you're talking my fucking language . . .'

Allenby looked him in the eye. 'General, there's no need for that in here. Thank you.'

Kydd squirmed and Walker smirked to himself as he watched the soldier's evident discomfort. *Great to see the cocky bastard put down*, he thought to himself. *This girl's sussed him out and put him firmly in his place. That's more than the PM's managed so far.* He caught her eye and gave her an encouraging nod.

Allenby ignored him and continued, 'But, more specifically, we also wanted to get inside the nuclear command and control system and take control of that . . . I'll come back to that in a moment.'

'So, what can you do about the Russian General Staff command and control system?' The Prime Minister was intrigued but also, Walker knew, on a very tight timetable.

'Our tactic was no different from hackers anywhere looking to achieve what's known in the trade as Distributed Denial of Service – DDoS. That involves taking control of multiple computers by installing a worm these guys invented.' Allenby gestured to the three young men on either side of her. 'Once Rasputin, that's the name we've given our particular worm, is inserted into one computer in a botnet – that's what we call multiple computers linked together under illicit control – it spreads like wildfire. As it spreads, the computers in the network come together to shut down websites or portions of the network by flooding the servers with data requests. This massive flow of data requests causes buffer overflow, jams the servers and makes them unusable.'

'So, effectively what you are doing is using the computers in the network to block the network,' said Little slowly, but looking somewhat confused; as well he might, thought Walker.

'Exactly, Prime Minister,' replied Allenby crisply. 'But the really clever thing about Rasputin is that we can activate it when we want to. Most worms go into action as soon as they enter the system. But Rasputin sits in their system, dormant, until we want it to create chaos.'

'OK . . . So how do you get into the network in the first place?'

'Good question, Prime Minister,' GCHQ Director Berry

intervened. 'Initially we tried to mount an operation with the CIA and MI6 to break into the servers of Russia's National Defence Control Centre, the NDCC, while it was being built. However, to give them credit – and the Russians are seriously good at this sort of thing – we failed. One reason is that their servers are Russian-made, which maximises their resistance to our offensive cyber capabilities. That by the way, Prime Minister, is another conversation for another day, about our own foreign-built servers . . . but I digress . . . Anyway, any defence is only as good as its weakest links. And Nicola here found a way in.' He smiled like a magician producing a rabbit from a hat, before pointing back to Allenby and so inviting her to explain.

'You'll appreciate, Prime Minister, that any computer connected to the internet is susceptible to infiltration and take-over. We had to find a way to access a closed network like the one used by the Russian General Staff. So we looked for an individual with access to the closed network into whose open-network computer we might be able to install a virus.'

'And . . . ?'

'PJHQ hosted a visit a few years ago from a group of Russians who were setting up the NDCC, before Crimea – when relations were still OK. Well, naturally, my predecessor took advantage of it and laid the ground work. The team monitored the computer usage of a number of the colonels when they were back in their hotel and managed to get IP addresses and other details. Roll the clock forward and one of those colonels is now a general in the NDCC, so we continued to monitor his usage and hacked into his computer with the details recorded from that time. We had clocked that he was a regular subscriber to a couple of dodgy websites and we also knew that he was in the habit of taking work home and transferring work from his laptop onto his office computer.

'The next step was to infect the websites he was downloading with Rasputin. So the next time he logged into one of his favourite porn sites, his computer was infected. Then he made the mistake of transferring a military presentation he'd written at home on his laptop onto the desk top in his office at the NDCC. His desk top is on the military net and that was that – we'd penetrated the system.'

The Prime Minister looked impressed. 'Ingenious . . . and very, very far-sighted,' he commented.

'That's the nature of our work, Prime Minister.' Berry once again took over. 'Thanks to Nicola and the team we can take down the Russian General Staff network on call. However, we must assume they'll have some form of reversionary mode and be able to get back up and running again very quickly. How quickly we have no idea. So, to get the best result for the operational boys, we'll have to initiate the Rasputin attack with maximum precision. And that means the closest possible coordination with the operational plan. Which is why the military team are here today.'

'Impressive,' said Little. 'But doesn't that still leave the nuclear command and control?'

'Yes, Prime Minister, but we can fix that.' Then Berry explained how the Russian system, on the face of it, depended on authority for launch from the President, who was always accompanied by an aide who carried the nuclear launch briefcase. 'Cheget is connected to Kavkaz, the senior government officials' communication system. That is connected to Kazbek, the broader nuclear command and control communication system. But, and this is the really good bit, it's possible for more junior people to intervene in the system.'

'Go on,' said Little, 'I think I'm still with you.'

'The Russians have a back-up system called Perimetr – literally 'dead hand' – which is designed to launch an attack in the event of a massive strike that has decapitated the Russian leadership. It's a sort of last-ditch revenge strike, which would send us all to oblivion: a modern-day version of *Doctor Strangelove*.'

'You're having me on,' the Prime Minister exclaimed. 'Life imitating art in the most ghastly way . . .'

'Exactly, Prime Minister, and I wish I was having you on. But what matters for today is that, by using Rasputin, we can now break into the operating system and insert a malicious code with a Trojan Horse, one that will not only give us access to Perimetr, but allow us to control it. So instead of Perimetr thinking that Russia's command and control has been destroyed and that it must now nuke the West, Rasputin will fool it into surrendering control to us. We will then have electronic control of the Iskander missiles in Kaliningrad. But, and again, for how long we just don't know.'

'But long enough to create . . . chaos?'

'We believe so.'

The Prime Minister leaned back. 'Pure genius,' he breathed. 'We hold the Russians to ransom with their own missiles.'

'Exactly, Prime Minister,' Berry said.

'And this is where Dave comes in, Prime Minister,' Kydd interjected. 'This will be a NATO operation although, of course, the US will be lead nation. Rasputin is the key to success so, if this is to work, it'll be very much down to the skill and ingenuity of GCHQ. And Dave is the key to linking Rasputin with the NATO plan. However, we shouldn't forget that, given the size of force we can offer these days, the US consider us as a junior partner alongside other European nations. It's just lucky that DSACEUR is still a UK post, but we can't take even that for granted indefinitely.'

'What do you mean?' demanded Little, turning to McKinlay. 'UK has always been a lead nation in NATO and punched well above its weight.'

Walker watched as McKinlay thought for a moment, as if pondering whether to accept the Prime Minister's line or to push back. Then he saw the Royal Marine's jaw set and his eyes narrow. He looked the Prime Minister directly in the eye and spoke.

'I've told the MOD many times that those days are over, Prime Minister. UK may think like that, but none of the other nations think that of UK. Sure, there's still a lot of respect for the quality of the people in the British Armed Forces, but the reality is that UK influence in NATO has diminished significantly, and that is entirely down to the constant reductions in defence capability of the last decade or so. And I say that despite the big equipment promises of the 2015 Defence Review. As far as our NATO allies are concerned, those were promises of jam tomorrow and not combat effectiveness today.'

'But . . .' Little started to protest, but having glanced at Kydd who was nodding in agreement with McKinlay's dire assessment, he instead gestured at him to continue.

'Thank you, Prime Minister . . . What is more, UK's position has been damaged by its reluctance to get involved in NATO operations and its willingness to let other nations carry the burden. Before all this kicked off, the Germans and Italians were heading the league table in terms of European contributors to operations in places like the Balkans and the NATO mission in Afghanistan. On top of that, no-one can understand why a maritime nation like the UK scrapped its maritime patrol aircraft.' He paused. 'And with the sinking of the *Queen Elizabeth*, that particular chicken came home to roost . . . Catastrophically.'

Walker was not surprised that Little was bristling at this criticism. 'Well, General,' he said sarcastically, 'you're a British officer, you'd better get out and tell NATO that we are stepping up to the mark again, especially with Rasputin.'

'I'm sorry, Prime Minister,' replied McKinlay quietly. 'Rasputin has to stay on the closest possible hold. Only SACEUR needs to know, together with his key Ops general in SHAPE, also an American. But it must go no further, even if it works out perfectly. Not even our Ambassador to NATO, Dame Flora Montrose, can know about it. Rasputin is an offensive cyber operation and NATO has made it very clear that it will only engage in defensive cyber operations. So, Rasputin must be seen only as a UK operation. And more generally, I'm not standing here as a British officer. I may be wearing a British uniform and no-one should doubt my loyalty to my country, but my first duty is to NATO. If I were to push a UK line, I'd lose whatever credibility I have and that could only disadvantage the UK in the longer term.'

Then, realising that he might have overdone it, he added, 'But, Prime Minister, it's not all doom and gloom. What I can say is that the rest of the Alliance, particularly the Americans, are very aware that there has been a change of direction.'

Walker could see that the Prime Minister had had enough of this criticism and was about to snap back, but Kydd intervened. 'I'm afraid to tell you Dave's right, Prime Minister. I'm getting exactly this from my US contacts, too. There's always the danger of listening to our own propaganda and it's no bad thing to have someone who's prepared to tell us how we're seen by others. Which you now have . . .'

The Prime Minister looked slowly from Kydd to McKinlay and back again. Walker saw the pugnacious look in Little's eye and waited for the eruption, but none came. Instead, the Prime Minister grinned disarmingly at Kydd. 'I knew what I was taking on when I appointed you, CDS. But I didn't expect there to be two of you . . .'

And now he also grinned at McKinlay. 'OK, I take the point. I don't like what you say, but I'm glad we've still got some generals who are prepared to tell it as it is.' Then he changed the subject. 'Could the Americans set up something like Rasputin?'

'Not without our help,' said Berry.

'Good,' said Little with a nod. 'Trevor, please set up a call to President Dillon just as soon as I'm back in Number Ten.'

1245 hours, Friday, 7 July 2017
GCHQ, Cheltenham, England

S OON AFTER THE meeting had concluded, the Prime Minister
left, accompanied by Walker. McKinlay was escorted back
to the car that was to take him to the small airport at Staverton,
near Gloucester, to catch the RAF HS-125 executive jet back
to Belgium. He was walking down the circular walkway that
runs through the building, known to all as 'The Street', when
he saw Nicola Allenby hastening to join him.

'General, I need to talk. Quietly please. If you have a moment,
that is . . .'

Allenby, who'd impressed McKinlay by her poise, self-confidence
and deep knowledge of her subject, looked concerned.

'Of course. How are we for time, Simon?' he asked his British
Army Military Assistant.

'The plane's not going without you, General . . . take as
long as you like. I suggest we head out to the garden. There's
plenty of space and we'll be able to find somewhere quiet.'

Their GCHQ escort, a middle-aged lady from Protocol, took
them into the open-air garden courtyard situated in the middle
of the Doughnut and they sat at a bench close to the memorial to the five GCHQ staff killed on active service in Afghanistan:
two Cotswold Stone circles, with the bronze heads of a young
woman and a helmeted soldier in profile, facing each other.

'You did well back there,' said McKinlay bluntly, once the escort was out of earshot. 'I don't mean just the op you've set up . . . but you weren't fazed by that little weasel with the PM – his Director of Communications, Walker . . . Odious man. Always looking to get something on you that he can trade later.'

Allenby brushed off the compliment with what seemed to McKinlay her trademark briskness, but he wondered as he observed her, was it really shyness?

'Thank you, General, but it happens all the time with those types.'

He nodded at her to continue.

'Look, I know you're heading back to SHAPE, but there's something you should know that I can't pass on via the usual channels . . . Which is why I wanted to grab you before you left.'

McKinlay was intrigued. 'I'm listening.'

'It's about the team of Mercians we've got in Latvia – at least they started in Latvia. As you'll know, they've now infiltrated into Kaliningrad from Lithuania. They've just completed a close target recce on the nuclear command and control bunker at Pravdinsk, in order to prepare the way for US Special Forces to seize it once we've activated Rasputin and established the electronic control I briefed the PM about.'

'OK,' said McKinlay.

'There are two issues of concern you should know about. First, we've picked up from the Russian nets that they've almost certainly identified the team. Not only that, but the Russians know they were responsible for humiliating the President with the helicopter shoot down at Ligatne. And second, we've picked up that the President has personally ordered the Spetsnaz to capture Tom Morland, the Mercian team commander. They want to make a spectacle of him. Before disposing of him, no doubt.'

'How did they manage that?' asked McKinlay.

'By the signature of the data transmissions. Without going into the technicalities, the team signaller has a particular way of putting together the message. He's good, but he's not SF, so he hasn't been trained in the techniques to avoid detection. We've picked up on it, so we're assuming the Russians have, too. They're brilliant at this sort of thing. We're now assuming that the Russians picked them up first in Latvia, which would explain how they were able to zero in on the team and then launch that camp attack, which only just failed. Since then, although they've only transmitted very occasionally since, they'll have been tracking the guys through Lithuania . . . and now we believe that the Russians know they're in Kaliningrad. So, although their last transmission was some distance from Pravdinsk, it has to be a fair bet that the Russians will put two and two together and work out that they're probably looking at the nuclear command and control facility there.'

McKinlay rubbed his chin ruminatively. 'I see . . . but I can't say I'm surprised. It was probably only a matter of time before the Russians caught up with them. So, what you're saying is that by tracking their radio signature, they may have inadvertently led the Russians to Pravdinsk?'

'Well, General, I was thinking more of the team walking into a trap.'

'Yes, I can see that. They've done incredibly well and had amazing luck, but luck usually runs out eventually. The secret of survival, not that I am one to talk,' he smiled as he rapped his artificial leg with his knuckles, 'is knowing when it is time to say enough. I think you are telling me that it's time this chap Morland did just that.'

'Yes, General. Exactly. Although the important news for our plan is that we aren't getting the sense that Moscow think they are doing anything more than looking.'

'Long may that last. Is there any satellite or radio information that shows troops being moved into the area?'

'No, General.'

'So even though they probably suspect that our boys are going to recce Pravdinsk, they aren't worried. Haven't reinforced, or anything?'

'No, General.'

'As I guessed. Or we'd have aborted the mission already. Correct?'

Allenby nodded.

'All of which makes sense, if you think about it. They're only five soldiers. Not even Special Forces. With a few Forest Brothers. I cannot imagine they will worry the Russians unduly. And yes, I do agree with you, it does look as if they will be expected.'

McKinlay looked hard at the girl as he spoke. Important as this information was, she could just as easily have briefed someone more junior. He had a sense that this girl, who had been so impressive and direct in front of the PM only moments before, was not letting everything on. 'Is there something you want me to do?' he asked, trying to keep any gruffness out of his voice. He had a plane to catch and a war to plan.

'Well . . . PJHQ know all this but refuse to warn them.'

'Let me guess,' McKinlay was thinking of a couple of his spook chums and their convoluted way of thinking, 'because, if you do warn them and they are captured, then the Russians will torture them and discover what they know, and therefore what we know . . . and, don't tell me, you haven't informed these Mercians what we are planning or their role in it.'

'Exactly, Sir. In case they're caught.'

'In case they're caught . . .' McKinlay mused, thinking through the variables before replying. 'Trouble is, and callous as it sounds, I have to agree.'

'But, Sir. It gets worse. They've identified a hidden minefield, which would totally stymie the American SOF forcing an entry into the perimeter.'

'Well, I guess there's only one solution then, if this is going to work,' McKinlay replied. 'Morland and his team will have to meet up with the US SOF when they infiltrate and guide them through or around the minefield.'

'Straight into an ambush by the Russian special forces, who we know are tracking them and are probably waiting for them . . .'

'Quite probably. We'll just have to hope that Morland has thought through how he approaches the task. He sounds like a capable young officer. Let's just hope he stays lucky.'

'But . . .'

'It's what we soldiers are paid to do when we take the Queen's Shilling on the day we join – harsh though it may sound.'

He gave her an avuncular smile before pushing himself to his feet. Then he caught himself and remembered his sense of humanity. This girl, little older than his own daughters, was a systems geek. She might come across like the captain of the lacrosse team but, in reality, she played with computers and radios. And now something clever she had set up was probably going to result in men being killed; men she had been communicating with, men whose names she had come to know, men she wanted to warn but was not being allowed to.

Looking at the evident distress on her face, it must have come as a shock to her to discover that there was such a direct and human dimension to her work. He thought again of his own wife and daughters and their accusation that he lacked empathy. GCHQ was going to need the Nicola Allenbys of this world in the dark days that were certain to come and he knew he ought to try to show some concern and understanding.

'I'm genuinely sorry if that came over as heartless, Nicola. But there really is nothing you can do to help. You need to focus on the fact that what you *have* done has helped, *is* going to save countless lives. It's not your fault he's going back into danger and you cannot warn him.'

Deep in the dense forest, hidden in the carefully concealed patrol base, Morland, Krauja and Arvydas Lukša, the Lithuanian Forest Brother who had taken over responsibility for looking after the Mercian team, went through the detail once again of what they had learned from their recent reconnaissance of the Pravdinsk Iskander missile site. They were looking for any potential gaps in the plan for the next phase of the operation. Close by, Sergeant Danny Wild provided immediate protection, while around them the Lithuanians and Mercians cleaned weapons, rested or prepared their kit for that night's operation. On the edge of a clearing the trail bikes, their means of transport up until now, stood hidden under camouflage nets.

Morland kept his voice low as he summarised what they knew. 'We've got a pretty firm fix on the way the site's laid out: barbed-wire perimeter fence, arc lights and sentry towers – together with the least exposed approaches. Also, it seems that the guards tend to follow the same pattern in their patrolling. In and out of the same gate in the compound.'

Krauja nodded. 'And we know they always use the same track through that minefield along the northern perimeter too. I couldn't spot whether it was marked or not, but at least we know it's there. Thank God for that wretched deer blowing its leg off after straying into it. If we hadn't been watching the perimeter fence when it did, we'd have never have known the minefield existed.'

'I only wish it had been us who got the meat instead of the Russians,' grumbled Captain Lukša, the broad-shouldered, former member of the Lithuanian national wrestling team, now of the Lithuanian Special Operations Forces. 'We could all do with a hot meal.'

'Roger to that,' said Morland with feeling. Ever since they had crossed into Russian-populated Kaliningrad, they had needed to be even more careful and that had meant the cold rations of 'hard routine' for fear that fires would give them away. 'Now, once again, those patrols. You're sure the Russians will stick with the timings and routes we've logged?'

'You can guarantee that the Russians will be predictable,' Lukša answered with his usual smile. 'When I was younger, I made my living from smuggling cigarettes across the border from Lithuania into Kaliningrad. If we had been caught? Well . . . but we risked it, because we knew where their minefields and standing patrols were situated. Improvisation and initiative isn't something they teach their soldiers. Don't get me wrong. The Russians can be brilliant planners, but once they have a plan they stick to it, and woe betide anyone who doesn't follow that plan. That's why crossing the border was never a problem. That and knowing every track and hiding place . . .'

'Thank God for your dodgy past.' Morland grinned at him. 'We owe you guys a lot. If you weren't so brilliant at driving motorbikes down forest tracks in the middle of the night at one hundred kilometres per hour using night vision goggles, and scaring the living daylights out of us Brits, we wouldn't have even got this far. In fact, I can say this, hand on heart, I never want to get on a bloody motorbike ever again . . . But now it's time to get serious. Those American Special Forces guys are depending on us to guide them in to the bunker. This is your backyard, Arvydas. That means we are following you.'

Lukša thought before replying. 'This is where it gets tricky. We'll leave a couple of my guys here with the bikes, ready to extract us fast back across the border to Lithuania once we've completed the task. We'll be able to hide up much better there.' He looked at Krauja and Morland, who both nodded their agreement.

Morland knew the Russians would swamp the area with troops once the Americans arrived and did whatever they were planning to do. That meant the team needed to be as far away as possible before that happened.

'We'll move out from here on foot at 2200 hours, once it's properly dark. I'll go ahead as lead scout. Tom, you follow me with the rest of your team and Marina behind you. Two of my people will bring up the rear. I'll signal when we're in the LUP – the lying-up position – and then it's the usual hard routine for the rest of the night and through tomorrow. We'll only be five kilometres from the compound and that means no fires or lights or cigarettes, pissing and crapping where we are, no movement, complete silence. We'll move out after dark tomorrow night to link up with the Americans for their drop. Then we take them forward so they can get eyes on the compound. We've recce'd the routes. We all know where we need to be and what we need to do. We just need to keep doing what we've been doing to make sure that we remain undetected. No mistakes . . . ' He stopped and looked at Morland. 'Happy with that, Tom?'

'Spot on, Arvydas. Exactly what London wants.' Morland looked around the patrol base. Everyone had been briefed and was ready to go. He nodded at Wild, 'Time to get something to eat and a bit of rest. It's going to be a long night.'

Lukša moved over to his soldiers to confirm they all knew what was planned and had no questions, while Wild did the same with the three other Mercians.

Morland reached into his bergen and pulled out a tin of sardines from his Lithuanian ration pack, together with a packet of dry biscuits. He looked at Krauja. 'It's hardly cordon bleu, Marina, but have a bite.'

Krauja pulled a face. 'No thanks, Tom, I've got some of my own. I wouldn't want to deprive you. But thanks anyway.'

'If only we could cook something. I'm a dab hand at putting together a classic compo all in stew.'

'A what?' asked Krauja.

'Everything in the pack put together and heated up: baked beans, meat, veg, hard tack biscuits, cheese – with lashings of curry powder and tabasco sauce,' said Morland, with a faraway look in his eye as he thought about hot food.

Krauja smiled. 'I hadn't seen you as a domestic god, Tom. I might just hold you to that . . . If we ever get out of here, that is.' For a moment her control faltered.

Morland saw that for all her Baltic strength of character, Krauja was frightened. 'Don't you worry, Marina. We'll make it out.' He gestured at Wild and the three other Mercian soldiers. 'Those buggers have been in much worse scrapes. They're natural-born survivors and so are you!'

For the first time since he had known her, she looked unconvinced.

'I'm being deadly serious here, Marina. I don't know what the Americans are planning, but I reckon that the Russians in that compound are going to get the shock of their lives tomorrow night. If we keep to the plan, keep quiet, we should be in and out. After that, of course . . .' As he said it, Morland was all too aware that, while they had been living almost cheek to cheek, they had hardly spoken to one another properly since they came into the forest; the consequence of living and operating tactically and on the run for weeks on end.

He looked around and saw that, for a brief moment, they were alone. 'I've been wanting to thank you, Marina. I saw how pissed off Jānis Krastiņš was, when he handed us over to Arvydas Lukša and the Lithuanian Forest Brothers. I didn't understand a word he was saying but, from the look he gave me when he left, I'm guessing you insisted on staying and looking after us.'

'Yes . . . Well . . .'

For a moment there was a softness in her eyes when Krauja looked back at him and Morland thought he detected the faintest of blushes beneath the green-and-brown camouflage cream smeared over her cheeks. Then it was if she caught herself before giving him her normal, no-nonsense look.

'When you and I first met in Riga, Juris Bērziņš, my boss, ordered me to stay with you and look after you . . . whatever happened. He had predicted something like this years ago. He had no doubt about what he was witnessing when he asked you to visit him and he assigned me to be your liaison officer. I told him yes, and I am fulfilling my word to a man I respected. Major Krastiņš's view was that with Bērziņš dead and Latvia overrun by the Russians, my promise no longer applied. I disagreed. That's all.'

'Is that so?' said Morland, unwilling to pursue the matter further. She was with them and that was that, and he certainly didn't want her anywhere else right now. Then another thought struck him. 'Please don't say this to anyone else, Marina, but I'm guessing we are going to get pulled out of here sooner rather than later. Although I have no idea how or when . . . If we are extracted, I think you should strongly consider coming back to the UK with us. You've more than done your bit and, what's more, you're much more useful alive and helping our Int people back home than stuck in the forests and being hunted down by the Russians. And something else I'm sure everyone is very aware of but they don't want to articulate, I think it's going to get very hairy around here once we complete this mission.'

'Thank you, Tom. I appreciate your concern.' Krauja looked at him gravely. 'But I'm Latvian. My country is occupied by Russia. The only way we can fight the invaders is from the forests. My duty is to get back where I'm needed. Besides . . . the Russians killed my brother.'

From the set look on her face, Morland knew better than to push her. Anyhow, it was time to clean his weapon, prepare his kit for the long patrol back to the compound and get some rest.

Five hours later, long after they had left their patrol base, Morland saw the shadowy outline of Captain Arvydas Lukša, the Lithuanian Forest Brother who was leading, hold up a hand. It was the signal to stop. He repeated the signal to Sergeant Wild behind him and he, in turn, passed the message soundlessly back to the rest of the patrol. He checked his luminous army issue watch: 0255 hrs. Twenty minutes later than planned, but better to take longer and go quieter, than rush and be heard and caught.

The other four Mercians, Krauja and two other Lithuanians automatically spread out to take up a position of all-round defence. When Morland saw they were in position, he swung his daysack from his shoulders and lowered it to the earth. Suppressing the urge to flop down next to it and rest, he moved to each team member in turn, careful not to snap any of the twigs or branches that littered the forest floor, and confirmed with a suppressed whisper that they were now in their lying-up place. This is where they would remain until the following night.

Only when Morland saw the unmistakeable silhouette of Corporal Jezza Watson move away from the team to do the first sentry stag did he sit down and consult his map by the faint red light of his torch. He knew they were in exactly the right place, but he double-checked all the same. Now it was time to settle in for what remained of the short summer night. They would stay hidden here all the next day until the scheduled parachute drop of US Special Forces tomorrow night.

He swigged a mouthful from his water bottle, extracted his bivvi bag from his daysack, felt the forest floor to make sure he was not placing it over any stones or protruding roots that would keep him awake and then unrolled it. Next he took off his webbing vest and laid it carefully beside him, ready to pull on at a moment's notice, and wriggled into his bivvi bag, boots still on. If anything happened out here, this close to the Russians, there would be no time to pull them on and lace them up. It had only been this level of attention to infantry drills by every member of the team that had meant that when the Spetsnaz – and he was convinced that only their Special Forces could have got that close to their camp undetected by the Forest Brothers – had ambushed them in the forest, five long-and-gruelling weeks ago, he had been armed and ready for action in seconds.

Thank God though for those negligently fired shots and the machine-gun fire that followed it. Morland could still remember the sudden sound of the distant rounds as they shattered the silence of the forest, startling him into shocked wakefulness. He knew full well, and Wild had not stopped reminding the team since, that it was only the speed of their constantly rehearsed bug-out drills that had enabled them to escape the well-placed trap.

As he went through his now all-too-familiar 'lying-up' routine, he was conscious of the faint rustles of the others doing the same; quietly, systematically and professionally. In mere minutes the movements stopped. The forest fell silent, except for the hoot of an owl and the scuffling of a distant wild boar rooting around for food in the undergrowth.

However, desperate for sleep as he was, with their objective now so close by, Morland found himself on full alert, ears cocked, listening for anything that might indicate they'd been compromised. Try as he might to convince himself he was imagining things, he kept seeing the face of the Russian Spetsnaz commander who had stared so intently at him when he'd roared past on the back of an escaping scrambler bike as the dawn light penetrated the forest: medium height, early thirties, close-cropped, dark hair, and wearing green combats, with no identifying insignia or badges. The man who had orchestrated the riot in Riga, the man he'd seen talking into his radio just before the snipers opened up on the crowd in the Vermanes Gardens, the man who had ordered the cold-blooded execution of those young girls. One glance had been enough, but when they had finally stopped at the next secret bunker, he had checked the pictures on his camera. It was the same man.

Again, the same thought recurred: what was that Russian doing there, leading an ambush, when a man of his evident importance surely had more important things to do? And was it paranoia, brought on by fear and exhaustion and that single stare, that now had Morland wondering whether it was him the Russian had been seeking? If so, was the Russian still tracking him? Because, if the Spetsnaz commander had managed to find them once in the wilderness, might he be able to do so again? Was he closing in on them even now?

They had moved from hide to hide, never staying long enough to give away evidence of their occupation – tracks worn in the forests, the build-up of rubbish and bodily wastes, all potential give-aways to determined searchers with sophisticated kit. Some hides had been built so deep underground that they would defeat the most advanced heat-seeking drones. But after their near capture they had continued to move, regardless.

They had been equally disciplined in their infrequent use of the radio, always travelling some distance away from their hides to send information and receive orders; Corporal Steve Bradley, his Kiwi signaller, obsessive about never transmitting for too long. But still Morland worried; fears for which he had no answers, fears he had decided to keep to himself rather than alarm the others. They were all stressed enough as it was. Weeks of ambushes and intelligence gathering, followed by high-speed changes of location to throw off any pursuers, had taken them all to the edge.

Silence: time to trust the sentry and get some much-needed sleep. As he forced himself to relax, Morland caught the warm reek of his filthy combat kit and unwashed body. *We've pretty much gone feral*, he thought. Wild beards, matted, filthy hair and scrawny from living on the dwindling and ever-more basic field rations that the Latvians and Lithuanians had shared with them. Not that it mattered. They all smelt as bad as one another and they hardly noticed the stench. In fact, even if they had been able to, they wouldn't have washed as the smell of soap could be enough to give them away to a patrol or a wild animal, so drawing attention to their position.

He'd expected his guys to cope; after all, they were experienced infantrymen and recce men, and they had done so – despite the usual grumbles. The Lithuanians, like the Latvians, were naturals. But, and somewhat to his surprise, Krauja had been the star. She had put up with the hardships, had taken her share of the stags, and her surveillance expertise had made her invaluable recceing the compound. More than that, behind her natural Latvian reserve, she could display a soldier's sense of humour and, when minded, could banter with the best of them.

But now was not the time to be thinking about her; now was the time to go through his mental check list for tomorrow. Move out from here after last light, a five-kilometre tab through the forest to the final RV. Then move into position near the DZ – Drop Zone – ready to guide in the US Special Forces ODA, who were due to parachute in by HAHO – high altitude, high opening – with the radar transponder beacon Lukša had with him. Once they'd linked up with the Americans, the ODA would mark out an LZ – Landing Zone – for the helicopters bringing in the air assault force. His task was to then lead the Americans forward to recce the compound and bunker with its perimeter fence and minefield.

At the prospect of getting up close to the perimeter again, Morland felt the now-familiar cold grip of raw fear in the pit of his stomach. They'd chanced it last time and got away with it. To go back to that ring of steel and death was asking for trouble. But he consoled himself with the thought that, once they'd guided the airborne to the wire, it was job done. They were to step back and let the Americans do whatever it was they had come to do. The trouble was, in his rapidly increasing experience, he doubted it would work out like that once the bullets started flying. Plans seldom did. However, of one thing he was certain, there was nothing he could do about it right now. Instead, he closed his eyes and, body cushioned on a deep layer of last year's pine needles, he slept.

MAJOR ANATOLY NIKOLAYEVICH Vronsky marched into the temporary office of Colonel General Arkady Vasilyevich Kirkorov, the Commander of Western Military District, the man in charge of suppressing the Baltic insurgency.

Vronsky threw a smart, parade-ground salute. He then stood rigidly at attention, waiting for the general to speak, braced for another outburst of rage similar to the last occasion, five weeks previously, when he had debriefed him in St Petersburg on the failure of the camp attack on the British guerrilla team.

Ordered by the President to oversee the capture of the British terrorists, Kirkorov had exploded in fury when Vronsky had blamed the failure of the attack on the poor discipline, training and weapons handling of the conscripts from the general's beloved Motor Rifle troops. Vronsky was in no doubt that, but for the personal orders of the President, he would have been heading for the gulag.

Vronsky stood silent, eyes fixed firmly on the wall above the line of the general's shaven bullet-head as he studied a Top Secret file spread on the desk in front of him. The key to survival in these situations, he knew – whether you were a highly decorated Spetsnaz officer or the newest recruit – was never to catch the senior officer's eye.

Men like Kirkorov were not, in Vronsky's experience, easy to deal with. An old-school Soviet type, he had first come to the attention of his superiors in Afghanistan in the 1980s for the scorched-earth approach he had taken to root out the Mujahidin in the Panjshir valley, regardless of the casualties to the civilian population. Subsequently, his promotion had been guaranteed as a result of the equally brutal tactics he employed as a Motor Rifle regiment commander in the Chechen wars; what he described with pride as 'bringing discipline to the territory of the Chechen Republic', but which left thousands of men, women and children dead, the capital city Grozny looking like Stalingrad, and a lasting legacy of hatred of Russia among the Muslim population of the Caucasus. A hatred that made it very much harder for the new generation of Russian Spetsnaz, like Vronsky, to establish networks of informers among the locals in order to root out and crush the insurgents.

The general was now doing much the same in the Baltics, but Vronsky's current concern was not with them. His sole mission was to capture this British officer. Succeed and he would have the gratitude of the President. Fail and . . . he did not even want to think about it. His plan called for a sophisticated ambush by his Spetsnaz team, waiting downstairs for the 'go' order right now. However, he had little doubt that the general would prefer to simply blitz the area and the British with it. And that was not what the President had ordered.

'Explain your thinking, Major,' the general finally said.

Vronsky caught the general's piggy eyes looking up at him. He did not make the mistake of looking down. 'Colonel General. Ever since the failed ambush, SIGINT has been trying to monitor the terrorists' movements. They got a break when they realised that their patrol signaller has a distinctive way of signing off after a transmission. They then replayed all recorded intercepts and were able to track him as he moved south. First down through Latvia, then into Lithuania, and finally into Kaliningrad.'

'Kaliningrad!' the general exploded. 'That's Russian territory – and our Iskander batteries are there. They'd never dare . . .'

Vronsky waited and when the general said nothing more, he continued. 'That's our conclusion as well, Sir. They'd never dare. Also, we now know for a fact that this is a team of five ordinary infantry soldiers.'

The general began to growl in anger and his hands clenched on the desk. 'Exactly what are you implying, Major?' the general demanded.

'Military Intelligence is categoric, and the FSB has confirmed that this is the case: the British always use their Special Forces as the tip of their military spear. Find the location of their Special Forces and you will find where they are going to attack. This is not only common sense, but it has been demonstrated time and again. Just as Spetsnaz always lead our attacks.'

The general thought about it. 'Go on.'

'There are no Allied Special Force units in or near Kaliningrad. However, we are already picking up indications that they are trying to infiltrate British SAS and SBS, together with American Deltas and SEALs into Estonia and Latvia. Precisely where NATO will attack. If it is foolish enough . . .'

'So?'

'So, these five British infantrymen were in Latvia conducting training and were caught behind our lines when we recovered our Baltic Provinces. They have been left there. The border is so closely guarded by land, sea and air that nothing can get in and nothing can get out. They are stranded and making mischief. And that's it. Nothing strategic, just being nuisances.'

'They've certainly succeeded in that,' the general growled, with the first hint of a smile of recognition for a fellow professional.

'I know, Colonel General. Which is why I'm here . . . Anyway, we believe they are on a recce mission. No more. No less. They are with a handful of Forest Brothers. However, each missile battery is guarded by a reinforced company and each is based in a highly defended complex. What possible threat could these few British constitute to us? What can they hope to do?'

'Attack our missiles . . .'

'With what, Colonel General? When I saw the British officer he was on the back of a motorbike, looked half-starved, and was armed only with an infantry rifle. What can he hope to do with that? And, even if he were to attack them, NATO knows the President will reply with nuclear missiles. They'd be mad. Which is why their Special Forces are nowhere near here. These men are lying low, trying not to be caught. Doubtless trying to do something useful, like reporting back our troop dispositions.'

'Your conclusion?'

This is your opportunity, Colonel General. The President wants this British officer. Were it not for that I'd bomb them from helicopters and drones and send in our airborne to pick up the remains. Because that's all that would be left of them. But the President wants us to give him this man to put on television. Alive . . .'

'Take a seat, Vronsky . . . Sasha!' he bellowed at the closed door.

A terrified-looking ADC opened the door and saluted. 'Yes, Colonel General?'

'Vodka, two glasses, and a plate of 'salo'.* And quickly. Major Vronsky and I have a plan to put together.'

The general turned back to him. 'Your plan?'

'Colonel General, early this morning we intercepted another radio transmission. Same radio, same operator. It's the British. This was about twenty kilometres north from Pravdinsk, in the forest south of the River Pregolya.'

'Pravdinsk . . . Our command bunker . . . and one of the

---

*The salted pork fat beloved as a taster to vodka.

Iskander batteries. If you're right, a target well worth a reconnaissance, but not one they'd ever dare attack. More an opportunity not to be missed than a specific threat. Hmm . . . and I suppose there's nothing they will see there that their satellites have not photographed already.'

'My thoughts entirely, Colonel General. My plan is to bring my Spetsnaz team of fifteen to reinforce the garrison. We'll either catch them when they go in to do their recce, or we'll zero in on them and catch them when they send their situation report back to London. Now we know what we're looking for, we'll locate them in minutes. Either up against the wire at Pravdinsk, or when they transmit . . . They'll never know what hit them.'

'Very well, Major. But on your own head be it,' Kirkorov growled, pouring two glasses of vodka before unbuttoning the top button of his tunic.

Following the general's lead, Vronsky drank the vodka in one gulp and quickly followed it with a piece of salo to line his stomach. Unless he could persuade the general otherwise, it was going to be a long, wasted afternoon and he still had much to do. 'Colonel General, my men are hoping you will do them the honour of inspecting them before they depart. And I need to get them to Pravdinsk long before the British arrive. Would you perhaps care to . . . ?'

The general gave him a sharp, suspicious look. He had obviously been looking forward to telling some stories as they drank the vodka. 'Go. I will inspect them in fifteen minutes.'

Vronsky drew up his men of the 45th Guards Spetsnaz Regiment in the vehicle hangar adjacent to the headquarters of the Kaliningrad Special Region and quickly explained the situation. An inspection like this was the last thing they needed, but Vronsky calculated that getting the general to inspect his soldiers right now was the best way of getting on his way before he got drunk and, perhaps, changed his mind. Besides, with only fifteen men in the detachment, Kirkorov would soon be finished.

As he stood, ready to greet the general by the door, Vronsky had time to think through his plan once again. Was he making a mistake?

From their radio transmissions, the British captain and his team were clearly heading for the Iskander nuclear missile battery, south of Pravdinsk. He could not imagine what they planned to achieve there, other than a recce of the bunker. They could not hope to seize a missile, at least not without starting the next world war and that seemed simply stupid. And he would not allow anything stupid to happen. Not with these men in the hall behind him. No, if the President really did want this man alive – and it seemed he really did – then ambushing him like this was the best solution. Decision confirmed, he and his men stood and waited.

The ADC arrived thirty minutes later and announced that Kirkorov was on his way with the base commander.

Vronsky ordered his men to attention.

The general, smelling slightly of vodka, strode in and, ignoring Vronsky, went straight to the line of men.

Despite himself, Vronsky was impressed at the way he went from man to man, taking a keen and intelligent interest in the specialist equipment that no conventional Russian soldier would ever see, but with which each Spetsnaz soldier was equipped. The new generation helmets and body armour with chest and back plates made of titanium and hard carbide-boron ceramics, impervious to the NATO standard 5.56 millimetre ammunition with which the British would be equipped; the grenade launchers; the AS Val assault rifles, so suited to operating with stealth and giving a minimum signature with its heavy, subsonic 9 millimetre, high-performance, armour-piercing ammunition, and magnified day and image-intensifier night sights; plus the collar and helmet-mounted radios that allowed them to communicate hands free.

Eventually the inspection finished. Kirkorov turned to Vronsky, who braced up to attention once again.

'Major Vronsky, your soldiers are impressive. Now, I have one question.'

'Sir?'

'You are certain that these terrorists pose no threat to our Iskander missiles?'

'They are five men and a few Forest Brothers. What threat could they pose to your company of highly trained guards and my Spetsnaz? No, Sir. They are obviously conducting a recon-naissance. And that is the last mistake they will ever make. The President will be forever grateful you allowed me to capture and hand them to you.'

The general smiled, looked at his ADC and pointed. 'You. Make a note of Major Vronsky's confidence and assurance.' Then he looked hard at the line of Spetsnaz. 'Make sure you succeed in this mission. The President is depending on you. Russia is depending on you.'

Vronsky saluted, now doubly impressed: Kirkorov knew exactly how to play dirty politics as well as crush dissidents. He should never have allowed himself to be manoeuvred into a statement like that but, had he demurred, he had little doubt the ambush plan would have been cancelled.

'Thank you, Sir. My men will not let you down . . . Now, Sir. May I have your leave to carry on, Sir. Please?'

'Do so. The Motherland will be watching you.' Kirkorov gave a perfunctory touch to the peak of his cap by way of returning Vronsky's parade-ground salute and walked out of the hangar, followed by his ADC and the base commander.

'Arsehole,' muttered one of the men in a stage whisper, as soon as they were out of earshot.

'I heard that, Lev Davidovich,' said Vronsky without turning around, not least to stop his men seeing the grin of relief that was breaking across his face at seeing the back of the general, and the imminent prospect of finally settling his score with this British officer. However, in that moment of triumph, he realised that he had allowed his mission to become personal. 'I'm getting as bad as the President,' he muttered to himself, before turning to face his men.

'Mount up,' he ordered and they clambered up into the Ural-4320 trucks, which were to take them to Pravdinsk.

Just over an hour later, Vronsky and his men dismounted by the perimeter of the Pravdinsk command bunker. This was close to where the radio sked had come from and, unless the British were playing some double bluff, this is where they were heading for. But even if they were, so what? All that mattered was that he had arrived here before them and this time he had the benefit of surprise. He and this British captain were going to meet again and soon.

He looked at the luminous dial of his treasured Rolex diver's watch: five and a half hours to sunset. Plenty of time to set up the ambush.

1500 hours, Saturday, 8 July 2017
The President's Office
The Kremlin, Moscow

FYODOR FYODOROVICH KOMAROV, the President's Chief of Staff, could see that his boss was uncomfortable. Despite his lack of height, the President had a presence that had always commanded respect, if not fear. But, Komarov observed to himself, since the sinking of the *Queen Elizabeth*, things had not worked out as expected and people were saying in ever louder whispers that the President had lost that sureness of touch that had been the hallmark of his rise to absolute power in the Kremlin. Was the President losing that reputation for strength that had guaranteed his position up until now? He looked at the expressionless faces around the table and wondered which of them was, even now, imagining themselves in the President's chair.

The President's pale, bloodless face was now flushed with anger, the pale eyes protruded more than usual, and sweat glistened on the bald patch where the hair had receded. Instead of speaking with his usual cold menace when less than pleased, he had of late been prone to outbursts of anger, shouting at his personal staff for the smallest apparent misdemeanours.

He was shouting now. This time at General Mikhail Gareyev,

Chief of the Russian General Staff, who sat at the conference table in the President's austere office in the Kremlin.

'Now you listen to me, Mikhail Nikolayevich,' he raged. 'Just over a month ago, you assured me that you would have the insurgency in the Baltic states under control! And now you tell me that you have lost freedom of movement, except when moving in force, on all but major roads because of the actions of these Forest Brother guerrillas! Was it for this that you thinned out the troops in Ukraine and the garrison in Kaliningrad? And what about detaining that British captain I ordered you to find? Still no sign of him? He's making a monkey of me . . . and you for that matter. I won't have it. Do you understand? If you can't deliver him, I'll find someone who can!'

Gareyev stayed silent. He knew better than to interrupt the tirade and Komarov assessed that, with the President in this mood, he would soon switch targets. He was right. The President next turned on the Director of the FSB, Merkulov.

'A month ago you assured me, Lavrentiy Pavlovich, that NATO was in disarray! And yet you now tell me that all your stations in NATO capitals report a renewed unity and sense of purpose and a determination to do whatever needs to be done to take the Baltic states from us! How do you explain that?'

As head of the FSB, the feared State Security and Counter-intelligence service and heir to the KGB in both reputation and practice, Merkulov, despite his mild, bespectacled appearance was deadly. Komarov saw him as the only man in Russia capable of frightening the President.

Quietly, almost nonchalantly, he murmured, 'Vladimir Vladimirovich, you should recognise that it was the unfortunate sinking of the two mine countermeasures vessels and *your* decision to torpedo the *Queen Elizabeth* when it posed no threat to us in the western Baltic that united NATO. And, if we wanted to ensure that America stepped up to lead the Alliance, we couldn't have done better than slaughter those American airmen and women at Lielvārde Air Base in Latvia. If we had left the Americans well alone, they would not be threatening us now. And NATO without the Americans is nothing. That simple. But we didn't and they are. Which is the problem we are facing now. What else is there to say?'

There was silence around the table. However, nobody moved to reprimand or distance themselves from Merkulov and that told Komarov much of what he feared: it increasingly looked if he was inextricably linked to the wrong man.

The President visibly curbed his rage. As an ex-KGB operative and former head of the FSB himself, he knew the power Merkulov wielded and that he needed his support.

In an effort to regain the initiative for him, Komarov changed the subject. 'Vladimir Vladimirovich, may I recommend that we ask for a report on NATO dispositions.'

The President looked at Gareyev. 'Go ahead, please,' he grunted in an effort to appear magisterial.

'Vladimir Vladimirovich. NATO, under American leadership, has mobilised significant forces. In the western Baltic, the Alliance has amassed an amphibious force based on 2nd Marine Expeditionary Force, that's an air-ground task force of around divisional size. Supporting it is the American 6th Fleet with two carrier battlegroups and a total of forty ships, with one hundred and seventy-five aircraft. All in all that's a sizable force in its own right. At the same time, the Alliance has concentrated a strong corps of three divisions under Headquarters ARRC, that's the Allied Rapid Reaction Corps, the British-led NATO High Readiness Force Land headquarters. They are now in north-east Poland, just south of the Lithuanian border.'

'Does that mean we are outnumbered?'

'No. But our forces are dispersed throughout the Baltic states, whereas NATO can concentrate all their effort to achieve decisive effect and we'll be heavily outnumbered at that point.'

The President thought about this for a few moments. 'So the strategic situation is still in our favour. If the Alliance is foolish enough to concentrate its forces at one point, which they must to launch a successful attack, they can be eradicated by just one of our tactical nuclear warheads?'

'Correct, Vladimir Vladimirovich.' The general gave a grim smile. 'There may be a distinction between tactical and intercontinental warheads, but the reality is that even the smallest modern warhead is many times more powerful than the bomb the Americans dropped on the Japanese in 1945. Just one well-placed tactical warhead will rip the heart out of an army corps. Those not incinerated on the spot will be too traumatised to continue fighting. Many more will die in the following days and weeks.'

'And they can do the same to us with their Cruise missiles . . .'

'Exactly. The difference is that Russia is such a vast country that we can disperse and hide and enough of us will survive. Western Europe is heavily populated. Their electorates would never permit such a thing. What is more, their politicians know we really will push the button if we are attacked.'

The President nodded, calmer now. 'As you say, Mikhail Nikolayevich, *exactly*. So, is this force they are pretending to threaten us with in the Baltic entirely American? What about the three divisions under the ARRC?'

'Vladimir Vladimirovich, you're correct that the Baltic naval and amphibious force is largely American, but not entirely. The British have deployed their Commando brigade headquarters in HMS *Albion*, an amphibious ship, together with a Royal Marine commando, while the Dutch have committed a marine battalion in the *Rotterdam*, their amphibious ship. Besides that, the British have also deployed HMS *Ocean*, a helicopter carrier, together with all the escorts they can muster. Add to that the French carrier, *Charles de Gaulle* and a number of escorts –

frigates and destroyers – from Germany, France, Italy, Spain, Portugal, Norway, Denmark and Belgium, to say nothing of, probably, hunter-killer subs from UK, France, Germany and, of course, America. So, the European members of NATO can certainly say to each other that they've stepped up to the mark. And, that is what our informants tell us they are saying to each other at leader and foreign minister level. The key point to make here is that, even with all their command and control problems, this force is significantly bigger than our Baltic Fleet. And that *would* be worrying if we thought that they were ready to risk nuclear retaliation, which . . .'

'They are not,' said the President interrupting, ignoring Gareyev's concerns. 'What about the divisions under the NATO corps in north-east Poland?'

'The strongest by far is the US Fourth Infantry, but on top of that there is the UK's Third Division with a British armoured brigade and a French Foreign Legion light-armoured brigade. We've also just heard that the Italians are sending the Ariete armoured brigade, which has always had a very close relationship with the ARRC. Most of the combat support – the artillery, engineers, reconnaissance and other support – is British, but with a fair representation from a number of other nations. And, of course, every nation will be contributing logistic units to support their own people.'

'And the Germans?'

'Yes. We've all been surprised by the Germans. First Panzer Division is now deployed and ready to roll in north-east Poland. And it's strong. It has also been reinforced by the Polish Tenth Armoured Cavalry Brigade.'

'Poles fighting alongside Germans. That must be a first. We certainly have united the Alliance . . .'

The President's attempt at a weak joke was met by an awkward silence around the table.

Even a fortnight ago, Komarov thought, there would have

been guffaws of fawning laughter. Not now, though, as the size of the forces building up on their border and the magnitude of their potential military miscalculation began to sink in.

Quickly the President moved on. 'What do you assess is NATO's intention?'

Gareyev replied, 'Vladimir Vladimirovich, we have considered this question in great depth and our assessment is based not only on the Alliance's deployment of forces and its capabilities, but we have also drawn extensively on both signals intelligence and human intelligence. We have called in every favour we are owed and risked exposing our top assets in the West to get at the truth of what is really going on. More than that, we have war-gamed and conducted operational analysis on several different scenarios. Finally, I have put all that mass of information to one side and asked myself the key question: what would I do if I was Admiral Howard, the SACEUR?'

'And what would you do, Mikhail Nikolayevich?'

'My view is that SACEUR's intention is to surround and neutralise our Baltic Fleet in Baltiysk, their base in Kaliningrad, and be prepared to conduct an amphibious landing on the coast of Estonia. Meanwhile, the NATO Corps in north-eastern Poland is poised to conduct an invasion with three divisions into Lithuania. All this would be preceded by a massive air campaign to knock out our air defences and neutralise our air force. Effectively, NATO is threatening an envelopment of our forces in the Baltic states by sea, land and air, with the aim of forcing our withdrawal from the Baltics.'

'What about deception?' probed the President.

'Very difficult for NATO,' replied Gareyev. 'I know from my own visit to SHAPE and discussions with senior NATO staff, when they were still allowed to meet us in Moscow, that the NATO military authorities are allowed to do nothing without the agreement of the North Atlantic Council. That makes it very difficult to conduct a deception operation because surprise would be impossible to achieve. Any strategic military decision must be authorised by the NAC. That is the NATO convention. As soon as a plan is put on the table, we will know about it within hours . . . Whatever security they try to put in place.'

'But,' mused the President, ever the conspiracy theorist. 'Surely . . .'

'I too have asked myself this,' General Gareyev interrupted, again something he would not have dared to do even a few weeks before. 'I have concluded that NATO, as an organisation, is incapable of the lateral thought required for successful *maskirovka*, or deception, hence the total surprise we achieved three years ago when we invaded Crimea. The situation is compounded by the NAC, which insists on retaining political authority for all operations. NATO has always had the problem of being too large, but once they expanded to twenty-eight members they became impossibly large. The politicians thought that the more members the better but, as we know, Vladimir Vladimirovitch, less can often be more.'

The President looked thoughtful. 'And our conventional response?'

'Despite their numbers we are ready for them. The Baltic Fleet will harass and interdict NATO's naval and amphibious forces as it sails east to conduct landings on the Estonian coast. Even if the invasion force succeeds in getting through and landing on the beaches, 6th Army has established strong defensive positions on the Estonian coast on all the likely invasion beaches, while maintaining mobile armoured reserves in depth ready to counter-attack. In the south, 20th Guards Army is deployed on the southern Lithuanian border. I can also report that 2nd Guards Tank Army has moved from its garrison in central Russia, at Samara, and been transferred to Western Military District. Meanwhile, the forces we withdrew from Kaliningrad and Ukraine will continue to contain the Forest Brother insurgency across the Baltic states.

'As for the air battle, NATO will be unable to win air superiority. Our Vorozneh radar in Kaliningrad is the match of anything they have and it can cover out to hundreds of kilometres. That's enough to keep all of Eastern and Central Europe under surveillance and capable of tracking more than five hundred aircraft simultaneously. Once detected, NATO aircraft will be easy meat for our S-400 and S-500 air defence missile systems as well as our own interceptors. So we are confident that we will retain the air superiority that will allow us to defeat NATO decisively on the ground.'

'What about Kaliningrad? Is there a danger that NATO could try and attack us there?'

'We think not, Vladimir Vladimirovich,' answered the Foreign Minister, who had remained quiet up to now. 'NATO goes on endlessly about being purely a defensive alliance. It is one thing to implement Article Five of the Washington Treaty to defend a member state, but quite another to attack Russian sovereign territory. NATO will never get the agreement of the NAC to do that. Apart from anything else, our friends in Athens and Budapest have confirmed they would veto any such proposal.'

Gareyev intervened. 'We know that the Americans and British use their Special Forces as the tip of their spear. We have been watching them carefully and I can tell you there are no Special Forces anywhere near Kaliningrad.'

The President looked satisfied; very much more his old self.

Because if the Alliance does attack, Komarov thought to himself, *and Russia does see them off as Gareyev clearly believes they would, then the President's position, and mine alongside him, would be sealed for the rest of his life.*

If NATO did the sensible thing and rattled their sabres, but no more, then the result would be the same: the President would have won. He and the President were only at risk if Russia were defeated and were that to happen, every man around this table would be in the same sinking ship. No, on reflection, although these were dangerous times, the President's fate was firmly linked with that of Russia and it was the same for these men.

The President had not finished, though. 'And, of course, just in case any of you are in any doubt, I will not hesitate to send a missile strike into Warsaw or Berlin the moment NATO attacks.'

'Yevgeney Sergeyevich,' he said, looking at the Foreign Minister, 'how confident are you that the Americans wouldn't take our use of tactical nuclear weapons as a pretext for an intercontinental strike?'

'A difficult one, Vladimir Vladimirovich,' came the reply. 'On the one hand the Americans won't risk Armageddon for the sake of a European city or a purely European military target. But, on the other, any use of tactical nuclear weapons on NATO forces, at sea or on land, will inevitably result in American casualties on a massive scale. That's because of the preponderance of Americans in the force. If any Americans are nuked, then all bets are off. They'll certainly respond with tactical battlefield weapons and I certainly wouldn't rule out the American use of intercontinental ballistic nuclear missiles.'

'So the message is to keep any usage strictly limited to the Europeans,' the President said briskly.

Komarov, however, was not fooled by this effort to be decisive and positive. If they were even discussing firing nuclear weapons then something had gone very wrong with the President's plan. It wasn't meant to be like this. A month ago he had sensed the tectonic plates were shifting. Now it was clear that they had shifted. The question was: how far and to whose benefit?

2200 hours, Saturday, 8 July 2017
Forest south of Pravdinsk, Kaliningrad, Russia

Eighteen hours later, an hour after sunset, Morland and the team moved out of their lying-up position. They'd all had more than enough rest, a few mouthfuls of water and something to eat; in Morland's case some dry biscuits and a can of cold meat from a ration pack he'd managed to find space for in his daysack. *Not much*, he thought, *but better than nothing*.

The night was clear and the light drizzle that had fallen as they lay in their hide had cleared. However, the moon had yet to rise and, even when it did – as a waning crescent moon – it would shed little light. They needed luck tonight and the lack of moonlight felt like a good omen. Lukša was once again lead scout and with Sergeant Wild now bringing up the rear as tail-end Charlie, they moved slowly and carefully, following the route they had already recced to the edge of the Drop Zone for American Special Forces. Occasionally they stopped to listen; each time moving into all-round defence and taking up fire positions as a standard drill while they did so. They were listening for danger ahead and off to the sides – sounds they might not hear as they moved through the forest – and also behind, for anyone following them. But all remained quiet.

After a couple of hours, Lukša halted and raised his hand. They were on the edge of the DZ. Again the patrol took cover and moved into all-round defence, this time, though, in a very tight circle, each person's ankle crossing the ankle of the person to the right of them: now was the time to present as small a target as possible to any roving patrols or wandering civilians.

Morland checked his watch. Twenty-five minutes to go, well ahead of time and roughly as planned. He pointed at his watch to Lukša, who was carrying the radar transponder beacon.

He gave a thumbs up in response to signal his understanding.

The time passed all too slowly. Then it was fifteen minutes to go. Morland again confirmed the time with Sergeant Wild and Lukša, and each compared times on their luminous watches. A thumbs up from each. Now they were on the countdown.

Exactly at a quarter past midnight Lukša activated his hand-held radar transponder beacon. It would transmit a response when interrogated by the incoming signal from the descending Special Forces parachutists and would guide the Americans in.

Meanwhile, somewhere thirty kilometres to their south, 30,000 feet above northern Poland, those Americans had jumped from their aircraft about fifty-two minutes earlier. Deploying their parachutes soon after leaving their aircraft, they had crossed into Russian airspace and were now descending by Hi-Glide canopy at around 28 kilometres an hour towards the DZ, guided by the GPS strapped to their wrists and, hopefully, undetected by radar. Right now, as they neared their destination, Morland knew they would be keenly awaiting the return signal from the radar transponder, telling them that there were friendly guides awaiting them at the DZ.

As for Morland, he was suddenly desperate to hear reassuring American voices, backed by American muscle, an indication that he might be taking the first step on his route back to home and some sort of normality.

He didn't have long to wait. Mere moments later, he was conscious of a faint whispering sound and to his front, in the open field beyond the tree line, he saw the silhouette of a parachute descending rapidly with a helmeted, oxygen-masked figure wearing night vision goggles dangling beneath it, followed in quick succession by several more. The American Green Berets had arrived.

2330 hours, Saturday, 8 July 2017, Central European Time
0030 hours, Sunday, 9 July 2017, Eastern European Time
Comprehensive Crisis Operations Management
Centre (CCOMC) SHAPE headquarters,
Mons, Belgium

IT HAD BEEN a long day but, nevertheless, the night shift of the CCOMC, the nerve centre of NATO's strategic head-quarters, was a hive of activity. In the open-plan command centre, staff officers from all the NATO member states and several partner nations, civilian staff with impressive academic credentials and representatives from well-established partners like the EU and UN humanitarian organisations, planned and executed the campaign to eject Russia from the Baltic states.

In the Operations Centre, with its banks of computers, multiple media feeds from different 24-hour news channels and social media, and its real-time satellite and drone surveillance imagery, up-to-the-minute information was filtered, analysed and disseminated to the Command Group and supporting staff. Plans were then made and direction passed down to the Joint Command HQs at Brunssum in the Netherlands and Naples in Italy, as well as to NATO's Maritime Command at Northwood and Air Command at Ramstein in Germany.

In the brightly lit CCOMC Conference Room, Admiral Max Howard, NATO's strategic commander, together with

McKinlay and Major General Skip Williams, the youth-ful-looking American Deputy Chief of Staff Operations, were running through the sequence of events for the operation due to be launched imminently, early on Sunday morning.

Williams was talking. 'As you'd expect, SACEUR, there continues to be serious push back from the staff at Air Command. For an operation of this magnitude they'd expect to have several days to implement the air campaign or, at the very least, a thirty-six-hour window to guarantee even half-effective suppres-sion of enemy air defences. So, the idea of mounting the whole operation over one short July night is a major concern for them. They've pointed out that every war in recent history, even establishing a no-fly zone against an enemy as useless as the Libyans, has depended on an air campaign lasting several days.'

'That's the way it's going to be, Skip.' Howard was firm. 'We're in a different type of war and the old norms don't apply here. An extended air campaign followed by a major land operation is old thinking. It's exactly what the Russians will expect. We've got to be more agile. We know the inte-grated air-defence system covering Kaliningrad and Eastern Europe is exceptionally capable. I'm very aware that their S-400 system has missiles capable of engaging out to four hundred kilometres and they have shorter-range missiles for killing fast, manoeuvrable targets, so the Russians have the potential to make our air forces' job about as difficult as it can be.

'However, our aircraft are world beaters, so I'm confident that with F-22A Raptors and the B-2A Spirit Stealth bombers leading the way, we've got the capability to carve holes in the Russian air defences to allow our other bombers through to attack targets on the ground. And don't forget the new version of HARM, the High-speed, Anti-Radiation Missile our aircraft are carrying. The GPS allows it to pinpoint the location of the

SAM, surface-to-air missile, radar emitters. Even if they switch off their radars, it will still hit them smack on the nose.'

McKinlay was impressed. He had not expected Howard to be so well-briefed on technical issues.

But then, he thought to himself, *as an ex-naval aviator who had commanded a carrier battlegroup, he shouldn't have been surprised. This technical stuff was essential bedside reading to aviators.*

Howard continued. 'But the bottom line is this. I'm counting on surprise and concentration of force in one massive attack by air, and Tomahawk missiles from the sea, to neutralise the Russian capability. And, of course, the key to it all is when the Brits activate Rasputin. The Russians won't know what the hell is happening. Except that there will be a total collapse of their integrated air-defence system, as well as their nuclear and other command and control systems.'

'We know that, Sir. But the problem is Com Air, the Air Commander, at Ramstein doesn't. He thinks he is putting his people into a suicide mission,' pointed out Williams. 'In fact, "taken leave of our senses" was one of the milder expressions he used. Couldn't we . . .?'

'Skip, I get it,' Howard interrupted. 'I've spoken to him. We're old buddies. But rightly, the Brits are keeping the circle of those in the know ultra-tight. God forbid, but they may need to use Rasputin again in the future, so we have to keep its very existence contained. I'll have another word with him to reassure him . . . And of course it's tough for those flyers. But that's the way it's got to be.'

The direction for McKinlay had been very clear – only Howard and Williams were cleared to be briefed about Rasputin and the circle was not to be widened. Even the SHAPE Chief of Staff, General Klaus Wittman, a German, was not being brought into the secret. But under the so-called 'two eyes' protocol, such sensitive intelligence could only be shared between the British and Americans, and then only those with an absolute need to know. Such restrictions created real resentment in an Alliance where shared endeavour was a fundamental principle; particularly for the French, who complained bitterly about this privileged Anglo-Saxon club.

'We need to move on, Skip. Run me through the sequence again.'

Williams pressed the switch on the remote control and ran through a series of briefing slides. Once Rasputin had been activated by a phone call from McKinlay to GCHQ direct, the window of opportunity was uncertain. The briefing at GCHQ from Allenby had been very clear and had not changed: Rasputin would have a devastating impact on all Russian command and control systems, integrated air-defence and nuclear included, but it was uncertain how long it would be sustainable.

The most GCHQ felt able to guarantee was an eight-hour window – and even that was assuming an hour or two of confusion while the Russians worked through what was happening in the middle of the night and then started to fix the bug – after which the Russians would regain control of both their air-defence and nuclear systems. Hence the critical importance of the short, sharp operation to suppress Russian air defences.

'We estimate that in the JOA, the Joint Operational Area, the Russians have got somewhere in the region of three hundred SAMs, organised into over a hundred firing batteries, with approximately five thousand Anti-Aircraft Artillery, supported by hundreds of overlapping early-warning, search-and-acquisition radars,' continued Williams. 'That means that, once Rasputin is activated, there'll need to be a constant flow of allied aircraft pouring over southern Lithuania, Kaliningrad and western Estonia to hit the batteries and other ground assets while the C2 is down. The targeting has been done very precisely and, as long as we achieve surprise, the Joint Force Air Component Commander, the JFACC, will be able to achieve air superiority before the air assault goes in.

'I'm not sure who'll be more surprised: the Russians when their systems crash, or our flyers when they find they've got an open door and no incoming SAMs. Or, let's put it like this, no coordinated SAM defences. It's entirely possible that individual batteries may be able to go into manual override and fire on their own initiative. Which raises a rather juicy prospect.'

'And that is?' asked Howard

'If it's an uncoordinated free-for-all up there, which it could be if Rasputin lives up to its name, then the Russians may not dare put their own planes into the air in case they get shot down by their own batteries.'

'That I like!' exclaimed McKinlay. GCHQ had not briefed him on that possibility.

Howard only nodded. 'That would be an unexpected bonus. But if Rasputin doesn't work, then we'll implement the contingency plan?'

'We're ready for that, SACEUR. It'll be a conventional and potentially very attritional campaign. Air Com has a contingency air-tasking order that assumes it will take thirty-six hours to neutralise the Russian Integrated S-400 Air Defence system. When that's been achieved . . . or not, it'll be your call. If it's looking good, it'll be a case of reinforcing success by letting the Allied Rapid Reaction Corps loose into southern Lithuania and going ahead with the 2nd Marine Expeditionary Force landing in Estonia. If not, you can mission-abort at any stage and let the politicians start talking.'

The room was silent. The prospect of mission failure was too grim to contemplate.

'And it could get far worse,' interrupted McKinlay. 'There's a high chance that the Russians will go nuclear.'

'I've talked to Washington about that, Dave,' replied Howard. 'The US has now moved to DEFCON 1. That's ready for nuclear release. They'll be making it very clear to Moscow through diplomatic channels that any recourse to nuclear, even battlefield, tactical weapons, will result in the launch of US ICBMs – which would mean the total destruction of several Russian cities for starters. The President has also talked to the Brits and the French, who have reduced notice to fire for their submarine-launched ICBMs to fifteen minutes. They've commenced targeting and prepared launch codes. We're looking MAD, mutually assured destruction, in the face.'

'Do you really mean that, SACEUR? Will President Dillon really put US cities in the firing line?'

Howard reflected for a moment before speaking quietly. 'Everything I've seen of President Dillon tells me she is serious about this and won't blink first. She realises only too well that if she hesitates today, chances are that she'll face the same problem tomorrow. But next time without NATO to support her. She's a very different animal to the last President and we've got to make sure the Russians understand that.'

'That makes Rasputin critical,' commented McKinlay. 'If it fails, it's either mission abort or we're into a bloody conventional fight with the near guarantee of nuclear exchange . . . There's a lot hanging on the shoulders of that young woman at GCHQ and her geeky mates.'

'Let's move on. Skip, take me back to your comfort zone,' said Howard. 'Even strategic commanders occasionally need to get into the tactical detail when there's so much hanging on it. I'd like to go through the op to secure the nuclear command bunker at Pravdinsk again. After all, that's the fulcrum on which everything else hangs.' It was time to be positive.

'As you know, SACEUR, the air assault will be preceded by a twelve-man ODA from the 1st Battalion, 10th Special Forces Group, based in Stuttgart. They're being inserted covertly by HAHO parachute drop, ahead of the main heliborne force. They're good to go on your final order.

'The Brit team which infiltrated in from Lithuania – the guys who've been working with the Forest Brothers – are waiting for them right now. Once they've joined up they'll be the pathfinders for the main air assault. They're also trained to immobilise the C2 circuitry of the Iskander nuclear-missile batteries once we've broken through the defences and suppressed the compounds.'

'And then?'

'This slide shows a satellite photo of the compound south of Pravdinsk.' At this point Williams pointed out the ground: the small town of Pravdinsk and, four miles to its south, the compound with the nuclear command and control bunker. Next he pointed to the forest line to the north, with the open ground to the north of that selected as the LZ, the helicopter landing zone.

He flicked on a second slide, next to the photo, and continued, 'These are the Special Forces Component Commander's phases for the operation. Phase One is when the Special Forces ODA arrive on the LZ. Rasputin will be activated on DSACEUR's call at 0100 hours, Kaliningrad time. That will trigger Phase Two, the air battle to suppress the Russian Integrated Air Defence System. Assuming Rasputin takes down their C2 that will give the ODAs two and a half hours before Phase Three, the air assault, starts at 0330, local Kaliningrad time. Obviously, if Rasputin does not work, we will not send in a heliborne assault anywhere near the Russian air defences. It would be a massacre.'

'Two and a half hours between Rasputin going live and the helicopters landing?' queried Howard. 'Surely it needs to be a lot tighter than that?'

'Ideally yes, SACEUR,' replied Williams, 'but we have to take account of the inevitable friction of war. During that time the air forces *have* to neutralise the SAM sites, so they don't take out the airborne on their way in. And that's assuming Rasputin has worked.'

'Skip's right, SACEUR,' interjected McKinlay. 'That's the reality.'

'Got it,' replied Howard. 'What happens when the airborne land?'

'The ODA will be followed by a beefed-up air-assault company. One for each of the three Iskander sites. The land component commander has had to make some compromises here: ideally he would want at least a three-to-one advantage over the defenders, which means at least a battalion task force. However, putting a battalion on the ground so close to the enemy is asking for trouble. He's therefore decided to reduce the air-assault landing force to an extra-strong, reinforced company group, but to give them plenty of air support to keep enemy heads down during their assault on the compound. We're also confident that the air strikes will be so precise that they will not risk setting off the Iskanders.

'The other issue at Pravdinsk is a minefield, probably anti-personnel only, which the Brit team have identified next to the perimeter wire and is covered by fire from the watchtowers. However, they've also identified a route through. Their job, once they've marked the LZ, is to guide the air-assault company right to the wire. Once they're in, they'll have engineers prep the site for demolition, in case it looks as if the Russians are getting their missiles back on line, or it looks as if we are going to be overrun. While they're doing that, the ODA will be physically disabling the circuitry inside.'

'And the other sites at Yuzhny and Ozyorsk?' queried Howard.

'Effectively the same concept of operations,' replied Williams. 'Although we've had good intel from other Forest Brother groups, it hasn't been to the same level as the Brits have provided. There may be minefields. We just don't know. If there are, and we're assuming there are, then we'll have to clear them. But Pravdinsk is the key to the plan as command and control to the other two sites is routed through there.

'So, once in, they'll disable the nukes at all the sites. My last point is that they'll then prepare for follow-up air-assault landings by 82nd Airborne at each site. At Pravdinsk we reckon we can build up a brigade on the ground within around six hours. That is more quickly than the Russians can launch an effective, co-ordinated, multi-brigade counter-attack. Any immediate and localised counter-attacks we're confident can be dealt with from the air. When the Russians realise what's happening and get their act together, they'll come at us with everything they've got. Unless, of course, us seizing the nukes persuades the Kremlin to back off. Which is what we are banking on happening.'

He stopped.

Howard was deep in thought, facing the eternal dilemma of the commander who must make the decision to commit men to battle with all its deadly consequences. He turned to McKinlay. 'What do you reckon, Dave? High risk if the Russians counter-attack before we can build up an adequate force on the ground. Even if we do and we send in the ARRC to reinforce them, we've got precisely the attritional, conventional, land battle we're looking to avoid. Besides, I'm not sure the Alliance will hold together if we get stuck into a major punch-up in Kaliningrad.'

'Especially as it's a battle they did not even know we were going to start, so they can say it's a battle they never authorised,' McKinlay mused.

'Are you now saying you're not sure, Dave?'

'No, SACEUR, I'm not saying that. In fact we are only a few hours away from capturing the Russian nuclear batteries. There is no indication the Russians have any idea about what is to hit them. Which means the deception plan is working. Which also means we have a fall-back plan, of sorts.'

'What do you mean, Dave?'

'The moment we have their missile bases, the whole strategic picture changes. That's always been our thinking. And, even if Rasputin does not work, or only works for a short time, then we still have our hands on one hundred Russian nuclear missiles . . .'

'Sir?' It was Skip Williams.

'Yes?' Howard looked momentarily irritated at the interruption.

'DSACEUR's right on the money. The ODAs each have a couple of guys who've been specially trained on the wiring of the Iskanders and more are going in with the air assault. They reckon that it will take about thirty-plus minutes to turn one missile round and, under our control, to target Russia. Once they've sorted out how to do one, the next ones will be far quicker. They plan to get a minimum ten Iskanders in each battery facing the Russians before there is any counter-attack. That really is a potent threat to back off or else.'

Howard listened intently. 'I like the sound of that, Skip . . . I guess if we only have ten Iskanders ready to launch at Russia, that'll be enough of a propaganda coup to humiliate the President and force a climb-down. Then it'll be up to the politicians to offer him a way out. Whatever happens, even if Rasputin is overcome and they recapture the batteries, the Russians will have no idea how many nukes will work or what they'll do if they fire them. Once we've had control of them, for even a short time, the Russians won't dare to use them until they've all been stripped down and checked . . . Hell!' He slapped his thigh and grinned. 'This is like a nightmare terrorist plot, on speed. And for once we're the goddamn terrorists – we're the ones doing it! It sure makes a change from being the ones being kicked, doesn't it, Dave?'

McKinlay laughed as well. The Admiral was right: it nearly always felt better to be attacking than defending. 'Full marks to us for lateral thinking. And it's not a plan you'd find in a Staff College solution anywhere west of Syria. Which is why the Russians won't have thought of it. But if Rasputin works – which it will – it offers us the genuine chance of winning the war at a stroke. We'll hold the Russians to ransom with their own nuclear weapons until they extract from the Baltic states. It is a solution that will see the minimum number of casualties for the maximum amount of effect. Which is why I have always supported the plan . . . as you know.'

Howard nodded his agreement and so McKinlay continued. He knew that, while the buck stopped, ultimately, with the Strategic Commander, as his deputy he was there to support, reassure and share the burden of command. And that meant committing properly to the plan.

'To summarise: high risk, but not yet a gamble.'

'Thanks, Dave. I appreciate your full support. I believe we're decided then, gentlemen.'

'There's one other thing, SACEUR,' added McKinlay. 'Thanks for agreeing to 3 Para helping to secure the site at Pravdinsk. That's a good call for us. They've been training with the 82nd Airborne. I'm told they've even been jumping out of American planes with American parachutes. Not that they're going to jump tonight, of course.'

'Too right,' added Williams with a grin. Decision made, it was time to lighten up. 'I gather they've been having an airborne ball and not a Marine has dared to show his ugly—'

'Hang on . . . ,' McKinlay immediately started to protest.

'It's good to see the Special Relationship is alive and well, guys,' Howard said, interrupting and shaking his head in amusement at the age-old rivalry between the green and red berets.

Then he turned to Williams, his face now grave and obviously all too aware of the consequences of his next order. 'Let's roll, Skip.'

0045 hours, Sunday, 9 July 2017, Central European Time
0145 hours, Sunday, 9 July 2017, Eastern European Time
Command Bunker, Iskander Missile Battery
Pravdinsk, Kaliningrad

MAJOR ANATOLY NIKOLAYEVICH Vronsky put his head round the office door, only to see Major Pyotr Petrovich Luzhin, the Pravdinsk Guard Force commander, slumped over his desk, head on his arms and snoring loudly, a half-finished bottle of vodka open beside him.

Typical MVD, Internal Troops, he thought to himself, *and these are the people responsible for guarding strategic assets like our Iskander batteries!*

Picking up his body armour, helmet and webbing from where he'd left it in Luzhin's office, he slung his AS Val assault rifle over his shoulder and walked down the corridor to the Guard Force Ops Room, where his team were monitoring the surveillance equipment covering the approaches to the perimeter wire. Underneath the Guard Force Ops Room, in the bunker below, was the Top Secret nuclear command and control room, with access only for those cleared at the very highest level.

Vronsky could understand Luzhin's annoyance. He had arrived the day before with his men and equipment in two trucks. The fat, puffy-faced major with the colourless face had been surprised by the arrival of the Spetsnaz officer wearing no rank or insignia on his combat smock. Surprise had then turned to barely repressed anger when Vronsky had told him that, on General Kirkorov, the Commander of Western Military District's orders, he was taking over command of the defence and protection of the Iskander compound.

'But Anatoly Nikolayevich,' protested Luzhin, 'my men are more than capable of defending this compound. I have a well-planned programme of mobile and foot patrols to ensure that the ground defence area out to five kilometres is properly covered. The perimeter is guarded, as you can see, by watch-towers, each with night vision devices and machine guns, which also cover the minefield. I also keep a Quick Reaction Force at immediate notice to move and I insist that my officers are out regularly to check that the soldiers are performing their duties in accordance with my orders. I can assure you, no enemy has dared come near this compound. What more can the general want?'

'I understand, Pyotr Petrovich.' Vronsky was diplomacy personified as he explained the position to his fellow major. 'I appreciate that it is unorthodox for one major to give instructions to another, but I regret that I can say very little. I am here by Presidential direction, so I have to ask for your full support. This mission is of strategic importance to Russia and hence a task for Spetsnaz. I will report to General Kirkorov that I found everything here in first-class order, but please withdraw your patrols into the compound. However, I will ask that you maintain your QRF at immediate notice to move and double up the guards in the watchtowers.'

Luzhin, after the inevitable – and procedurally correct – radio call to headquarters, recognised that he had no alternative but to comply and took himself off to his office to drown his frustration.

Vronsky, meanwhile, accompanied by Senior Warrant Officer Dimitri Prokofitch Razhumikin, his Ops NCO, conducted a reconnaissance of the immediate vicinity of the compound based on a careful study of the map and aerial photos he'd brought from Kaliningrad. The ground suited his purpose admirably. The most likely route for the enemy approach was from the direction of the forest, to the north of the perimeter. It would give the terrorists the best cover and get them closer to the command bunker. His deduction that this was their target was further reinforced by a report from HQ that a drone with forward-looking infrared had picked up a heat source in the forest five kilometres north of the compound.

'That's it,' he said to himself. 'The bastards are on their way . . . and they're not getting away from me this time.'

An hour after finishing his recce, Vronsky gave orders to his team to allow them plenty of time to get into position.

'Listen in guys and welcome to Operation BORODINO,' he said to the Spetsnaz team, assembled by Razhumikin in the Guard Force conference room. 'First, the preliminaries. You've been split into four groups: Gun Groups One and Two, each equipped with the PKP Pecheneg, 7.62 millimetre light machine gun and AGS-30, thirty-millimetre grenade launchers, plus normal small arms and grenades; next is the Korda group, equipped as you'd expect from the name by one of my favourite weapons, the Korda 12.7 millimetre heavy machine gun – a beauty which got me out of trouble in the second Chechen war several times. Finally, there's the reserve group. Note, too, that I've marked the map with a number of named spot points to avoid having to send grid references.' He paused to allow his men to take notes and check their maps.

'Mission: capture the British infiltration team as they move forward to conduct a reconnaissance of the compound. I won't say more about that, as Senior Warrant Officer Razhumikin gave you the intelligence picture previously. The key point I want to make is that I want the British officer alive. We'll do it by surrounding the team on all sides with a curtain of fire.

On my order, the reserve group will move in and take them prisoner. Do what you need to do to subdue them, but the President wants the officer alive and looking photogenic on TV. Moving on to tasks. Gun Group One, you are to set up the unattended ground sensors along the southern edge of the forest line to pick up the intruders as they head towards the minefield. On my order, you are to engage them from a position you are to recce and prepare on the southern edge of the forest line.

'Gun Group Two. You are to act as cut-off group, ready to engage them from a position in the scrubby area north-east of the minefield, here. Again, recce and prepare a position that will prevent any escape from the killing area.' And he indicated on the map where he wanted them located.

'Next, Korda group. You are to set up in the watchtower on the perimeter fence, here. You are to engage the enemy on my order – and I plan to be in the tower with you – as they move into the killing area. For all of you, the Korda opening fire is your signal to engage.'

Finally, my reserve group. I want you ready to move out from the back gate of the perimeter fence to capture the enemy on my order, when they've been neutralised.'

Then he concluded, 'If they do what I expect them to do, they'll enter into the killing area we've prepared for them and be trapped between the minefield and watchtowers along the perimeter fence and the two cut-off groups. We hose them down and, when they realise it's surrender or die, we put them in the bag.'

Finally, he ran through the timings and other coordinating instructions quickly, in order to give the groups as much time as possible to do their recces and get into position.

All was set and Vronsky knew it was likely to be a long night. But he'd had plenty of those and waiting in an easy chair, drinking coffee with the radio watchkeepers in the Ops

Room, was infinitely better than lying in a damp forest, as he'd had to do last time he was on the trail of these terrorists. Anyway, he needed to be close to the team monitoring the seismic and passive infrared images transmitted from the un-attended ground sensors. He also needed to hear what was happening on the 'all-informed' Guard radio net. When things kicked off, as he expected them to either tonight or tomorrow night, he'd be able to run from the Ops Room and up the steps into the watchtower with the Korda. That commanded a clear view of the killing area and the two cut-off positions. It was from there he'd direct the operation.

As he walked back into the Ops Room, he saw instantly that something was very wrong. The images on the closed-circuit TV screens covering the Iskander site were alternately freezing, then breaking up into small squares and then crashing completely. Computer screens were disintegrating into wavy lines with psychedelic patterns and crazy colours. From the radio loudspeaker came only loud mush and white noise. Signallers were desperately checking their radio sets. Only the team monitoring the unattended ground sensors, which oper-ated on a different waveband from the signals radios, reported no interference.

'Anatoly Nikolayevich,' reported Razhumikin, 'we've got a real problem here. All radio communications have suddenly gone down. The CCTV coverage of the Iskander site has gone crazy and computers in the command network appear to be closing down without reason. Worse, we've just heard from the nuclear command bunker downstairs that the Kazbek nuclear C2 system has crashed and that Perimetr, the back-up "fail-safe" system, is not responding to commands. They're reporting that it seems as if their systems have been taken over by an alien command net. What's just as worrying, as the systems are down we cannot tell headquarters what is happening. They don't even know we've got a problem.'

'Can't you use a landline to warn them?' Vronsky demanded.

'No,' said one of the Guard Force watchkeepers. 'We don't have one as that would be a breach of nuclear protocols. The only way information can come into or out of this compound is through the nuclear command and control net.'

'Which is now malfunctioning . . .'

'Correct, Sir.'

Then Vronsky stopped dead, his mind racing. The 45th Guards Spetsnaz Regiment had just established an offensive cyber-warfare wing to look at how they might destroy enemy command and control through Distributed Denial of Services: infecting communications systems with a Trojan. Had they been beaten to it by NATO?

At that moment the alarm linked to the unattended ground-sensor monitor unit sounded. Razhumikin took one look. 'Contact. Intruder. Spot position Bagratian, south-east corner of forest. Activate BORODINO now!'

Vronsky was running out of the door and pulling on his kit before Razhumikin had finished his sentence.

0100 hours, Sunday, 9 July 2017, Central European Time
0200 hours, Sunday, 9 July 2017, Eastern European Time
Over Wroclaw, Poland

As always, major Philip Bertinetti was struck by the pure joy of flying his F-16C multi-role fighter aircraft; small, nimble, with acceleration like a bullet, it felt as if he was wearing the aircraft rather than sitting in it. Today, though, he could feel a slight sluggishness from the additional weight of a full load of ordnance: a pair each of Sidewinder and AMRAAM air-to-air missiles for aerial combat, two GBU-31, Mark 84, 2,000-pound bombs fitted with the JDAM kit, which converted a 'dumb' unguided bomb into an all-weather 'smart' munition and was known as 'the Hammer' for its destructive power, plus a HARM, High-speed Anti-Radiation Missile, for knocking out ground-based radars and a laser-guided Maverick missile for any other opportunity targets.

In addition, there was comfort in knowing that he could also rely on the 20 millimetre six-barrel cannon in the port wing, capable of a firing rate of 6,000 rounds per minute to help get him out of trouble, although, given the overall ammunition load, this would not last long.

Now he was once more heading to war, this time leading an eight-aircraft sortie from 510th Fighter Squadron – the 'Buzzards'. Their mission: to conduct a low-level attack against the Voronezh radar system operating from the Pionersky Radar Station at the former Dnuyavka air base in Kaliningrad. Once they'd destroyed the radars, they would head back into Poland to refuel before returning to mount a CAP, a combat air patrol, to intercept and destroy the anticipated counter-attack from Russian aircraft against the airborne operation that was to follow them.

The 'Buzzards' were part of a massive multinational air armada pouring into Kaliningrad from all over Central and Western Europe. Bertinetti knew that the largest sortie, a joint US Air-Force–Navy Suppression of Enemy Air Defences, or SEAD, mission consisting of fifty aircraft, was already approaching its targets. The sortie was designed to look like a bombing raid on Kaliningrad and the base of the Russian Baltic Fleet at Baltiysk. However, it was, instead, fitted out with decoys, drones and HARMs, to overwhelm and destroy the air defences protecting the approaches to the critical points: the Pionersky radar station and the nuclear missile sites at Yuzhny, Pravdinsk and Ozyorsk. Take them out and, in two bold strokes, Russia lost much of its offensive capability.

As he hurtled through the night above Poland at 30,000 feet and at a cruising speed of 435 knots, he felt the familiar nerves in the pit of his stomach, as the unreality and scale of what he was involved in hit him. Only that afternoon, in lovely sunshine, instead of the normal family Sunday afternoon spent by the officers' club swimming pool, he had kissed his wife farewell at the gate of their married quarter by the air base at Aviano in northern Italy, before heading in to prepare for the mission. He might be a combat veteran with three confirmed kills – hence the three small Russian flags his ground crew had painted on the side of his F-16 – but he was wise enough and modest enough to know that only luck had protected him from the insane randomness of war. And, like courage, luck was an expendable commodity.

Forcing himself to focus on his head-up display, he saw that in two minutes they'd be within the 400-kilometre range of the Russian S-400 Integrated Air Defence System.

'Don't dwell on it,' he urged himself. 'Only worry about the things you can change . . . and think of your guys.' He glanced to his right and there, in the darkness, just to his rear, covering his six o'clock and keeping perfect station, were the flashing anti-collision, navigation and formation lights of his wingman, Captain Mike Ryan. Sure, he'd had his baptism of fire over Lielvārde in Latvia a couple of months ago, but he was still pretty new on the squadron and needed all the reassurance he could get. On either side and to his rear, and also keeping perfect station, were the six other aircraft making up the bombing attack. All the pilots knew from the briefing that they were moments away from the death zone, and that meant they would all need the reassurance of good leadership. A quick radar transmission from Bertinetti and he knew they'd stay alert for each other and were ready for incoming SAMs.

Another look at the colour flat-panel, liquid-crystal multi-function instruments and, right on time, the helmet-mounted cueing system told him that they had entered the danger area for the S-400. Automatically, the airborne radar flicked into air-ground mode to initiate simultaneous multi-target tracking by the planar antenna array installed in the aircraft's nose.

'Won't be long now before the radar locks onto us,' he muttered to himself, in the knowledge that the Voronezh system could track 500 aircraft simultaneously at ranges beyond 600 kilometres – in plenty of time to launch the S-400 40N6 missile with its range of 400 kilometres. At its speed of Mach 6.2, Bertinetti calculated that a missile would take just over three minutes from launch at that range to hit his sortie. And he was lead aircraft.

'Any moment now,' he muttered again, trying not to tense

up and wanting to keep his hands and arms as relaxed as possible. When his radar picked up the incoming missiles, he was going to have to fly as he had never flown before if he was to be one of the aircraft that survived – if any survived – the impending carnage. The only slight consolation, he told himself as he waited for the warning from his alarm systems, was that as soon as a radar locked onto him, his HARM would fly straight back down the beam, provided he was close enough. That should mean, unless the Russians had some countermeasures he did not know about, that the following wave stood a very much better chance of getting through. And the wave after that a better chance still, until the Russian defences were first breached and then overwhelmed.

Another check of his instruments. Everything was doing what it was meant to do, but there was still nothing. And they were closing fast on Kaliningrad.

Then the radio in his helmet burst into life.

'Apollo, this is Giant Killer, are you receiving me?'

'Affirmative, Giant Killer,' Bertinetti replied – thinking, *what does ground control want?*

'Apollo, we're receiving reports that lead SEAD sortie is on target and has received no incoming, repeat no contact. They've had a clear run onto target and have taken out multiple SAM systems.'

'Roger, Giant Killer. Guess they're keeping it for us then.' Bertinetti tried to make light of this surprising news.

'Apollo, on the contrary, we're getting multiple reports that enemy C2 is totally scrambled. All their systems appear to be down.'

Bertinetti was dumbfounded. That could only mean one thing: something massive must have been initiated to coincide with the air attack. How else would the feared Russian integrated air-defence system crash?

But this was no time to be complacent. It was time to prepare for their own run in to the target and to pray that the gods of war were looking after them as well.

An hour later, Bertinetti knew that something extraordinary had taken place. As they had prepared for the mission, the 510 Fighter Squadron pilots had all assumed their attack on the Pionersky radar station would require them to penetrate the most sophisticated, integrated air-defence system on the planet. It would probably be a suicide mission. But something unaccountable had plunged the Russian command and control systems into chaos, for there had been no incoming SAMs.

True, the vehicle-mounted, four-barrelled, ZSU-23-4 anti-aircraft guns had put up a fair amount of 23-millimetre flak, but a hit from one of those now-elderly anti-aircraft systems, while deadly, would have seemed more like bad luck than anything else, given the other modern weapon systems arrayed against them. But no SAM missiles were fired at them and the few uncoordinated attacks by Russian air defence MiG-29 Fulcrums and MiG-31 Foxhounds had been easily seen off by teams of roving F-15 Eagles providing top cover above the F-16s.

In fact, the raid had started like a night training-run in the Nevada desert. Led by Bertinetti, they'd gone down to very low level shortly after entering the 400-kilometre S-400 range and, guided by their LANTIRN infrared navigation and targeting systems, they'd approached the target at no more than 100 feet, streaking across the tree tops with the ground flashing by in the darkness below. Seventy kilometres from the target they had linked up with the eight F-15 Eagles above them. They carried advanced, counter-electronic warfare jammers to neutralise the radar systems of the SAM-6 batteries and ZSU-23-4 anti-aircraft guns guarding the Pionersky radar station.

As they closed with the target, Bertinetti led the sortie in a gradual climb to 5,000 feet. A few individual ZSU-23-4s started to put up a massive barrage of manually aimed flak. So, just short of the target and conscious of the streams of Russian tracer flashing past his canopy, he had overcome his natural instinct to turn and dive to make for a more difficult target and had, instead, gritted his teeth and held his course and height before releasing his two GBU-31, Mark 84 bombs. Guided by the JDAM kits, they hit the radar station in the centre of the roof with a massive explosion. Pulling left and climbing aggressively to escape the flak and join the circling F-15s, he had seen the building erupt as the two bombs buried themselves deep inside – only to be followed by the other seven F-16s, also achieving perfect hits.

Extraordinary, thought Bertinetti. Although they had not said as much, HQ had sent out his eight F-16s in the hope that one or two might get through. And one direct hit would probably have been enough to knock out the radar. Instead they had all survived and all had scored. What was really going on down there in Kaliningrad, he wondered. Because someone had been, and was still being, very clever indeed.

'Giant Killer, this is Apollo. Mission accomplished.' Bertinetti spoke coolly into his radio to ground control. 'Now heading to link up with tankers before getting back on CAP.'

'Apollo, copy that. Tally ho and good hunting.'

0115 hours, Sunday, 9 July 2017, Central European Time
0215 hours, Sunday, 9 July 2017, Eastern European Time
Forest north of Pravdinsk Iskander Battery, Kaliningrad

FACE BLACKENED WITH cam cream, Captain Jack Webb, commander of the elite US Special Forces ODA team, which had just jumped in, whispered urgently to Morland. 'I'm happy with the LZ preparation. It's tight, but workable. I'm leaving two of my guys to control it from here. I now need to get up close to be ready to laser target-mark enemy positions for air strikes to allow the company to assault the compound.'

The twelve men of the Green Beret ODA team had worked fast since landing. After hitting the ground, each man had bundled up his parachute and hastened into the cover of the forest. Parachutes, oxygen masks and other kit necessary for the high-altitude jump were quickly hidden under bushes. Once they were ready, they had moved out of the forest and onto the main landing zone, all the while covered by Morland's team and the Lithuanians as they worked.

Given the imminent arrival of the air-assault company, preparations had been rudimentary but everything took time, especially in the dark and while trying to maintain operational security by making no noise and showing no lights. The centre of the LZ was marked by nine infrared Cyalume lightsticks – invisible to the naked eye – in the shape of a large letter 'A', which would easily be picked up by incoming Chinook pilots wearing night vision goggles. A similar Cyalume was placed on the trailing edge of the LZ to indicate the direction in which helicopters were to depart from the LZ. Finally, the team conducted a quick recce to confirm that there were no major obstacles on or around the LZ; a Chinook landing on some abandoned farm equipment could be fatal.

'Right, Jack, here's how we're going to approach the perimeter,' replied Morland, acutely conscious that the only way to maintain their luck was to keep moving with the utmost care and deliberation. He did not want to lose surprise at this late stage. Once the heliborne troops that Webb had told him would be following had landed, all hell would break loose, but right now, all was quiet and the Russians had not reacted in any way. He was praying that nothing had alerted them to the arrival of the Green Berets.

He pulled out his map and with a shaded, red-bulbed torch, showed Webb the route: three hundred metres due east through the forest, then south-east along the edge of the tree line for a kilometre and a half. They'd follow the trees around what looked like the heel of a foot at the corner of the forest, before heading due south towards a sunken lane with a scrubby hedge running along one side, around 300 metres north of the compound.

This would give them some cover from which they could observe the anti-personnel minefield, the perimeter fence, watch-towers and the Command Bunker. Although, as Morland pointed out, they would need to listen out for the sound of engines, as that would indicate the hourly roving patrol was heading out of the compound. From Morland's previous recce, he had calculated that it would then take no longer than three minutes before the patrol, if it turned in that direction, would be heading down the lane. And if they were caught in the sunken lane, it would be game over.

Webb took it all in and indicated that he was content with a brief thumbs up. Then, in a whisper, Morland outlined the drills so that Webb could brief his men before they set out. They would move in three groups, maintaining enough distance between each to provide mutual support in case one was hit. Archer and Watson would form the gun group and would move first through the forest, taking up a fire position with the GPMG and night vision goggles on the eastern side. They would then cover the scout group, with Lukša leading and consisting of Webb, his ODA engineer sergeant, Morland, Krauja and Bradley. Once the scouts had started their move down the outside of the forest, the reserve group, made up of Sergeant Wild, the two Lithuanians and the remaining eight men of the ODA team, would traverse the forest and wait on the edge of the tree line, ready to guide the reinforced company forward for its assault on the compound, or to be called forward to assist if required.

'That's the plan. But tell your guys to stay flexible. It all depends on how we find the ground. We haven't been near the wire, for obvious reasons, only observed it from a distance. The enemy seem stuck into a pretty fixed routine, but who knows what they'll do when they hear our helicopters.'

'Sure, Tom. Give me ten.' And Webb crept back to brief his ODA on the plan.

Shortly afterwards, after a whispered 'good to go' from Webb and a thumbs up from Morland, the shadowy figures of Archer and Watson moved off into the forest. A brief shaft of moonlight through the clouds glinted on the belts of ammunition they had draped off their shoulders, giving them the appearance of Mexican bandits. But there was no affectation about it. They would be cursing the extra weight and the risk of snagging the linked rounds on branches as they moved through the trees. However, they all knew that if something went wrong, the GPMG would burn through ammunition at an alarming rate. That was why the rest of the team, him included, were all carrying an extra belt of 200 rounds, 'just in case'.

After ten minutes, a whispered message in the earpiece of the personal role radio, given to him by the Latvian Forest Brothers, told him that the gun group were in position and ready.

Wordlessly Lukša followed with the rest of the scout group. Fifteen minutes later, they were through the forest and moving south-east along the eastern edge of the tree line. Morland felt a faint breeze bringing the scent of newly cut hay from a distant field. The moon was still low in the sky, its silver light, thankfully, still mostly obscured by clouds.

Then Lukša stopped and pointed ahead to Archer on the gun and Watson lying beside him, ready to feed in the belt of ammo now stacked in a neat pile to the left of the gun on a poncho, to stop the ammunition getting dirty. Perfect, but Morland would have expected no less from these two.

They took up positions in all-round defence. Morland tapped Watson on the shoulder and he tapped Archer. The gun group, carefully and quietly and making no effort to rush, re-shouldered the ammunition before moving off to their next fire position, on the heel of the forest covering the open ground.

Morland's stomach clenched involuntarily and his mouth was dry with fear. They were about to go into the unknown; away from the comforting proximity of the forest into the open ground beyond.

Look at the others, thought Morland. *They're equally scared, but they're just carrying on as if it's a walk in the park.*

He glanced surreptitiously at Krauja; face streaked with cam cream in the moonlight, blonde hair scraped back under a borrowed Latvian army combat cap, her combat smock with the overlong sleeves rolled up, Heckler & Koch, 5.56 millimetre assault rifle – standard issue to Latvian infantry – tucked into her shoulder as she covered her arcs of fire. She looked professional. And deadly. If she was scared, she was not showing it.

Another wait. Another short radio message from Watson. The gun group was in position and ready.

They stood up and left the edge of the forest. Four hundred metres ahead of them Morland could see the hedge running along the edge of the sunken lane – and beyond was the perimeter fence of the Iskander Battery site.

Something's not right, thought Morland. *The lights were blazing earlier . . . they've turned off the lights. Why . . . ? Are they expecting us?* But it was too late. The air assault troops were on their way and they were committed.

As they left the cover of the forest, they shook out as planned into diamond formation: Lukša leading, the ODA engineer sergeant forward right, Webb just behind him, Bradley as tail-end Charlie watching their rear, Krauja on the left with Morland front left. As they walked, they swung their weapons slowly from the hips to cover their individual arc of fire; front, left, right and back again, listening for any suspicious sound, looking for any movement. As they moved they peered into and through the darkness, watchful and as alert as leopards hunting the African bush at night. Finally, they entered a field of thigh-high, half-ripe barley, damp to the hand from an earlier rain shower. Now they moved carefully, deliberately, slower than walking pace. After ten minutes they had only covered 350 metres and Morland's heart began to race. Ahead, he could now see the distinct outline of the hedge along the sunken lane and he realised that dawn was on its way.

Only another fifty metres. We're going to make it!

And then it happened.

All his mind could register was noise and light, the crack of bullets and a crazy, flashing kaleidoscope of intense colour: orange-and-white explosions and the vicious red of tracer rounds smashing through the air as they ripped past him in the darkness. And then, almost blinded by the light of explosions and gunfire, another noise engulfed him. It was louder than everything else and all the more terrifying for it – the deep, steady *whump–whump–whump* of a heavy machine gun. Morland risked peering for a brief moment over the heads of the barley. There, from a darkened watchtower, came the unmistakable muzzle flashes as the machine gun pumped round after round at them.

Then, to their rear right and also to their left, he picked out the very much faster, higher-pitched, chainsaw-like *rat-ratta-tat-tat* of what sounded like 7.62 machine guns, the tracer rounds shattering the darkness and cutting strips in the barley off to either side of their group. And as if this wasn't enough, there was the crump of what could only be a mortar or heavy grenade launcher. It was already bracketing them; loud explosions and shrapnel whistling through the air. But all off to the flank, which did not make sense. In fact, how he had survived the initial maelstrom of steel was an even bigger mystery, but he was not complaining. However, and of this he was in no doubt, the Russians had been waiting for them.

And then instinct and training kicked in. 'Take cover . . . !' Morland yelled as he jinked forward and dived down, then rolled to his left, trying to ensure that anyone targeting him would no longer know where he was. He then willed his body deep into the ground to get away from the hell above. His nose was full of the smell of fresh earth, while all around the cacophony of tracer racing past, explosions and mind-bending, psychedelic light continued.

Deep in the barley he saw nothing.

That means they can't see me . . . Check on the others . . .

He screamed out names to make himself heard above the din and could just make out faint answering shouts. There was nothing for it, he had to get round to everyone and find out for himself. And stay low.

They can't see you if you stay below the level of the barley.

He crawled back to where Krauja was lying; eyes wide open now, unfocused with terror. But, thankfully, unharmed.

He shook her until she focused on him and he gave her a

421

smile to try to reassure her. 'We'll be OK . . . Just follow me!' he yelled above the noise.

The moment of terror passed and she nodded her agreement. Next they crawled back to find Bradley the giant Kiwi signaller, also unhurt, holding his SA80 above the corn and firing back on automatic, the fierce light of a Maori warrior in his eyes.

'Well done Brad . . . stay close. Aimed shots, if you can. Without getting your head knocked off . . .'

On Morland crawled around the circle. He found Webb, the ODA captain, speaking into his radio. 'I've sent a TIC – troops in contact report. There's aircraft up there on call, so we should have close air-support pretty soon.'

'If we can survive that long,' replied Morland.

Slowly he peered above the barley. There were tracer and muzzle flashes from their left, more sporadic now. That had to be that machine gun. More to their rear right. And then, from the perimeter watchtower, the constant fire of the heavier machine gun. It was as he had first thought: they had walked straight into a trap. What was it his instructor had drilled into him in the 'Reaction to Ambush' lesson at the School of Infantry at Brecon: 'Those caught in the kill zone, assault through using fire and movement.'

Bollocks to that! Whoever wrote that had never been ambushed by the Russians. Time to return fire. Even if there was no possible chance of winning a fire fight with three machine guns. Then find cover.

He yelled at the others, throat straining in an effort to make himself heard above the noise. 'Form base line! Rapid fire! Peel off and skirmish to sunken lane!'

Then he tripped over something in the barley. It was the ODA sergeant, lying spread-eagled on the ground. Morland knelt beside him: no movement. He looked to have been hurled backwards and onto his side by a burst of machine-gun bullets, which had taken him across the chest. Gouts of blood were still pumping out onto the earth from a series of gaping exit wounds across his back.

Webb, who was following him, joined him, felt the pulse on the sergeant's neck and shook his head.

Leaving the body, they crawled to where Lukša had been point man. And there, as the fire continued to play all around them, they found the Lithuanian slumped in the barley, left shoulder soaked in blood and left arm now a bloody stump from the elbow.

Krauja pushed forward, ripped open her first field dressing and wrapped it around the remains of his arm. A second dressing was strapped around his shoulder. The others passed forward more dressings and while Krauja put on all the pressure she could, Morland pulled his field tourniquet from his webbing, wrapped it around Lukša's upper arm and tightened it. Slowly the blood flow eased. He reached back into his webbing and grabbed a morphine syrette.

'Hold tight, Arvydas. I'll just give you a shot of morphine to ease the pain.'

Lukša looked at him with gritted teeth. 'We Lithuanians don't feel pain. Just stop the blood and I'll be fine. I want to keep my head clear for killing fucking Russians.'

Morland looked at him in stunned admiration and, in that moment, knew that with soldiers like Lukša, they'd get out of this somehow. He felt a surge of adrenalin kick in. And anger. Unaccountably the fear had gone. He looked at Bradley, SA80 again on automatic, continuing to fire above the barley.

'Boss!' Bradley shouted. 'The gun group are in action. The fire is easing off.'

Morland risked another look above the corn. From the corner of the forest behind them was the unmistakable and pleasingly familiar noise of burst after burst of GPMG. Cleverly sited in defilade, it was out of sight of the Russians manning what had to be a 12.7 millimetre heavy machine gun. Had the Russians been able to see them, it would have been no contest: Archer and Watson would soon be dead meat. Instead, they were doing good work and he could see their tracer landing all around the machine gun position to their left. Then the fire coming from that direction stopped. And that gave them the briefest of respites as the Russians turned all their fury on the GPMG.

Bradley grabbed Lukša and, helped by Krauja, dragged him on his back through the corn like a life-saver pulling a drowning man to shore, while Morland and Webb continued to engage the enemy.

Inch by inch, foot by foot, they fought their way forwards through the corn. Never had fifty metres taken so long but eventually, sweat streaming down their faces, they reached the edge of the sunken lane, slid under the hedge and into the bottom. How they had not all been killed was still a complete puzzle to Morland; they had been little more than stationary targets out there in the corn. Moreover, the compound guards were bound to have sophisticated night sights in those watchtowers – which was probably why the lights had been switched off – and that Korda could have hosed them down in seconds. The more he thought about what had just happened, the less sense it made.

Morland took a quick pull on his water bottle. His throat was raw with all the shouting and he needed all the energy he could muster. Leaving Krauja to continue to administer first aid to Lukša, Morland and Webb crawled up the other side. The heavy machine gun from the watchtower had given up trying to hit the GPMG team and now switched back to them. Tracer was smacking into the barley fire fifty yards behind them, where they'd originally been contacted. However, the rounds coming from their rear left had suddenly stopped; Archer and Watson must have knocked out that light machine gun, although fire was still coming from the machine gun to their right. They might be safe for the moment, but they were not going anywhere. They were trapped.

'I've given the reserve group the grid of the enemy gun

group on the edge of the forest line to our rear right!' yelled Webb in Morland's ear. 'They've got plenty of fire power so they should be able to suppress them.'

'What about air?' asked Morland, marvelling at how laid-back he was now feeling after the initial terror of the ambush. 'There's no way we're going anywhere until that heavy machine gun is knocked out. And the air assault is due in any minute.' The luminous dials on his army issue G1098 watch told him it was 0315.

'Don't worry about that. My guys at the LZ can guide them forward. And I don't think the air assault will need much guiding in. They're getting the full light show after all . . .' Webb gave him a grin. 'We'll stay put and help look after you guys. Anyway, I've got to guide the air onto the compound, and for that I need eyes on.'

Webb stopped and listened to his earpiece. He then turned back to Morland. 'F-16 with Maverick inbound. Time on target, five minutes. Time to paint the target.'

With that he reached into his daysack and pulled out his An/PEQ-1 SOF Laser Marker, a hand-held, laser target-designator, the size of a small video camera. He switched it on and pointed it at the watchtower where their tormentor was located, looking through the optical sight as he did so. As he held it steady on the ground, an intensely focused laser beam – invisible to the men in the tower – shone at the target. It would be picked up by the sensor on the incoming aircraft; the muzzle flash of the Korda being Webb's aiming point.

They waited, Webb locked onto his target as if he was on the range and firing a rifle. Then, high above them and just audible, even above the firing, Morland heard the familiar scream of a fast jet engine.

'Won't be long now,' muttered Webb. 'Stand by for impact . . .'

*0200 hours, Sunday, 9 July 2017, Central European Time
0300 hours, Sunday, 9 July 2017, Eastern European Time
25,000 feet above Kaliningrad*

'GIANT KILLER, THIS is Apollo, refuel complete. Now on station as CAP.' Bertinetti spoke briefly into his microphone as his F-16 soared high above the flatlands of Kaliningrad, with Captain Mike Ryan tucked in close on his starboard side and just astern.

'Copy that, Apollo. Be aware. You've now got NATO's Boeing E-3A Sentry aircraft providing air surveillance in case of enemy air attack. An Airseeker RC-135 Rivet Joint SIGINT aircraft from the RAF is also airborne and reports Russian C2 still down. SAM threat is minimal.'

'Roger, Giant Killer. Send sitrep regarding air assault landings.'

'Giant Killer. H-Hour confirmed, 0330, Apollo.'

Bertinetti breathed a sigh of relief. It was one thing to have flown in fast and low, hit the Pionersky radar site as ordered and then to extract quickly, but at the mission brief he had been less than happy to be told that the Buzzards of 510th Fighter Squadron would then be required to provide a two-ship CAP, combat air patrol, following their bombing run. At the time, expecting few if any of them to survive the attack, he had felt that was an order too far. However, he knew the drill well enough: just get on with it. There was no way he was

426

asking anyone else to take on the extra tasking. Mike Ryan had caught his eye and nodded; he was Bertinetti's wingman and that was an end of the matter. He was coming, too.

Mission complete, the other six aircraft had headed straight for home. The pilots would first debrief and then creep home and into bed, almost as if nothing had happened.

However, it was still very much happening for him and Ryan. Far to the east, and invisible in the dark forests far below, the first fingers of dawn were beginning to lighten the faint curve of the horizon. He checked the time: sunrise in an hour and then they too could return to Aviano. He stifled a yawn and tried to stretch his legs. He had been strapped into his seat for four hours now; his G-suit felt too tight against his body and he longed to remove his helmet to scratch his head. The F-16 was always a great aircraft to fly, but it was well past time to count his blessings and head home before his luck ran out. Nevertheless, he set his instruments, activated auto-pilot and settled back to cover the area of sky above south-central Kaliningrad in a series of 'racetrack' – long loop – patterns.

It was not long before his radio burst into life again.

'Apollo, this is Giant Killer. Are you receiving me? TIC now.'

'Apollo, Roger. Send details.'

'Troops in contact, enemy grid 893456, south of Pravdinsk. Under fire from heavy machine gun. They have laser designator and are ready to paint the target. Be aware, target on edge of Iskander compound, possible that nuclear warheads have been armed. Accuracy essential.'

'Apollo, copy that. Out.'

At the words 'nuclear warheads armed,' all the fatigue of a long night flight and his body's craving for sleep vanished. Bertinetti checked his position. He entered the enemy grid reference into LANTIRN. The infrared navigation and targeting systems updated itself, giving him a time on target of five minutes. He called ground control again to get the marker to lase the target.

'Giant Killer, relay to TIC. Time on target five minutes. Paint the target in two.'

Then he called Ryan. 'Ghost One, this is Apollo. Cover my six o'clock while I go in.'

He put the F-16 into a dive and it responded like a thoroughbred racehorse let loose from the stalls. Flying low and fast, Bertinetti selected the stores management system page on his right-hand multifunction display, before punching the appropriate button around its perimeter to power up the Maverick. As he did so, the missile gyro ran up to speed in preparation for launch and lit the cockpit indicator, showing it was ready to fire. As he reached his pull-up point, he climbed and instantly picked up the target in the inky black below him. Flying at 3,000 feet, it was all too easy to see the streaks of tracer fire burning into the darkness. Without emotion, Bertinetti depressed his cage switch, allowing the missile to start to look for the laser marking the target.

Immediately the weapon-seeker symbology appeared on his head-up display in front of him, the signal for him to line up his aircraft with the target . . . He counted the seconds down from twenty, as he had done so often on the firing ranges on Exercise Red Flag, back home in the Nevada desert. At fifteen seconds his head-up display indicated target-lock on. The sensor on the Maverick missile had detected the laser beam as it bounced off the 'painted' target being marked by the laser operator on the ground.

'Hold it steady, boy. Hold it steady,' Bertinetti urged the unknown operator.

The laser beam remained rock steady.

This guy's a serious pro. He's done this before. And he's under fire.

Bertinetti felt, once again, the respect an airman feels for the man on the ground, close up and personal with the enemy.

Bertinetti had encountered much worse target designation on a peacetime range with no-one shooting back.

I'm not going to let this guy down. He's done his job perfectly and now I'm going to do mine.

As he closed in, he concentrated on holding the aircraft steady. Get this wrong and he would not only blow himself and the Iskanders to eternity, he would go down as the man who sparked the nuclear exchange that ended civilisation. That was if there was anybody left alive to remember it.

'Now!' he told himself, as he pressed the weapon-release button on the top of his stick with his right thumb. The missile fired forward off its launch rail and, as it blasted into the blackness in front of him, he was momentarily blinded by the flaming propellant. He felt the wing rise a fraction as the weight was removed and he automatically moved to correct the aircraft trim.

Below him, the missile accelerated towards its target.

0225 hours, Sunday, 9 July 2017, Central European Time
0325 hours, Sunday, 9 July 2017, Eastern European Time
Close to the Pravdinsk Iskander Battery, Kaliningrad

HIGH ABOVE THEM, Morland was conscious of the scream of a fast jet engine.

'Won't be long now!' shouted Webb. 'Stand by for impact . . .'

Morland looked up and, in the sky above the muzzle flashes, the first faint streaks of dawn light illuminated a dark, cigar shape, which descended rapidly towards the watchtower where the Korda continued to pump out a steady stream of tracer. It flew inexorably, a creature with a computer brain of its own.

Morland and Webb dropped into the bottom of the sunken lane and were conscious only of a blinding flash lighting the horizon above them, followed a split second later by an ear-splitting roar as the Maverick missile, fitted with laser seeker and 298-pound penetrative-blast, fragmentation warhead, hit the watchtower and eradicated it with the precision of a sniper's bullet. From his position three hundred metres away, Morland was surprised by how little blast there was; all the energy appeared to have gone downwards. He scrambled up the edge of the sunken lane and peered at the perimeter through the base of the hedge. The crack and thump of incoming machine-gun fire had disappeared and when the smoke cleared, there was no longer any watchtower.

'Neatly done,' said Webb. 'Bullseye . . . and all without setting off the nukes.'

'Shit, that I hadn't thought of . . .' muttered a suddenly very relieved Morland, as a figure in a para smock, face smeared in cam cream and framed by a British airborne ballistic helmet, unexpectedly appeared beside him.

Morland realised he must have been temporarily deafened by the noise of gunfire and explosions as he had not heard the man approach. He looked over his shoulder and saw two similarly equipped soldiers on either flank, covering the lead man. One was carrying an SA-80 assault rifle and the second a Minimi, 5.56 millimetre, light machine gun.

The lead man knelt beside him. 'Sergeant Atkins, Recce Platoon, 3 Para. We're the advance party. Main body of the company is approaching the LZ right now,' he said in a strong Brummie accent.

Morland looked up at him. 'Captain Tom Morland, Recce Platoon commander, 1 Mercian. What kept you?' he said with a grin, as a massive sense of relief swept over him. Somehow, with 3 Para here, he knew it was going to be alright.

Behind them, Morland now heard the steady, rhythmic *whack, whack* of double rotors as Chinook helicopters landed beyond the forest to the north. And then the brief silence was shattered as multiple streams of tracer again lit the sky. This time, though, the firing came from above the trees to his rear left. Apache attack helicopters, laden with lethal ordnance and equipped with thermal and night-imaging sights, were putting down concentrated fire onto the compound perimeter, prior to shooting in the assault company attack and blasting any surviving defenders into surrender.

Epilogue

Sunday morning in Oxford in August, out of university term time and before the bus loads of tourists arrive *en masse* to flood the city, is usually quiet and that morning was no exception. The sun shone on the elegant buildings where St Giles merges into the Woodstock Road as Captain Tom Morland opened the door into Brown's, where he'd agreed to meet Nicola Allenby for a late breakfast.

Ever since his return from the Baltics, he had been keen to catch up with her. Seeing her again over the satellite VTC in Latvia, before the war had started, had been a shock and he now wanted to have that long overdue talk. However, ever since his extraction by helicopter from the nuclear bunker outside Pravdinsk, his time had not been his own. There had been a series of debriefs, 'lessons learned' sessions, and a friendly chat with the Regimental Medical Officer, who gave him some pointers to help him identify any warning signs of post-traumatic stress disorder downstream.

Fortunately, one of the debriefs had been with Allenby at GCHQ. After hearing in detail how GCHQ and, no doubt, the Russians had tracked their progress through the Baltics, Morland had given his account of their time in the forests, with a particular focus on radio and communications. The team

432

at GCHQ had been particularly interested in the cyber-attack he had witnessed when the Russians had first knocked out the Latvian command and control systems as a prelude to their invasion.

Afterwards, he and Allenby had somehow contrived to bump into one another and both agreed to meet. But Allenby was also in demand and it had taken until now to coordinate their diaries. Morland had arrived in Oxford early, but Allenby was already seated at a table with a copy of *The Sunday Times* spread out in front of her. They greeted each other awkwardly; more as colleagues rather than old friends.

'You're looking a lot more civilised than when I last saw you – you were pretty scrawny when you first came back,' Allenby commented, in an obvious effort to ease the atmosphere.

'It wasn't exactly Jamie Oliver-style cooking in the forests . . .'

Allenby smiled back, ice temporarily broken.

Breakfast ordered, Allenby pointed to the massive, front-page headline: *Russian President Missing in Helicopter Crash in Siberia*.

'Seen this?' she asked.

'I heard it on the car radio. I can scarcely believe it. I thought he was indestructible.'

Allenby turned the newspaper so they could both see. It was full of stock shots of the President in action-man mode: riding a horse bare-chested, hunting bears, diving for archaeological artefacts in the Black Sea and fishing for salmon.

'It says he'd flown there to do a thing about climate change to re-establish his political credentials after his disaster in the Baltic states. Another presidential alpha-male stunt, but this time to demonstrate his new green credentials. He always insisted on using his old Mi-8 'Hip' Soviet Russian workhorse helicopter, rather than anything state of the art. And look where that's ended up . . .'

'Deep in the tundra, I'm glad to say.' Morland drank a mouthful of coffee and looked at the headline. 'I can hardly believe the bastard has finally gone. I thought he'd be around for ever . . . He certainly planned to be.'

Allenby looked around. The restaurant was near empty and there was no-one close enough to listen in to their conversation, but she still lowered her voice. 'You and the Forest Brothers certainly played a part in undermining him.'

'Really?' Morland exclaimed.

'Really,' Allenby answered. 'But don't expect anyone to thank you. For us to even acknowledge your contribution would invite the Russians to investigate how we might know what they are thinking . . . After his OTT reaction to the falling helicopters we started picking up chatter about potential successors and how best to replace him. The one thing that keeps you in power in Russia is a reputation for strength. Once he started losing that, it was only a matter of time. In fact, we don't believe he's been in control for some weeks now.'

'Are you saying that the helicopter was pushed, rather than fell?'

'That's what I think. Of course, helicopters do fall out of the sky . . .'

'Please tell me this is this good news and that someone who's less of a bastard will take over.'

'Maybe not,' replied Allenby. 'We've been picking up that his likely successor is even more of a hardline nationalist, which is a real worry. He's been ranting about enemies within and the stab in the back; the need to take revenge on NATO for the Russian defeat and the fact that they had to return the Baltics to get Kaliningrad and their missiles back.'

Morland was thoughtful. 'Yes, I can see how that must have hurt Russian pride.'

'Well, that was the NATO plan.'

'I hear that you might have had something . . .'

'Enough, Tom. You know I can't go into any of that. Anyway, you've certainly been through the mill. You were lucky to get away with it after the President put that Spetsnaz guy on your trail.'

'Yeah, so you told us at GCHQ.'

'Did you know he set up the ambush at Pravdinsk?' said Allenby.

'I didn't, but I can't say I'm surprised. I saw him order the snipers to open fire on those Russian girls in Riga and then, there he was, leading the camp attack in Latvia. It seemed a pretty massive coincidence and I began to wonder if he had been told to track us down. When I saw the compound lights had gone out, I suspected we might be walking into a trap, but it was far too late to back out by then. Tell me. Was he killed in the air strike?'

'We don't know. It's strange. We've not picked up anything on him at all, although we were able to track pretty much everything else. It's as if the Russians are deliberately not saying anything to cover his tracks.'

The atmosphere chilled slightly, as they both contemplated the possible consequences of that.

Closing the newspaper and with it the subject, Allenby turned the conversation back to Morland. 'What is the Army going to do with you?'

'The CO hasn't told me what he wants me to do next. I've been hanging around barracks, trying to keep busy. To be honest, I'm not sure about staying in the Army. I've loved my time, but I guess I've already had more than my share of excitement. The problem as I see it is that, with these endless cuts, there isn't much of a future any more for people like me.'

'That bad?'

'Yes, that bad. Did you know that Sergeant Wild has PVR'd – resigned – and with him going, Archer and Watson are talking about following him into civvie street. It's not as if I have any arguments to stop them.'

'You don't think the politicians will have learned from their lucky escape this time . . . Maybe improve things?'

'Come on, Nicola! Not a chance of it,' Morland said bitterly. 'There'll be lots of eye-catching, big-ticket items. Like lashing out on money for Special Forces, or jam-tomorrow equipment purchases that will make for great headlines. But precious little of what really matters. What's needed is for the powers-that-be to recognise the need to put some genuine muscle back on the bones from where it's already been hacked away. Don't tell me that the Baltics were won back by air strikes, cyber and smart bombs alone.

'Sure, they were essential props. But without the right people doing the right things at the right time, shiny toys will only get you so far. And the unavoidable fact is that the Russians only had a go at the Baltics in the first place because the President reckoned our weakness gave him that opportunity on a plate. Putting that right is going to cost real money and I just can't see it happening. As any politician will tell you, there's no votes these days in spending money on defence. Even after what so nearly happened. That simple.

'What's more, the political leadership needs to understand that it's all about people. Once you get rid of well-trained professionals, you can't just wave your wand and expect them to reappear as if by magic, just because you need them again. Our forces are as formidable as they are because of our training. Day in day out, year in year out. Getting better at our jobs all the time. Just as in any line of work. But you can't be a banker or a plumber and a reservist and train your heart out for a few weeks every year and then, come the crisis, expect to put your uniform on and hope to be a fraction as good as a professional. It just doesn't work like that, however much the politicians wish it did and tell us it can. In battle you need to survive the first encounter and to do that you need to be a highly trained professional, who is part of a highly skilled team.

'History is full of ill-trained armies that broke when they hit smaller bands of professionals who knew their trade and had the right kit. Britain has understood that for the last few centuries and look where it took us . . . but no longer, it seems. Trouble is, and I'm sorry if I'm sounding too much the cynic, there's no headlines to be had in well-motivated and well-supported soldiers just quietly getting on with their jobs . . .' Morland realised his voice had risen in agitation at what he saw as the betrayal of everything he believed in when he had joined the Army.

He saw Allenby give him a quizzical look and then, thankfully, she changed the subject. 'And you, Tom. How do you feel about it? Your time in the forests . . . ?'

'Well, you know . . . It takes a bit of time to wind down and get back to normality. It's good to be back with the Battalion . . . but I find I'm still spending time with the guys who were there with me. There's no-one else, apart from Marina Krauja and the Forest Brothers, who could begin to understand what it was like out there.'

'What about Marina? You must have got pretty close to her? She sounds like quite a girl.'

Morland was quiet for a moment. 'She's a great girl.'

'Will you see her again?' asked Allenby.

How best to answer Allenby's question? Because it was a question he had been asking himself ever since his rushed farewell with Krauja as she had been unexpectedly put on a helicopter bound for Poland, while he'd been directed to an RAF C-130 Hercules about to head to RAF Brize Norton.

'I'm sure I will . . . some time. When we were in the forest, and on the run, we did get pretty close in some ways. Who wouldn't, given everything that happened? But it was hardly the time or place. She's pretty tough. Especially after her recent experiences. She's also a woman with a mission. She's determined to help rebuild things in Latvia. Her brother was killed when the Russians attacked the airport and her parents need her around – which is all fair enough. I can only respect her for that . . .'

Which he knew, and even as he said it, was not really an answer. Allenby, of course, picked up on it and probed deeper.

As she did so, Morland recognised the parallels between the two of them. In so doing, he realised how much he had been looking forward to seeing Allenby again. And how much he was enjoying being with her now.

'I'd like to meet her one day,' announced Allenby.

'You'd like her. You've got a lot in common.'

Glossary

ACE – Allied Command Europe. An element in the Cold War NATO command structure. No longer exists

ACTORD – Activation Order

ACTWARN – Activation Warning

ADC – Aide de Camp, a general's junior personal staff officer, usually a captain

AMRAAM – Advanced Medium Range Air-to-Air Missile

ARRC – Allied Rapid Reaction Corps. British led multinational NATO formation

Article 5 – Article in Washington Treaty of 1949, the founding treaty of NATO, which states that: 'an armed attack against one or more of (NATO member states) in Europe or North America shall be considered an attack against them all' and binds other member states to take 'such action as it deems necessary, including the use of armed force, to restore and maintain the security of the North Atlantic area.'

ASAP – As Soon As Possible

C2 – Command and Control

CAP – Combat Air Patrol

CCOMC – Comprehensive Crisis Operations Management Centre, the nerve centre of **SHAPE**

CDS – UK Chief of Defence Staff

CEO – Chief Executive Officer

CIA – Central Intelligence Agency. The USA's foreign intelligence service

CMC – Chairman of the Military Committee, NATO's senior military officer and the principal military adviser to the Secretary General and the North Atlantic Council.

CJSOR – Combined Joint Statement of Requirement. The list of forces required for an operation

CO – Commanding Officer

COM EUCOM – Commander US European Command

Der Spiegel – influential German weekly news magazine

DDoS – Distributed Denial of Services. A form of cyber attack

DSACEUR – Deputy Supreme Commander Europe, NATO's deputy strategic commander

DSO – Distinguished Service Order, a prestigious British military award for meritorious service in war

DZ – Drop Zone for airborne forces

ERV – Emergency Rendezvous point

FSB – Federal Security Service of the Russian Federation and the successor to the KGB

G1098 – an item of British military equipment for personal issue

G7 – Group of Seven an informal bloc of industrialized democracies that meets annually to discuss issues such as global economic governance, international security, and energy policy (biggest economies). Was **G8** until Russia was expelled following invasion of Crimea

GCHQ – Government Communications Headquarters. British intelligence and security organisation responsible for providing signals intelligence (SIGINT) and information assurance to the British Government and Armed Forces

GDP – Gross domestic product

GPMG – General Purpose Machine Gun

GPS – Global Positioning System

HAHO – High Altitude High Opening. High altitude insertion by parachute

HARM – High Speed Anti-Radiation Missile. Designed to destroy active radar

HEAT – High Explosive Anti-Tank

HUMVEE – High Mobility Multipurpose Wheeled Vehicle (HMMWV), commonly known as the Humvee, a four-wheel drive military light truck

ICBM – Inter-Continental Ballistic Missiles

IED – Improvised Explosive Device

JFACC – Joint Force Air Component Commander

JFS – Jet Fuel Starter on F16, single engine multi-role fighter aircraft

JOA – Joint Operational Area

KGB – principal intelligence service of the former Soviet Union

LANTIRN – Low Altitude Navigation and Targeting Infrared for Night, a combined navigation and targeting pod system.

LZ – Landing Zone for helicopter borne forces

MA – Military Assistant. A middle ranking staff officer to a senior officer

MEF – Marine Expeditionary Force.

MI6 – name commonly given to **SIS** (Secret Intelligence Service), British foreign intelligence agency

MOD – UK Ministry of Defence

MVD – Russian interior ministry controlling internal troops

NAC – North Atlantic Council, the decision-making body of NATO

NATO – North Atlantic Treaty Organisation

NATO Sec Gen – NATO Secretary General, invariably a distinguished international figure who is responsible for leading the North Atlantic Council

NDCC – National Defence Control Centre. Russian principal military command centre

NRF – NATO Response Force

NSA – National Security Agency. US intelligence agency responsible for global monitoring, collection, and processing of information and data for foreign intelligence

ODA – Operational Detachment Alpha. 12 man basic unit of US Special Operations Forces

'O' Group – Orders Group. Conference at which military commander issues orders to immediate subordinates in the chain of command.

OTT – Over the top (excessive)

PJHQ – Permanent Joint Headquarters at Northwood in Middlesex, England

PM – UK Prime Minister

PR – Public relations

PRR – Personal Role Radio

PSO – Principal Staff Officer to a very senior officer

PVR – Premature Voluntary Release

RNZS – Russkiy Narodov Zaschita Sila or Russian People's Protection Force, a fictional militia

ROE – Rules of Engagement

RV – Rendezvous point

SA80 A2LA85 – British army's standard infantry rifle

SACEUR – Supreme Allied Commander Europe, NATO's strategic commander

SAM – Surface to Air missile

SAS – Special Air Service. UK Special Forces

SBS – UK (principally maritime) Special Forces

SEALs – US Navy's primary Special Operations Forces

SF – Special Forces. UK term for Special Operations Forces

SIGINT – Signals Intelligence

SHAPE – Supreme Headquarters Allied Powers Europe, NATO's strategic headquarter

Siloviki – Russian term denoting politicians with a background in military or security services. Much favoured by the Russian President

SNMCMG – Standing NATO Mine Countermeasures Group

SOF – Special Operations Forces

SONAR – (**SO**und **N**avigation **A**nd **R**anging) is a technique that uses sound propagation (usually underwater, as in submarine navigation) to navigate, communicate with or detect objects on or under the surface of the water, such as other vessels

SOP – Standard Operating Procedures

STRIKEFORNATO – Naval Striking and Support Forces NATO. The Alliance's premier maritime battle-staff and the Alliance's primary link for integrating US Maritime capabilities with NATO's

TIC – Troops in Contact

USAFE – US Air Force Europe

VIP – Very Important Person

VHF – Very High Frequency. Radio waves between 30-300 MHz

VJTF – Very High Readiness Joint Task Force
VTC – Video Teleconference
VVIP – Very Very Important Person

Acknowledgements

THE INSPIRATION FOR this book came from the many good friends I made as a result of a number of trips to Latvia, Estonia and Lithuania. Not only have they shown me great kindness and warm hospitality, but they have shared their personal and family histories of the brutal period of Soviet occupation. The courage with which they regained their freedom in the dying days of the Soviet Union is nothing short of inspirational, hence the dedication at the front of this book. Those events took place more than a generation ago and have passed into history. But in the face of a resurgent Russia, once again a potentially existential threat on the eastern frontiers of the Baltic states and to all members of NATO, they must never be repeated.

But that inspiration needed a catalyst and this book would never have been written without Roger Field. It started at a Sandhurst reunion with a conversation about what I would do when I left the Army. With the irrepressible enthusiasm that has always been his hallmark, he urged me to consider writing. After what seems now feeble resistance, perhaps because some-where within me I had always wanted to write, I gave in and this is the result. But Roger Field has been much more than agent and editor. A published writer himself, he brought a novelist's eye to the project and I owe him profound thanks for his creative imagination, eye for detail and the rigorous red pen of his many suggestions, extensive additions and corrections that have gone far beyond the normal call of duty for an editor and agent. In addition, I owe Mark Booth of Hodder and Stoughton particular thanks. I am deeply grateful to him for the enthusiasm and interest he has shown from the start of the project, together with his wise, extensive and detailed advice, to say nothing of the time he has put into the project.

Much of what I write about is based on my own experience – and I plead guilty to simplifying the complex for the sake of the story. However, I have depended on professional advice from those who have operated at the sharp end, particularly at sea and in the air. Maritime advice has been freely given by a former colleague who wishes to remain anonymous, while the advice on air warfare has come from Henry Salmon, a former fast jet pilot.

While many of the characters and names in the events of 2017 are purely fictional, others are based on, or named after, individuals I have known. I am indebted to those who have generously allowed me to draw on their individual character-istics or to name fictional characters after them. I trust you will understand if I do not acknowledge you all individually.

The foundations of this project have been my family without whose encouragement, support and objective criticism the book would never have been completed. In particular, my loyal companions Delilah and Maisie, our two springer spaniels, have been instrumental in applying the adage '*solvitur ambulando*' – 'it is solved by walking', which has overcome many an impasse. But more important than anything else, and utterly consistent throughout the nearly thirty-six years we have been married, the rock on which everything has been built has been my beloved wife Sarah-Jane, to whom I owe more than I can ever say. No thanks and gratitude can ever be enough for what she has done, and continues to do for me.